ISAAC ASIMOV'S

THREE LAWS OF ROBOTICS

1.

A robot may not injure a human being, or through inaction, allow a human being to come to harm.

2.

A robot must obey the orders given it by human beings except where such orders would conflict with the First Law.

3.

A robot must protect its own existence, as long as such protection does not conflict with the First or Second Laws.

ISAAC ASIMOV'S
ROBOT MYSTERY

CHIMERA

AVAILABLE NOW

THE ALFRED BESTER COLLECTION
The Deceivers
The Computer Connection
re: demolished

THE ROBERT SILVERBERG COLLECTION
Sailing to Byzantium
Science Fiction 101: Robert Silverberg's Worlds of Wonder

ISAAC ASIMOV'S ROBOT CITY
Volume 1
by Michael P. Kube-McDowell and Mike McQuay

Volume 2
by William F. Wu and Arthur Byron Cover

Volume 3
by Rob Chilson and William F. Wu

ISAAC ASIMOV ROBOT MYSTERIES
by Mark W. Tiedemann
Mirage

THE EDEN TRILOGY
by Harry Harrison
West of Eden
Winter in Eden

Arthur C. Clarke's Venus Prime: Volumes 1, 2, 3, and 4
by Paul Preuss

Callisto
by Lin Carter

The Dream Master
by Roger Zelazny

Moebius' Arzach
by Randy and Jean-Marc Lofficier

The Touch
Created by Steven Elliot-Altman

COMING SOON

Return to Eden
Volume 3 of the *Eden Trilogy*
by Harry Harrison

Damnation Alley
by Roger Zelazny

ISAAC ASIMOV'S
ROBOT MYSTERY

CHIMERA

MARK W. TIEDEMANN

ibooks
new york

An Original Publication of ibooks, inc.

Copyright © 2001 Byron Preiss Visual Publications, Inc.

An ibooks, inc. Book

ibooks, inc.
24 West 25th Street
New York, NY 10010

Asimov's Chimera
ISBN 0-7394-1876-9

Edited by Steven Roman

Cover art by Bruce Jensen
Cover design by Jason Vita
Interior design by Michael Mendelsohn at MM Design 2000

Printed in the U.S.A.

For Donna and Henry Tiedemann
Mom and Dad
with love, respect, and thanks

ISAAC ASIMOV'S
ROBOT MYSTERY

CHIMERA

PROLOGUE

... brief touch, contact with the data port, numbers names dates prognoses, all flow from the brief touch, a tiny surge that feels the way nerves should feel, the stimulation of a hair drawn lightly along a fingertip, but inside, along a conduit less than a hundredth a hair's width, to a smaller place where it grows and explicates and becomes meaningful in translation, revealing location disposition architecture security, an excess of data that gives access, all from a brief touch ...

Director Ortalf stopped complaining about the lateness of the hour the instant he saw the hole cut in the wall of the cafeteria at the Seth Canobil Hospice Center, where he worked. His irritation turned quickly to confusion, then embarrassment, and finally fear. He walked up to the opening and reached out to touch the edge, but withdrew his fingers centimeters from brushing the too-smooth cut. In the flat light it shone mirror bright.

"Ah ..." he said, looking around. The police officers

who had brought him here stood impassively, their faces professionally expressionless. Director Ortalf looked around at the people milling about the area. They moved in groups of threes and fours, some in uniform, most in civilian clothes. Ortalf started at the sight of a drone moving slowly across the floor, its sensors inspecting every centimeter of the tiles.

"Forensic," explained a deep, male voice nearby.

Ortalf looked around. A tall man in somber gray was watching him, his face as ambivalent as everyone else's— except for his eyes, which glistened expectantly.

"Ah," Ortalf said again. "Are you . . . ?"

"Mr. Ortalf," the man said, ignoring the question. *"Director* Ortalf."

"Yes?"

"You run this facility?"

Ortalf nodded sharply. "What is going on? Who—?"

"A routine maintenance monitor detected a power outage here," the man explained. "According to its logs, this was listed as a class-B primary site. It attempted to restore the lines, but found irregularities. It then alerted the local authorities."

"Power outage . . . but we have a back-up."

"Had."

"Redundant system . . . *had?"*

"How many people work here, Director Ortalf?" The man—who must be some sort of inspector, Ortalf surmised— walked away, forcing Ortalf to catch up and walk with him.

"Um . . . six permanent staff," he said.

The man paused briefly, then continued walking. "I understand you have nearly three thousand wards here."

Ortalf tried to think. "Your people got me out of bed not even half an hour ago, Inspector. I haven't had time to shower, to get breakfast, to—three thousand? Yes, that sounds about right."

"And only six staff."

"Six *permanent* staff, I said. We have several interns and part-time volunteers, but even so, almost everything is automated."

They left the cafeteria and started down a long corridor. Emergency lights glowed dimly along the floor and ceiling, even though the regular lights were on.

"Who was on call tonight?" the inspector asked.

"I don't—please, Inspector, *what* is going on?"

At the end of the corridor a short set of stairs led down into a nurse's station. Banks of screens showed a bright orange STAND BY flashing on them. Ortalf's gnawing apprehension worsened. He moved toward the main console, but the inspector gripped his upper arm tightly.

"Please don't touch anything. Who was on call tonight?"

"I don't remember. Joquil, I think. Yes, Kilif Joquil."

The inspector gestured toward a door that opened at the rear of the station. Ortalf pushed it wide open. Sprawled over the cot that hugged one wall of the cubicle lay a large body, face down.

Ortalf thought for a moment that the man was dead. But a sudden, labored breath heaved through the torso. Dread gave way to impatience.

"What is going on?" the director demanded.

The inspector nodded toward the sleeping male nurse. "Did you know Kilif Joquil used Brethe?"

"What? Now look—"

The inspector aimed a long finger at the nightstand at the head of the cot. Ortalf stared at its contents for a long time before he recognized the inhaler and an unlabeled vial.

"We screen our people carefully," he said weakly.

"I'm sure you do."

Ortalf looked at the inspector. "Habits can start any time. We scan every six months."

The nurse shifted in the cot again, then lay still. Ortalf turned and left. The inspector said nothing, just followed, as the director headed for the door to the first ward.

Ortalf stopped at the entrance. The room stretched, nearly a hundred meters on a side, dwarfing the half-dozen or so strangers now wandering the aisles of matreches. Ortalf searched the field of metal and plastic, looking for the telltale difference: a flaw, damage, a sign of disruption. His pulse raced.

"Not this one," the inspector said quietly, just behind him. "Number Five."

Ward Five was two levels down. Ortalf's breathing came hard when he reached it. Twice the size of the first-level wards, it contained the same number of matreches. These, however, were larger, more complex. More was demanded of them; the lives within required special care.

Ortalf spotted the damaged units at once. He staggered toward them, dodging down a jagged path between the intact incubators, till he reached the first one.

Sticky fluid covered the floor around it. The shell had been removed and the sac within punctured. Ortalf expected to see an asphyxiated, dehydrated corpse in the bed, but the cradle was empty. The tubes of the support system lay severed and useless on the cushions, a couple of them still oozing liquids. Ortalf made to reach in, but hesitated—touch would tell him the same as sight, that the child was gone. He looked around, confused and close to panic. Nearby he saw two more violated matreches.

"But . . . but . . ." He stopped when he found the inspector watching him. "I don't understand," Ortalf said finally.

The inspector came to a conclusion. Concerning what, Ortalf could not be sure, but he recognized the change in the inspector's face, from glassy hardness to near pity. The inspector nodded and gestured for them to return to the administration level.

Ortalf let himself be escorted back, dazed. He barely noticed the people and machines that roamed through his facility. Police, forensic units, specialists—insurance adjustors, too, for all he knew, and within hours the lawyers would be calling.

The inspector brought him to his own office and closed the door.

"What's happened?" Ortalf asked. He had wanted to make it a demand, but it came out as a pale, exhausted gasp.

"I'd frankly hoped you might be able to tell me, Director Ortalf. But . . ." He sat on the edge of Ortalf's desk and gazed down at him. Some of the hardness had returned, but mixed now with sympathy.

"From what we've been able to reconstruct so far, the entire clinic was severed from outside communications. There was one independent oversight program with a direct line to your maintenance chief, but after ten minutes even that was cut. Most of it went down with the power. You may well have a number of fatalities to deal with. I'm not sure how critical these systems are to each unit—"

"Each matreche has its own power unit to protect from a complete outage."

"So I gathered from the manufacturer's specs. Are they all up to par?"

"So far as I know. You'd have to ask our maintenance supervisor, Kromis—"

"We'd love to, but we can't find her."

"She . . . have you been to her apartment?"

"Police are there now. I'd like to have her employment file when you get a moment. In fact, we'll want the employment files on all your people, even the consultants, interns, and part-timers."

"Do you really think it could have been one of my people?"

"Not alone, no. But it's clear that whoever it was had a thorough knowledge of your systems."

"Of course. Um . . . do you know how they broke in?"

"Once the power was down and the security net with it," the inspector explained, "a hole was cut through the point where there would least likely be a back-up alarm they could know nothing about—nobody alarms cafeterias—and from there they went through the clinic, cutting the rest of the power and finally deactivating even your passive monitoring systems."

Ortalf blinked. "It could take days to get everything back up." He stared off toward a wall, his thoughts an anxious jumble. "How many are missing?" he asked.

"Twenty-four, I think. All from Ward Five."

"All?"

The inspector nodded. "Who were they?"

"I don't . . . you mean, who do we maintain in Ward Five? A special group, I'm afraid. Very special."

"Isn't everyone in your facility special?"

Ortalf studied the inspector, unsure if he heard sarcasm in the man's voice. The face, though, remained impassive.

"Some more than others," Ortalf said. "Those—Ward Five—have the most severe situations."

"UPDs, aren't they?"

"Yes. Untreatable Physiological Dysfunctions."

"Lepers."

Ortalf started. "I'm sorry?"

"Nothing." Impatience flashed across the inspector's face. "Ancient reference. It's not important. Tell me, can you think of any reason someone would want to kidnap them?"

"No."

"Blackmail? Ransom?"

"I doubt any of them will live long enough outside their matreches to be of any use in that regard."

"Why is that?"

"The matreches—each one is specifically modified to its occupant. They're unique, like the individuals they support. They change over time, with the condition of their charge. It would be nearly impossible to duplicate those specifications in another unit quickly enough to save a removed occupant. I have no doubt that a number of them are dead already."

"I see. That leaves revenge. Who were they?"

"Revenge?" Ortalf stood. "You're joking! What could any of these children have done—"

"Not them," the inspector said calmly. "Their parents."

"Their histories are completely confidential. Inaccessible."

"Really? You do that as efficiently as your employee background checks?"

"*I'm* the only one who can access those records."

"And will you inform the parents when you've done so, to let them know that their children have been lost?"

Ortalf, uncomfortable, sat down and shook his head. "That's not the arrangement we have."

"They don't want to know, do they? That's why you have them in the first place."

"You have to understand, a lot of them have no family to begin with."

"Discards. Abandoned."

"Yes."

"I'd be willing to wager that many of those whose records are so carefully sealed are children *with* families."

The inspector stood, and for a moment Ortalf expected to be struck. He closed his eyes and waited, but the blow never came. When he looked up, the inspector stood in the doorway, his back to the director.

"The records will be required," the inspector said. "Please make yourself available for further questioning."

Ortalf watched the man walk away. Nearly a minute passed before he realized that he still did not know the inspector's name. At that moment, he was just as glad not to.

TWENTY-FIVE
YEARS LATER . . .

ONE

Coren Lanra watched from behind a grime-encrusted refuse bin in the recess of an old, unused loading dock. A sneeze threatened, teased by sharp odors and the chill air. Across the wide alley, members of a third-shift crew emerged from an unmarked door. Even if they saw him they would pass him off as one of the ubiquitous warren ghosts, homeless and destitute, that haunted the districts surrounding Petrabor Spaceport. Coren wore a shabby, ankle-length gray-black coat over worn coveralls; four days' beard darkened his pale face beneath oily, unwashed hair. He itched.

Three hours still remained in the third shift. Coren counted fifteen people through the door—all but one of the full crew compliment of the largely automated warehouse. They were unlikely to get into trouble—Coren recognized their supervisor among them, marked by the thick silver rings around his upper arms. They strode noisily up the alley, boots crunching on scattered debris, laughter echoing off the walls, heading for a home kitchen or a bar. They rounded a corner. Coren listened till their voices came as whispers in the distance.

He dropped from the lip of the bay and hurried to their exit door, propped open by a thin sheet of plastic he'd stuck there earlier to jam the lock and disable the tracking sensor that kept a log of when the door was used. Just inside, he found an ID reader set in a heavy inner door. He slipped his forged card into the slot and waited to see if he had gotten what he had paid for.

The light on the reader winked green and he slipped through into a locker room. Forty-eight lockers, sixteen per shift. Coren wondered where the last worker was inside the mammoth complex.

From one of the oversized pockets in his coat he took out a small button and pressed it on the frame of the exit door. Should anyone follow him through, the button would warn him with a strong signal pulse tuned to a receiver on his wrist.

He went to the shower room.

Water dripped from some of the shower heads; the floor was damp. He turned on a jet of hot water and removed several blocky objects from various pockets. He placed them beneath the steaming spray and stepped back. Quickly, the scan-occluding resins melted off a number of devices. Coren shut off the water and gathered them up, shaking away the excess water.

He hurried down a short hallway that let into a large office area, then threaded a path through the maze of irregularly-spaced desks and chairs to the transparent wall that overlooked the main warehouse space.

Immense square blocks formed a grid below the enormous ceiling. Within each block, stacks of cubicles, nacelles, skids, crates—all manner of packaging—filled the volume. Turnover was constant. The space between each block extended down several levels and buzzed with transports, bringing loads up from below or, coming from the bays along the far wall, descending with newly arrived cargo to the proper location. The contents were monitored by a very sophisticated AI system—not alive, no, but as close to machine awareness as Terran prejudice and law allowed.

Walkways followed the grid pattern; staircases led down into the hivelike labyrinth. Coren wondered just how far he would fall if he lost his balance while walking along one of those narrow paths. He pressed close to the wall and looked straight down and could not make out the bottom.

He turned away, head swimming in a brief wash of vertigo. At least there was a roof above . . .

Coren took out a few of his vonoomans. The little machines clustered in the palm of his left hand. He turned slowly, surveying the office. Satisfied, he knelt down and set them on the floor. He lightly touched them, and each glowed briefly as it activated.

"If Rega knew I used you," he whispered to them, "he might . . ." He grunted, self-mocking, and touched each one again. The devices stirred for a few moments, then shot off in different directions, seeking out the specific energy signatures of communications, monitoring, and alarm systems. Once in place, Coren would be able to range wherever he wished within the warehouse, free of detection.

He took out a palm-sized pad and switched it on. Less than a minute later all the telltales winked green.

He sat down at one of the desks, jacked his palm monitor into the computer keyboard before him, and initiated an access sequence. The security code was not very sophisticated; his decrypter gained entry in less than thirty seconds.

Coren keyed quickly. The scheduling chart came up on the screen, showing incoming and outgoing traffic for all the bays on the far side of the warehouse. He studied the times.

Most of the bays were tightly scheduled. One showed a half-hour period with nothing going out, nothing coming in. He tapped queries. A shipment had been canceled at the last minute. Three shipments, in fact, all belonging to a company called Kysler, and all cancellations routed out of the Baltimor ITE oversight offices. Baltimor . . . practically the other side of the globe. Odd. There was an ITE oversight office in the Laus District and another up north in Arkanleg, both of which should have had responsibility for supervising traffic in and out of Petrabor. Still, there was no reason Baltimor would be necessarily barred from such duties . . .

He opened the manifests. Mostly raw synthetic materials, exotic molecular structures, exported by an Auroran-owned wholesaler. One bin contained electronics manufactured by Imbitek. Coren studied the ID tags for a few moments. Kysler Diversified was the distributor. All the lots had destination codes which he could not read.

Coren closed down the station. He unjacked his monitor, checked the status on his little interference runners once more, then headed out. He knew now which bay he needed.

Coren followed the transparent wall till he came to an exit. A short staircase took him down to the walkway that bordered the labyrinth. He produced another handful of vonoomans, smaller than the first group, from a different pocket. Activated, they scurried along the walkway and disappeared. The first group gave him security, interfering with the warehouse systems; *these* would find people for him.

Automated tractors following invisible guide signals sped through the canyons, a constant loud humming and rush of cold air that whipped at his coat. The place smelled of oil and ozone, metal and hot plastic, and, under all that, an organic odor: yeast or mold. Rot.

The walkway took him to a broad receiving area fronting a row of large bay doors. As he neared, the sounds grew thunderous: doors opening and slamming shut, transports rumbling through in both directions, the wind now almost constant. And beyond that, in the distance, deeper, sepulchral, the heavy thunder of the port itself: shuttles lifting off and landing irregularly, disrupting any possible rhythm to all the noise.

Between the edge of the storage hive and the bays lay six meters of ancient, stained apron. Except for small piles of boxes and litter, Coren saw nowhere to hide. He set free another handful of machines and retreated to the nearest staircase leading down into a canyon.

Fog lay heavily a few stories below. Coren descended half the height of the block, until the cold bit at his face and filled his sinuses with warning hollowness. He sat down on a step and pulled his palm monitor out once more.

It unfolded four times to give him a display showing the locations of all his little spies against a map of the entire warehouse. The surveillance blocks still showed operative. Now he saw blue dots where all his other machines had secreted themselves. He pressed the half-meter-square screen against the wall beside him and waited.

Ten minutes.

One blue dot turned red. Coren looked up, surprised. The intruder had come from the nearby loading bays. *The sixteenth member of the crew,* he thought. Coren looked down at the fog, twenty or more meters below, and wondered if he should move—into even more bitter cold. But numbers flashed beside the dot on his flatscreen, coordinates that told him the precise location of the worker, who waited near one of the bay doors, showing no sign of coming any closer to Coren. After a few seconds Coren felt confident that he would not be seen—not by this one, at least.

Twelve more minutes passed.

Three blue dots turned red, far down the row, back near the offices. As he watched, his machines focussed on the new intruders, coordinates proliferated over the screen, and he counted bodies: fifty-one.

The number surprised him. He had expected no more than a dozen, at most fifteen.

They came as a group down a walkway, heading this direction, obviously for a meeting with the waiting dock-worker, who now moved a few steps from the wall.

Coren folded the screen back down to palm-size and crept up the stairs to the lip of the walkway.

The dockworker stood just inside the warehouse by an open bay door several meters away, his back to Coren. Hands in pockets, the man shifted minutely from foot to foot as if keeping time to a tune only he heard. Coren looked across the grid of walkways to the approaching group. From this distance he recognized no one. All of them wore black, all of them carried small packs.

Five or six children accompanied the adults.

Coren glanced at his palm-monitor. The communications and surveillance dampers still showed green. He estimated that he had another twenty minutes before the AI figured out why its internal security system was down.

Coren peeled off his overcoat.

As the fifty-one refugees gathered around the dock-worker, Coren stepped silently from the stairwell and moved smoothly up to the perimeter, then cautiously worked his way through them. He looked at no one, aware only that a few people gave him quick, nervous looks. They were frightened, tense, too careful perhaps in some ways, careless in others. None of them would want to believe that they had been followed or infiltrated or caught, so unless it was made obvious that he did not belong here, they would explain him away to themselves. At least, for the time being.

Long enough to reach the front of the gathering.

"—no changes," a woman said tersely. "Canister BJ-5156. Don't tell me about some other canister—"

"It can't be helped," the dockworker said calmly. "I'm sorry. The one segregated for you was found and impounded."

"Why wasn't I informed?"

"I'm informing you now. I'm informing you that we have back-up. We were prepared. It's the same as it was, only different. A new canister. I could point out that you were supposed to be a party of fifty-two and you're missing one. Bad security. But, hey, we understand—people get scared and back out at the last minute." He gave her a crooked smile. "We *are* professionals."

The woman was tall, almost gaunt, sharply featured. Her head sat forward, angry and demanding, as she glared at the dockworker, who gazed back at her evenly. Coren admired his nerve under that displeased inspection.

After several seconds, she nodded slowly. "All right. But if this turns out to be anything but copacetic I'll peel your skin off with pliers. Tell your people we're ready."

The worker nodded and walked through the bay.

Coren started forward.

Something closed on his right bicep. He tugged at it

automatically, to no effect. He turned around, left hand curled to give a palm blow, and froze, abruptly and utterly terrified.

A robot regarded him blankly through mesh-covered eye sockets.

"I apologize, sir," it said quietly, "but I must ask that you come with me."

The robot drew him back through the crowd, which now watched him with open fear and shock. Some cringed back from the robot, but most stood fast, staring outrage at Coren Lanra.

The robot walked him down the row of bay doors, to the fourth one from the group, and waited, still holding him, firmly but harmlessly.

"Damn it, Coren."

Coren glanced around at the voice. He looked at the woman he had come to talk to. He waited as long as he could before speaking, taking advantage of the opportunity to simply look at her. Finally, he said, "Good to see you, too, Nyom."

She let her breath out through her teeth, slowly, and Coren felt himself smile.

"Don't tell me you're surprised to see me," he said.

"I'm not. That's what bothers me."

Coren gestured toward the robot. "Umm . . ."

"Coffee, go see to our arrangements."

"Yes, Nyom."

The robot released Coren's arm. He congratulated himself that he did not immediately step away from it. Instead, he watched it walk back toward the group of refugees.

"What are you doing?" he asked the young woman. "Running baleys?"

"You know I am. I have been."

"I'd hoped I'd been misinformed. Are you insane?"

She shook her head impatiently. "That's good, Coren, appeal to my vanity. You always had a way of making me feel special."

"I'm serious. Do you know what you're doing?"

"Usually."

Coren waited, but she said nothing more. Abruptly, he felt awkward and slightly foolish. He glanced toward the baleys.

"Where'd you get the tinhead?" he asked. "Your father would love that."

"To hell with my father and to hell with you. What, did he send you to find me? What are you going to do, throw me over your shoulder and drag me back home?"

"The thought had occurred to me."

She snorted, but took a step back. Then she gave him a narrow look. "What *are* you going to do?"

He met her gaze evenly, trying to think of a suitable answer. Finding none, he shook his head. "I didn't know you had a robot."

She laughed. "You don't have a plan? Rega didn't send you. You came on your own."

"Not exactly. He *did* tell me to find out what you're doing and–"

"And what? Sit on me till the election is over? That's what this is about, then. Rega is afraid his little girl's activities might botch his election. Tell him not to worry. I think he can ruin his chances all on his own; he doesn't need my help. In fact, you can give him some good news: He won't have to worry about me anymore at all. I won't give him any further cause for concern."

Coren waited. He recognized the tone of voice, the half smile, and a small point of fear burned at the back of his throat. He slipped his hands into his pockets, the right one finding a small plastic bag. He squeezed it till it burst in his palm.

"Nyom," the robot interrupted. Coren started and Nyom laughed.

"Coffee won't hurt you," she said. "What is it, Coffee?"

"Time," the robot said.

"I'll be right there."

Coffee retreated.

"What do you mean, Nyom?" Coren asked.

She sighed and stepped closer. "Tell me the truth now, Coren: did you tell the authorities? Am I going to be arrested by Immigration and Trade Enforcement?"

"No."

She studied him. "You really just came all on your own."

"Too many people are hard to control."

"That's not it." She frowned. "It's still personal, isn't it?" When he did not answer, she smiled. "I'm really flattered. And I'm sorry." She touched his face lightly and turned away.

He grabbed her arm. "What did you mean, Nyom?"

"I'm going with this bunch, that's all. My turn to exit. Nothing personal, Coren, but if you found me, then it's only a matter of time before the authorities find me. I'm taking this ride."

Coren felt his fear grow, becoming panic. "Go *where?*"

"Nova Levis."

Coren released her. He wanted to argue. More, he now really *did* want to drag her out of here. But it was clear from her expression, from the waiting baleys, and the robot watching everything that he would not be able to.

"Well," he said, shrugging. "I can die happy now. I know

you really *are* insane." He cleared his throat. "You *do* know that Nova Levis is under blockade, I suppose?"

"We'll make it." For a moment, Nyom looked sad. "Sorry. I wish . . ."

"Nyom. Please don't."

She shook her head. "Gotta go. You shouldn't be seen. My contacts aren't as understanding as I am."

Nyom sprinted back to her flock of baleys. Seconds later they filed through the bay door. Coren backed quickly up against a wall, standing motionless until they had all passed out of the warehouse proper.

Behind him, one of the bay doors began to open.

Coren broke for it and slipped around the edge just as a huge hauler rumbled through, carrying a four-meter-high stack of cubes. Its slipstream almost knocked him down.

Just on the other side of the opening, Coren found a massive support rib rising to the ceiling high overhead. He pressed into the corner and waited till the bay door sealed, then pulled another device from his pocket.

He raised the optam to his eyes as he peered around the column of composite metal.

Seven or eight meters from the wall, the pavement ended and a tangled maze of thin tracks spread out, delta-like, busy with huge transports carrying large containers, bins, and packages from the tunnel system that led directly to the shuttle pads dotting the landing area of Petrabor field. The surge and rumble of shuttle traffic drove through him, vibrating his bones.

He was annoyed that Nyom had read him so easily. He had hoped she would assume that he had brought back-up— the police, immigration authorities, other company security. He thought he could talk her out of it; that, after loading her latest troop of misguided would-be Settlers aboard whatever means of transport she had arranged, he could convince her to come home and suspend operations for a time. Until the end of the election. He had hoped she might finally want to stay with him.

He had hoped . . .

The view through the optam showed the party of baleys, a few dozen meters down, on an empty patch. While Coren watched, a huge pod drifted out of the writhing traffic and came to a stop before them. The end developed a seam and opened smoothly to one side. Four people stepped from its dark interior to meet with Nyom.

Coren stiffened. Two of the four were robots. One looked a bit more sophisticated than the other, almost human, but the dull sheen that outlined its sleek head and body gave it away. It moved with an unusual grace, a fluid, almost organic motion, uncharacteristic of any robot with which Coren was familiar. It circled the baleys, slowly, as if taking inventory. It stopped before Nyom's robot, Coffee, then seemed to come to a decision and rejoined its companions.

Coren touched a contact on the side of the optam and sound came through the bead in his ear, but he only heard the muffled, unintelligible sounds of a discussion. He lowered the optam and tried to adjust the aural filters to compensate for the noise, then raised it again.

The strange robot was gone.

Coren dropped the optam; he saw the robot clearly. When he raised the magnifier again, the robot did not appear. He could see the other robot easily, a machine slightly smaller than Coffee, a bit sleeker. But the first robot remained invisible.

Masked . . . ?

Coren tensed, preparing to act. The baleys began filing

into the big container, and he realized that he would do nothing. *Nyom knows what she's doing,* he thought. *At least as far as procedure goes.* She did not act alarmed, so he had to assume she knew these people, these machines. It unsettled him, though, to watch her, the last one, walk up the ramp, accompanied by Coffee.

The masked robot followed a minute later, causing Coren's pulse to accelerate again. The other contacts, human and robot, closed up the container, then walked away.

Five minutes later an automated hauler hooked onto the container and pulled it into the maze of tracks and out of Coren's reach.

Abruptly, Coren felt a wave of bitterness. Failure did that. It would have been so simple, so much easier if she had just come with him. Now . . .

He opened his palm monitor and keyed for a new signal. A bright yellow dot glowed on the small screen. The smear he had placed on Nyom had transferred from fabric to metal to plastic, a clever seeker code built into the tiny molecules that imparted a kind of machine instinct to find a suitable place to use as a conductor and enable them to transmit.

He pocketed the optam and the palm monitor and slipped back through the bay door on the next cycle, just ahead of another huge pallet. All he had to do now was get out of the warehouse—and all the communications damping he had put in place—and signal his contact on Kopernik Station.

He imagined how angry Nyom was about to be.

"So what?" he mused as he recovered his overcoat. "Better she's righteously pissed off at me than dead from some trigger-happy blockade station." He glanced back at the bay door. "Nova Levis! What are you *thinking,* Nyom? Or *are* you thinking." He trotted along the walkway toward the offices, muttering. "You've never been particularly impulsive, but when you are, you are absolutely unpredictable. Nova Levis. Damn."

When he reached the locker room, he punched a code into the palm monitor. All the little machines he'd released thoughout the warehouse began to eat themselves into dust. Nothing would be left to analyze, if anyone ever found them. Just minuscule piles of refuse.

He checked the time, estimated that he had about six hours before that bin reached dockside on Kopernik. He could even clean up before he made his call . . .

He recovered the small button he had placed in the exit and stepped into the alley. He saw no one and quickly bounded across to where he had been hiding when the nightshift crew had left. He fished one more device from an inside pocket and opened it. He tapped in a code and waited for the comm to upload for him.

The screen remained blank. He ran a diagnostic. LOCALITY ERROR scrolled across the small screen. Coren hissed, annoyed. Something around here was interfering with the link. He should have tested it first. Probably being this close to the port was causing problems. He closed up the comm unit and headed down the alley.

He splashed through the accrued seepage and hunched his shoulders against the random drops of condensation from the unseen ceiling high overhead. He rounded the next corner and headed up a broad alleyway littered with abandoned shipping crates, refuse dumpsters, old and broken transports, and the scraps of traffic.

"Hey, gato."

Coren glanced to his right, at the source of the throaty voice. A tall man came out of the shadow of a receiving bay and loped toward him, hands in the pockets of a long overcoat. Coren's hand moved for the stunner he carried in his jacket. The stranger coughed heavily, a phlegmy hack Coren recognized as one of the recent strains of sublevel tuberculosis. Not contagious usually, but Coren liked to keep his distance.

"Not tonight," he said.

"Hey, that's not sapien," the man said. "Just wanting a share, you know."

Coren reflexively pulled out a few credits from his pocket and tossed them.

The man scooped them up with more alacrity than Coren would have guessed.

"Thanks, gato," he said and touched a finger to his hat.

Coren turned away.

A hand clenched around his throat between one breath and the next. Coren grabbed the wrist and pushed forward to relieve the pressure, but the hand held. The wrist, wrapped in a thick sleeve, seemed like steel. Coren tried to turn away from the encircling arm and drive an elbow back. He missed, tried again, and then dropped to his knees under a sharp blow to the left shoulder.

He choked. Sparks danced around the edge of his vision. He tried to sweep a hand around to catch the knees of his attacker, but he was too off-balance.

He closed his eyes, and the pain went away.

Coren came awake lying on damp pavement, his throat burning as he choked on the sourness in his mouth. His shoulder throbbed and would not support his attempt to push himself up. He rolled over and stared up at dark walls, too close. He had been moved. He lay still for a minute or more until the acid subsided and his breathing calmed. He managed finally to sit up.

He was about three meters from the end of a narrow

hallway, but still in the same general area of Petrabor, from what he could see beyond. His head spun and his legs trembled as he got to his feet. He needed to get to a medical unit, he knew, but not down here; no telling what kind of treatment he might get from the quacks practicing in the sublevels. He needed to get to a comm sooner.

He patted his pockets. His stunner was gone, as were his optam, palm monitor, and comm unit. But they had missed his ID, and he still had a few credits in a calf-pouch.

Coren tried to figure out what had happened. He was not a small man, and he had been trained well during his years with Special Service, but whoever had attacked him had handled him as if he were a child. Possible, but not the panhandler. Surely not.

He sighed heavily and coughed.

Later, he thought, stumbling from the hallway. *Figure it out later. . . .*

TWO

When he returned to the hostel, all Coren wanted to do was fall into bed and sleep. He leaned against the door of his room, eyes shut, feeling his bruises and weariness. He had been beaten up once before, years ago, but the brain did not remember the pain.

He forced his eyes open. The clock above the bed said NINETEEN-TEN LOCAL.

"Damn. Five hours."

He lurched to the small desk and pulled a briefcase from beneath it. He threw off his overcoat and tapped in the release code on the case, then took out his personal datum. He jacked it into the room comm and entered a string of numbers. He sat down then, anxiously watching while the link assembled itself through a secure channel.

"Come on . . . come on . . ."

"Palen here," a voice crackled sharply from the comm.

"It's Coren, Sipha. The package is on its way up."

"Already tracking it. We'll have it in the bay in . . . two

hours and a bit. Where have you been? I expected your call—"

"I'll tell you later. I was delayed unavoidably."

"You still coming up?"

"As soon as I get clean. I'll be on a shuttle in an hour."

"If we get the package in station before you get here?"

"Can you delay opening till I'm there?"

"Within limits."

"I'm moving as fast as I can, Sipha. Thanks."

Coren entered a new number and read over the shuttle schedules that scrolled onto the screen. Hand trembling slightly, he booked one, and closed down the link. He considered trying to contact the data troll who had told him about tonight's clandestine emigration, but that could scare her. She had been nervous anyway; their meeting had not gone smoothly. Coren had been in too big a hurry to question her anxiety, but now he wondered about it. He unjacked his datum and put it away.

He assembled his luggage quickly, then stripped off the grimy clothes. He showered, depilated his face, and dressed in tailored black and dark blue. The overcoat and coveralls went into the recycle chute.

Coren snatched his briefcase and single duffle, gave the cubicle a last look, gaze lingering on the bed. *I really need sleep,* he thought. On the shuttle, he decided, and left for the port.

Coren gripped the armrests, unable to make himself relax. He knew the shuttle was in motion and, though he felt nothing, the knowledge made him sick. He forced himself not to slouch, grateful that the nausea was not worse.

"Big brave policeman," he muttered sourly, "scared of a little spaceflight."

He glanced at his fellow passengers. One man slept soundly by induced coma—an option Coren found more repellant than the flight itself—and the only others he could see clearly seemed to be Spacers, tall and elegant and gathered together in one section in the front of the cabin, talking animatedly, unfazed by the fact that they were hurtling through space with less than thirty centimeters of hull between them and vacuum.

Coren closed his eyes and tried to think about what had happened to him.

It was possible that Nyom had hired someone to cover her back and that the panhandler had been her muscle. Possible, but inconsistent with Nyom Looms—at least, not the Nyom Looms Coren thought he knew.

Perhaps he no longer really knew her. He had made an assumption, relied on old data, and gotten hurt.

But assuming for the moment that the panhandler had not been her man, then who was he? Coren's shoulder and neck throbbed; the bruise would be spectacular.

Definitely have to have a talk with that data troll, he thought. The idea that he had been set up troubled him, but it was not unlikely. Baley running attracted an undependable variety of conscience, people committed to various causes but with a weakness for money that worked against their revolutionary principles. The few True Believers were unapproachable in any ordinary sense—those from whom Coren could extract information were, by definition, untrustworthy.

The troll who had supplied him with the data for last night's shipment—a woman named Jeta Fromm—should have been more reliable. Coren used a clearing house for people like her: Data Recovery Systems, Ltd. An innocuous name, considering how much borderline illicit trade they dealt in. But they guaranteed the work of their operatives—

sometimes in heavy-handed and unpleasant ways—and would not take it well to learn that one of their people had betrayed a client. Still, he had not gotten that impression from Jeta Fromm. She did not seem like the sort who would indulge in doublecrosses. She had been anxious, but the data she supplied had been accurate. If anything, she had seemed preoccupied. Coren relied a great deal on his intuition about people—he had occasionally been wrong, no system is perfect—and he thought he had judged her correctly. Perhaps he had and something else was involved. It would not do to act before he knew, which meant he had to find her on his own and not go through the clearing house. They might misunderstand. At best, he could cost her employment. At worst . . .

The other possibility was that Number Sixteen third shift dockworker who had met with Nyom. But Coren had not seen him clearly and with his optam stolen he had no images to work with. Perhaps he could find out who he was through the ITE office in Baltimor. He knew someone there. It would be interesting in any case to find out what connection existed between that branch and a Petrabor baley-smuggling operation.

At least he knew he could rely on Sipha Palen and accomplish his mission.

Nyom would be furious with him.

No matter, so long as she was safely back on Earth and out of circulation for a while. Rega owned a villa in Kenya Sector where he often went to be alone—Coren himself had overseen its security. It was the safest place he knew to tuck Nyom away while the election ran.

"Your attention please," an automated voice said. "We will be docking at Kopernik Station in fifteen minutes. Please be sure your safety field is on and secured and any personal objects are stowed in the appropriate compartments. Remain in your seats until the green debarkation light is on. Thank you."

Coren sighed gratefully. Fifteen minutes. Good. He looked up at the group of Spacers and briefly caught one's eye. For a moment he thought he recognized an expression of sympathy. But it passed and she laughed at a joke from one of her companions.

He shifted uncomfortably. His safety field had stayed on the entire trip. His skin prickled slightly from the faint pressure. His shirt stuck to him from the sweat; he would need another shower as soon as he debarked.

He felt a brief lurch and clutched desperately at the armrests.

"We have completed docking at Kopernik Station, Bay two-one-seven. Please remain seated until we are ready for debarkation. We hope you have enjoyed your flight and we thank you for traveling Intrapoint."

Coren bit back a snide comment and concerned himself with shutting down the safety field. His legs hurt from the constant tension.

A row of green lights winked on overhead the length of the cabin. An attendant came through to help anyone who might need assistance. Coren stood, thankful his legs did not shake. He pulled his briefcase from the cubby beneath his seat and made his way to the exit. As he walked down the white-walled tunnel away from the shuttle, he began feeling more confident. He emerged into the brightly-lit, cheerily-colored, close-ceilinged reception lounge feeling a bit foolish about his fear. He slipped on his jacket while he scanned the waiting crowd.

Sipha Palen stood off to the left and gave him a nod, then strolled off. Coren checked in at the security desk and retrieved his duffle. He caught up with Sipha halfway down the concourse and fell into step beside her.

Sipha stood at least twelve centimeters taller than him, with broad shoulders tapering into what she called a "swimmer's build"—slim-hipped and sinewy. Pale amber eyes stood out sharply against her brassy-brown skin; she wore her copper hair in a thick queue than hung to just between her shoulderblades. Her ivory suit hinted at "uniform" without being obvious. She smelled of hot metal and flowers.

"How was the flight?" she asked nonchalantly.

"Don't," he said.

She gave him a wry smile. "You should fly more often. You might learn to like it."

"It's good to see you, Sipha," he said, ignoring the jab.

"Likewise. The package arrived four hours, twenty minutes ago. We have the bay secured—just my people. Do you want to go right there or tidy up first?"

"Let's get it over with. Maybe I can enjoy the rest of my stay afterward."

Sipha made a dubious noise, but increased the pace slightly. She led him to an in-station shuttle car.

"By the way," he said as he strapped in, "there are two robots in there. One looks pretty ordinary, but the other one was invisible to my optam."

"Masked?"

"I can't think of another explanation. So let your people know to be careful."

They made the transit in silence, Coren staring at a spot just above Sipha's right shoulder. The car slowed to a halt and Sipha stepped lithely out. Coren followed her down a service corridor into an immense bay.

The security people standing around straightened when they saw Sipha. She strode across the pale gray floor toward the cargo bin sitting near its center. Coren's heartbeat quickened upon seeing it—relief, he realized. It was here, safe, and soon Nyom would be on her way to even more safety.

It is still personal . . . he thought.

A pair of uniformed techs, expressions tight, approached Sipha. They spoke in low, terse tones.

"Open the damn thing now!" Sipha shouted.

She sprinted the rest of the distance to the bin. Coren dropped his luggage and ran after her. Techs, galvanized, lurched into motion.

People converged on the bin. Coren stopped outside the huddle of technicians working to open it and waited, impatient and anxious.

The seal parted and the door folded down.

Coren shouldered his way through the uniforms.

Sipha entered the bin first.

"Get me some light in here!" she called, her voice hollow.

Coren bumped her, stopped at the edge of darkness. The spillover from the bay lights picked out disconnected details of a squat bulk just before them and lines that might be the edges of shelves or cots. Coren heard a faint, rhythmic buzzing.

"What—?" he began.

Techs came up behind them with hand-held floodlamps. They switched them on and raised them.

Coren blinked at the sudden glare.

The air smelled faintly burnt . . .

"Shit," Sipha breathed.

Racks of couches crowded the walls all around, three deep, with barely a meter between levels. Each pallet contained a body. None of them moved; Coren detected no breath pushing at clothing, no hint of life. Dead bodies, an umbilical running from each facemask to the large apparatus in the center of the cramped open space directly before Sipha and Coren.

On the opposite side of the big machine, Coffee knelt, motionless.

Coren's ears sang with blood. Sparks teased at the periphery of his vision and he felt cocooned, separated from his surroundings. He made himself step forward. He looked in at the nearest corpse. She had been strapped into the couch. Her hands had clutched spasmodically at the fabric beneath her.

The couch above her held a child, its eyes staring blindly.

He made his way around the apparatus, stepping carefully over the tubes running from its base, up the railings, and into the couches.

Coffee's hands were frozen on a control panel. Coren bent over to see what the robot was touching. DISENGAGE. Coren glared at the robot. He felt his hands curl instantly into fists.

"You piece of—"

"Coren."

He looked up at Sipha. She still stood at the entrance. She pointed up.

Coren looked.

Dangling from the ceiling of the bin was another body. Hanging, suspended, it shifted ever-so-slightly right to left and back in the movement of air coming from the bay. It was a woman, her head angled sharply to the left. Her eyes were wide, tongue extruded between her lips.

Nyom.

The tea in his cup had gone cold as Coren watched Sipha's people remove the bodies. The air in the office cubicle was a few degrees too cool. He stared fixedly through the window at the forensic dance around the crime scene.

Nyom would be brought out last, he knew, because her condition was so different.

Sipha entered the office and sat down heavily behind the small desk.

"Fifty-two bodies," she said. "We don't have the facilities to store them in our morgue. I'm having stasis units moved into an equipment locker nearby. Best we can do till we know how to handle this."

Coren looked up. "Fifty-two? There were fifty-one baleys."

"We've got fifty-two now."

"All human?"

Sipha nodded. "Maybe one was already in the bin. Who knows?"

"What about the other robot?" Coren asked.

"No second robot. Just the one. Sorry."

"I saw it enter the bin with them. You're telling me it got out?"

"You saw it get in at the warehouse dock. After that, who knows? Once on board its shuttle, it could have left. Or it might not have even gotten on the shuttle." She grunted. "We could ask the one we *do* have, but it's collapsed."

"How convenient," he said. "What ship was this bin scheduled for?"

"It's not even in dock yet, won't be for another three days. A Settler cargo hauler, slated for a direct run to an orbital facility owned by a company called the Hunter Group."

"Three days . . ." Coren shook his head.

"So," Sipha said after a time, "what do you think happened?"

Coren shuddered briefly and set the cup aside. He folded his hands in his lap. "The other robot. It must've glitched or malfunctioned or . . . something. It killed Nyom, then suffocated the others by switching off the rebreather unit."

"What about Nyom's robot? Why would it have allowed that to happen?"

"They must've been in it together."

Sipha said nothing. Coren turned his chair to face her. She wore a skeptical expression.

"That's what you *want* to believe," she said.

Coren nodded. "Trouble is, I don't have a viable alternative. Do you?"

"No. But I'm not sure I can accept that one robot could kill. You want me to accept that two of them were cooperating in a mass murder."

Coren grunted. "Since when have you gone Spacer?"

She frowned. "Since when have you lost the ability to think?"

Coren glared at her.

"We partnered for two years in Special Service," she said. "I thought you were more reasonable than that. Maybe I was wrong. Maybe working for Rega Looms has loosened your grip on objective reality. What do you think?"

Coren worked himself back from anger and tried to think it through. Sipha had come into the Service directly from the military, a different path than his more direct route of applying to the Academy for Civic Defense, Forensics, and Criminal Interdiction. Despite their divergent backgrounds, Coren had come to trust her. He still did. It had surprised him when, after he had left the Service, she had taken this position as head of security for Kopernik Station.

But it put her in almost daily contact with Spacers and

Settlers, both factions of whom had embassy branches on the station.

Nevertheless, he trusted her. That, he recognized, had not changed.

"All right," he said slowly. "Tell me your reasoning."

"That robot is collapsed. Positronic nervous breakdown. Something happened to cause it, and if it could break down like that then it could not have harmed any of those people. If it were still walking around, calmly trying to do its business, then I might agree with you." She sat back. "I've been up here five years, Coren. I've learned a little bit about robots. Have to, when you deal with Spacers who won't leave home without them. I had to learn to discount my own prejudices a long time ago if I wanted any chance of running my department efficiently and doing my job honestly. It wasn't easy—I still don't like them—but I know their limitations. It wasn't the robot. Not that one, anyway. And I doubt it was this other one—there's no in-built compunction that prevents a robot from harming another robot, especially in the defense of humans. As far as we've been able to tell, that second robot wasn't even on board when this happened." She gestured toward the bay. "Besides, what motive? Suicide? Bringing along a robot would have been the best way to *fail* to commit suicide. They're programmed to save our lives for us, whether we want them to or not."

Coren nodded. "All right, that's all logical. As far as it goes. Sorry about the remark."

"Forget it. So—how do you want to proceed?"

"Why do I get a say? Isn't this official now?"

Sipha pursed her lips thoughtfully. "Maybe." She seemed to consider carefully. "See, this bay is Settler. When you contacted me about this little favor you wanted, I called in a few favors of my own. Right now, this whole business exists in an official vacuum. No one knows but you, me, and my immediate staff." She stabbed a finger in the direction of the cargo bin. "And whoever killed all those people."

"You'll have to make it official sooner or later."

"True. But maybe by then we can figure this out."

Coren studied her for a moment. Something in her expression teased at him.

"There's something else," he stated.

Sipha still pondered, then nodded. "I agreed to do this for you because I need you."

"I'm flattered. But I'm also private now."

"Oh, I think we can change that if we need to. But . . . I have a problem I can't take to my superiors. I'm not even sure who among my own people I can trust with it. I need outside help. I didn't know how I was going to get it till you called."

"Is it related?"

"I wouldn't be surprised. Probably. It has to do with baleys, at least. Dead ones, too, though this is the first load of corpses to show up on my station."

Coren raised an eyebrow in amusement. "'Your' station?"

Sipha smiled wolfishly. "Oh, yes, old partner mine. Never doubt it. *My* station. It has trouble and I want it fixed." She gazed past him, into the bay. "As I say, this is the first load of corpses. The occasional body has been turning up from time to time. The sorts of people who easily get crushed when they learn the wrong thing, or know too much, or who just show up where they shouldn't. Most of them have been thoroughly professional kills . . . till about three months ago."

Coren waited. She seemed to come to a decision and

activated the datum on the desk. The paper-thin screen extruded and winked on. She worked intently for a couple of minutes, then crooked a finger at him to have a look.

"We found this in one of our detention cells," she said.

On the screen Coren saw a body, laid out on a morgue table. It had been a woman—the basic shape was still intact—but he had never seen a body so thoroughly bruised: blue, green, and sickly yellow marks ran from the scalp to the toes. Faint red laceration marks interrupted the mottling here and there.

"What was it? Explosive decompression? Something fall on her?"

"In a detention cell?" Sipha asked wryly. "She was alive when we put her in there. Small-quantity Brethe peddler, nothing major, ever—public nuisance, more than anything else. She was supposed to be, you see, because she worked for me."

"Regular cop?"

"No, she really did used to deal in black market. I made her a better deal. It worked out. She worked the Settler section for me."

Coren felt himself smile. "And when there was something really important to report ... ?"

"She got herself arrested. This hadn't been the first time she'd visited one of my cells. The next shift, we found her like this. Very simply, every bone in her body had been broken. A lot of them were crushed."

"What was she reporting?"

"I don't know. She came in 'under the influence.' I was tied up with arranging all this for you and didn't get a chance to talk to her."

"No one heard or saw anything?"

"Evidently not. That's why I'm not really sure about my people. Can you think of a way that could happen and no one on watch would know about it?"

Coren shook his head. "What about surveillance?"

"Blank for that section. I suspended two of my officers for negligence, but I honestly don't think they were the ones who did it. Someone with a bit more expertise fiddled the recorders. The problem with that is, I have at least five people on my staff who *could* have done it, but none of them has a motive." Sipha gestured toward the image on the screen. "Besides, look at that and tell me how it was done. A couple of adjusters with clubs? I don't think so."

"But since you don't really suspect your two discipline cases, you have an idea."

Sipha nodded. "During autopsy we came up with this." She tapped the keypad. "The bruising is uninterrupted over the entire body and none of the fractures are consistent with blows."

The screen changed, showing an image of a shoulder, blackened like rotting fruit. Sipha adjusted the scan and one shape emerged, slightly darker than the surrounding bruise. Coren stared at the vague outline of a hand. An odd hand, to be sure, the fingers too thick and short, the spread too wide.

"Was it clear enough for any kind of prints?" he asked.

"No prints. Perfectly smooth except for a couple of joints. And the bone beneath this impression had been ground nearly to powder. No, partner mine, this isn't a human hand."

"A robot?" He shook his head. "But you said—"

"I said *that* robot—" she pointed out at the bay "—didn't do it. But that's still my best guess. And if a robot did this—" she gestured at the screen "—if a robot—maybe your second mystery robot—got into my cells and did this, then I have a serious problem." She looked up at him. "Will you help me?"

"I—" Coren began.

The door opened. One of Sipha's men leaned in. "Chief, you need to see this."

"Couple things," the older man—Baxin, Sipha's staff pathologist—said when Sipha and Coren entered the bin. He pointed at the rebreather unit. The umbilicals had all been disconnected and had retracted into the unit. "That's a standard Fain-Bischer rebreather. About six years old, out of date, but still in good working order. No reason it won't last another hundred years once it's been cleaned out."

"Cleaned out of what?" Sipha asked.

"We don't know yet, but it's evident from the postures of the deceased that they've been poisoned. Something in the rebreather, we assume. Something clever, too. The filtration system should have blocked it, but it didn't." He nodded sharply. "That's one thing. The other . . ." He pointed up.

Nyom's body had been taken down and now they could see how she had been suspended. The roof had a crack in it, about half a meter long and perhaps five to eight centimeters at the widest. The metal around it was discolored, heat-scored.

"The bin was pressurized," the tech explained. "The air leaked out through that crack. My guess is that the body was drawn to it during freefall. The fabric of her pants got caught in it."

"Did decompression kill her?" Coren asked.

"No. A broken neck did that. She was dead before she got stuck in the ceiling."

Coren looked down at the rebreather. "Why? If everyone

else was poisoned . . ." He looked around. "Where's the robot?"

"I've got it in an impound locker," Baxin said. "I didn't know where else to put it."

Sipha extended her hand. "Give me the tag. I'll take care of the robot. How long on autopsies?"

"Fifteen, twenty hours," Baxin said. "A few preliminaries sooner than that maybe."

"What made the crack?" Coren asked. "It looks intentional."

"It is," Baxin said. "Heat induction, industrial grade drill or welder, crystalized the metal, made it brittle."

"What kind?"

"We don't have it. There's nothing in here that would do that."

"Not even the robot?"

"No, I don't think so. Specialized tool, in my opinion."

Coren gave the hole in the roof a last glance, then left the bin.

When Sipha joined him, he said, "Doesn't make sense. Who broke her neck if Coffee didn't?"

She glanced at him. " 'Coffee'?"

"That's what she called the robot." He saw Sipha's expression. "Don't ask me, I don't know why. But who else could have broken her neck?"

"We'll check the bodies to see if time of death matches in all cases. But I still think you're wrong about the robot. Maybe it knew they were being poisoned—that's what it was trying to stop."

"*How* did it know? And who—"

"I know, who broke Nyom's neck. Maybe the same one who crushed that Brethe dealer?"

"And which one would that be? Which dead one in that

bin who had never been to Kopernik before would that be?" Coren asked sarcastically. "Oh, wait, I know. The same one who cracked a hole in the bin with an inducer that no one can find."

Sipha snarled at him. "I don't damn well know, Coren. So I repeat: will you help me?"

He nodded. "Oh, yes. I'll help you. No question." He mulled his options for a few seconds. "I'm going back down. You can handle the autopsies without me. Also, I'll need ID on all of them."

"What's down there?" Sipha frowned. Clearly, she had thought they would be working together for a few days.

"I have a couple of people to talk to. For one, the data troll who put me onto Nyom in the first place. I want to find those people Nyom was dealing with, and she's my best chance right now." He drew a deep breath. "And we're going to need a roboticist."

"There's a lab full of them here—"

"Do you trust them?"

Sipha scowled, then shook her head. "Not till I find out who killed my Brethe dealer."

"I'll see if I can take care of that, then."

"I suppose you know a roboticist?"

"*Of* one, yes. I think it's best to stay away from anyone involved directly with the Spacer sector on Kopernik."

Sipha nodded. "I'll get you on the next shuttle back to D.C."

"No, not D.C. Lyzig District—that's where my informant lives. I'll take the suborbital back to D.C. after I talk to her. Send me the autopsy data when you have it."

"What are you going to say to Looms?"

Coren shook his head. "I'll worry about that when I see him."

THREE

The flight down frightened him more than the trip up to Kopernik. Perhaps it was the idea of falling, but Coren felt at the edge of panic from the moment the shuttle left dock till he walked, legs trembling, into the concourse at Lyzig Station. It did not make sense—he never reacted this way on a semiballistic—and he resented the idea that it was all psychosomatic. He went directly to a public restroom and rinsed his face in cold water, then sat in a stall till the sweating and nausea passed.

"Never again," he muttered as he finally gathered himself up. He checked his watch—twenty minutes wasted getting over his reaction—and left the restroom.

He rented a locker and shoved his one bag inside, then headed for the station lobby.

Lyzig buzzed with first-shift traffic. The warrens swarmed with people going to jobs or shops or meetings. Coren liked Lyzig: Clean, robust, a polished politesse substituted for the unmannered friendliness of other Eurosector districts, as if the residents were conscious of a long history—an important past they were obliged to honor.

At the station gate he flagged a taxi and gave his destination. The driver's eyebrows raised speculatively, but all he said was "Very good, sir," and moved into the vehicular lanes. The short ride ended at an ancient hotel. Coren tipped the driver and stepped out.

The taxi pulled away and Coren began walking in the opposite direction. His shakes were gone by now and he walked purposefully, in imitation of resident Lyzigers.

He had three options to find Jeta Fromm. He had already decided against contacting Data Recovery Systems, through which he had originally found her. He had to assume that whoever had killed Nyom had gotten the same information about the baley run, and that meant a competitor. He had no way of knowing yet where they would have gotten the data—it might have been Jeta Fromm herself, or her handlers, or some as yet undetermined third source. He could too easily reveal his interest by going through the usual channels.

The second option was not worth considering at this point. Local police could find her and pick her up, but he would be effectively destroying her career and perhaps hurting several other people associated with her. A significant part of the work he did depended on clandestine resources. Damaging them by "going local" could cost him his reputation and impair his ability to do his job. Using the local police, then, was a course of last resort.

His best option, then, was to find her himself. He had met with her twice, at different locations of her choosing. Her nervousness had bothered him, so he had traced her back to her hab—just in case he needed to find her quickly and confidentially. Like now.

The area he now entered was very old, and the signs of wear and neglect became more evident the further he walked. The fast pace and energy representative of Lyzig faded; people here were in no hurry to go anywhere—a few were even sitting in doorways, or gathered in small groups near shops or in the cramped public spaces that passed for parks in this part of the urbanplex.

Coren automatically imitated the lethargy around him, moving slower, keeping his head down. He tucked his hands in his pockets and searched the corridor signs till he found one marked BETRAGSTRAS. He walked down the narrower corridor to a steep metal staircase that ran up the window-less wall to his left. The ghosts of old graffiti discolored the surfaces, scrubbed endlessly by automated cleaners that, over time, failed to remove all the paint.

At the top of the stairs, Coren found a broad rooftop upon which stacks of single-unit cubicles formed a small, cramped village. Light glowed from open doorways, and the thick smell of cooking almost covered the odors of plastic and sweat and unprocessed waste.

Faces appeared at doorways, lingered for a few seconds, then retreated.

Coren estimated about a thousand people lived in this precariously overbuilt shantytown, lived quite illegally and with little fear of eviction, but with the constant possibility of having the entire makeshift construct tumble down on them. Many of the residents worked legitimate jobs that paid too little to afford them a decent domicile and do whatever else they found more important—sending children to better schools, subscriptions to expensive entertain-ments, paying off a debt, or saving for the chance to emi-grate—but just as many worked on the edge of legality: dealers in stolen data or controlled substances, informants, runners, small credit fences, rented muscle. Others simply had nowhere else to go and had fallen here, fortunate to at least have a place to sleep and a source for food.

Coren took out his palm monitor and made his way through the maze of passageways, up a ladder, and down a short gangway to an unlit doorway. The signal from the smear he had deposited on Jeta the second time they met was weaker, but still traceable. The self-replicating vonoomans exhausted themselves after a few days and decayed unrecoverably. He ran the sensor up and down a scale to test it. Satisfied that Jeta Fromm had at least stayed here for more than an hour, giving his tiny tracers a chance to proliferate in the environment, he pocketed the monitor. He palmed a flash and switched it on as he kicked in the flimsy plastic door and stepped through.

In the harsh blue-white illumination, the cubicle leapt into sharp relief. A cot stretched against the wall to his left, a sleeping bag and extra blankets wadded up at the head. A makeshift desk stood along the back wall, cluttered with objects that formed an indecipherable tangle. Along the wall to the right was a trunk, the lid open, the contents spilling over the edge—clothing, from the look of it.

Immediately to the right Coren found a lamp propped on a three-legged table. He switched it on and turned off his own light.

Vacant. He closed the door behind him.

He studied the room carefully. Jeta Fromm had struck him as a fastidious person, neat and methodical. This place did not. He sat down on the edge of the cot.

Disks, small pieces of paper, items of clothing, scraps of unidentifiable detritus littered the floor. A chair lay on its side to the left of the desk. The cot itself was angled away from the wall.

It appeared to Coren that she—or someone—had left in a hurry, possibly in a panic. Jeta peddled data—rumor, software, illicit downloads, even documented fact when she sold material to the newsnets as a stringer—so any of a number of deals could cause her to run.

She had been very professional when he met her, but it seemed to him now that there had been an undercurrent of desperation. She managed it well and he had been in a hurry, so he had neglected to pay it enough attention.

Coren stepped up to the desk. The clutter consisted mainly of components from old, salvaged readers, scanners, and bits of datum units. He saw a control panel from a commline. Tools lay mixed with the debris. Two bare spaces suggested removed equipment. He guessed, given her range of services, that she owned a pathburner, a very expensive microcircuitry cutter. Probably a very good decryption datum. The cost of those two pieces would be more than his own yearly salary.

What he saw here convinced Coren that Jeta was on the run. Someone—maybe the same someone who had rolled him in Petrabor—had come looking for her. She had duly disappeared.

He knelt down and shuffled through the papers and disks on the floor. The disks were labeled by numbers. He could go through them, but he doubted she would have left anything behind worth the trouble.

The papers mostly contained scribbled comm codes, cryptic notes—"Jam on B-stras, 3s" or "Cram Seef for Rudo, level 12"—and a couple of doodles. One caught his eye that said "B meet at seven's place, 2shift" followed by a comm code. He slipped it into his pocket and stood.

He turned off the light and stepped outside.

To his left he glimpsed someone watching him from a

doorway. The door slammed shut. Coren reached the cubicle in three long strides and shouldered his way in.

In the pale light he saw a small man shoving himself in the corner behind a large chest of drawers. Coren shut the door and stepped closer.

"I didn't! Stop! I didn't!" the man cried.

"You know Jeta?" Coren demanded. "She ask you to watch her place?"

"I don't—nothing to say, gato—please—"

"Don't 'gato' me, shit. Dump it now. You're a friend of Jeta's?"

He nodded once. He was not quite as small as he at first seemed, but the clothes he wore were too big and his head was long and shaved bald. His sleeves half-covered his hands.

"You're watching for her, right? Who came to visit before me? Who's looking for her?"

The man shook his head a little too quickly. "Don't know."

"Don't know what? Who, if, when?"

"Never saw them before."

"Them? Two? More?"

"Two. Man and a woman."

"The man," Coren said. "Short, stout, yellow skin?"

A scowl flashed across his face. "No, it was—I don't know. Leave me alone."

Coren resisted the urge to grab the smaller man. Strong-arming would do no good, but he wondered just how far subtlety would get him.

"Listen, gato," he said gently, "Jeta's in trouble. If I don't find her first she'll be dead. Savvy? Now, who came?"

"Never—I—" The man swallowed loudly and closed his eyes. "Dead?" he whispered.

"*Very* dead."

The man nodded weakly. "She—two days ago, third shift, she says time to go, she's sorry. Be back in a few days for her jumble—"

"Her what?"

"Jumble—her stuff—"

"All right, go on."

"Asks me just to spot who comes looking. Like you guessed."

"And?"

"Three hours later this tall gato, long coat, tosses her cube. Didn't see me. Stayed in her place maybe twenty minutes."

"Tall. Anything else?"

"Dark skin, like he's seen sun or something. Didn't blink."

"Didn't blink . . . his eyes?"

"What else you got that blinks?"

"Did he talk to you?"

"No," the man said indignantly. "I *said* he didn't see me."

"You said a woman?"

"Came yesterday. Looked around Jeta's cube, stayed maybe an hour, then left."

"What did she look like?"

"Wore a mask. Not too big, though, but—"

"Nobody stopped her?"

"The other one was with her, stayed outside."

"You don't know where Jeta might have gone?"

"No," the man insisted.

Coren grunted. He took a gamble. "Who's Seven?"

The man frowned. " 'Seven'? I don't know . . ." He seemed honestly ignorant, so Coren dropped it.

"Did these gatos talk to anybody else?"

"Might have." The man paused, thought it over for a

moment. "Yes, did. Cobbel and Renz. They got the first cubes at the edge."

Coren suppressed a smile. "What did this tall gato sound like?"

"Kind of raspy-voiced, like he had trouble breathing. But it came out of his chest, real deep. Cobbel and Renz didn't like him too much."

"Did the woman talk to anyone?"

"No."

Coren considered. Then he stood. "All right, thanks. I'm not here to hurt Jeta. You tell her the gato that paid her twice market for that last data she sold needs to talk to her again. Tell her to find me if she wants to stay alive. Savvy?"

"How'll she find you?"

"Same way she found what I wanted. She'll know. You see her, you tell her to stay on the move, though."

"Serious shit?" the man asked.

Coren nodded. "Very."

He backed out of the cubicle and reentered Jeta's cube. He took out his palm monitor and adjusted it, then turned a slow circle till a light flashed red.

From up in the corner, tucked in a crack between the wall and the ceiling, he removed a small button. He repeated the scan and found another one, on her desk amid a jumble of electronics, pretending to be a relay switch.

If there were more, his monitor missed them. He opened a slot in the side of the monitor and dropped them in. They barely fit.

At the edge of the hab collection, he paused. Then he knocked on the nearest door.

A woman looked out at him. She said nothing, only waited expectantly.

"Cobbel or Renz?" Coren said.

"Renz. What?"

"The tall gato talked to you about Jeta Fromm."

She frowned. "What about him?"

"Did he give you a code to tap if you found Jeta?"

"You police?"

"Private."

"Ah." She stepped out. She was quite a bit shorter than he, surprisingly so. "He tapped us. Ears all over the place. Cobbel's still looking for all of them. We figured that, when he *didn't* give us a code."

"He knew you'd lie."

Rena shook her head. "Wouldn't lie." She smiled. "Wouldn't tell him *anything.*"

"What was he like?"

She frowned again, thoughtfully. "Scary shit. Never blinked. Skin looked wrong."

"Wrong how?"

"Don't know. Just wrong. Diseased, maybe. Too smooth. No veins." She studied him narrowly. "Jeta's in trouble."

"Looks that way. Bad trouble."

"You trying to help?"

"My fault. Trying to cover accounts."

Renz nodded. "You won't find her. Best *she* finds *you.*"

"If you see her, tell her. I need to talk to her."

"Ain't seen her in a few days. She knows how to find you?"

Coren nodded. "I don't think there's much Jeta can't find. Do you?"

That elicited a sly smile.

"Just out of curiosity," Coren asked, "how long has she lived here? People in her profession move a lot, I know."

"Long enough," Renz said. "Longer than most—three months or so."

Coren nodded. That was a long time—for a data troll.

"I'm going," Coren said. "You see her, tell her. I need to talk to her soonest."

He went to the steps. He glanced back and saw people watching him now, openly. Something had passed through here that had scared them.

Coren hurried down the steps.

On the way back to the tube station, Coren stopped at a public comm and punched in the code he had found. The screen flashed DISCONNECTED SOURCE. He studied the note for a time, trying to decide if it would be worth his while to try to find this Seven. In the end, he fed the paper into a recycler. No time to be as thorough as he wanted. He tapped in the code for the Auroran embassy and began making his way through the maze of connections to find the person he needed to speak to.

Third shift was just beginning in Petrabor Sector. Coren's timing was close, arriving at the warehouse just ahead of the crew.

He stood across from their entrance and this time they noticed him as they filed in by groups of twos and threes. He no longer wore the tattered leftovers of a warren ghost but the fine suit of someone in authority—an inspector or manager or perhaps a cop. As they saw him their friendly chatter died away, replaced by suspicion and silence.

Coren had about half an hour before he needed to catch a semiballistic to D.C. He studied the faces that passed before him, matching them to his memory, but the sixteenth crewman failed to appear. No surprise.

The foreman emerged from the employee access and came toward him. He was a short man, middle-aged and just beginning to lose the firm lines of a body made powerful during time working the bays instead of just supervising others.

"Can I help you?" he asked, stopping a meter away.

Coren held up his ID, which contained the emblem identifying him as a licensed independent security investigator. The foreman almost took a step closer to examine it, but Coren shoved it back into his pocket.

"Last night," Coren said, "you took your crew out during on-duty time. A place called Dimilio's?"

The foreman's eyes became wary. "What about it?"

Coren shook his head sorrowfully. "That's not contract."

"The Guild send you? Management?"

"What do you think would've happened if the routers had glitched with no one there to shut it down?"

"Routers never glitch!"

"They do if they're hacked."

Now the wariness turned to fear. "Hacked . . . " He swallowed. "You're talking about—"

"I'm not talking about anything yet. I'm asking. Why did you think it would all right to walk out midshift, en masse like that, for a few drinks?"

The foreman scowled at him. "I don't have to talk to you."

Coren nodded agreeably. "That's right, you don't. But if that's what you decide to do, the next people you talk to will be ITE inspectors. They don't give a damn about contract protections."

The foreman took a tentative step closer. "Look—it was Oril's birthday. Not yesterday, but the day before, but there wasn't time then to do anything. Busy shift. Things slowed down yesterday, there were a couple of windows, we figured, what's an hour or two? We've never had a problem—"

Coren sighed dramatically. "Contract says someone has to be on duty—"

"There was! We left the sub here. He didn't know Oril anyway, no loss."

"The sub. I didn't see any sub listed—"

The foreman looked pained for a second. "Farom was out, he's been having trouble with his kid. He's already past his allotment for personal time and sick days—any more and he gets written up. We paid the sub out of our own pocket to come in for him so Farom wouldn't get the reprimand."

"I need the sub's name."

"I'm telling you, Farom's a good worker—"

"The sub's name." Coren leaned closer and softened his voice. "If I can keep this off the record I will—it'll save me a lot of trouble. I don't need the extra datawork. I just have to verify that you didn't leave your shift unattended. Word is that management has some losses to explain to shareholders. You know how that is. Now there was a glitch in the logs for the time you were all toasting Oril's good health. If it was operator error, then we can correct it on our end and leave you alone." Coren reached out then and grabbed hold of the foreman's coverall. "But you pull that kind of shit again, I'll have your ass in front of management *and* the Guild conciliators. Understand?"

"Yuri Pocivil," the foreman said quickly. "He's normally Second Shift at the Number Four yard. He had personal time."

"How did you come to call him?"

"We used him before."

"Covering for Farom?"

The foreman swallowed. "As a matter of fact, yeah."

Coren released him. "Yuri Pocivil. I'm going to have a talk with him. He explains the glitch to my satisfaction, you won't see me again."

"We've never had any problems with him before."

"Happens when you step out of contract. Go back to work."

Shaken, the foreman almost bowed as he backed away. He'd recovered his composure by the time he reached the entrance. He gave Coren a last look—to which Coren returned a reassuring nod—then disappeared inside the warehouse.

Yuri Pocivil had failed to report to work that day and his apartment was vacant. Coren was not surprised, but he *was* disappointed. It would have been simpler had he found him. Pocivil was a more direct line to whoever was running the operation.

He made his way to the station, mulling over his next move. The routing had been modified in Baltimor. That, at least, was convenient to his next stop.

FOUR

Derec Avery watched the screens with mild interest. The central view was a complex collection of concentric, overlapping rings. Where some of the lines crossed, pockets formed containing patternless amalgams of small shapes, like froth or dried, cracked mud, or a cloud of midges. The right-hand screen showed a similar view but without the pockets. The left showed only chaos.

As he watched, the rings on the central screen expanded and shrank minutely, as if jockeying for position in a crowded container, occasionally sending waves through one or more of the broken pockets. One pocket suddenly dissolved, quickly forming its own node and growing a set of rings. On the opposite side another pocket, this one filled with what appeared to be different-sized pebbles, wavered on the brink of dissolution. The pocket changed shape, narrowing, nearly splitting in two, then reinflating. Abruptly, it solidified, the pebbles merging to form a smooth surface. Then the wall burst and pebbles spilled across the orderly waves of circles, rupturing them, forming new pockets of disorder, and within seconds the screen lost all sign of pattern.

"Disappointing," said a calm, genderless alto voice.

"What happened, Thales?" Derec asked, though he already knew.

"I lost a primary anchor in the matrix," replied his office's Resident Intelligence. "When it went, it caused a cascade."

"Did you know it was a primary anchor?"

"No. That is, of course, the problem. I have to assign anchor points without knowing how they relate to the entire matrix. Some are unimportant and stable, others are primary and stable, but a few are primary and corrupted. When they go, they corrupt the entire system."

"Maybe you'll get lucky next time, Thales."

The positronic intelligence did not reply. Thales had long since catalogued most of what it called Derec's "sympathy concessions": meaningless phrases used to soothe hurt feelings or disappointments that, according to Thales, seemed important to people not for what they contained—because they contained nothing useful—but for the fact that they were said. For the moment, it appeared Thales did not consider a response necessary.

The chaos filling the screen in front of Derec, so far resistant to Thales' attempts at restoring pattern and function, showed all that remained of Derec's ambition: the flexibility of a human mind expressed in a positronic matrix. He had always wanted to build a robotic intelligence that could cope with trauma—with failure—and recover from the brink of collapse. He had hoped to build a robot that would work through Three Law violations and retain a coherent structure, preserving memory and identity in the face of the unacceptable.

He had failed.

The physical fragments of what had been the robot Bogard filled a crate, awaiting shipment . . . somewhere. The positronic remnants of Bogard's mind filled a buffer in Thales' gener-ously large, though currently abbreviated, memory. Bogard's collapse had resulted from the death of Bok Golner—a death for which Bogard had felt responsible, indeed had inadver-tently caused. Golner had been a killer, an anti-robot fanatic, and had been about to kill Derec when Bogard came to his cre-ator's rescue. But none of that mattered in the absolutist struc-ture of a positronic brain which prohibited the taking of a human life, intentions notwithstanding. Thales believed the key to Bogard's failure could be pulled from those shards. But after nearly a year, they had proved indecipherable. Thales continued to express optimism; Derec was not as sanguine.

"Perhaps," the RI said, "I should make a copy of each stage so that I can reset one step back rather than do the entire construct over. Of course, that would require a larger memory buffer than the one to which I now have access."

"Oh, well," Derec said, standing. "Sorry."

"I understand, Derec. No need to apologize."

Perversely, Derec felt a pang of guilt. That lack of mem-ory had been a problem throughout Thales' attempts to reorder Bogard's matrix. Thales simply did not have enough in its present configuration. Derec counted them both lucky to have as much as they did. Of course, any less might begin impairing Thales' normal functions.

"I can try to make another request . . ." he said.

"If you think it will help."

No, he thought, *but it might make me feel better to try . . .*

Derec reached to the screen of chaos and touched an icon. The screen went blank.

"Do you wish me to continue, Derec?" Thales asked.

"Sure. I'm . . . I have some other things to tend to."

"Of course."

Derec drifted into his living room. Against one long wall

a subetheric showed two political candidates soundlessly debating. He frowned, recognizing one of them: Rega Looms. For a moment, Derec felt confused, then remembered that Looms was running for a senate seat in the upcoming election. He had declared in opposition to Jonis Taprin, who had replaced Clar Eliton the previous year in a recall election. Taprin ran now on a revised, anti-robot platform, a complete about-face from his position not fourteen months earlier when, as Eliton's vice senator, he had supported what had become known as "Concessionism" and a gradual reintroduction of positronics on Earth.

In retrospect, Derec did not know how much he had ever believed it could be done. In Earth's long history of social change, fickle politics, and policy-by-trend, the ban on positronics had lasted the longest and tenaciously resisted reform. Hard to believe, on a world where once the newest and brightest and best technologies had been created and dispensed and embraced with almost childlike passion for novelty.

Curious, Derec turned on the volume.

"—travel to other worlds has diluted Earth's reservoir of genius," Looms said, jabbing the armrest of his chair with a stiff finger. "I'll concede that you now hold a position with which I have long been in agreement, that positronics should not be allowed a return to Earth, but I feel that you don't go far enough. Positronics is not the only threat."

"Mr. Looms, with all due respect," Taprin said smoothly, clearly the more practiced public figure, "you can't expect us to shut down commerce. What you suggest would break the back of our economy."

"No, sir, I think that's alarmist and misleading. Economies are artificial constructs, just like any other machine. We make them what we want them to be. I am simply saying that we should change the way in which we operate our economy so that we can eventually sever all ties to other worlds."

"But, sir, you must take into account that there are citizens—Terrans—who simply don't want those ties severed."

"There are *also* Terrans who want positronic robots," Looms countered. "We don't let *them* dictate policy."

"The numbers, sir, the numbers—"

Derec switched off the subetheric. Looms' campaign strategy seemed to be to try to become more reactionary than his reactionary opponent. A year ago Derec would not have given that tactic a chance of success, but Earth always surprised him.

"You have a call, Derec," Thales said. "Ambassador Ariel Burgess."

Derec considered telling Thales to say he was out. Instead, he went to the comm and pressed his thumb on the ACCEPT. "Hello."

"I hope I'm not interrupting anything, Derec, but are you busy right now?" Ariel asked crisply.

The visual was off, so Derec allowed himself a wry smile. "Nothing pressing."

"Would you come up to my office? I need—I'd appreciate your opinion on something."

" 'Something.' For instance?"

There was a pause. "Please."

Derec blinked. *Please . . . ?* "I'll be right there."

"Thank you."

The connection broke and Derec stared at the comm, baffled.

"Thales, I'll be in Ambassador Burgess's offices for a while," he said, moving to the door. "In case anything comes up."

"Very well, Derec."

*   *   *

Ariel's offices consisted of four large chambers in the main diplomatic quarter of the Auroran Embassy. The lone robot at the reception desk magnified the impression of emptiness: Only one robot, out of a staff of four robots and eleven people a year before.

"Ambassador Burgess is expecting you, sir," the robot said as he entered. "Go right through."

"Thank you."

Derec pushed open the door to Ariel's personal office.

He hesitated. Hofton stood behind and to the left of Ariel's chair, hands folded appropriately before him, posture straight and attentive, looking as if he had not been absent for most of the last year, transferred to another office. He inclined his nearly hairless head in greeting but otherwise said nothing, face professionally expressionless.

A man sat in one of Ariel's highback visitor's chairs. He stood as the door closed behind Derec. Tall, wide-shouldered, with short, gray-flecked hair, dark eyes set deep below pale eyebrows, and a too-straight nose that hinted at cosmetic retouch, he looked familiar to Derec.

"Mr. Lanra," Ariel said, "this is Derec Avery, special attaché to my department."

Derec gave her a sharp look.

"Derec," she continued smoothly, "this is Coren Lanra, head of security for DyNan Manual Industries."

Derec gripped Lanra's hand. "I've heard of you, of course. Mia Daventri said you helped her out during the Managin . . . situation last year."

"Indeed," Lanra said. "And you're the head of Phylaxis Group."

"Once upon a time."

Lanra frowned.

"I've asked Mr. Avery," Ariel said, "to sit in as an impartial witness. He's attached to my office but he doesn't work for me, unlike Hofton."

Lanra sat down. "I'd hoped to confine this meeting to just you and I, Ambassador Burgess."

"Humor me, Mr. Lanra. The past year has made me wary of private meetings."

Lanra almost smiled at that. "Very well. I have a problem which may interest you. I'd like to enlist your expertise."

"In what capacity?"

Derec moved to the other visitor's chair and sat down. Lanra seemed to be deliberating, lips pursed, hands pressed together meditatively.

"You must understand," he said slowly, "that this has nothing to do with DyNan. This is a private matter concerning Rega Looms and myself."

"If you say so," Ariel said dryly.

Lanra sighed wearily. "Rega Looms' daughter was found dead less than twenty-four hours ago on Kopernik Station. She was involved in running baleys and was apparently accompanying a group of them. All fifty-two are dead."

Ariel winced. "I'm terribly sorry. But how—"

"She had a robot in her possession."

Derec sat forward, startled. Hofton moved his hands behind his back, which made him seem even more attentive. Ariel stared at Lanra, openly amazed.

After a long silence, Ariel cleared her throat. "This hasn't been on the newsnets."

"Not yet," Lanra said. "I hope to keep it that way for a few days. Longer if possible, but sooner or later someone is going to make some connections, find a source—something."

"That's . . . unique, Mr. Lanra . . ."

Lanra said nothing.

"The daughter of Rega Looms," Derec said, as much to break the silence as to confirm what he had heard, "had a robot."

"Yes, Mr. Avery."

"Her own?"

"I presume so."

"And where is it now?"

"On Kopernik, under security lock."

"Forgive me," Ariel said, "but I still don't see how this concerns us."

Derec frowned at her. "This robot, it was collapsed?"

"Uh . . . yes," Lanra said. "Frozen up, unresponsive. But there's activity—at least, there's current still running through it. I don't know enough about them to know if that means anything."

"Well—" Derec began.

"I repeat," Ariel interrupted, "I still don't see how this concerns us."

Lanra shifted uncomfortably. "Forgive me, but it was my understanding that you are the liaison from the Calvin Institute here on Earth."

Ariel pursed her lips, inclining her head as if to say *And . . . ?*

"This is a robotics issue," Lanra said. "Your field. Positronics." His expression darkened. "I don't know any-one else here. If there *are* other specialists, I'm not aware of any—at least, none I can get access to."

"And none you'd want to confide this to in any case," Ariel said. "I suppose you want us to try to recover its mem-ories, if possible."

"Something like that."

Ariel laughed sharply. "How much do you know about our situation, Mr. Lanra? Mia surely told you something about our current problems. I can't believe you'd come here like this without having done a little background work."

Lanra straightened in his chair and the hint of a smile tugged at his lips. "I know that you aren't held in very high esteem by your own people. Last year's events with Senator Eliton—"

"*Ex*-Senator Eliton," Ariel said crossly.

"—didn't come out in your favor, as perhaps they should have."

"That's generous of you, Mr. Lanra," Derec said.

"Generous? No, Mr. Avery, merely fair. *Ex*-Senator Eliton's duplicity cost us all a gram or two of flesh. We were both under scrutiny for things Eliton engineered."

Faking his own death to discredit positronics, Spacer diplomacy, ruin a long-overdue reconciliation with Earth, Derec thought bitterly, *and wrecking my own ambitions as a side-effect ... yes, that* was *an expensive experience.*

"Involving ourselves in Terran affairs," Ariel said slowly, "cost us perhaps a bit more than you know."

"I may be able to help you defray some of those costs."

Ariel shook her head. "Based on the chance that Rega Looms will be elected to the Terran Senate? You have to know how ironic that would be to us." She stood. "I'm sorry, Mr. Lanra, but I don't really think there's anything we can do to help you."

"You haven't heard everything yet," Lanra said, rising.

"I'm not interested."

"Then why did you agree to see me?"

"Simple courtesy, Mr. Lanra. You were helpful to us last year. I'm sorry we can't return the favor, but the situation is too complicated just now. If you'll excuse me."

"But—"

Derec watched Ariel end the interview with a firm shake of her head. She glanced at him, then left the office, leaving Lanra staring after her.

The door closed and Lanra sighed heavily. He looked at Derec. "I don't suppose *you* can do anything?"

"Like what? Talk her into something that I agree is a bad idea?"

"I thought you'd be interested in the problem. I thought you might welcome a chance to—"

Derec shook his head.

"You're *not* interested?"

Derec laughed. "Of course I'm *interested*. That's beside the point."

"You're a private citizen, Mr. Avery. Would you consider taking the job as a consultant? I imagine Ambassador Burgess could order you to stay here, but would she if you took this up of your own choice?"

Lanra's eyes danced knowingly, as if he knew something about Derec no one else did. Under other circumstances, Derec decided, Coren Lanra might be an interesting man to know.

"We misjudged you," Derec said. "You knew exactly what our problems were before you came in here, didn't you? I'm not exactly a private citizen, not in any way that gives me the freedom of movement to do what you ask. Aurora's entire policy is one of wait and see, don't move, stay still and maybe the situation will change. So even if Ariel might want to help you, it's doubtful Ambassador Setaris would allow it. But you knew all this. Why pretend otherwise?"

"I didn't want anyone to feel pressured. People work better if they think they have a choice." Lanra shrugged. "A pleasure to meet you, Mr. Avery. Perhaps under other circumstances . . . " He headed for the exit. "If you reconsider—"

"I have your code, sir," Hofton said.

"Thanks."

The door closed softly and Derec let out a heavy breath. He considered for a few moments doing exactly what Lanra suggested: taking the job, whatever it was, and chancing Ariel's anger.

But she had a good point—what chance was there that Rega Looms could win his run for the Senate? And if he did, how likely would it be that he would help the very people he most wanted off Earth?

"I hate it when she's so right," Derec said. He looked up then at Hofton, who seemed amused. "You were awfully quiet."

"Not my place to interject opinion," Hofton said. "Besides, I concur with Ariel's assessment."

"What are you doing here anyway? I thought you had been assigned to another department."

"Which has been shut down. I'm taking leave from official duties for a time. Ariel asked me to attend this meeting as a favor."

Another department closed . . . The Auroran presence on Earth shrank a little more each week. Ariel kept these offices only because they had no other use for them. She retained her title and, presumably, her perks for appearances only, but Derec knew that Ambassador Setaris would ship her back to Aurora in an instant if she could. Derec, too, for that matter. They were embarrassments to the Auroran mission here; they stayed only because admitting it to Earth by recalling them would be more embarrassing.

But it would not take much to shift that balance.

Still, to get his hands on a complete positronic lab would be worth a few risks. He might be able to get Thales the extra memory buffers then, might be able to set up a more thorough analysis protocol on Bogard while working on Lanra's problem, might—

"Derec." Ariel stood in the doorway. "Don't even think about it."

"I know you too damn well." Ariel poured them drinks.

Hofton sat now in the chair vacated by Coren Lanra. Derec reflected idly that he had never before seen Hofton relaxing. Ariel handed him a scotch, then gave another to Derec.

"You were just as tempted as I was," Derec said.

"I doubt it. I've had enough of being burned by Terrans."

Derec sipped at his drink. "But think of it! Rega Looms, the great Luddite, has—had—a daughter who owned a robot."

"If I may point out," Hofton said, "Mr. Lanra said a robot was found in her company. He never said she owned it."

"She was a baley runner," Derec said. "That's what Lanra said: she was running illegal emigrants, she was in charge. I don't think a baley slipping by ITE would be allowed to bring along a robot. Therefore, it's only logical that it was hers."

"Lanra probably thinks the robot killed her," Ariel said. "He wants us to substantiate his suspicion. That would be convenient, wouldn't it? Any help Rega Looms might have been able to offer would evaporate when we hand him verification of his worst fears."

"Come on," Derec protested. "How could that be? From his description, the robot is collapsed. Obviously a Three Law violation occurred—"

"*You* had a robot that collapsed after it killed someone."

Derec stiffened. "That was an accident."

Ariel shrugged. "Whatever. So might this have been. Would Rega Looms appreciate the difference?"

"It's doubtful in any event," Hofton said, "that Mr. Looms—should he win the election—could do anything on our behalf under any circumstances without compromising his newly-won mandate. Should he win, he will do so as the avatar of the anti-robot faction and, unless I've misunderstood his rhetoric, the anti-Spacer faction as well. Added to that, his daughter was engaged in illegal activities that ran counter to his political position and the rhetoric of his church. That can't be explained away. I suspect Mr. Lanra is offering what he cannot guarantee."

"If Coren Lanra has his way," Ariel said, "none of this will ever become public. He's doing damage control."

"Precisely," Hofton said. "And with no public reason to do so, Looms will have no private reason to fulfill any obligations his agents may make without his knowledge."

"Rega Looms has a dead daughter," Derec said. "Someone's going to notice."

They sat in silence for a time, brooding. Derec began to resent Lanra for bringing something to them that offered the possibility of rehabilitating their situation. Raised hopes crumbled too easily under analysis.

"It would be interesting," Hofton said finally, "to know where she got a robot. And how she managed to keep it with her." He finished his drink and stood. "I have a few chores to tend to. Thank you for the chance to act the part of your aide once more. It was fun. Should you need further performances . . ."

"You'll be the first I call, Hofton," Ariel said, smiling wanly. "Thanks."

Hofton bowed his head. "Ambassador." He walked out.

"I'm going to miss him," Ariel said.

Derec shot her a look. "Have you heard something?"

"No, but how much longer could it be?" She leaned forward and turned her glass idly on the desk. "I still do a little liaison work so I get to keep track of some of the numbers of illicit robot traffic. There's still activity, but it's declined precipitously in the last year."

"Is that a surprise? ITE must be working overtime now that they feel they have permission."

"Mmm. Mostly, I get to do P.R. work with irate Spacer businesses. The latest was a complaint about a five-hour delay in shipping. An unscheduled route change out of Petrabor spaceport." She shrugged. "Five hours. You'd think the world was ending to hear the complaint. Too much excitement sometimes." She smiled grimly. "Did you know Alda Mikels is being released next week?"

"I thought he was sentenced to ten years for public endangerment."

Ariel shrugged. "Terran jurisprudence. Damned if I can see what's prudent about it. But how long after that do you think it will be before he starts haranguing us in public or trying to bring a suit against us? That might just convince Setaris to ship us home."

Derec closed his eyes and swallowed more scotch. Alda Mikels: head of Imbitek Heavy Industries, industrialist, engineer. And murderer. The trial had lasted nearly two months—scores of witnesses, experts and counterexperts testifying . . . but not one positronic specialist. Derec had been deposed, as had Ariel, but neither of them had been called to the stand. Something about their status as noncitizens, it seemed; Derec never did get it entirely straight.

Mikels had sabotaged the complex Resident Intelligence

of Washington D.C.'s Union Station, the showpiece on Earth for positronics. The fragile treaties and agreements that had allowed it to be built in the first place as an intercultural zone where Earthers might come to see for themselves how positronics worked, the first step in a hoped-for reintroduction of robots to Earth, shattered in the aftermath of that very system's failure and the subsequent slaughter of so many Spacer and Terran diplomats.

A failure Alda Mikels had implemented.

But the end result had been that Mikel's sabotage had been poorly understood and therefore the harm he'd done had been rendered less his responsibility than the unpredictable nature of positronics. Derec had watched, amazed, when the lesser indictment of "Public Endangerment" had been handed down.

It had all been part of a larger scheme to discredit positronics and any possible diplomatic advancements in Spacer-Terran relations. At its center had been Senator Clar Eliton, a man who had convinced Aurora of his honest intentions to help bring robots back to Earth. For his part, Eliton had escaped prison because of the frail evidence to connect him to Mikels and the others involved—which included the former head of Special Service, who had vanished. At least Eliton had been recalled, losing his senate seat in the process.

Not that his replacement, Jonis Taprin, was much better. He was openly hostile to Spacers and robotics. Better that than the oily duplicity in which Eliton had indulged, Derec felt.

But it had been Mikels' technology that had undermined the positronic intelligence that ran Union Station and allowed a team of assassins to enter the main gallery and shoot down the gathering of diplomats who had arrived to commence the conference they had hoped would begin reconciliation.

Coren Lanra's employer, Rega Looms, had been suspected for a time. None of his people had been shot during the slaughter, which made him look very culpable. But that, too, had been a set-up.

Their own involvement—Derec's and Ariel's—had gotten them sequestered to the embassy, in a legal limbo, awaiting deportation at the convenience of Sen Setaris, the head of the Auroran mission on Earth. Ariel's confinement had been repealed after a few months as certain duties were returned to her, but as far as Derec knew she rarely left. He often wondered what was taking so long to deport them. It seemed cruel to leave them dangling like this, teasing them with possibilities. He had grown numb waiting.

He finished his scotch and went to the bar for another.

"My question," Derec said, "is how come we're being so careful? Do you *really* want to stay here?"

Ariel frowned. "I don't—"

"You're afraid to do anything that might get us kicked back to Aurora sooner. We both know that's what they intend to do anyway. Why are we being so careful? I repeat: do you *want* to stay on Earth?"

"I don't know." She looked at him. "Don't you?"

"Under these circumstances?" He shrugged and left the question hang. In truth, he was torn. Saying no would mean he had never found anything worthwhile here, which would be a lie. Saying yes meant he was willing to tolerate anything to remain, which would be a bigger lie. His affection for Earth complicated his thinking. He finished his second scotch and set the glass down. "Thanks for the drink. I have some time to hunt down and kill, so if you'll excuse me . . ."

Ariel raised her own glass in mock assent.

Derec left her offices and headed down the corridors, in the direction of his apartment, his mood muddied by the alcohol. He reached the elevator and punched the button.

"Mr. Avery?"

Derec turned slowly. Coren Lanra stood nearby.

"Forgive me," Lanra said. "I just thought you'd like to know—that you'd be *interested* to know—that we believe a robot was responsible for Nyom Looms' death."

Derec stared at him. *One more point in Ariel's favor . . .*

"That's impossible, of course," he said.

Lanra smiled thinly. "So you say. But I suppose you'll never know now. Thank you for your time. Sorry to bother you."

Derec watched Lanra walk away until the elevator door opened.

FIVE

A riel, you have a call."

Ariel squeezed her eyes shut and groaned. She rolled over, and the band around her skull tightened just enough to let her know that the muzzy warmth of too much scotch needed several more hours to sleep off. Too late. She opened her eyes.

R. Jennie stood at the foot of the bed, impassive and attentive.

"What? What did you say, Jennie?" Her mouth felt gummy, barely cooperative.

"You have a call. Ambassador Setaris."

"Hell . . . what time is it?"

"Two-twenty."

"In the morning?"

"I asked if it would be convenient for her to call again later, but she insists that she cannot."

"Of course she does," Ariel complained as she pushed herself up and swung her legs over the side of the bed. "That's what it means to be an Ambassador. Ambassadorial prerogative . . . plenipotent–potentiary authority . . . executive privilege . . ." She shook her head. "Two-twenty . . . what in–?"

"I brought coffee."

Ariel looked up at the robot. A tray with silvered urn and various cups waited on Ariel's dressing table. Ariel sighed. "Thank you, Jennie. Tell Ambassador Setaris I will be there in a minute. Or two."

"Yes, Ariel."

It seemed to Ariel that her robot left the room gratefully, as if relieved to have something to do other than watch Ariel struggle with a hangover. Impossible, really . . . or was it? Empathic mimicry was part of the positronic package . . .

Ariel stood, dismissing the thought. Too complicated at the moment. She stumbled only once on her way to the coffee. She poured without trembling and raised the cup of hot, black liquid to her lips. The aroma, usually welcome, made her shudder briefly, but she swallowed a mouthful without incident and decided that she would manage.

She caught sight of herself in the dressing table mirror and frowned at the deep circles under her eyes. Her black hair stood out in chaotic spikes and she noticed that she had the faint beginnings of jowls and a double chin. The rest of her seemed trim enough, though she had not paid serious attention to her body in nearly a year. She met her own eyes again–normally a clear blue, but cloudy now and slightly unfocussed–and saw the weariness. This past year had been a steady mix of boredom and anxiety, layered over a sense of helplessness. Instead of fighting it she had taken to sense-dulling indulgence. It showed.

She finished the cup, poured another, and pulled on a robe.

R. Jennie had kept the screen on the comm blanked.

Ariel sat down before the compact unit, ran fingers through her hair, and keyed ACCEPT.

"Good morning, Ambassador," she said, letting sarcasm leak into her voice.

"My apologies, Ariel, I realize this is an inconvenient hour," Setaris said smoothly. "I need to speak to you in person. Please come to my office."

Ariel glanced at the time chop in the lower left corner of the screen. "I'm feeling a little—"

"Of course you are. I imagine you have been for a while. Perhaps we can do something about it. Would you be so kind as to be here in an hour? We have some things to discuss."

"Um . . . of course."

"Very good, Ariel. See you then."

The link died and Ariel felt a hard lump develop just behind her breastbone. *What the hell . . . ?*

"Jennie, it looks like we may finally be taking that journey."

"Shall I begin packing, Ariel?"

"No . . . not yet. But do an inventory."

"Yes, Ariel."

Ariel had expected to be recalled to Aurora for nearly a year. That it had not yet happened worried her. Now that it seemed imminent, it worried her more.

The message light winked on before her. She automatically touched ACCEPT.

A single line of type scrolled across the screen.

WE HAVEN'T FINISHED WITH YOU, AMBASSADOR BURGESS. K.P.

Ariel stared at it for some time before she keyed for a trace. She knew it would not be backtracked, she had gotten messages like this before. Since last year's trial, a dozen or more of these had been a daily nuisance. Most had come from recognizably marginal obsessives—harmless in any real sense—but a few had come from people who might have followed up on the threats, implied or otherwise.

It had been a few months, though, since a message like this had shown up on her system. The screens the embassy had installed very efficiently and thoroughly blocked them all. That one had gotten through was a mark of how good the sender was at penetrating protected systems. Which also showed just how dangerous he or she might be.

The trace came back negative. No source could be located.

Ariel finished her coffee and went to dress.

Sen Setaris's offices dwarfed Ariel's. Even at this hour, embassy personnel scurried about constantly. Ariel counted five robots between the receptionist and Setaris's private office, and saw minor staff from at least four other Spacer legations waiting in the anteroom. The Auroran embassy contained the main meeting hall for all joint legation conferences, and at least four guest suites were attached directly to the offices. Ariel's own chambers, four levels below, were one of a dozen departmental offices with quasi-independent status. Their importance to the principle mission was reflected in their relative size.

Even so, Ariel was surprised to see so much business being done. Perhaps the entire mission was shutting down. She had heard nothing that would have suggested so drastic a move, but then she had been kept out of most embassy affairs.

Sen Setaris looked up from a flatscreen on her desk when Ariel entered. She appeared as elegant and austere as ever: thick, silvered hair forming wings around her narrow head, eyes large and brilliant green, and the ideal set of lines on her otherwise smooth face to give the impression of experience and intelligence without pointing up age. On Earth she was an anomaly in that regard, as were most senior Spacers: Terrans lived relatively short lives, aging quickly until death at around a hundred, while Spacers tended to live to two or three centuries. Ariel did not know Setaris's exact age, but it was well on toward two hundred.

She wondered if Setaris slept anymore.

"Ariel," Setaris said, smiling thinly. "How good of you to be so prompt. Sit down, I'll only be another minute or two."

Ariel suppressed a sarcastic smile and sat on the long sofa to the left of Setaris's desk rather than in one of the visitor's chairs. If Setaris noticed the small breach of protocol she gave no indication. She continued working on the flatscreen, touching it from time to time, until finally she picked up a stylus and dashed her signature on the screen. She shut the datum down and turned toward Ariel.

"What do you know about Nova Levis?" she asked.

Ariel raised her eyebrows. "Only what I've seen on subetheric. It's a Settler colony that's been blockaded. They refused inspections for pirate bases or something."

"That's essentially correct, though, of course, there's much more to it. Earth has requested Spacer cooperation. Ships have been provided to patrol the perimeter of the system, but they want more. They want an intervention."

"You mean an invasion."

"Exactly. It's out of the question, of course, but we haven't said no yet. They're offering us a chance to recoup our losses diplomatically. If we could give them something to mollify their paranoia we might actually recover ground from . . ." Setaris let the sentence drift off, her eyebrows raised suggestively.

"What do *we* have to do with Nova Levis?" Ariel asked.

"Nothing directly. But it has been a transfer point for a good deal of black market trade. That's what started the Terrans on this ill-advised military operation. Solaria is still providing a limited amount of access, though, and Earth has accused the Fifty Worlds of acting in collusion to thwart their legal mandate to investigate and control piracy."

"Do they actually *have* such a mandate?"

"They have ships around Nova Levis. The finer points of law are so much wind under the circumstances. It's in our interest, however, to be seen as supporting legality in this case. And because Solaria has elected to ignore requests to cease any and all transport to Nova Levis, it falls to us to represent Spacer adherence to law."

"And in return, Earth gives us what?"

"We gain credibility," Setaris replied.

The true currency of diplomacy, Ariel heard her finish. She wondered if the Solarians believed that. She was not sure she believed it herself, but certainly her own credibility was no longer bankable.

"Why would Solaria be so . . . uncooperative?" she asked.

Setaris grunted. "Do they need a reason? But seriously, we don't really know. I've asked Chassik and he keeps promising to look into it."

"Is Nova Levis hosting pirates?" Ariel asked.

Setaris frowned thoughtfully. "Probably. I'm afraid they

may be involved in something worse. But that's speculation. Whatever they're doing, it seems they think it necessary to hide it."

Ariel waited. When Setaris remained silent, she asked,
"What does this have to do with me?"

"Two things. ITE has suggested to us—without providing
much proof—" she gave Ariel a dubious look as if to say *as
usual,* then continued "—that Spacer businesses here are
connected to the illicit shipments going to Nova Levis. It
seems that—they suggest—baley-running and contraband
travel the same routes and that we are colluding in all this."

"That's ridiculous."

"I agree, but can you say for certain? Do you know what
our people are doing these days?"

Ariel stiffened, fully aware of the implied criticism. She
had been lapse, she had let things slide. She could not
remember the last inspection she had administered through
the Auroran manufactories on Earth. She found the idea
that Aurorans would be tangled up in running baleys as
well as contraband ludicrous . . . but she could not make a
case based on current knowledge.

And of course it was her responsibility. She *was* still
Trade and Business liaison . . .

"And the other thing?" she asked.

"You had a visitor yesterday. Coren Lanra, security chief
for DyNan Manual Industries."

Ariel managed to keep both surprise and disgust from
her voice when she answered. "Yes, I did."

"May I ask what he wanted?"

Don't you already know? "He wanted my help. He has a
problem with a robot."

Setaris pursed her lips.

"You're not surprised?" Ariel asked.

"Did you know that the daughter of Rega Looms is a baley runner?" Setaris asked instead. "She's been operating a successful underground emigration avenue for nearly five years." She nodded at Ariel's silence. "I just learned this myself recently. I was quite surprised."

"Did you know that she's now dead as a result?" Ariel asked.

Setaris frowned at that. "This . . . robot problem—"

"Relates to her death."

"Interesting. Did you agree to help him?"

"No, of course not."

"Why not?"

"Under the circumstances, I thought minimizing our involvement in what seems to me a Terran police matter would be the best course. Was I mistaken?"

Setaris folded her hands on the desk and seemed to study them. "Not entirely, no." She drew a sharp breath and looked up. "But . . . there are certain limitations official status imparts which can be very frustrating. All circumstances have boundaries. Mine may be more constraining than yours in some cases."

Ariel frowned. "Are you suggesting that I help Mr. Lanra?"

"The Terrans are very concerned with their baley problem. A growing fraction of them seem to be heading for Nova Levis. The place has acquired a certain status since the embargo, a faux romantic patina making it seem more attractive than other . . . less notorious colonies. It may be also that Nova Levis has the facilities for trans-shipping them to other colonies more efficiently than trying to get direct routes from here. That's one of the suggestions I've heard."

"You sound dubious."

"Most baleys get to where they want to go without a terrible amount of trouble—there are plenty of freelance pilots with ships for hire to take them. And, frankly, I'm not convinced Terran authorities really *want* to stop them. But Nova Levis is different. It requires blockade runners. This is a problem on an order of magnitude higher than simple illegal emigration."

"You think Solaria is involved in getting them past the blockade."

"It's one of those certainties one can't prove without creating an incident. It might be possible to prove it from this end with less incident."

"And you've been asked—unofficially—by Earth to see if you can do something about it."

Setaris almost smiled. "You know, you're very sharp, Ariel. I've always admired that about you . . . even when you're suffering the effects of alcohol poisoning. Imagine what you can do with a clear head and a purpose."

The sarcasm sank through Ariel like a wave of muggy heat. Ariel felt herself start to bristle, but checked it before she said something impolitic.

"I'm not entirely clear how rendering assistance to Mr. Lanra would help us with any of this," she said instead.

Setaris frowned. "Now you're being obtuse. Nyom Looms and Coren Lanra had a relationship once. We don't know why it ended or if it did. In either case, it seems logical that if she's running baleys then her father—or someone in her father's organization—is helping her."

Ariel laughed briefly. "Coren Lanra doesn't strike me as the type."

"Perhaps not. But the connection exists nonetheless."

Ariel nodded slowly, understanding exactly what Setaris was asking her to do. In a way, it made perfect sense—

Ariel was the most expendable member of the Auroran mission.

"Can I expect any kind of extra consideration should things work out well?" she asked.

"Ariel, you know extra consideration is always on the table for good work."

But what constitutes "good" work? Politically convenient or thorough?

"I'll want Hofton reassigned to me," Ariel said.

"I think you need an aide in any case. It doesn't look good to be all alone in your department."

Ariel stood. "What level of access do I have?"

Setaris looked genuinely surprised. "I don't believe your clearance was ever rescinded, Ariel."

"I would like confirmation of that."

Setaris regarded her for a long time before nodding.

"By this afternoon, if it's not too much trouble," Ariel said then, turning.

"Don't you feel sometimes that you've been on Earth too long, Ariel? That certain of their less admirable qualities have transferred?"

"I like to believe that it goes both ways, Ambassador." She made herself present a pleasant, innocuous, naïve smile, though she did not expect Setaris to be fooled. "If you'll excuse me, I have to make some calls."

Ariel expected Setaris to call her back and retract everything, but she made it to the door without hearing her voice. She wondered then what kind of confirmation she would actually get when she returned to her own office and checked.

Her heart hammered as she reached the main corridor. Her head still hurt, but for the time being she did not really mind.

* * *

Halfway back to her office she came to another conclusion and entered a general clerical station to call Hofton. An hour later, he joined her in the embassy restaurant at a table beside a bank of windows that overlooked an open air park on the roof of the building. False dawn gave everything a shimmery, vague appearance. Beautiful, she thought, and pitied the agoraphobic Terrans who could not enjoy such a simple, open view.

"I understand," Hofton said as he sat down, "that I'm working for you again."

"When did you receive notice?"

"Around midnight. I didn't bother going to bed. I gather you know something about this?"

Ariel chuckled. "She told you before she called me. That's interesting." Ariel gazed out the window for a time. The trees swayed in a breeze. Somewhere to the east lay the Atlantic Ocean, somewhere northwest was the spaceport. *It would be pleasant,* she thought, *to live on a world where you didn't have to make a special trip just to see open sky and trees . . .*

Hofton waited patiently. At some point during Ariel's reverie he had ordered an iced drink.

"Sorry," she said, turning back to him. "To answer your question: yes, I know something about it. Not enough, of course, but it seems we're being given a chance to redeem ourselves."

"At what cost?"

Ariel shrugged. The question was rhetorical—Hofton understood the machinery of politics better than she. "Ambassador Setaris would like us to render assistance to Mr. Lanra."

Hofton frowned contemplatively. "I suppose," he said, "we have no choice."

Ariel flashed a sarcastic smile. "Oh, sure. We have a choice."

Hofton looked skeptical, then raised his glass in mock toast. "Here's to damnation, then. Who do we have to kill?"

SIX

Coren kept a private office in an old quarter of D.C., far from the corporate warrens of DyNan. He had not used it in nearly eight months. When Looms had asked him to find Nyom, he hired the best cleaner he knew to find any and all eyes and ears. Only a few had turned up, and those had long since been severed at the receiving end. Coren set up a screen to let him know if any new ones turned up, and moved in.

The neighborhood was undergoing one of its period downturns in popularity. Not a year earlier, it was impossible to find available space here, but now even his own building was nearly empty. He had leased the space before accepting the position with DyNan, right before it had become really popular, thinking that he would go into private practice after leaving Special Service. He had never used it for business other than DyNan's, though, and sometimes thought about breaking the lease and letting it go. He was glad now that he had kept it.

He walked through the small reception area and into the main office. He shrugged out of his jacket and hung it on the pole by the door.

"Good afternoon," his Desk said. "Please verify identity."

Coren sat down and placed his palm against the ID scan on the desk top. He felt a moment's warmth as the machine explored his hand, body temperature, blood chemistry, and pattern of bone growth.

"Welcome, Mr. Lanra," the Desk said. "You have three messages."

"List," Coren said.

"One from Sipha Palen, one from Rega Looms, and one from Myler Towne."

"Who is Myler Towne?"

"Director ProTem of Imbitek Incorporated."

Coren drummed his fingers tentatively on the edge of the desk. "Play Rega Looms', please."

The flatscreen remained retracted—no video, typical of Rega. A crisp tenor voice snapped out of the air.

"Coren, I'm in Dukane District, code appended. I would appreciate an update on that detail I asked you to look into at your earliest convenience. I'll be here till tomorrow, then I'm going to—" He paused. "Going to Delfi. I'll forward the code when we get there."

Coren checked the time chop. Most likely right now Rega Looms' entourage was packing him up to leave Dukane. It would not be a good time to interrupt, especially with bad news. Besides, Coren thought, it would be best to tell Rega in person. He did not want to; for anyone else a comm dialogue would be sufficient. But not Rega.

"Desk, see if you can get me an update on Mr. Looms' itinerary for the next three days."

"Yes, sir."

"Play Sipha Palen's message, please."

This time the flatscreen slid up from the desk top and winked on. Sipha's face filled the field.

"Coren, we've got prelims on the autopsies. Atropimyfex, an atropine-based neurotoxin. Basic crystalline structure that gasifies on contact with moisture—in this case, the humidity of all those exhaling lungs. It has the same profile as certain beneficial pharmaceuticals, but my pathologist says it didn't need the camouflage since the rebreather's filter system wouldn't have caught it anyway. Baxin is really impressed, by the way. Says this is very sophisticated stuff, high profile. It's used mainly in terraforming work, suppression of indigenous fauna. Very expensive and not available legally on Earth. Someone way up the chain wanted these people dead. He's doing work-ups on all of them just to be sure, but he estimates that death came within five minutes of the first seizures. Paralysis in under ten seconds, then gradual destruction of the autonomic nervous system. It starts breaking down, then, and becomes very difficult to trace in a few days."

She glanced off-screen briefly. "Nyom Looms is a different matter. She was evidently smart enough to carry her own breather. We found it in one of the couches, crushed. She died from a broken neck. I'm having Baxin go over her for any foreign material—he found some fabric under her fingernails—but he says you can rule out the robot we found. Whoever killed her was still on board; there's no sign that anyone got out. So we have a suicide/murder. I know that's not what you thought we'd find, but . . ."

She shrugged elaborately. "No sign of the robot you told me about. The only thing we've gotten out of there are corpses. No telltale handprint on Nyom, either. This was a very clean break; anyone with the hand strength and the training could have done it. That's all the good news I have, Coren. I'm sending you an encrypted data package with everything we've got so far. Let me know what you turn up down there. I hope you come back up soon."

Coren suppressed a mild shudder. A return flight?

He had not hoped to find the second robot, but if the seals were intact from the inside, then someone had to have accompanied the baleys up. So one of Nyom's own baleys had committed the crime? It strained credulity.

But there *was* a missing passenger . . .

"Desk, code a reply to Sipha Palen, use same encryption. Sipha, we may still be looking at a robot, just not the one we have in the locker. The second one got out somewhere, and someone else might have gotten in. We don't know what the exact procedure is for this kind of smuggling. Keep me apprised of what you find under Nyom's finger-nails. I'm still trying to find my informant. She's disappeared, of course. I'll comm you later. Desk, send."

"Yes, sir. Message encrypted and sent. You have one message remaining."

"Wait."

Jeta Fromm posed a problem. Without her, tracking down the people Nyom worked with would take days, weeks. Finding the dockworker, Yuri Pocivil, would be even harder.

For now, though, he had no answers. Maybe she would contact him, but he doubted it.

"Desk, do a records search for Yuri Pocivil. Last known residence in the Petrabor District. Now play the last message."

Appearing on the flatscreen was a face Coren did not recognize, with a wide brow and short, black hair. Large, moist-brown eyes stared out at him.

"Mr. Lanra, please forgive the presumption. I'm Myler Towne, current administrative head of Imbitek. You may know our company." He smiled slightly at his own false modesty. "I'm familiar with you, of course, and with your record. We'd like to discuss the possibility of acquiring your services ourselves. If you're interested, please give me a little of your time and we can talk. My code is appended. I hope to talk with you soon."

The screen went blank and slid out of sight.

Coren laughed out loud, then sobered. Surely this was a joke! Or was Myler Towne, temporary mouthpiece for the company that had nearly ruined Rega Looms, so ignorant of circumstances that he thought this was a good and acceptable offer?

It might be amusing to meet with him and see how it goes . . .

"Do you wish to send a reply, sir?" the Desk asked.

"No. Not yet. Do you have that itinerary for me?"

"Yes, sir."

"Let me see it."

A list of destinations within the northeastern quadrant of the continent appeared on the desk surface. He skimmed it quickly, then touched one. Baltimor District. That would be convenient, but Rega would not be there for another two days.

Still, lacking any other worthwhile possibility . . .

"Desk, send a message to Rega Looms, informing him that I'll talk to him in Delfi. Then find the code for Brun Damik at Immigration and Trade Enforcement."

"Yes, sir. Do you wish me to connect you?"

"No, just give me a location."

"Baltimor District ITE headquarters, Level Five, unnumbered private office."

"Thank you."

Coren leaned back and considered what to do next. Brun Damik would be a place to start, at least until he found Fromm.

If he found her.

Time, time, too damn little time . . .

He really did not want to speak with Rega. He could put that off for a day. Brun Damik, though . . . so the man had a private, unnumbered office now. Coren chastised himself for not keeping better track of people he still knew in government service. The trouble was, he had left originally out of a desire to have no more to do with government service, so he was unmotivated to pay close attention.

Not very professional, Coren. Not very professional at all . . .

That was the reason he had bought the Desk in the first place, so he could overlook details like this without losing track of them altogether. He appreciated his Desk—it was the closest thing to full sentient awareness he could afford to buy on Earth, just shy of illegal positronics.

Illegal, but not unobtainable. Nyom had gotten hold of a robot, had even owned it long enough to name it and work with it under the noses of ITE.

Spacers kept robots within their own districts. The ban on positronics had many, many holes in it. There were even Terrans who owned robots—fetishists and self-indulgent social rebels who enjoyed flaunting the law and custom, even if only in private.

Holes Rega Looms wanted to fill in, an ambition that would suffer should his daughter's ideological treason become public.

Coren stood and went to the door to his workroom. A sofa sprawled the length of one short wall to the right, a low table before it. An alcove contained changes of clothes. To the left, three sets of shelves held a variety of boxes, bags, and objects—tech Lanra used from time to time, some of it illegal even for him to possess. He absently took a replacement optam from one shelf.

He locked the door and sat down on the sofa, folded his hands beneath his chin, and studied the shelves. After a time, he heaved himself to his feet and went to a lower shelf. He pulled out a shallow box and placed it on the table.

He took out a set of images and spread them over the table. Nyom Looms: laughing, smiling, contemplative, seductive, playful, clothed, naked, painted, bathed in light. The kind of pictures meant for one other person, exposed and cloistered at once. Old pictures—Coren checked the dates, though he knew it without thinking—from five years ago.

One image showed them both, together, holding each other.

"Frivolously romantic," so Nyom had pronounced them afterward, when it ended and she chose a life that discluded him. Disclusion—left out, overlooked, omitted—rather than excluded. She never barred him from joining her, but she did not invite him, either. Probably because she already knew what he would say.

They had argued, he remembered, and she had left him confused. It had taken some time for him to understand that part of what had hurt her was that he had not made a counteroffer. He had not asked her to stay with him. Coren Lanra did not think that way. Nyom had made a decision—

what right had he to ask her to turn her back on her choice?

On the other hand, perhaps he still did not know what it had been about.

Beneath the sheaf of images were three small boxes. One contained a silver-and-jade bracelet, another contained a set of rings in gold and platinum, and the third held the receipt for an apartment lease they had shared.

Coren stared at the pictures, left the boxes unopened, and grunted. This was all—the only evidence outside his memories of their relationship. All that remained of some-one for whom he had cared. All he would ever have of her, now.

"She's dead," he said quietly. "Nyom is dead."

And then, for the third time in his life, Coren Lanra wept.

The office of Immigration and Trade Enforcement, Baltimor District, occupied five floors of a hexagonal block near the Trade Mall, where thousands of Import-Export firms kept offices, adjacent to the warehouse warrens that occupied an apostrophe-shaped wedge around the lines of the ancient harbor. South of the District, spaceport facilities filled the upper levels and the urban canopy almost the entire dis-tance to D.C. Passengers debarked in D.C., at Union Station; cargo and its handlers came into Baltimor, through Customs and Dissemination.

Coren waited outside the administrative entrance, in a small café, watching. Brun Damik emerged a little more than an hour before his regular shift ended. Damik walked quickly for a man of his size, but being so tall it appeared to be his natural gait. Coren had some trouble keeping up with him and nearly lost him twice before Damik entered a restaurant.

Coren watched from the entrance as Damik was seated at a small table near the back of the dining room. When the maitre d'hôtel approached, Coren laid a credit note on his station and pointed at Damik.

"He's alone, sir," the maitre d' said. He palmed the note and turned his back while Coren, smiling, entered the restaurant.

He sat down across from Damik, who looked up from his salad, startled.

"What's good here, Brun? A little expensive for you, isn't it? Take must be good this year."

Damik's face lost all expression for several seconds. Then, slowly, a wide grin compressed his features. "You ass. Lanra! How are you?"

"Busy these days. But I thought I'd make time to talk to an old backstabber. How are your connections these days, gato?"

Damik laughed loudly and slapped the table once, sharply. "What are you drinking? I'm off-shift, so it doesn't matter."

"I'm not, so it does. Are you buying?"

"Of course."

"Nava."

Damik frowned briefly. "That's a Solarian drink, isn't it?"

Coren nodded. "Tastes like a good bourbon but without the alcohol."

Damik grunted. "Very Spacer. Riskless pleasure. Spineless ninnies."

Coren shrugged. "Good drink, though."

"Expensive." He gestured for a waiter and gave the order anyway, including a beer for himself. "What have you been doing, Coren? Still working for what's-his-name? Rega Looms?"

"I am."

"He pays you well enough to afford good food?"

"When I have time to eat it. What about you? You're not still counting canisters, are you?"

"Not by hand, no. They gave me my own department."

"They must be desperate."

Damik laughed again. Their drinks arrived and he raised his beer in a mock toast. Lanra tapped his glass and sipped.

"So," Damik said. "Pleasantries aside, what do you need?"

Coren reached into his jacket pocket and pulled out a small hemisphere that looked like polished foam. He pressed the base with his thumb and set it in the center of the table.

Damik cocked an eyebrow. "Does Looms know you play with toys like that?"

"I take it you've seen one or two yourself, then. No, actually, if Rega knew what I use in the course of my job we'd probably have a serious policy disagreement. Fortunately, he's not the sort of employer that pries a lot unless things go wrong."

Damik thought about that. "Has anything gone wrong?"

"We don't have to be coy now, Brun." Coren pointed at the hemisphere. "Maybe Special Service has something that can unscramble the interference that's generating, but it would take longer than our conversation."

"You're not staying for dessert, then."

"I don't think I'm staying for a second drink. I asked how your connections are. I meant it."

"I got a promotion, didn't I?"

"I'm talking about your black market ones."

Damik grinned. "So'm I. What do you need?"

"I stumbled on a diverted shipment recently. You gimmicked a bay assignment all the way over in Petrabor, some stuff for Kysler. I'm assuming it was you, or someone in your office."

"You 'stumbled' on it? How does that work?"

"Part of the job. Am I speaking to the right man?"

Damik shrugged. "What if you are?"

"Baley-running. How does *that* work?"

Damik stabbed a forkful of green leaves and pushed them around the plate listlessly. "How much are you offering?"

"Depends entirely on the quality of your data."

"Hm. Well, the cheap part is the actual transportation. Refitted cargo bins are popular. Usually, they only have to support life for a day or two till they get turned over to the ship that's going directly to the colony of choice. Then it's no different than steerage class. Most baleys, I can't understand why they bother—they could go legally."

"You know that's not true. ITE screening sorts out 'undesirables' and denies them visas. That means anyone with a political opinion, technical skills above a certain level, and money they might take with them. That's about eighty percent of the people who apply."

"If they're that well-off or that smart, why would they want to go?"

"I really don't care. Go on."

"The expensive part is the bribery. You need a customs inspector, a set of transit permits, and enough to pay off a warehouse crew. You need another customs official on the other end."

"At Kopernik."

Damik nodded. "But you knew all this."

"You left out the part I don't know. Who do you start the process through? Who fronts the credits and who parcels out the payments?"

"It's not that organized. We're talking about rats in the system, a few here and there. Whoever is taking money from the baleys themselves has to know who to talk to—"

"Not in every case," Coren said. "That might be true for small groups, but in the last two years the numbers have increased. There are shipments of up to three hundred people leaving in one group."

"That's a myth. Numbers like that, ITE would look totally negligent—or subverted—to let them through. No, the largest single group you'll ever see go through would be fifty or sixty. Even that's pushing it." Damik finished his salad. "So?"

"So that still means enough money to attract the people I'm looking for. Once they get a taste, they don't go away, they assume control."

Damik chuckled. "You never disappoint, Lanra. I can see why you left Service—those idiots wouldn't know what to do with a smart one like you."

"I assume that means I'm right. So who?"

"Depends on the colony. Each one has a gatekeeper."

"Reporting to who?" Coren asked.

"I don't know. I imagine you're right, there *is* some person or persons at the end of the chain, but . . . "

"Okay. Then give me a gatekeeper."

"Which colony?"

"Let's say Nova Levis."

Damik's eyes widened fractionally, just for an instant. He shook his head. "You don't have that kind of credit."

"How do you know?"

"Because you're overdrawn now and we haven't even talked price."

"I knew you were the right gato to talk to about this. I always appreciated your honesty."

"Ha ha. Your wit hasn't improved much."

"But my credit has," Coren said.

Damik regarded him skeptically. The waiter came and cleared away his salad plate, then set his dinner before him. Damik appeared to notice none of this, eyes fixed on Coren.

"Do you remember," Coren said as the waiter left, "all that business last year involving Clar Eliton and the assassinations at Union Station?"

"Lot of dead Spacers. So?"

"More than that—quite a few Terrans were killed or hurt, too. It was complicated. For a time, Rega Looms was suspected. In the course of doing my job—covering Rega's butt, technically—I learned a lot of details about a lot of people, mostly people I'll never meet and never deal with. But there've been exceptions. You, for instance."

Coren leaned forward, as if preparing to confide in Damik. "We knew each other for . . . what? Six years before I left Special Service?"

"Something like that."

"In all that time I never knew you were a Managin. Did you even know that yourself, or did you simply neglect to enter it in your file?" Coren spread his hands. "None of my business, really. Before last year, none of anyone's. But they turned out to be less than simply embarrassing to someone like you. They turned out to be—can you guess, Brun?—a security risk. Now imagine that. A bunch of fringe idiot anti-Spacer sociopaths an actual security risk. I'll tell you, Brun, I got a real laugh out of that when I heard it the first time. I thought, 'Don't those people at the Terran Bureau of Investigation have anything better to do than upgrade their lists of the possibly dangerous all day long? They should be after real criminals, real threats, real detriments to society.' "

"You thought all that, did you?"

"Yes, I did. I thought all that. But that was then. Today I thought, 'I wonder what the director of ITE would say if he knew his freshly-promoted chief of inspection at the Baltimor Station used to be one of those sorts?' And I decided to find out what *you* would think of it first."

Coren sat back and smiled across the table at Damik.

Slowly, Damik picked up a fork. "Is that all?"

"No, no, no. You were a real follower back then. I've got your name attached to at least four other groups like the Managins. But to be fair, only two of those ever got serious attention from the TBI." Coren watched Damik cut a piece of his cutlet and fork it into his mouth. "So, how's my credit now?"

"Still not good enough." Damik grinned crookedly. "I'll tell you this, they're all corporate types at the high end. I wouldn't be at all surprised if the guy getting out from rehab this week is one."

"Alda Mikels? Is he the one you deal with."

"I told you, I don't know names—"

Coren shifted in his chair, leaned on his forearms over the small table. "I asked, is that who you deal with?"

Damik moved back. He studied Coren with narrowed eyes for several seconds. Finally, he shook his head. "Mikels is in jail—how could he do anything with baleys? Look, Coren, that's as much as you get—"

Coren sat back. "Let's see, besides the Managins, you were part of the Campaign for Terran Rights—they were the ones who shut down the vats feeding Calcubay District several years back. About the time you were an active member, under the name of . . ." Coren looked upward in mock concentration. "Ah, I remember. You called yourself 'Damil Bruller.' Then there was—"

"Enough."

"What's the problem, Brun? No one can hear us." Coren gestured at his hemisphere.

"How big a file do you have on me?"

"Big enough. Come on, Brun, I don't have any desire to ruin your life. This has nothing to do with you. I just need to know how to find the people who would have had oversight on the last shipment of baleys out of Petrabor that you so innocently arranged. Seriously, who do you deal with? Who helps you afford real pork?" Coren took his own fork, reached across the table, and delicately worked loose a small piece of the gravy-soaked meat. He popped it into his mouth and smiled. "Very good."

"You don't need to know that."

"I'm afraid I *do,*" Coren said flatly.

Damik let out a long, low breath—nearly a growl. "Two people come see me to arrange things: a woman named Tresha, and a man named Gamelin. At least, that's what she calls him. He never speaks—I assume he's just muscle, he's big enough."

"Tresha what?"

"The bank is closed for the day."

Coren studied Damik's eyes, then shrugged. He picked up his hemisphere and dropped it back into his pocket.

"You don't ever come talk to me again, Lanra," Damik warned. "We're done."

"Oh, I wish I could promise that. I really do." Coren smiled. "Enjoy the rest of your meal."

Coren entered a bar down the corridor from the restaurant, ordered a drink, then went into the restroom. He shrugged out of his jacket, pulling it inside out, changing it from a dark green to a light blue. He broke a small vial in his hands and smeared the thick liquid through his hair, which turned black in less than a minute. He washed his hands before returning to his drink.

Damik walked by a few minutes later. Coren gave him several meters before he sauntered after him.

Damik went through the motions of surveying for a tail, but Coren suspected that his skills were long unused and inadequate. Within two intersections, Damik stopped looking behind him, and picked up his pace.

Coren followed him to a highspeed walkway that carried them south into the vast financial district that filled a lot of the area between Baltimor and D.C. He got off after ten kilometers and used a public comm. Coren counted off two minutes, twenty seconds. Damik left the booth and skipped across the accelerating lanes to continue south.

Another ten kilometers. Coren took off his jacket and tied it around his waist. Damik had apparently decided no one would follow him from here and never bothered to do another survey. Coren moved closer out of contempt, as if to dare Damik to recognize him, but the man never glanced back.

Damik got off in a warehouse sector. He descended three levels, to a home kitchen, and took a position leaning against one massive pillar. He stood out in this T-class area and drew a lot of odd looks, but he remained where he stood, feigning ambivalence.

Coren turned his jacket out again, slung it by one finger over his shoulder, and skirted the edge of the kitchen till he found a table recently vacated. He sat down before the remains of a late, vat-based dinner, the rich yeast-and-grain aroma thick in his nostrils. He gripped the nearly empty glass of beer and pretended to be enjoying the last of it, keeping Damik in the corner of his field of vision.

About ten minutes went by before anyone approached Damik. An older man in an innocuous black jacket and gray pants came up to him. Coren slipped his optam out, adjusted its range, and waited. Just before Damik and the old man were about to turn away, Coren smoothly raised the device and recorded them.

They moved away from him. The last Coren saw of them, the old man put his arm around Damik's shoulders and patted him in an incongruously paternal manner.

SEVEN

Coren swallowed a painblock. The throbbing along his neck and shoulder began to ebb. He did not want to take the time to see his doctor, though he knew he should—he still did not know how badly he had been injured in Petrabor.

He crossed the avenue to the open arcade. Shops alternated with private offices along both sides. Coren breathed in the mingled smells of several restaurants and food vendors. At this hour he saw few people. Later, the place would be as crowded as it had been during the height of the last shift.

The door he sought turned out to be plain blue bearing a small nameplate: RW ENTERPRISES.

The image he had recorded of the older man matched quickly to a name—Ree Wenithal—and the company he owned. The public record contained a brief description and little else: a general import-export firm specializing in textiles, licensed eight years ago, with Ree Wenithal listed as sole owner. No recent police reports, at least not in the last three years.

Coren had nearly paid a second visit to Brun Damik after his cursory check of Wenithal's company—what was their connection? Then he found the one detail that had brought him directly here: Wenithal had been a cop.

Coren pressed his fingers to the nameplate.

"Yes?" a polite voice asked.

"Coren Lanra to see Mr. Wenithal."

"Do you have an appointment, Mr. Lanra?"

"No, but I think he'll want to talk to me. I was given his name by a mutual acquaintance: a man named Damik."

Coren waited.

"Very well, Mr. Lanra. Please come in."

The door opened.

At the end of a short hallway, he passed under an arch into a wide, brightly-lit office area. Coren counted eight people working at desks.

A door at the rear opened and a neatly-dressed man with thin, pearl-white hair came toward him—the same man he had seen meet Brun Damik. He seemed tall from a distance but as he neared, Coren saw that it was an illusion: the man walked and carried himself as if he stood a head taller than anyone else.

"Mr. Lanra?" He extended a hand. "I'm Ree Wenithal. How may I help you?"

"A little of your time, a few questions."

Wenithal smiled and waved Coren in the direction of his door. Coren keyed the little hemisphere in his pocket.

The office was dark, expensively furnished with heavy chairs and sofas and polished woodwork. The desk was cluttered with disks and papers. A suit hung from the handle of a closet door to the right. Another sheaf of papers lay beside a half-full cup of coffee on an end table by an upholstered armchair that still held the imprint of its recent occupant.

Coren turned at the sound of the door clicking shut.

Wenithal's left hand was in his jacket pocket.

"There are easily four other ways to leave this office beside the way you came in," Wenithal said matter-of-factly.

"Do I need to know any of them?"

"I suppose that depends on what you have to say." His eyes narrowed. "You used a name I know to get in here. But I don't know you."

"But you know my type."

"TBI?"

"Special Service."

"But not anymore. You've gone private."

"It happens from time to time."

"Who do you work for now?"

"Rega Looms."

Wenithal's face showed a moment of confusion. Then he grunted, took his hand from his pocket, and went to his desk. "Drink?"

"No, thank you."

Wenithal poured a glass for himself and added ice, moving carefully, methodically. "So," he said, turning to Coren, "what does Mr. Looms want with me now?"

"'Now?' Has he wanted anything from you in the past?"

Wenithal frowned. "We've done business before. I admit, he's never sent his security people to negotiate a new contract, but . . ."

"Nothing. I'm not here at his behest. I'm following up on something else, unrelated to the company."

"What would that be?"

"I'm told that you're the man to see about baleys."

"Who told you that? It wasn't Brun."

"A mutual acquaintance."

Wenithal shrugged. "Suit yourself. I don't know anything about it."

"I could check."

Wenithal sighed. "I'm assuming you checked me out before you came in here. You know what I used to do. What I know stems from my investigations as a law enforcement officer. Most of that information is several years out of date. I'm really not interested in rehashing old cases with you."

"Old cases often refuse to go quietly into a file. Especially if they're big enough."

"And are mine big enough?"

Coren shrugged.

"You threatened Brun over this. You *are* the same man who spoke with him earlier, aren't you? What particularly do you want?"

"Names. Who were you investigating?"

"You don't know what you want, do you?"

"I hoped you might be able to help me narrow it down. I'm looking for a baley runner, the one who makes all the arrangements with the shippers before the runners themselves shunt their cargoes."

"A particular one, I imagine." Wenithal smiled sardonically. "Actually, at one time I was investigating your Mr. Looms."

"For what?"

"It didn't prove out. His name was on a list. You know how that goes. It was coincidental."

"So why mention it?"

"Just to remind you that we all have files. What would someone find in yours?"

"Less than you might expect. I've had a fairly dull career."

Wenithal looked surprised, then laughed. "My cases are all a matter of public record—you could look for yourself. Why bother me?"

"What I'm looking for won't be in your case logs. For one thing, I doubt very much if the people I'm interested in are part of the public record."

"Why not?"

Coren felt his patience fray. "Is this a test?"

Wenithal shook his head. "You've come into my business, you've asked questions that could be construed as accusatory, you've made requests you have no right to make and no authority to push through. I haven't heard one thing yet to convince me that I shouldn't call the police and have you escorted out."

"Nova Levis."

Wenithal's face hardened. His reaction lasted less than a second, but Coren recognized it and it surprised him. Dropping the name of the colony had been a gamble; Wenithal could easily have feigned ignorance. Instead, Wenithal now took this seriously. Coren wished he knew why.

"This had been slightly amusing till now," Wenithal said. "Leave. I no longer have any involvement in anything that might help you, and I resent the implication that I should. I'm a businessman. A *legitimate* businessman."

"Yes, well, you're in imports and exports. Coincidence?"

"Not at all. I learned quite a bit about the industry working on certain cases. When I retired it was easy to slip right into it. Now leave. This interview is over."

"That's unfortunate. I felt certain we could help each other."

"Why would you think that?"

"You said it yourself: I scared Brun. He came to you before anyone else. Why was that? Paternal advice?"

"As odd as it may seem, yes."

Coren raised an eyebrow skeptically. "Really. Well, if that *is* indeed the case, then perhaps we should both be concerned about the same thing. If I compromised him and you have his interests at heart, then—"

"If this is unrelated to Rega Looms, what is it related to? What's your concern in any of this?"

"I didn't say it wasn't related to Looms, I said it wasn't related to his company."

"Ah. Campaign stuff? You're private security, so part of your job is to clean up embarrassments. Let me guess—his daughter is in trouble."

"Why would you guess that?"

Wenithal shrugged. "Rumors. I hear things still. Conversations with old friends. She runs baleys, does she?"

"Not anymore. She's dead."

Coren had not planned to tell anyone, but he wanted to see Wenithal's reaction. He was not disappointed. Wenithal looked surprised and, for a moment, vulnerable. The bluster and firmness of the ex-cop vanished, replaced by an expression of informed terror. It metamorphosed slowly into a mask of sympathy and sadness.

"I'm . . . very sorry to hear that . . ." He turned away and muttered something more.

"What was that?"

"Hmm? Oh, nothing. I was just—my condolences to Mr. Looms. How—?"

"Running baleys."

"I see . . . yes, I can see that you would be interested. I'm very sorry, Mr. Lanra." He sat down. "I can't help you. I wish I could, but I'm long out of it. All I could give you are rumors."

"Rumors are often more reliable."

"Pah! Police superstition. You *hope* rumors are more reliable because usually they're all you get. When I was working I'd have taken a solid fact over rumor any day." Wenithal looked up, the wall back in place. "Now if you don't mind, I have a business to take care of. I'm not a policeman anymore. I did that for twenty-two years. No more. Go away."

Coren wanted to return to his private office and begin reviewing Wenithal's career. Instead, he took the tubeway west, to Delfi. From Wenithal's place it was only forty-five kilometers to Looms' hotel.

What is it about a Settler colony that would spook an ex-cop like that? His mention of Nova Levis had disturbed Wenithal. If he was part of a baley-running scheme, it might make sense. And if Nova Levis was the name that rattled him, then maybe he was the contact Nyom went through, in which case Coren would visit him again.

He dozed on the short ride, uneasily, the image of Nyom dangling broken-necked from the ceiling of that bin an unwelcome intrusion.

He tucked the earpiece of his portable comm in his left ear and keyed his office. The Desk answered.

"I want you to search police files for the case logs of Wenithal, Ree. Especially his last few cases and anything that might relate to baleys and baley running. Anything on Yuri Pocivil?" he asked *sotto voce*.

"Public records search positive result," the Desk

reported. "Pocivil, Yuri. Immigrant, work-pass issued six years ago. Originally from the Settler colony Cassus Thole. Resident of Petrabor District for the last four years. Employee of Improvo Shipping and Storage, Petrabor branch, last three years eight months. Current status, indefinite sickleave. Current location unknown."

Sick leave. *Dead more likely,* Coren thought sourly. He said, "Is there an image attached?"

"Yes, sir."

"Forward all this to Sipha Palen on Kopernik Station and continue search, locate. Any new messages?"

"New message from Myler Towne. Do you wish to hear it?"

"No. File." He hesitated. Then: "Make an appointment for me to see my physician, earliest convenience. End link." He plucked the earpiece out and tucked it back in the slot on the side of his comm.

Yuri Pocivil was a settler. Unusual for them to return to Earth. Unless he had been born on Cassus Thole and thought Earth had more to offer. It was easy to forget that the entire Settler program was less than two centuries old, with so many emigrants leaving Earth all the time.

He wondered who owned Improvo Shipping and Storage . . .

Rega Looms' entourage filled two floors of the Banil-Holbro, in the center of the theater district in Delfi. Coren stepped off the walkway directly onto the broad plaza fronting the polished false stone-and-gilt façade of the hotel.

Two of Coren's people stood just inside talking to the bellcaptain. Their laughter seemed distant and muffled in the lobby.

Both of them straightened when they saw Coren.

"Boss," Shola said. "Back from vacation?"

"No, don't worry, I'm not back yet," Coren said. "Where's Rega?"

The other one—*New man,* Coren thought for a moment. *What's his name? Lukas*—came up alongside him and they walked a few paces from the bellcaptain.

"Mr. Looms is in room four-ninety-one, sir."

"Thanks, Lukas. Everything copacetic? Any problems?"

"Other than lack of sleep?" Lukas smiled wanly.

Coren laughed. "That's what overtime pay was invented for," he said and walked away, toward the elevators.

Two more of his people waited in the hallway outside room four-ninety-one. They greeted him with silent nods. Coren knocked on the door and entered.

Rega Looms sat on the edge of a chair, staring at a datum screen on the table between him and Lio Top, his campaign manager. A spread of fruit and vegetables covered a sideboard, next to a big samovar.

Lio looked up first. "Hi, Coren," she said. "Didn't expect you back so soon."

"My compulsiveness is bothering me," he said, choosing a carrot from the tray. "Just wanted to see how things were going. Or not."

Rega Looms continued to focus on the datum. "Hello, Coren. Make yourself comfortable, I'll be with you in a few minutes."

Coren wandered to the far end of the room and sat down in a too-soft armchair. He ate his carrot without really tasting it. Now that he was here, in Rega's presence, he felt anxious.

"First thing in the morning," he heard Looms say finally.

Lio stood. Rega Looms closed the datum and rubbed his eyes.

"Six, then?" Lio asked.

Looms nodded. "That will be fine. Thank you, Lio."

She cast Coren a sympathetic look. "G'night, Coren." Coren's heartbeat kicked up a notch.

"Coren," Rega said. "Come sit down here."

Coren's legs felt leaden, but he took the seat vacated by Lio and made himself look at Rega Looms.

Too much of Nyom there, he thought, wincing.

"My daughter," Looms said.

Until this moment Coren had given no thought to what he intended to tell Rega. He justified—excused—this lapse by telling himself that *he* had yet to accept the facts. But that was facile, a diversion to keep himself from acknowledging the truth, that it hurt to say the words and it would hurt more to see his own reaction mirrored in Rega.

"She's dead, Rega."

Rega sat back as if slapped. He did not look at Coren, but stared at a point midway between them, eyes locked in place. He closed them slowly and his mouth opened wordlessly.

Coren's ears began to hum in the silence.

"How?" Rega asked, a faint whisper.

"I don't have all the details. She was running baleys and went with the last bunch. They all turned up dead on Kopernik Station."

"You didn't prevent her?"

"How was I supposed to do that?"

Rega's eyes snapped open and focussed on Coren. "I pay you to know how to manage those details."

"Dragging her out was my only option. Not feasible."

Rega did not look away, but the rage drained slightly from his face. Finally, he nodded.

"Now what?" he asked.

"I need a few days to find out why and who. I can keep

it out of the newsnets that long, but you better be prepared for it to hit. If I come up with answers, you could–" He stopped himself. He almost said, *you could turn it to your advantage.* It surprised him for a moment.

"That's Lio's job," Rega said, following his thoughts. He closed his eyes again. "Both of them now," he whispered. He sighed. "I have a campaign to win. Do what you have to do to find them. If it costs me the election, so be it." His eyes glistened now. He stood. "Thank you for ... for coming by, Coren. I know this wasn't easy for you."

"For either of us."

"Do you have any ideas yet?"

"Possibilities. Do you want to know?"

"No. Not till you finish. Then I want to know everything."

"Yes, sir."

As Coren started for the door, Rega caught his arm.

"Everything, Coren."

Rega let go and walked away, toward the bedroom. Coren waited till the door *snick*ed shut before he left.

By the time Coren returned to his office, third shift was just ending. His stomach churned–the carrot had triggered his hunger–so he stopped by a small carry-out within walking distance of his building and bought a sandwich.

"Good morning," the Desk greeted him. "Please verify identity."

Coren sat down and went through the procedure, unwrapping his sandwich with his free hand.

"Welcome, Mr. Lanra. You have two messages. One from Myler Towne, one from Ambassador Burgess, Auroran Embassy."

Coren stopped chewing. "Burgess? Time."

"Six-ten."

Half an hour ago.

Coren finished chewing and swallowed. "The one from Myler Towne—is it a repeat of the first message?"

"Yes, sir."

"File it."

"Yes, sir."

"No word from Jeta Fromm?"

"No, sir."

"Anything further on Yuri Pocivil?"

"No, sir."

"Ree Wenithal?"

"Yes, sir. Public records plus case logs, per parameters."

"Good, good. New search. I want to know who owns Improvo Shipping and Storage, and which freighter and passenger lines it does business with."

"Yes, sir."

Coren stretched lazily until his shoulder twinged. "Did you make that physician's appointment?"

"Yes, sir. Your physician has an opening six days from now, second shift."

Good thing it's not an emergency, Coren thought wryly. "Okay. What specifically do you have on Wenithal? Display."

The screen rose from the desk and file headers scrolled down. Coren caught the words "Nova Levis" and said "Stop. Case file number 82-791-AKB. Review."

"Infant abduction case involving several prominent families. Ree Wenithal primary investigator. Eighteen-month investigation culminating in sixty-two percent recoveries and the closing of eight orphanages and four bioremedial research laboratories."

"How does Nova Levis figure in?"

"R and D facility which came under investigation relative to Ree Wenithal's investigation. Laboratory cleared of any charges."

Cleared ... but the name scared Wenithal just the same ...

"Collate the particulars: names of families, the children involved, witness lists, and other sources."

"Yes, sir. Do you wish to audit Ambassador Burgess's message?"

"Not yet. Alert me two hours from now."

"Yes, sir."

He rubbed his face and eyes as if to massage away the fatigue.

He felt incompetent. Things had gotten away from him already. It had happened before, but he never got used to it. So much of police work relied on chance and luck—the rest was a question of tenacity. Coren had a good track record of wearing a case down until he solved it. But that took time, and right now he did not have that luxury. He needed to know *now*.

He had lost Jeta Fromm. That was his one chance of finding out about that strange robot quickly enough to find Nyom's killers before the murders went public. The more time passed, the less likely he could wrap this up before the news broke.

Going to Brun Damik had been a gamble. Not a bad one, Coren thought, considering the rearrangement of shipping schedules out of his office for Petrabor. And Damik *did* know something. But instead of the answer that would have made Coren's life easier, he led him to Ree Wenithal. In truth, despite the curious fact that Damik had called Wenithal first after Coren's visit, Coren would have walked away from Wenithal as a useless lead.

Except for Wenithal's reaction to the name Nova Levis. But now Coren knew that Nova Levis was the name of a research lab. How did that relate to the colony? And what did kidnapping have to do with it?

"Desk, display data package received from Sipha Palen."

The screen came up. A menu scrolled across it. Coren read through the choices—autopsy, crime scene, material forensics—and touched the icon over crime scene.

The screen showed the cargo bin. Coren hesitated, then accessed the internal view.

Bodies stacked in couches crowding the walls . . .

He reached for the screen and accesssed the image of the dead Brethe dealer, then gazed at it thoughtfully. "Desk, I want a search for all manufacturers of prosthetic devices. Find a match for the hand pattern found on the woman's shoulder, and the type of prosthetic capable of doing this kind of damage."

"Yes, sir."

"End," he said. The screen went blank. "I'll go over it later."

"Yes, sir."

He scooped up his sandwich and went into his private space. He was tired and hungry and the painblock had worn off sometime in the last hour. It would do no good to rush into anything as unexpected as this.

The images of Nyom still covered the table. He gathered them up and placed them back in the carton. He sat down then, and finished eating.

EIGHT

He woke up with a stiff neck on top of the bruises. He swallowed another painblock and went to his desk.

"Good morning, sir," the Desk said. "Analysis and collation on the provided data completed. Do you wish a summary?"

"In a moment. I need coffee right now." He switched his samovar on. The machine hummed gently to life. Dark, steaming liquid filled a cup below the spigot. Coren breathed in the steam. "Any more messages?"

"None. Do you wish to review those in the queue?"

"Play Ambassador Burgess's."

Coren heard the flatscreen scroll up from the desktop, but he stood by the samovar, eyes closed, sipping his coffee.

"Mr. Lanra, I would like to apologize for any abruptness I may have exhibited with you yesterday. It has come to my attention that our interests may intersect. I would appreciate another opportunity to talk about it. I'll be in my office the rest of the day."

Coren opened his eyes. "Hm. I wonder what I disturbed. Connect to Ambassador Burgess."

"Yes, sir."

A few seconds later a crisp male voice said, "Ambassador Burgess's office, how may I help you?"

Coren went to the desk. On the flatscreen he saw the face of Burgess's aide, Hofton. "Coren Lanra. I'm returning the Ambassador's call."

"Of course. Wait one moment while I put you through."

The screen went pale gray, then Ariel Burgess appeared. Her eyes looked slightly puffy; perhaps she had gotten as little sleep as he.

"Ambassador Burgess."

"Mr. Lanra, thank you for returning my call so promptly."

"I admit I'm puzzled at this turnaround."

"No more than I am. Perhaps between the two of us we can make sense of some of it. Would you care to meet with us again?"

"When?"

"As soon as convenient for you."

"Right now, frankly, nothing is convenient. How about—" he glanced at the time chop "—ten. That'll give me a chance to clean up a little."

"That would be excellent. Here?"

"Certainly. I know the way."

She almost smiled at that. "Till then, Mr. Lanra."

The screen blanked.

"Desk, give me a summary of the analysis on the data I gave you."

"Specify order."

"Um . . ." He rubbed his eyes, remembering. "Update on Yuri Pocivil?"

"No further progress."

"Improvo Shipping."

"Improvo Shipping and Storage is a subsidiary owned outright by the Hunter Group. It has been in operation for thirty-eight years with ninety-two facilities within Sol System and fifty-one facilities located on various Settler worlds. The Hunter Group itself is an offworld company, headquarters on Cassus Thole."

"Really. How many employees within this system?"

"Six hundred seventy-two thousand."

"How many of those are immigrant?"

"Two thousand seven hundred."

"How many of those are natives of Cassus Thole?"

"Eleven hundred twenty-two."

"Uh-huh. Interesting. No list of board members?"

"No such list available at this time."

"Continue search, see if you can find one. Also, I want a list of all Hunter Group holdings. Next, the data from Wenithal's case file."

"The last case he worked on was a major kidnapping ring. It developed from an investigation into a single instance which led him to uncover a global operation with offworld connections. Infants were being sold through various vendors—primarily orphanages and child hospice centers—to offworld buyers."

Coren's interest spiked. "Go on. That sounds familiar. What's in the case file?"

"The record obtained from the public police database contains categorized tables, names cross-referenced in hierarchical tabulations according to assigned probabilities."

"Sounds like his interview and suspect lists."

"Correct. Three hundred seventy-nine names listed, all time-indexed over an eleven-year period beginning twenty-nine years ago, ending eighteen years ago. Of those with current public record files available, two hundred and ninety are deceased—"

"Stop. Two hundred and ninety dead?"

"Correct."

"Pattern analysis. Common factors?"

"One hundred thirty fatalities occurred within an eight-month period. Ninety-seven died of age-related factors. Eighty-three died as the result of fatal accident. Sixty-eight died as the result of fatal interaction—"

"You mean homicide."

"That is a legal definition not applicable in all instances."

"They were killed by other people."

"With certain qualifications, yes."

"Continue."

"Thirty-nine died of causes unverifiable due to inaccessibility of data."

"Explain."

"Deceased were offworld at the time of death. There were irregularities in subsequent reporting."

"Hard copy, names, places, dates, and cause of death." Coren watched while the Desk produced a disk for him. "Give me current disposition of surviving members of the list."

"Of the eighty-nine remaining names, forty-three are serving sentences in rehabilitation clinics, eighteen have emigrated to Settler colonies, and five are residents in hospice centers. Displaying list of remaining twenty-three."

Coren read down the rows until he came to a name he recognized. He whistled.

"Alda Mikels . . . interesting." He read on. "A few of these people are prominent public figures. I—" He stopped, startled. "Rega Looms."

Coren stared at the name for a long time. He retrieved his hemisphere then and set it into its niche on the desktop.

"Desk, download contents of last recorded exchange."

"Done."

"Play back."

Coren listened to his conversation with Ree Wenithal again. When he reached the point where he told Wenithal that Nyom Looms was dead, he said, "Stop there. Subject said something below normal range of hearing. Amplify and enhance."

From the desk speaker he heard Wenithal, in a raspy whisper, say "Both of them now."

"End playback." Coren looked at Rega's name on the screen. "'Both of them now.' What does that mean?"

"Unknown," the Desk said.

Rega had said something very similar. *Both of whom?*

"Desk, give me a hard copy on these names, then file and return to standby."

Coren went into his private room to clean up and change clothes. He wanted to go back to his apartment and stretch out for several hours' decent sleep, but he lacked the time.

He slipped the disks into his pocket and drummed his fingers on the edge of the desk. Several years ago, Coren remembered, Alda Mikels and a few others invited Rega Looms to join a business consortium which seemed to Looms at the margins of legality—gray market at least, if not black market. Some of those people were on Wenithal's list. Considering Looms' attitude toward most of them, Coren wondered why they would have approached him in the first place. Perhaps the association went back further than Rega had told him.

"Desk, I want a review of the last twenty-three names, those surviving and still on Earth. Initiate a records search and correlate common associations for the past twenty years."

"Parameters?"

"Education, business, investments, public service, children." He hesitated. "If nothing turns up, expand search to thirty years."

"Yes, sir."

Coren disliked investigating his own employer. Sometimes, though, protecting Rega Looms required that he know things Looms probably preferred he did not.

"Also, get me a thorough background on Ree Wenithal. Retired, law enforcement, currently runs his own import-export firm."

"Public file previously referenced—"

"I want a deeper background."

"Yes, sir."

"Also . . . also, display crime scene image from Sipha Palen's data."

The view spread across the screen. He stared at the bodies as the view rotated slowly through three-hundred-sixty degrees. Fifty-two people.

"Give me a copy of this, too," he said. One more disk extruded from the slot.

He ran down the list of instructions just given and tried to think of anything overlooked. Nothing came to mind but he could never quite shake the feeling that he had missed something. Without Jeta Fromm or the dockworker Pocivil, all he had was Nyom's collapsed robot.

There's never enough time to do this right. . . .

The Spacer Embassy occupied a huge area on the eastern edge of D.C., in the heart of the government districts.

Embassies, really, as the structure contained the missions for all the Spacer Worlds. Most had one set of offices, usually unoccupied. Of the Fifty Worlds, only a dozen maintained full-time staffs on Earth, Aurora and Solaria being the largest.

Just living on Earth marked these people as unique. Most Spacers disdained other worlds, especially the one that spawned them so long ago. But no group is completely homogeneous, and Spacers proved no exception. The total Spacer population on Earth never exceeded a few tens of thousands—a handful compared to populations in the many millions—but their presence made a powerful impression on Terrans.

Of them all, Coren reflected as he entered the main gallery of the Embassy, he preferred the Aurorans—they were the most approachable, the least defensive, compared to the xenophobic Solarians. To be sure, those Solarians living here did not share the degree of paranoia exhibited by most of their people in dealing with outsiders, but they still came across as standoffish and mistrustful.

Coren signed in at the reception desk and patiently received directions to the Auroran arm of the embassy building. He then retraced his path from the previous day.

Hofton met him in the reception lounge of Ambassador Burgess's offices. "The Ambassador is expecting you, Mr. Lanra. Mr. Avery is here as well. I trust this is acceptable."

"Completely."

Hofton escorted him into Burgess's office and closed the doors.

Ariel Burgess looked tired, with the beginnings of dark circles under her eyes. Derec Avery seemed much the same as he had yesterday.

"Mr. Lanra," Burgess said, rising from her seat and coming around the desk to clasp his hand. "Thank you for giving us a second opportunity to discuss your problem with us."

"Thank you, Ambassador. I have to tell you, I'm a little dismayed."

"I'm a little surprised myself. It seems we have a parallel interest in your situation."

"Parallel interest . . . quid pro quo, then."

"If that's satisfactory."

"I don't have the luxury of time, Ambassador. What I need is a roboticist to see if anything can be salvaged from a collapsed positronic brain—the robot I told you about yesterday."

"It allegedly witnessed a mass murder," Derec Avery said. "Which would probably have precipitated the collapse."

"Possibly."

"Let me guess," Burgess said. "You think the robot itself committed the crime."

"*A* robot, certainly."

"Why?"

"We have no other viable suspect," he said. "Everyone who boarded the cargo bin used to shuttle the victims to Kopernik is accounted for—all dead. There was no way for a human to get out of it without breaking the internal seals in place inside the bin. So we're left with a suicide-murderer, or . . ." He pursed his lips. "I saw another robot board the bin with the victims. It was . . . unusual."

"A second robot," Ariel said. "You didn't mention this yesterday."

"I didn't know if you'd be helping me or not."

"That might have changed our minds sooner."

Coren held up his hands apologetically.

"You said it was unusual," Derec said. "How so?"

"It didn't register through my surveillance equipment. I could *see* it, as I see you, but through an optam it was invisible. Masked—what they used to call 'stealthed.'"

"We don't make robots like that," Ariel said. "That function is useless except for military or criminal purposes, and we don't—can't—use robots for either of those things."

"Nevertheless, I witnessed just such a robot."

"And when the bin was opened?" Derec asked. "Was it there?"

"No. Only Nyom Looms' robot was present. Here." He handed the disk containing Sipha's reports. "Go to the crime scene."

In a moment they huddled around Ariel's desk, gazing at a full holographic image of the interior of the cargo bin.

"This is what the security people on Kopernik found when they opened it up," Coren explained.

"What is that the robot is working on?" Derec asked.

"A rebreather unit. It contained a poison that caused neurological damage and paralysis."

"Who is this?" Ariel asked, pointing to the body hanging from the bin ceiling.

"Nyom Looms. She wasn't poisoned. She had her own rebreather. Her neck was broken, instead."

"Fifty-one others," Hofton said. "How did she get attached up there?"

"The bin was cracked. The air leaked out fairly quickly—not all at once, but in a vacuum it must've created a current. We think it drew her to it. Her clothing was pulled through."

"Cracked," Ariel mused. "Big enough for your robot to slip through?"

"Hardly. You can see the dimensions for yourself."

Ariel frowned and gave Derec a look Coren could not

read. "It would be unlikely, I think," she said. She sighed. "You still haven't given us a convincing argument to indict a robot." She pointed to the image of Coffee. "What do you think, Derec? A modified DW-12?"

"Looks like it. But it's not possible, Mr. Lanra. There is no way to modify a positronic brain to subvert its Three Law constraints. Tampering at that level would destroy the brain. The fact that it's collapsed proves that its programming was consistent with its original protocols. It witnessed the deaths of humans ostensibly in its charge. It failed to protect them. It collapsed."

"As I recall," Coren noted, "a positronic brain was modified at Union Station to cause the deaths of a good number of people."

Derec stiffened. "That's . . . inaccurate. It was modified to ignore a lethal situation. It *caused* nothing. And it collapsed shortly after it realized what had happened." He frowned thoughtfully. "What was this robot doing at the rebreather controls?"

"As far as we can tell, trying to shut it off."

"You've said 'we' a few times now. Who else is involved in this investigation?" Ariel asked.

"Kopernik Station's chief of security is working with me on this," Coren replied.

"How are you keeping it out of the newsnets, then?"

"The bin was delivered to a Settler dock. She has an arrangement with the Settler security people. It's isolated, outside the usual legal channels. For the time being, it doesn't exist. That won't last long."

"And the robot?" Derec asked.

"Stored."

"Still in the Settler section?"

"In Chief Palen's morgue."

"We need to have it."

"There's no way I can bring it down here. Not in time, anyway. I need someone to go to it."

Ariel looked at Derec. "What do you think?"

Derec shook his head. "A risk. I'm still not sure what my status is."

Ariel looked at Coren. "Our . . . range of free movement may be somewhat curtailed. Especially Mr. Avery's."

"Mine isn't," Hofton said. "I could accompany Mr. Avery up to our embassy branch on Kopernik." He glanced at Derec. "You'd be in the diplomatic pouch, so to speak."

Derec grunted, smiling thinly.

"Excuse me," Coren said. "There's no question here, is there? You're *going* to help me."

"You wouldn't be talking to us otherwise, Mr. Lanra," Ariel said.

"Why?"

Ariel looked thoughtful. "Before I answer that, let me ask you something. Where was Nyom Looms taking this group of baleys?"

"Nova Levis."

"Why there? I can think of at least a dozen other Settler colonies that would accept baleys that aren't under blockade."

"I don't know. Nova Levis is . . . romantic."

"That's hardly a reason. But even so, the next question is, why kill them?"

"Her father is running for office," Coren said. "Something like this—"

"Just letting it out that she ran baleys would accomplish as much," Ariel said, shaking her head. "What was there about this run that warranted murder?"

Coren said nothing.

"That's the question, then," Ariel said. "Answer the why, you discover the who. Theoretically, anyway. And it won't be a robot."

Coren leaned across her desk and touched an icon on her flatscreen. "I'd like your opinion on these, then."

The image from Ariel's desk projector vanished, replaced a moment later by the autopsy images Sipha had sent him of the Brethe dealer who had died in her holding cell. The sight brought a sharp hiss from Derec Avery; Burgess paled.

"At first we thought this was unrelated," Coren explained. "Maybe it is, but I'm guessing not. Frame sixteen—" he gestured for Ariel to find that image "—is an enhanced display of a handprint left subdurally. Tell me what you think."

Ariel touched her projector control and the autopsy images shifted. The false color view of the oversized handprint bloomed.

"Too big for a human hand . . ." Derec mused.

Coren watched Ambassador Burgess. Finally, she nodded. She glanced at him, frowning briefly, and looked away.

"I'd have to agree with Derec," she said. "A human hand didn't make that. But that still leaves the field open to a number of explanations. Prosthetics, for one."

"I ran a catalogue check for any prosthetics commercially available that match that pattern. Nothing turned up. That doesn't rule out a custom manufacture, of course, but . . ."

"But you still think it's a robot."

"Something managed to slip past all the security in a police cell block to do this. I already told you the robot I saw was blind to my optam. It may be the same technique in this case: a masked robot, invisible to surveillance monitors."

"So now it's a conspiracy of robots," Derec said. "Less and less likely."

"Can you give me a *better* explanation to account for the damage?" Coren asked sharply.

"Isn't that what we need to find out?" Ariel Burgess said. "You asked why we're helping. What you've proposed here is a good enough reason for me. Earthers think the worst of robots on a good day. This—" she waved at the projection "—validates all your fears, if true. A chance to head this off and perhaps prevent a very ugly purge would be a good enough reason, don't you think?"

"For your part, that seems plausible. But that's not the only reason."

Ariel bowed her head in mock acceptance. "Of course not. Illegal emigration is a point in common between us and Terra. There's a quid pro quo in that, too."

"You're working with ITE?"

"No. We're working with *you.*"

Coren looked from one face to the other, returning to Ariel. He expected them to keep things from him, most of it details of their involvement that really did not concern him. But he also expected them to be subtle about it. Instead, they were very obviously not telling him something. If he did not need their expertise . . .

"What specifically are *you* getting from this arrangement?" he asked.

Ambassador Burgess gave a faint smile and a slight shake of the head. She gestured at the image of the dead woman on her screen. "Who was this? Why was she killed?"

"According to Chief Palen, she was a small-time narcotics dealer," Coren lied. "Could be any number of people she may have crossed in the course of business."

"This seems excessive for a bad debt," Ariel said. She drew a deep breath, slowly released it. "Aurora has been asked by Terran authorities to look into the Nova Levis situation. That involves a lot of baleys. I was asked by my immediate superior to lend you aid. Partly, we may have a problem with Spacer businesses shipping illegally from Earth. It's being suggested that Spacers are colluding in bypassing immigration and trade laws. I presume they believe we'll find things that will be mutually helpful. Is that sufficient answer for you, Mr. Lanra?"

Coren folded his arms across his chest. "It will do . . . for now."

"In that case," Ariel said, smiling uneasily, "how do you want to proceed, Mr. Lanra?"

NINE

W e have work, Thales." Derec started feeding disks into the reader on Thales' console. "Load these." "Has Phylaxis been revived, Derec?" the RI asked.

"No. This is an embassy assignment. Sort of." Derec slid the last disk into the reader, then pulled a chair over. "To be honest, I'm not sure about this. There's a possibility that our situation could get worse."

"Then, is it advisable to accept?"

"We don't have a lot of choices, Thales. Ariel has been handed this by Ambassador Setaris. I get the impression that Setaris is just passing on instructions from Aurora." He leaned back and laced his fingers under his chin. "We're to assist the chief of security for DyNan Manual Industries, a man named Coren Lanra, in an investigation concerning the death of Rega Looms' daughter, baley running, and a possible robot involvement."

A few moments passed before Thales responded. "Based

on the data I have just reviewed, am I correct that Mr. Lanra suspects a robot in the deaths?"

"He does."

"That is not possible."

"I explained that to him. But he's an Earther—he believes positronics are inherently evil. Still, I don't have a better explanation for the body found in the holding cell."

"The damage is singular."

Derec grunted. "That's one way to look at it. For now, though, I want you to give me a program for a remote presence. I have to go up to Kopernik Station to try to salvage the DW-12 they have. It may be the only witness to what happened in the cargo bin. I'll need you to help me sift through what's left of its brain. I don't think I can take all of you, and even if I could I'm not sure I want to risk you outside Auroran territory."

"According to my memory, the positronics laboratory on Kopernik is more than ample for our purposes. Do we have a free comm channel to the Auroran branch on Kopernik? I will need to establish that they have the facilities."

"Ariel's setting that up now. I'll be on a shuttle in less than five hours, so we have to set this up quickly."

"I have analyzed the data provided."

"Good. I'd like to hear your assessment."

"There are a number of inconsistencies, primary among them is the connection between the death of the Brethe dealer and the deaths of the baleys. Except for the suggestion that a robot is involved, there is no basis I can see for the link between them. If a robot is not involved in one or the other or, as is more likely, both, then the Brethe dealer is an entirely separate issue and a complication in the investigation of the murdered baleys."

"And if a robot *is* involved?"

"The likelihood of finding a robot capable of such crimes being as remote as it is, then there would be grounds to link the two, as it would be logical that only one such robot exists. But that prompts a number of questions, all of which require factors of chance and coincidence that recomplicate the central question. Such a robot would need to be transported to and from Kopernik on a regular basis, in a short period of time."

"Increasing the chance of discovery," Derec noted.

"Precisely, even given the capabilities described by Mr. Lanra of a robot able to hide from surveillance tools. It should be pointed out that it is not accurate to suggest that only a robot could use masking capabilities. For a robot, however, the risk of discovery in this instance would be unnecessarily higher. There is nothing in the data provided concerning the baleys that implicate a robot. This crime could just as well have been committed by humans."

"How would the assassin escape? Everyone in the cargo bin was dead and the seals showed no indication of having been opened between the time the baleys boarded and Chief Palen's people opened it up on Kopernik."

"Human history is overfull with examples of suicide assassins. However, barring that, I lack sufficient information to rule out all possible methods of escape."

"What about the crack in the bin?"

"There is insufficient information for me to speculate productively about that. It could be a structural flaw in the material."

"All right, set that aside for the moment. Can you still access Terran data sources?"

"Of course."

Despite the fact that it was incapable of emotion, Derec nevertheless heard a note of smug pride in Thales' statement.

"Of course," he echoed. "I want you to run a search for any recent murders or accidental deaths that bear similarities to the Brethe dealer."

"That will require me to access certain law enforcement datums."

"Is that a problem?"

"No, but it will take more time. I may not have that information for some hours. Unless you do not care about detection."

"Do it right, Thales. I don't want the TBI on our backs about this. You said there were a number of inconsistencies. Continue."

"All the passengers but one succumbed to a neurotoxin. Why not all of them? Nyom Looms carried her own rebreather. The question is why? Did she anticipate trouble? Was she sharing the primary rebreather before donning her own? And if there was time for one to remove the rebreather mask, why not more? The DW-12 unit appears to be trying to shut the rebreather off. This suggests that the bin was pressurized and contained sufficient atmosphere that shutting down the rebreather would not constitute further threat to human life."

"The crack."

"Why would they use a damaged bin? It is reasonable to assume that an inspection would have revealed the crack prior to its transfer to an orbital lifter—unless, as I already suggested, it was a structural flaw which manifested only after lift-off. But it also seems reasonable to assume the crack was made specifically to force the passengers to continue using the rebreather, as the air would leak out, thus guaranteeing that they would be poisoned."

"So the crack was made after the bin had been transferred," Derec said.

"If it was intentional, that is reasonable. But by whom?"

"Or what. That brings us back to the robot hypothesis."

"Which remains unlikely. The opening is too small for a robot to pass through, and since the DW-12 is the only one present—and is still present—in the bin, then we can rule it out."

"The masked robot?"

"Being undetectable by surveillance equipment would not render it invisible to plain sight. It would still have been in the container. There are other possibilities for creating such a crack."

"Coren Lanra says he saw it board."

"But it was not there when the bin was opened. Either it left before arrival on Kopernik, even before it left Earth, or Mr. Lanra is mistaken."

"Agreed," Derec said, nodding. "But there are no tools in the bin. It appears that whoever made the opening also left."

"Unlikely."

"Again, I agree. Continue."

"There is evidence of an absence. Not all the cradles in the bin are occupied. Two appear to have been empty when the bin was opened. One can be accounted for by the victim found suspended from the ceiling. The other was simply empty. Both were provided with rebreather masks. From the appearance of both empty cradles, one *was* occupied."

Have to ask Lanra about that, Derec thought. "So? They miscounted."

"One assumes these bins are prepared in advance. That they would contain the exact number of cradles necessary for a single shipment seems unlikely. However, if they *did* outfit this one to specific requirements, why would there be an extra?"

"Possibly someone elected not to go at the last moment?"

"Not an unreasonable hypothesis, Derec."

Maybe one of the late Nyom Looms' charges still lived, then. One not involved in the murder, at least, since that empty cradle remained unaccounted for.

"I have a question, Derec," Thales said.

"Yes?"

"Should I suspend my work on Bogard's positronic matrix for the duration of this assignment?"

"Why would—? Oh."

Memory, Derec realized. Normally Thales possessed far more memory than either of these chores required, but already Bogard's problem took up more than Thales possessed. The hasty move from their former housing at the defunct Phylaxis Group building meant a good portion of Thales' auxiliary memory buffers waited, unused, in storage. Having access to Kopernik's buffers, however, represented an opportunity for Thales to once more utilize its full potential.

"We'll wait," he decided. "Find out what facilities you can use on Kopernik. Maybe you can divide functions."

"I would appreciate the opportunity to test several hypotheses concerning Bogard. Kopernik's facilities would offer that chance."

"We'll find out. Is there anything else?"

"Yes. Will identification of the deceased be provided?"

"I don't know. Is it important?"

"Finding commonalities among them may bear upon discovering who would want them all dead."

Derec blinked. Sometimes he felt like an idiot. "Of course. I'll ask." He scratched his chin idly. "Speaking of Bogard, do you have an update?"

"No change since last report. I do not possess sufficient memory to operate at a more effective level."

"Okay. I didn't expect anything, but . . ."

"There is a possible solution to the total problem."

Derec hesitated. "You mentioned hypotheses . . ."

"Part of Bogard's unusual make-up was based on unorthodox hardware configurations. I have attempted to simulate these, but like the human brain, the physical matrix itself represents a necessary and unpredictable condition of awareness. Given the limitations within which we are forced to work, I have compiled a protocol whereby it may be practical to encode a new positronic brain with a composite persona: Bogard's, and myself."

Derec considered for a few seconds. "What good would that do? Bogard's matrix is completely collapsed. Trying to load it into a new brain would either be rejected by the load protocols or result in a duplicate encoding, collapsed condition and all."

"Normally, yes. The encoding protocols require a stable framework for reception to work. I am suggesting that I can provide that framework while allowing those elements of Bogard that match a viable positronic template to load within it."

"A combination?"

"I could not predict to what extent the result would be a combination—how much of each source matrix would encode in the new brain—but in essence, parts of both Bogard and myself would transfer together."

Derec shifted in his chair, intrigued. "The result could be only a slightly less coherent matrix. Collapse would occur at the first challenge."

"Possibly. I am running simulations to account for as many variables as possible based on my own composition."

"What, uh, would be the point?"

"You would have a functioning persona capable of self-analysis. It might be possible to simply ask it why it failed."

Derec felt eager to try. He wanted to say yes. He distrusted the impulse, but the idea excited him.

"Continue running the simulations until I can find out more about Kopernik's lab."

"Yes, Derec."

The light on the comm winked on. Derec leaned closer: Ariel was calling. "We may have that answer now," he said, and reached for the ACCEPT button. His hand trembled slightly; he clenched it into a fist for a moment, then pressed the contact.

Hofton brought the link to Derec's apartment. Derec opened the small metal case and ran a diagnostic on the device.

"Our shuttle lifts in an hour, twenty minutes," Hofton said. "Are you packed?"

Derec pointed to a single large case by the door. "This'll take about half an hour," he said, patting the side of the link. "Thales, we have a Mark-Six Collaborative Transcriptor."

"You requested a Mark-Four."

"Is this a problem?"

"No, this is a considerable improvement. Refresh periods can be at greater intervals and more thorough."

Derec looked at Hofton.

"I took a few liberties," the aide said. "No one was using this one."

Derec smiled. "I didn't realize you were such a good scrounger."

"The position of 'aide' is descriptively vague for a reason," Hofton said.

The diagnostic winked green. "The unit checks one hundred percent, Thales. Are you ready?"

"I have modified the download pathways to accommodate the superior unit. Start with nodes eight through fourteen."

Derec opened a panel on Thales' console and began attaching thick connectors. "Did you happen to find out who's running the lab on Kopernik?"

"Yes," Hofton said. "Rotij Polifos."

"I don't know him. Is he good?"

"He's been director for the past seven years."

"Hm. Anybody else?"

"There are two specialists and six interns. From what I saw, I think you'll be pleased. I also did some background on Mr. Lanra and his friend on Kopernik."

Derec rechecked the connections, then pressed a contact labeled OPEN CHANNEL. He watched the indicators for a few seconds.

"Coren Lanra used to be Special Service," Derec said.

"Yes, he did. So was Sipha Palen. In fact, they partnered together in Service."

"Why'd they quit?"

"Ideology, apparently. In Mr. Lanra's case, he disapproved of the changes in Terran policy toward positronics. He resigned roughly at the time we were beginning work on the Union Station RI. Ms. Palen requested reassignment after being attached to Senator Kolbren's office."

"Kolbren . . . isn't he the one that sponsored the legislation attempting to bar all Spacers from public areas? For health reasons, if I recall."

"In essence. It was a quarantine measure. It didn't even get out of committee, but Kolbren keeps winning reelection. Ms. Palen asked for a new position and was refused. She resigned. Shortly afterward, she accepted her current position as chief of security for Kopernik."

Derec grunted. "Odd. She resented working for a rabid anti-Spacer, and her former partner resented growing cooperation with Spacers. How did they get along as partners?"

"I'm not psychic. Your guess is as good as mine. I suppose they found other things upon which to base their relationship."

Derec looked at Hofton. He could never tell when the man was being sincere or sardonic. It annoyed him that Ariel seemed to like Hofton so much—Derec's own dry wit irritated her.

"Both, however," Hofton continued, "had exemplary records while in Special Service."

"And now he works for a man who wants to see us all thrown off Earth." Derec shrugged. "So we cooperate with him."

"A quandary. It *is* odd."

"Any ideas?"

"None I'd be willing to share at the moment."

Hofton's expression remained politely attentive, betraying nothing more. He had worked for Ariel for nearly three years. Before Hofton, she had gone through four other aides in something over two years. Derec had never asked about them or asked why Hofton was different. He wanted to ask now.

Instead, he said, "Hofton, you're perfect."

"One tries, sir."

Derec laughed, and was rewarded by a faint smile from Hofton.

"Anything else I need to know about these people?" Derec asked.

"I'm not sure. One curious fact about Mr. Lanra came up. He's an orphan."

"Really."

"Yes, sir. He matriculated from the Connover-Trinidal Youth Asylum, a life-long resident. I find this remarkable because many people from the same background don't enjoy much success."

"He never knew his parents?"

"No. And, of course, the records are sealed. But as far as I could tell, he never tried to look into them."

"Hm. What about Palen?"

"Very much the opposite. Large, extended family, prosperous, the best schools, etcetera." Hofton waited a beat. "Should I continue looking?"

"Not on my account. Maybe Ariel would like to know more. Is Lanra accompanying us to Kopernik?"

"No, sir. He has lines of investigation down here . . . so he says."

Derec gave Hofton a curious look.

"The shuttle up to Kopernik two days ago," Hofton said, "was his first trip offworld."

For a few seconds, Derec did not understand. Then: "Oh. Well, then, I suppose it's just as well he has things to do down here."

Hofton nodded. "I think it's for the best."

"Probably."

"We may find Ms. Palen more cooperative anyway, simply because she doesn't work for Rega Looms."

"That's certainly a possibility."

They fell silent then, and Derec stared at the link until a light winked on requesting the next phase of its setup. Derec worked silently, rearranging the connections, reconfiguring part of the device to match the next part of Thales' requirements.

Hofton softly cleared his throat. "May I ask a question, sir?"

"Sure."

"Why are you involving yourself in this?"

Derec straightened, trying to compose an explanation of the link and why Thales required it due to the distances involved and the complexity of the job, but stopped, comprehending the question a moment later.

"You mean with this investigation?" he asked.

"Yes."

"I could ask you the same." Hofton waited and Derec nodded. "I love this," he said, waving at Thales. "Working with positronics. Working, period. I hate inactivity."

"You could do calisthenics in that case."

Derec laughed briefly. "I'm doing this because I can, because it might give me a chance to do something I want to do. Because the chance to get my hands on the tools to do some serious work is worth the risk."

"You'd like to rebuild your robot, Bogard."

"Of course I would, but it's more than that."

"There are several good reasons for you to refuse."

"I know. I'm not going to think about them." Derec looked at Hofton. "You?"

"You mentioned inactivity. Do you have any idea how

dull diplomatic work can be?" He smiled wryly. "Seriously, though, I have been with perhaps a dozen senior diplomats. The work was interesting—more so in the beginning, before the desensitizing produced by overfamiliarity and intimate contempt—but rarely challenging. Even so, had my various superiors been in the least worth the bother, I would never have complained, much less transferred. I never thought I'd find myself working for someone like Ambassador Burgess. It was very difficult when I was forced to leave her service last year. I admit, I'd begun to take her for granted. But I just finished several months with a man named Cotish Valgas, who is a deputy overseer in Furnishing and Accoutrements. Yes, there *is* such a department—I was shocked myself. Suffice it to say that I'll never take Ms. Burgess for granted again."

"She's special, isn't she?"

Hofton nodded slowly, his eyes bright and sharp. "She is that, sir."

"So why is *she* doing this?"

"Because she's been ordered to."

Derec shook his head. "No, no. You've known her for all this time. Is that the Ariel you know?"

Hofton frowned. "She's more disciplined, I think, than you give her credit." He blinked and folded his arms. "But, no, not really. She could easily refuse. She's been expecting a recall to Aurora anyway."

"So?"

"I think she wants a chance to get even."

"With who?"

"All of them, sir. All of them." He glanced at his watch. "We have an hour before the shuttle leaves. Will you be done?"

Derec checked the monitors. "Five more minutes."

Hofton cleared his throat, and shifted uncomfortably on his feet. "Um . . . I spoke perhaps too openly, Mr. Avery—"

"She'll never hear about it from me." Hofton looked mildly relieved. "Under one condition."

"Sir?"

"Call me Derec."

"I'll do my best, sir."

TEN

Three people were waiting in his office when Coren returned. Two of them wore the look of professional security—well-dressed but practical, no clothing that would bind and impede a wide range of movement—while the third looked very administrative. Coren recognized none of them other than by type. He resisted the immediate urge to run; right now he did not have time for further complications.

"Mr. Lanra," the administrative type said. "I'm Del Socras. I work for Mr. Myler Towne of Imbitek. Forgive the intrusion, but I was instructed to convey Mr. Towne's regards and extend his invitation to lunch."

Coren glanced at the security, both of whom had risen to their feet upon his entrance. "I really am rather busy, Mr. Socras."

"Mr. Towne realizes this. It will be a brief lunch."

Coren considered his options: run, call the police, or comply. From the look of the pair of security types, it was even odds that he could get away. Dragging in the police might complicate things to the point that his investigation of Nyom's death would have to be postponed or abandoned. It always seemed to be the petty things that interrupted one's plans.

That was the problem, though. If it were petty, why would Towne be so insistent? Reluctantly, he concluded that his only viable option was to go along and find out.

"Very well. Shall I meet him somewhere?"

"We have a car, Mr. Lanra."

"Of course you do." Coren made himself smile. "Shall we, then?"

"One moment, sir," one of the security said and pulled out a palm monitor that looked remarkably like Coren's own. He walked around Coren twice, then reached into Coren's pocket and removed his hemisphere. He handed it to Towne.

"I don't think you'll need this, Mr. Lanra," Towne said, setting it on the Desk. "Our security is very good."

"I'm sure it is," Coren said tightly.

Socras led the way out of the building and across the avenue to the garage.

The drive lasted fifteen minutes, during which time Socras made a few attempts at polite conversation which Coren ignored. To his credit, Coren thought, he took the hint and lapsed into a polite silence.

The windows were all darkened. When they stopped, he had no idea where exactly he was.

He was shocked to see a garden.

Outside? No—he saw delicate ribbing overhead, supporting a high vaulting ceiling. Relieved, he surveyed the rest of the chamber. A garden, yes, and an expensive one.

A large dead patch off to the left, an area that looked as

if some withering blight had eaten the life out of the very air around it, spoiled the placid beauty around him. Even the pavement and wall nearby were blackened.

A touch on his elbow prompted him to move forward.

Myler Towne sat behind a small table covered with dishes. He dwarfed his chair and made the people around him appear small. He looked up as Coren stopped.

"Mr. Lanra," he said, his voice surprisingly gentle. "I'm pleased you accepted my invitation."

"Is that what it was?"

"Of course. It's illegal to coerce people."

"Of course it is. What can I do for you, Mr. Towne?"

"Come to work for me."

Coren held back a laugh.

Towne looked at him, scooped a mound of mashed potato onto his fork, and smiled.

"Neither of us," he said, "has time for banter. I have some questions before you answer me. You saw the damage when you came in?"

"Yes . . ."

"I used to take my lunch there."

Coren glanced back at the dead patch. "You mean that was an attack?"

"Did you engineer it?"

Coren started. "Excuse me?"

Towne smiled briefly. "I didn't think so. Have you ever worked for Imbitek?"

"I think you'd know."

"Possibly. I don't have all my predecessor's records." Towne waited, ate another bite of potato, then pushed the plate away a thumb's width. "Did you?"

"No."

"You *were* involved in that imbroglio last year that put Mr. Mikels in prison, weren't you?"

"No."

Myler Towne glanced around at his people. "I was misinformed? I was under the impression that you met with the Auroran liaison from the Calvin Institute. Was that on some other matter? I ask, you see, for a number of reasons, not all of which may be immediately connected—"

"My employer was under suspicion for the events that put your employer in prison, Mr. Towne. I was doing my job, seeing to his security. I was not, however, involved in any of it."

"Hmm. Indeed. Then why have you been twice to the Auroran embassy in the last two days?"

"Your first message to call came before either of those meetings, so I assume your reasons had nothing to do with that. Have they changed?"

"When I hire someone I want to know about them."

"You aren't hiring me."

Towne gave a mock frown of disbelief. "You're turning my offer down?"

"I am."

"But you haven't even heard it."

Coren sighed. "Must I?"

Myler Towne stood. He was an enormous man, easily head and shoulders taller than Coren, and not, as Coren first suspected, run to fat. For his size, he had a trim waistline, which implied that the shoulders filling his smock were solid and powerful.

"It's such a *good* offer," Towne said.

He came around the small table and an attendant immediately began clearing off the dishes. Another removed the table, and a third took away the chair.

Towne took Coren's upper right arm in a massive hand that nearly encircled his bicep. "Walk with me, Mr. Lanra."

Coren moved without thinking. There was no question of refusing.

Towne guided him deeper into the arboreta. The scents of various flowers mingled, almost too sweet. The colors competed for his eye.

"Do you like it?" Towne asked.

"It's . . . astonishing."

"Not entirely decorative. Beautiful, yes, but this is a working facility. There are several plots of non-Terran plantlife."

"Isn't that . . . ?"

"Illegal? No, we have permission. Well, for most of them. A few unexpected forms got in with the authorized seeds and have proven useful. We do a substantial business in pharmaceuticals, as well as our industrial divisions."

Coren glanced back in the direction of the "accident" and shuddered.

"No, that wasn't caused by an alien plant," Towne said. "Not directly, at least. We manage the biospheres here better than that. What you saw was a deliberate attempt to kill me. A very fast-acting substance—something we call a decompiler—was introduced in a standard defoliant. The plants we grew there possessed a method of self-defense that produced a cloud of protein molecules as they tried to rid themselves of the infection—in this instance a hopeless task, but it kept the poor things spewing vapor. I liked to eat there because the molecules so produced have a very pleasant aroma and a side benefit for the palate. Anyway, the moment this compound, which the plants continuously kept in the air, came into contact with flesh, it reacted with the adiposa and began to work faster. Much faster. One of my gardeners wandered in there just before lunch a few days ago. The entire plot was reduced to the state you saw in about ten minutes."

"Um . . ." Coren worked to keep the image out of his head and failed. "So someone is trying to assassinate you?"

"Absolutely."

"What does this have to do with me?"

"Nothing. That's why I called you. I live within thick layers of security, Mr. Lanra. For someone to get that close . . ."

Coren nodded, understanding perfectly. "You don't trust your own staff."

"There are a few, of course, but I'm not sure I would secure the results I need if I were to put them to finding the traitor. I think it would be better done by an outsider, someone not overly familiar with the situation or the personnel involved."

"I suppose it's pointless to ask if there was surveillance."

"Constant. We have nothing. We've reviewed the record and nothing unusual happened. I have one gardener for that plot—*had*, I should say—and he was the only one recorded tending the area. I doubt he would have been stupid enough to step into his own trap had he laid it."

"It would be extreme. Any idea who ordered it?"

"Oh, yes, I have a very good idea. I can't prove it. And I'd rather not say just now."

At that point, Towne released Coren's arm and stopped. Coren turned to face him.

"I would rather wait till I hear your answer," Towne said.

Coren shook his head. "Any other time, Mr. Towne, I might consider it. But just now . . ."

"I'll pay you half a million credits. Half now, half when your investigation is successful."

Coren's breath exploded as if he had been punched.

"Don't be shocked, Mr. Lanra, I'm very serious. This is worth considerably more to me than a half million."

"Forgive me, Mr. Towne..." Coren swallowed. "You must know that I can't accept. I have other responsibilities right now—"

"Looms' election? You can't think he'll win. Besides, I know that you've essentially delegated his security to your subordinate."

"That's not the only thing, but I *do* owe some loyalty to Mr. Looms. How would it look if I left his employ now?"

Towne nodded. "It would look bad. I won't try to tell you that his election would be an inconvenience to Imbitek. Seeing him fail would hardly be unwelcome. But I think he will, anyway. So do you. Or you're not as smart as I thought."

"Still, I'm engaged in a project that I can't let drop. In a few days I might be able to reconsider—"

"In a few days I could be dead."

"Then let me recommend another—"

"I want *you*, Mr. Lanra. I'm not interested in second best." Towne cocked his head to one side. "More money? Name your price, we can negotiate."

"This is a personal matter."

"Very much so."

"For me. I'm afraid I can't. Not right now."

Towne looked about to say more, then closed his mouth. He shrugged. "I'm sorry, then. I'll have my people take you back to your office. Don't fret, Mr. Lanra, I'm not the vindictive sort." He pursed his lips. "This personal issue. Perhaps I could help. I'm not without resources."

Coren hesitated. Towne's offer took on new possibilities. He could not use his own security people to find Nyom's killer, but it would have been good to have the help. He ran through a number of ways he might take advantage of Imbitek's security.

No, it was too complex. He did not have the time to work it out, build the appropriate firewalls, exercise the desired level of control.

"That's very generous," Coren said carefully. *Damn, it's tempting . . .*

"I think I can wait one more day," Towne said. "Let me know." He looked to his left then, and gestured. "Thank you for taking the time to talk with me, Mr. Lanra."

The pair of security that had accompanied Socras appeared then. They escorted Coren back through the lush garden. He paused before the dead foliage on the way out, fascinated in spite of his decision.

Decompilers? he wondered.

He instructed his Desk to run a thorough sweep on the office for eyes and ears. When the Desk reported none, Coren was surprised. He hefted his hemisphere, wondering how else they might set up surveillance.

I don't have time for this . . .

"What about the searches? Report."

"Of the twenty-three names you designated for records searches, partial correlations have been found as far back as twenty-eight years. Eight of them attended the same university together. Sixteen have military service records. Twelve share relatives through marriage."

"Give me the highest factor of commonality."

"Investment."

No surprise there, he thought. Every one of those twenty-three names was moneyed. "Any particular stock?"

"Nova Levis Corporation. All of them were primary shareholders."

"Nova Levis? The colony or the lab?

"The lab."

"You said 'were.' They are no longer investors?"

"The corporation ran for eight years without showing a profit and was consequently closed."

"Sold? To who?"

"Purchased outright by the Kysler Diversified Group. Debt paid out of available funds plus sale of equipment and patents."

Kysler . . . the same company that owned those shipments diverted to make room for Nyom's baleys . . . ?

"What patents?" he asked.

"Unknown at this time. Do you wish another search?"

"Yes. Who was on the board of directors?"

"Unknown."

"Did any of those twenty-three sell early?"

"Three: Kyas Vol, Tenebra Patis, and Rega Looms."

"How early?"

"Joint sale, three years after purchase of shares."

"Did any other shareholders who are not on this list of twenty-three sell at that time?"

"One. Gale Chassik."

"The Solarian Ambassador?"

"Presently. He was not ambassador at the time."

Coren considered. "I want a complete dossier on Nova Levis Corporation. For the time being, though, how does this figure into Ree Wenithal's career?"

"Ree Wenithal was an operative of EuroSector Bureau of Criminal Investigation. His last case involved research into Nova Levis Corporation as one of several laboratories suspected as collusive entities in a kidnapping ring. Results proved inconclusive, no action taken."

So that's where his reaction came from . . .

"Synopsis of his last investigation."

"Three-year investigation of kidnapping and infant brokerage, leading to the discovery of a child-selling trade operating between Earth and a Settler colony named Tau Regis. Agent Wenithal received a commendation for excellence in police investigation, three citations for exceptional public service, and a merit commendation for valor after exposing the ring and overseeing its destruction. He retired one year afterward with full pension and lifetime honors awards. He opened his own business two years later, a small private security firm which failed after four years. He remained retired then until starting the present firm of RW Enterprises."

"Hard copy the dossier on the investigation."

"Only the public record is available. Details are under security seal pending review."

"Very well, the public record, then." Coren tapped a fingertip against his chin, thinking. "Question: If Wenithal's case only lasted three years, why is there an eleven-year spread concerning the names in his files?"

"Subjects related in prior investigations from various districts. Collated by Wenithal under his own investigation for related details."

"So this was not the first time these matters had been investigated?"

"No. Ongoing investigations in five separate jurisdictions extending back seven years prior to Wenithal's case."

"Are any of the investigating officers available?"

"No. Eighteen officers, all deceased."

"What about staff? Are any of the people who worked for Nova Levis still alive and available? The principle researchers, what happened to them?"

"Five researchers. Three are listed as deceased, one

emigrated shortly after the lab closed, and the fifth is listed only as Missing."

"Missing. Name?"

"Kyas Vol."

"One of the primary shareholders who baled out early."

"Correct."

"Just missing, no last known address? What about his file? Who was he?"

"An immigrant, native of Spacer world Theia, resident director of research at two medical centers prior to accepting directorship of neurobiology department of Nova Levis."

Spacer...?

"Did he return to Theia?"

"The record does not so indicate."

"Missing." That could mean anything.

"The one who emigrated—destination?"

"Nova Levis."

Coren grunted. "Why am I not surprised."

"Unknown."

Coren felt himself smile at the Desk's literalness. "Very well. Continue search. In the meantime, link me to Sipha Palen, encrypt protocols."

The screen emerged from the desktop and winked on. Coren waited patiently while the machines exchanged the proper codes to set up the link. A few minutes later Sipha's face filled the screen.

"About time," she said. "I was beginning to think you'd forgotten all about me."

"No chance. I've had an interesting time since last we spoke. Listen, I'm sending you a positronic specialist."

"You're kidding. You really know one?"

"Two, actually, but you're only getting Derec Avery."

Sipha frowned for a moment, then whistled. "I *am* impressed, partner mine."

"You know about him?"

"I know someone who knows him. You would think he was the reincarnation of Susan Calvin to listen to this person."

"Who? Oh, yes. Never mind. Anyway, he should be on his way up within the next hour or two. He's coming in company with an officer of the Auroran embassy, a fellow named Hofton. Meet them, keep the heat off them, and get them to their embassy branch as quietly and quickly as possible. Avery's position with Terran authorities is . . . what would be a good word? . . . fluid. I don't want him busted and deported before he can do us any good."

"Consider it done. Nobody arrests anyone on my station unless I say so."

"Good, good. I'm also sending you a list of names. This is a fishing expedition, frankly, but it might turn up something. See if any of the deceased match in any way."

"I'll do what I can. Have you found your informant?"

"No. Someone else is looking for her, too. It might be a race." He thought about that. "Keep your people alert to her coming through Kopernik. If she's on the run she might try leaving Earth."

"Got a description?"

"I'll forward you an image. What about on your end? Anything new?"

"We found some fibers on the bin that match fibers taken from Nyom Looms' fingernails. She fought. Our target may be banged up a bit."

Somehow I doubt that, Coren thought. "What kind of fibers?"

"Synthetic of some kind. We're still analyzing it. I'll let

you know when we identify it." She paused. "You're sending Derec Avery up. Does that mean you're staying down?"

"Afraid so. I've got some things to follow up."

"And you really don't want to get back on a shuttle, do
you?"

Coren smiled wryly. "No, not really. Sorry."

"You're going to have to get over that some day. Especially if you ever expect me to continue our friendship."

"We'll see."

"Uh-huh."

Coren shrugged. "Hey, can I help it if I'm just an ordinary Terran?"

"You aren't, though. That's why your aversion annoys
me."

"Yes, well . . ." He felt awkward, caught wordless.

"Did you tell Looms?" she asked.

"Um . . . yes. He took it better than I expected. Or maybe
not. It's hard to read him, sometimes."

"Does he want you to keep looking?"

"Yes."

"You would, anyway."

"Yes."

Sipha nodded as if understanding something else about
him. "Let me get back to work. I'll see to it Mr. Avery gets to
the Auroran embassy."

"Right." Coren started to reach for the disconnect, then
hesitated. "Sipha, have you ever caught anyone smuggling
stolen children through Kopernik?"

She stared at him, momentarily stunned. "No. Why?"

"Something . . . just a peripheral bit of information I
stumbled on. An old case, nothing current. Just thought I'd
ask. Thanks."

"Talk to you later."

The screen went blank.

Coren cleared his throat and shrugged, as if trying to physically reset his thinking. "Desk, do you have that public file on Wenithal's last case?"

"Yes."

"Display it, please."

The screen filled with text. Coren leaned forward and began to read.

ELEVEN

Union Station D.C. looked much the same as always, but Derec never felt at ease with it—not after the assassinations and the subsequent ruin of his company and his hopes. The floor had long since been cleansed of blood and now shone with the high polish of smokey mirrors. People hurried about their business beneath its cavernous arch, announcements echoed over the P.A., and no one seemed to notice how much it had changed.

As Derec walked toward the customs desk, Hofton behind him carrying a large bag and a columnar container, he kept looking around, searching, until he realized what it was he sought.

Robots. There were no robots.

Union Station had once, for a short time, been a kind of free zone where robots worked openly. The Terran Senate had passed special legislation to allow positronics here, as a testing ground to see how Earthers would react, and to show Earthers the nature of robots. Spacers came through Union

Station D.C. and no other port on Earth, so it was convenient to provide them with a reception area that offered familiar accommodations. A Resident Intelligence had been installed to supervise the complex operations of the facility and manage all the robots. Derec's company, the Phylaxis Group, had overseen its installation and had been contracted to do the maintenance and troubleshooting for it, but subsequent events took all that away. And more.

He was nervous here: partly because it had been months since he had visited Union Station and his last memory of it held death, and partly because this was the first time since the trials at which the conspirators in the assassinations were found guilty and sentenced he had left the embassy. Though treated primarily as witnesses, Derec's staff had been detained and questioned for several weeks, and at least one person had been arrested on a minor charge tangentially related to Phylaxis and its activities. In the aftermath, it had been made clear to Derec that his presence on Earth may be required indefinitely. He was to make himself available to the court.

His passport had been confiscated.

Later, Ariel had let him know that she had interceded in his arrest. His Auroran citizenship was reinstated and he received a new passport, but his position became tenuous in the course of action taken by ITE to challenge the new document, and an injunction resulted barring him from leaving Earth.

"Legally," Ariel had explained, "this is absurd. It's a gesture. They can't keep you from leaving unless they arrest you. They can't arrest you on Auroran soil. If you *do* leave, your Auroran passport won't be questioned anywhere else and without criminal charges being filed, there are no grounds for extradition. They're trying to keep you here because they don't know what they want to do with you. You frighten them. We all do."

I have news for you, Ariel, he now thought as he placed his one small bag on the customs desk, *they frighten* me . . .

Hofton set his burdens on the desk beside Derec's and extracted a disk from his jacket. He handed it to the attendant.

"I didn't even have a chance to find out anything about the director of the lab," Derec said. "Rotij Polifos. Never heard of him."

"*I* had a chance," Hofton said.

"And?"

"I think later . . . ?"

Derec looked at the customs attendant, who seemed totally absorbed by their documents. "Sure," he said.

In retrospect, Derec realized that he saw the attendant push the button. She closed out one screen, turned smoothly, and her hand brushed across a depression on the desk to the right of her keypad. A second later, she handed Hofton a disk.

"Derec Avery?"

Derec turned to the voice and found himself confronted by three men in uniform and a fourth in a dark suit. One of the uniforms stood closest.

"Yes?" Derec replied, his pulse picking up.

"Port Authority," the uniform said. "Would you come with us, please?"

"Um . . . I . . ."

"Excuse me, officer," Hofton said, stepping forward. "Is there a problem?"

"We have some questions for Mr. Avery."

"You may ask them here. We have a shuttle to catch."

The uniform frowned. "Who are you?"

Hofton extended his ID. The officer slipped the disk into a palm reader, then showed it to the man in the suit.

"We are on Auroran embassy business," Hofton said. "Unless you have specific issues that you are willing to state publicly, you have no legal grounds to detain us. Our passage is to Kopernik Station and we will be staying at the embassy annex there. I can cite you the relevant part of the diplomatic accommodations code if you like, but I believe you already know it."

"There's no need to—" the man in the suit said.

"Identify yourself, sir," Hofton said. "Are you *also* Port Authority? If not, please produce a valid warrant."

"Warrant . . . ?"

"If you wish to detain Mr. Avery, I believe a warrant is required—you may not do so on spec. If there *is* such a warrant, we are permitted to return to the Auroran embassy here for consultation with our law department. Mr. Avery is currently working under a brief from Ambassador Burgess. You may check that. The brief extends her diplomatic immunity to her agents. You may check *that* in the code as well. But you may not detain us while you do so unless you have a valid warrant."

"What is the nature of your visit to Kopernik?" the man in the suit asked.

"You have not yet identified yourself," Hofton said. "Mr. Avery is not obligated to answer that."

"Are you a lawyer?"

"No, sir. If I were I would have settled this matter by now. I'm giving you the benefit of a less predatory disposition."

The man in the suit stepped forward, his face reddening. "That man," he said, jabbing a finger at Derec, "does not leave this planet."

"I repeat," Hofton said calmly, "do you have a valid warrant?"

Derec watched, stunned, as if time had stopped. Hofton did not flinch, did not smile, did not do anything that might have looked like an actionable gesture. The man in the suit reddened further.

"You have no authority to prevent him," Hofton said finally. "If you attempt to do so, the Auroran embassy will file a formal complaint. If you do not have that warrant, I can also promise that you will no longer hold the position you currently do. Now, there's an easy solution. Kopernik is technically Earth. A satellite, true, and not on the ground, but if you check you will see that it qualifies as Earth. Mr. Avery is not leaving Earth."

"That's facile," the man in the suit said.

"Yes. But legal."

One of the uniforms was smiling. The man in the suit stepped back.

"I'll be contacting my people on Kopernik," he said. "We'll have this conversation sooner or later."

"You'll have plenty of time then to enjoin Mr. Avery from further travel outsystem," Hofton said. "Now, if you don't mind, we have a shuttle to catch." Hofton turned to the custom attendant. "Please return my original disk now."

The attendant paled visibly and handed over another disk.

"Thank you," Hofton said and grabbed the container and the bag. "Mr. Avery?"

Shaken, Derec managed to walk toward the debarkation concourse.

Halfway to the shuttle, he glanced at Hofton. "How true was all that?"

"Mostly," Hofton said. "I was guessing that they had no

warrant, which is the only reason I could think that might prevent them from detaining us. As for what the Auroran embassy would do if he had insisted—which he could have . . . well, I rather doubt they'd risk an incident over you."

"You bluffed," Derec said in amazement.

Hofton nodded. "Successfully, I think."

Derec took his briefcase from the Kopernik customs inspector, nodded curtly, and walked forward, into the debarkation lounge. From space, Kopernik Station resembled a child's construction from struts and blocks and spheres, additions over time added to the original dumbbell configuration giving the impression of an abstract modelbuilder's idea of a tree. Symmetry could be sensed but not directly observed.

The interior looked no different from any brightly-lit warren on Earth. The debarkation lounge resembled the foyer of a hostel. Derec had dozed during the last half-hour of the flight and felt slightly muddled. He searched for signs directing him to the Spacer section, which should be nearby. He noticed a pair of women off to his right who seemed to be waiting for someone.

Then he saw a station security officer to the left, also watching for someone. Anxious, he increased his pace.

"Mr. Avery?" a man called from behind him.

A sickly warm sensation erupted within him, spreading out from his stomach.

"Sir," Hofton called.

"Mr. Avery—" the man repeated.

"Derec, wait," a woman said.

Derec hesitated at the familiar voice, almost turned to look, and stumbled a few steps. A passerby caught his arm, steadying him. Derec jerked away. "Sorry," he muttered. "Thank you."

"Derec," Hofton said, coming around to block his path.

"Derec," came the familiar-sounding voice again. Female. Where—?

One of the two women he had noticed grinned at him. Thick mahogany hair haloed her rounded face. She wore a loose-fitting shift and pants, Auroran-style. Derec stared at her, sure he should know her and unable to name her.

Standing beside *her* was the second woman—taller, dark-skinned, athletic, dressed in a suit that suggested a uniform. She radiated authority and he wondered what trick or bluff Hofton could do now to get them to the Spacer embassy. He swallowed hard and made himself stay put.

"Sir," Hofton said. "I believe our contact is here."

"Hi, boss," the familiar woman said.

Derec stared, recognizing her now. "Rana . . . ? Rana Duvan . . . ?"

Her grin widened.

"Mr. Avery?" the dark woman asked quietly, stopping within arm's length.

"Y-yes?"

"I'm Sipha Palen," she said, extending a hand. "Coren told me to expect you. I apologize for being late."

Tentatively, Derec clasped her hand. The grip was dry and strong. Abruptly, he felt very foolish.

"Ms. Palen, yes. I—" He looked past her at Rana. "Would you excuse me?"

He set his briefcase down at Hofton's feet and embraced Rana. Her arms came around his back and squeezed him.

"I don't—" he began.

"It's good to see—"

"—what are you—?"

"—too long—" she commented.

"—can't believe it, you look—"

Derec's breath escaped in a heavy sigh, simultaneously with Rana's sharp laugh. He stepped back. Her eyes glistened and she wiped at them impatiently.

"What are you doing here?" Derec asked.

Rana smiled. "I'm your embassy contact."

"Embassy . . . ?"

"Long story," she said. "Later." She nodded in Sipha Palen's direction. "Business."

Palen watched with a bemused gleam in her eyes, hands clasped behind her back.

"Sorry," Derec said. "Rana and I used to work together. It's been a while since we saw each other."

"Of course," Palen said.

"Um . . . yes, Mr. Lanra said you'd meet us. You're chief of security?"

"Every bit of it," she said, smiling. "Welcome to Kopernik."

"Thank you. I believe I'm supposed to oversee an excavation on a positronic brain?" He looked at Rana, who shrugged.

"We haven't let it out of our lockup yet," Palen said. "Now that you're here, we can get started."

"Rana is more than qualified—"

"Coren and I have agreed to a certain protocol in this case. You are part of it."

"I see. Well, then, let's get started. I understand there's a time limit?"

"There is. I'll take you to the robot directly and we'll all escort it to the Auroran embassy, if that's acceptable to you, Ms. Duvan."

"I'm not in charge of the embassy," Rana said. She glanced at Hofton. "If it's been cleared with Yart, then . . . "

"I've already secured the appropriate clearances," Hofton said. "Ambassador Leri is aware that certain unusual circumstances prevail. We have his cooperation."

"Good," Sipha Palen said. "Then . . . ?" She made a gesture for them all to proceed.

Derec retrieved his briefcase and they fell into a group, he and Palen in the lead, Hofton and Rana following. As they passed beneath the arch leading to the main concourse, Derec glanced to the left and saw a tall man in a knee-length ivory coat. His face was almost as pale as his coat, but mottled, as if from scarring. The faintest trails of hair traced across his scalp above a high forehead, and sharp, golden-green eyes shifted slowly, intently. He stood facing the customs aisles, as if waiting for someone, but as they walked by, he turned to watch Derec and his companions. It seemed to Derec, just for a moment, that the man smiled. Too brief to get a firm sense about it, but Derec thought he recognized a sign of familiarity and satisfaction in that expression.

Then Derec was through the archway and out of sight. He had never seen the man before. He knew he did not want to meet him. The reaction was irrational and after several steps he dismissed the entire episode as a leftover of his anxiety.

Must be Palen's man, he thought. It made sense. By the time they reached the embassy branch, Derec had forgotten all about him.

Palen's section looked cramped. The doors were narrow and the passageways claustrophobic. The main desk nearly filled the front office, the bulkheads behind it filled with communications equipment that appeared constantly active. As they entered, two uniformed officers looked up from where they sat behind the long, heavy counter.

"Chief—" one started.

"Not now," Palen said. "Where's Oler?"

"Back in the lockup," the other officer said.

"Chief," the first one said again, "you've got a message here from an Agent Harwol, TBI. He says it's urgent, would you—"

"Later," Palen cut him off.

Without another word, Palen led the way around the end of the desk and into a corridor. At the other end, they emerged into a wide, low-ceilinged chamber lined with cells. Derec counted three people behind the transparent doors, none of whom bothered to look up as Palen's group filed through. One, though, caught Derec's eye—a Spacer, judging by the clothes.

Adjacent to the cell block was another chamber about the same size, but without the cells; instead, tables, chairs, and a few couches littered the floor. Against one wall stood an autochef and a samovar.

A short woman with no hair sat at one table, bent over a reader, one hand wrapped around a tall cup. She looked up.

"We're here to get the tinhead, Oler," Palen said. "Get us a gurney, will you?"

The woman nodded, paused to finish reading something, then walked out. Palen went to a plain door opposite the autochef. With a passkey, she opened it and stepped inside.

Derec followed Palen into the storage locker. Shelves stacked against the left wall to the ceiling, boxes and canisters piled on the floor to the right. At the far end lay a robot, legs bent up in the small space.

"You stored it here?" Derec asked.

"It hasn't moved since we found it," Palen said. "What would you have me do, put it in a cell where it could be seen? Most of our guests don't stay very long. I thought it best to keep rumor to a minimum."

"I understand, but I thought you'd have it in your forensic pathology lab or something."

"I repeat: I wanted to keep rumor down. I already have the people who were there when we found it assigned exclusively to the crime scene and a communications block around that bay." Palen frowned. "Besides, my people were a little nervous about it."

"I thought you were used to dealing with robots," Derec said. "That's what Lanra implied anyway."

"More used to it than the average Terran, but considering the possibility that this one committed murder, that was more faith than I was willing to ask of my people."

"You don't believe that, do you?"

"No. But it wasn't me I was concerned with. Now, do you want to look at this thing or criticize my methods some more?"

Chastised, Derec stepped past her and knelt down. As he expected, it was a DW-12—a very versatile laborer, basically. In the inadequate light of the closet, it seemed physically in reasonably good condition, but it was hard to tell. He lifted one heavy arm and pulled it straight. Relieved, he set it down—at least it had not locked up.

"It should be easy to move." He stood. "What have you done to it?"

"I had my chief pathologist go over it for physical evidence, but honestly not much beyond that. It was in his lab for about an hour, then we put it in here. I thought it best to just wait for you."

"Fine. Let's get it to the Spacer embassy, then."

"Mr. Avery." Palen stepped closer to him. In the tight space she seemed to tower over him. It was an effort not to back away. "What are the chances of recovering anything from it?"

"There's no way I can give you an estimate yet. I have to see how badly collapsed it is first."

"But statistically—"

"Any numbers I give you would be meaningless. You'll just have to wait till we can start the excavation." He waited, but she continued to stare at him. He shrugged. "I'm sorry."

"Fine. Then let's get you situated."

Yart Leri looked very much an Auroran: slim, face smoothly ageless, large, clear eyes, and a politely attentive demeanor that nonetheless discouraged intimacy.

"Welcome, Mr. Avery," he said, meeting them in the embassy reception area. A robot occupied the desk. "We've arranged quarters for you and Mr. Hofton. I've been instructed to lend every assistance. The resources of the embassy are, within certain limits, at your disposal."

"Thank you. I'd like first off to see your positronics lab."

"Certainly. I'll have Rotij show you around. That's Rotij Polifos. He's our chief roboticist. He'll be assisting you, should you require it."

"With all due respect," Derec said, "might I be allowed to choose my own lab assistant?"

Leri blinked. "Of course."

"I'd like Rana."

The ambassador almost frowned. "She is not, I believe, fully credited—"

"Nor is she Auroran. I understand that. But we worked together before. I found her most adequate."

"I see no objection," Leri said.

"In that case, I'd like to see the lab as soon as possible."

"I understood this would be a priority situation. I've had Rotij prep an area just for your use."

"Shall I wait for you?" Palen asked.

"Yes, if you could," Derec said. "This won't take that long. Then I'd like to get the robot here as quickly as possible."

"May I ask," Leri said, "what robot?"

"You haven't been briefed?"

"Not in all the particulars . . ."

Derec did not know what orders Leri might have had from Sen Setaris. Best to say nothing, he decided, and sort out the protocols later.

"I'll leave it to higher authority, then," he said. "I'm sure Ambassador Setaris will update you as needed."

"But—"

The lab, sir?" Derec prompted.

Leri frowned. "This way."

Derec caught a look from Rana. She rolled her eyes as if to say *now there's going to be trouble,* then nodded for Derec to follow Leri.

The small reception area gave no indication of the volume the embassy occupied. Leri led Derec, Hofton, and Rana down a hallway to an elevator. Four levels down, it opened onto a lab area Derec guessed at about five hundred square meters.

Derec took a few tentative steps forward, surveying the equipment neatly arrayed across the room. He recognized most of it, but a few pieces looked unfamiliar.

"We finished a complete overhaul six months ago," Rana offered.

Derec whistled appreciatively, Terran fashion, then saw Leri's puzzled look. "I'm very impressed, sir. It doesn't look like you want for anything."

"This is a working lab, Mr. Avery," Leri said with a mixture of pride and contempt. "Kopernik hosts a large population of robots in the Spacer sections. We service the positronics of all the incoming and outgoing Spacer ships."

"Including the Solarian?"

"The Solarians do not possess such a lab. They contract us to do their service and repair work."

A small cluster of people huddled together in a far corner, talking among themselves. Derec counted five and wondered which among them was head of the lab.

"Rotij," Leri called.

One of the group looked toward them, raised a hand, then excused himself from the discussion. He approached with long strides; he was typically tall, with a Spacer's indeterminate age.

"Yes?" he said, stopping before them.

"Rotij Polifos," Leri intoned, "this is Derec Avery and his aide, Hofton . . ." Leri blinked at Hofton uncertainly.

"That's correct," Hofton said.

"Hofton, from the groundside mission. The people I spoke to you about, from Ambassador Burgess's office . . . ?"

"Yes, of course," Rotij said. He seemed distracted and mildly put out. "Honored, Mr. Avery. I know your work."

"Thank you."

"Rotij," Leri continued, "is chief roboticist and director of this positronics lab." He looked between them for a few moments, then nodded, satisfied. "According to my instructions, you're to be accorded every service of the facility. Should you require anything else, please feel free to see me."

"Thank you, Ambassador," Derec said. "You're very kind."

"If I may, I'll leave you to Director Polifos—"

"I need a minute, Yart," Polifos said.

Leri blinked. "I'm sure we can get together later and—"

"*Now.* If you please."

"Mr. Avery requires immediate attention. Afterward, of course." With that, Leri spun around and returned to the elevator.

Polifos glared after Leri for several seconds, then laughed caustically. "Busy man." He turned toward Derec with a sigh. "Well. How can I help you? Ambassador Burgess's instructions were vague except on the point that you're to have the run of the place. I'm afraid I'll have to ask that you leave us *some* area to do our regular work—"

"I need a single station," Derec said. "For one robot, full range diagnostic ensemble, and a large memory cache for an RI direct link."

The Director's face lost expression. "Well . . . I don't see a problem . . . did you say an RI direct link?"

"Yes," Hofton said. "And it's quite heavy."

Polifos wanted very much to watch while Derec set up the link to Thales, but his attention was divided by the work he had been supervising when Derec and Hofton first arrived. He was both relieved and disappointed when Derec made it clear that he wanted to work with Rana.

The instant Polifos returned to the huddle on the other side of the lab, Rana began reconfiguring a commlink station for Thales' requirements.

"I assume nothing's changed," she said, fingers moving deftly over the board.

"Thales' configurations? No, only location and peripheral memory cache. Here are the numbers." He scribbled out the address and the current parameters.

Rana frowned. "How did you get all of it into that small of a buffer? Thales must feel absolutely claustrophobic."

"Daily complaints. I didn't have much choice. The move into the embassy was rather hasty. I'm lucky it wasn't confiscated."

"I was going to say, I'm surprised you still have him."

"'Him'? That's very Spacer of you."

"I'm working on it." She flashed him a smile. "I never expected to see you again."

"Ever?"

"Well, not this soon, anyway." She glanced over her shoulder, across the lab. "I'll see about having this area shielded. Then you can tell me what the hell is going on."

Derec followed her gaze. Hofton had left with Palen to fetch the robot. For the moment it was only Rana and himself and a couple of technicians on the far side of the room, intent on their own work.

"Is there a problem?" Derec asked quietly.

"Nothing overt. Rotij can be a pain sometimes." She shook her head.

"What are *you* doing here?" he asked.

"Qualifying for Auroran citizenship."

"Seriously?"

"Perfectly. This is what I salvaged. Frankly, it's more than I ever expected. The TBI was *really* upset with us, you know. I have a chance to go to Aurora and maybe study at the Calvin Institute. It would have helped if . . ." Rana shrugged.

"If Ariel had retained some cachet?"

"To put it mildly."

"We're working on recovering some. That's part of what this is all about."

Rana finished configuring the board. She pulled a cable from the case containing Derec's link and connected it to the console. She pressed a contact and waited. After a few seconds, she entered more commands.

"You're very good," Derec said.

"I should be. You trained me."

"I think you were a better student than I was a teacher."

Rana initiated a long encryption sequence, then turned to another, smaller board. She watched it briefly, touched one button, and sighed.

"All right," she announced, clapping her hands dramatically. "Unless someone is trying very, very hard, we're secure from eavesdropping."

"Do you think anyone would?"

Rana gave him a wry look. "Our Ambassador Yart Leri is a jealous little god and is not at all happy at being kept ignorant about your mission. He wouldn't do it out of malice, just vanity."

"What about Rotij Polifos? He seemed unhappy about all this."

"This? Maybe. But one of our interns was arrested yesterday and he's naturally upset about it. I don't consider Rotij the jealous type. Not that way."

"I saw a Spacer in Palen's lockup. What was the charge?"

"Disorderly conduct. It doesn't mean anything, it's just an excuse for Palen to haul someone in for questioning. What her questions might be, who knows? Just have to wait for Masid to be released and find out."

"Polifos. Is he good?"

"Competent. Secretive. I don't know a lot about him—he never talks about himself."

"Anyone else I should be concerned with?" Derec asked.

"No one comes immediately to mind, but this *is*

Kopernik. I doubt your presence is even known on the rest of the station, but I don't like taking chances." She glanced at her encryption, then sat down. "So. What is this all about?"

"We're doing a favor for Rega Looms."

He waited while Rana digested this. A smile worked at her face. "You *are* joking."

"No. Not in the least. Of course, that's not all of it. I don't know what it's about on Ariel's end, but Looms' problem apparently dovetails with a project Setaris gave to Ariel. Hofton will be returning with what looks like a standard DW-12 that witnessed a murder. It's collapsed, we need to see if we can recover anything."

"I haven't heard about any murders. Not recently, anyway."

"Baleys. Fifty of them, looks like. You haven't heard anything because Palen is working on the same favor and keeping it silent as long as she can."

"How long has it been so far?"

"Two, two and a half days. I'm guessing."

"And how exactly does Rega Looms fit into this?"

"His daughter was one of the victims."

Rana stared at him blankly. Then: "I see."

Derec coughed softly. "So, tell me about this Auroran citizenship."

Rana shrugged. "A gamble. When the dust settled last year, I applied for emigration. ITE refused, based on essential skills, but I couldn't get an employment stamp, either. So I went to Ariel and asked if she could help. A few referrals later, it looked possible that I could get Auroran citizenship due to the fact that I'm an undesirable."

Derec started. "What?"

"I'm a positronic specialist." She grinned wryly.

"Absurd, isn't it? But just the fact that I worked in a field that was for all intents and purposes outlawed on Earth put me in a special category of almost-but-not-quite foreign spy. I have the entire law in my apartment and I occasionally read through it for a laugh. Anyway, we started the data flowing. I've gotten this far, a transfer to Kopernik. The longer I work here, in this lab, the less desirable I become to Terran authorities." She smiled. "When the Aurorans here found out I was a positronics tech, they didn't know whether to believe me or throw me out. When they learned how I'd become one, they wanted to hand me off to someone else. Anyone else. Ariel got dragged back in. Her suggestion was to hire me as a contract worker and go from there. I've had to start the application process over three times now. I can't blame them for being cautious. But it's in the works now. My application has been forwarded to Aurora. All I have to do now is to continue proving that I know what I'm doing." She bobbed her eyebrows. "So that's where I stand. Waiting. Like I said, six months ago we upgraded the whole lab. I did most of the conceptual work with Rotij—who's very good, by the way. Rotij has added his name to my list of sponsors."

"I'm glad. It would be interesting to watch you at the Calvin."

"I might shake them up a little?"

"Just might."

Rana smiled. "What about you?"

Derec shrugged elaborately. "Like you—waiting. Only difference is, I don't have any clear path. Ariel got my Auroran citizenship renewed, but there's some ... complication ... with the Terran authorities. I'm stuck in the embassy unless I want to be barred from Earth forever."

"I thought you were cleared of any charges?"

"Not quite that simple. This *is* Earth, after all. I suppose it would make everything easier if I just packed up and left."

"Would that be so bad?"

"I don't know. Yes . . . no . . . maybe. It's . . . I like Earth. For all its maddening irrationality, there's so much here. They have history. Thousands of years of history. There's something intoxicating about it." Derec felt clumsy, as if groping to make sense. "It's the first place I really came to know after I recovered from amnemonic plague. I might as well have been born here."

"I forgot about that. Sorry."

"Don't be." Derec disliked talking about his past—lack of past, really. The one thing he shared with Ariel that would never change: both of them were recovered amnesiacs, victims of Burundi's Fever. The damage the disease caused left them permanently incapable of recovering memories from before its onset.

But they had rebuilt their lives. Derec had used Earth as a focus, a home base, a place from which to find . . . what he needed to find.

"Ariel doesn't share your appreciation," Rana said.

"She told you that?"

"We had a couple of long talks. She needed a sympathetic ear, I think, that would go away later."

"Well. I don't know, though. She's here. She requested an Earth posting."

"Hm. By the way, not to change the subject but . . . what about Bogard?"

Derec sighed. "Bogard. Most of Bogard is in a crate stashed in a lockup in the embassy. Thales keeps teasing at his matrix. Of course, without sufficient memory, there's only so much Thales can do."

"We've got the memory here."

"Believe me, the thought *did* cross my mind. And Thales'. If possible . . ."

Rana smiled conspiratorially. "I don't see a problem. We'll do what we can."

He gestured at the encryption sequence. "How big is this?"

"I'm using a five-digit key."

"Five. Isn't that a little excessive?"

"All these years on Earth and you're still not paranoid enough. Actually, I'm encrypting against positronic intrusion. I'm letting Thales choose the key. That way you or I can't give it away."

"And Thales won't. Impressive."

"Thank you." She regarded him thoughtfully. "And thanks for wanting to work with me again. I hope I can help."

"Believe me, it helped just seeing you."

Rana looked startled, then laughed nervously. "I missed you."

Derec felt a warm rush of blood flow through his scalp and face. Surprised, he looked away.

A tone sounded, and Rana looked over at the comm console. "Ah. We have security." She tapped in a command. "Thales?"

"I am online, Rana. How are you?"

Half an hour later, the robot arrived, encased in a dull gray canister, rolled on a gurney between Palen and Hofton. Its entry attracted attention from the huddle of technicians, who watched it all the way across the lab until it disappeared behind the blind Rana had erected.

Derec waited for Palen to open the case. The lid peeled back with a soft *snik*. It was much as he had seen in the storage closet: An older model DW-12—or perhaps even, now that the light was better, a DW-10 with modifications—stretched out like a corpse in a coffin. Derec pressed two fingers against the place where its ear would be. A small panel on the chest slid away to reveal a screen. Derec touched the screen, setting it aglow. A string of alphanumerics scrolled rapidly over it, stopped, then disappeared, leaving behind a flashing red dot.

"It didn't hurt to try," he said. "Thales, the self-diagnostic is junk. We'll have to do this from first principles."

"I am prepared, Derec," Thales replied.

Palen frowned at the link perched on the console.

"Resident Intelligence," Derec explained as he began connecting cables to various jacks in the robot's head and torso. He had to wipe accrued grime off a couple of them. "A disembodied positronic brain configured to act as a primary systems processor."

"Uh-huh," Palen said. "Like the one that went crazy in Union Station last year?"

Derec hesitated. "Basically. Only this one is mine and no one has tampered with it but me. So you needn't worry about it hallucinating." He finished the connections. "Run synchronous pattern test, Thales. Test link."

"Working, Derec." A moment later: "The link is fine. We can proceed."

"Is there anything left in there?"

It took nearly two minutes for Thales to answer.

"Damage is considerable, Derec, but I detect a few orderly sectors. Memory nodes have not been corrupted."

Derec exchanged grins with Rana.

"What does that mean?" Palen asked.

"It means," Derec said, "that we have a good chance of salvaging something for you."

TWELVE

Ariel felt a momentary surge, like the rush from falling, as the limo left the embassy. She could not pin down in memory the last time she had been outside the Spacer mission. She swallowed dryly, waiting. The further the transport carried from the garage, the calmer she became; after a time, she laughed at herself.

She opened her datum and accessed current files. A list of reports scrolled down the screen—detail work she had neglected for months. The complaints sorted themselves automatically in a separate column, apart from the regular stock and shipping reports all Aurorans were required to file. Three firms came up more often than any other, one of them filing eighteen complaints over the last six months, all of them having to do with delayed or lost exports.

Carsanli Intercomp built domicile environmental control units, adaptable to a wide range of habitats. Their principle customers were Settler colonies. Ariel was impressed with their logic—they built the units on Earth, using part Spacer technologies and part Terran, and shipped through Terran distributors, which minimized their Spacer presence. A lot of Spacer firms conducted business in a similar fashion, but often had a difficult time in the manufacturing end due to restrictions on factory space and local regulations concerning employment and vending requirements. In an unusual arrangement, Carsanli leased a factory already owned and operated by a Terran firm—Imbitek—from whom they also bought the Terran components.

The company kept its offices in the Convention District of D.C. Ariel recognized the area as she entered it. She used to come here twice a week, before so many Spacer businesses had abandoned Earth. There was still a large Spacer presence, though, and she had no sound reason for having neglected her duties.

The limo stopped at the main entrance to the offices. She stepped out and looked around. This was a warehouse area. People in worktogs or officewear filled the passages as First Shift opened. She caught a few frowns and curious looks from passersby, but ignored them. Steeling herself, she entered the building.

"Ambassador Burgess," said a tall Auroran who greeted her. Behind him stood a broad reception desk and the company seal on the wall: an oblate disk filled with a moil of multihued shapes that reminded Ariel of feathers. "Welcome to Carsanli Intercomp. I'm Farin Holiye, general manager. This is most unexpected."

She grasped his hand briefly. "Things have been unusually complicated recently. I apologize for taking so long to come down."

Holiye smiled brightly. "Not at all, not at all. Please, this way. We can talk in my office."

Ariel followed him through a door and up a short flight of stairs. He waved her into a wide, dark-panelled office.

"May I offer refreshment?" he asked, heading for a sidebar.

"No, thank you. I have a rather full schedule today. But I wanted to see you first."

"Ah. Yes, well . . ." He gestured to a pair of plush chairs on opposite ends of a low table. "I don't wish to begin with a complaint—"

"I'm aware of the number of reports you've sent," Ariel said, sitting. "I'm here now."

"Yes . . . well, the basic problem is that several consignments of product have gone missing; I think it's accurate to say stolen. Insurance has compensated for them, of course, but we've lost three major customers over it."

"You sent them replacements?"

"Of course, but those went missing, too. It was very aggravating."

"Shipments to the same clients . . . that's very interesting. May I see the manifests?"

"Certainly." He went to his desk and returned with a slate. "I had them prepared for you."

Ariel scanned the columns. Four very large orders purchased by a construction firm on Epsilon Coriae never arrived. As Holiye had claimed, insurance covered the loss, but the Settler company canceled the contract. ITE attributed the loss to piracy and pled lack of jurisdiction once the shipments left the solar system. She scrolled further and noted several other shipments lost. All of them had been slated for Settler companies.

"You also complained about delays?"

"Several times," Holiye said expansively. "We thought it

was a problem with our exit port so we tried to get it changed, but the request was tangled up and has still not been acted upon." He pursed his lips. "This is one of the things I understood your office dealt with . . ."

"Of course. Again, I apologize. I'll look into it immediately. What port are you using?"

"Petrabor."

Ariel looked up. "Was any reason given for the delays?"

"A number of times they claimed a routing glitch in their logistics programs. Once they simply said that the shipment had been overlooked by the dock crew. I found that intolerable."

"How long has this been going on?"

"We've always had a few problems," Holiye said, "but we expect some loss and delay. Space is vast and people are people. But I'd say in the last two years it's become chronic."

"I see . . ." She handed back the manifest. "How long have you been working with Imbitek?"

"Years."

"Any problems?"

"No. In fact, since the previous chairman was replaced, things have gotten even better. The new CEO seems very dedicated to providing service."

"Mmm. How is it you drew Petrabor Spaceport?"

"The main factory is in Kiv Sector, just south. Petrabor is the closest port capable of handling the quantities in a timely fashion."

"Of course if they keep losing or misplacing shipments . . ."

"Exactly—the benefit of faster service from larger capacity is offset by the nuisance factor."

"Well, if I recall," Ariel mused, "the Arkanleg port or

even Kyro should be able to handle the traffic. I'll look into getting you rerouted." She stood. "Um . . . the stolen shipments . . . is there any pattern? Anything about them that strikes you as consistent?"

"Well, no. We usually always use the same shipping line, as we always have. The destinations are always different, too."

"I see. Well, thank you. I'll look into that, too, but I can't promise anything."

Holiye stood. "I appreciate you taking an interest, Ambassador."

Finally, Ariel heard in his voice. She nodded, shook his hand, and let him see her out.

Several hours later, Ariel let herself reluctantly into Derec's apartment. Her head buzzed with too much information. She had visited four more firms, following up the complaints. Between the sense of guilt over neglecting her duties and the amount of abuse these companies had suffered from lost shipments, unexplained delays, and shabby treatment by warehouse managers and shippers, Ariel felt humiliated and angry.

All of them shipped out of Petrabor.

Terran authorities had paid no attention because they were Spacers.

And the pattern included her.

Negligence is a disease, she thought bitterly, *and I caught it.*

Holiye's assessment that the problem had become chronic in the last year appeared accurate. Someone was taking advantage of her truncated authority. The abuse was clear and unmistakable, but since her office was the clearinghouse for the complaints, no one had bothered to put it all together. Why should they? It was her job and she had stopped doing it.

Time to straighten it all out ...

She would have preferred transferring Thales to her own rooms or even into a standard lab facility, but either option would have taken too long. She considered running a real-time link from here to her apartment, but the more remote access existed, the greater the chance of eavesdropping. The Terrans, especially—as backward as their tech seemed in some areas, they were disconcertingly advanced in others.

She stood in the living room for a few minutes, quietly letting herself grow used to the idea of being here. It surprised her sometimes how difficult it was to continue knowing Derec. They got along well enough, but there were limits, and she did not know them all.

She looked around. Too little furniture, she judged. Austere. One sofa, one chair, a low table, and a subetheric. No carpet, just a plain tile. The table was still cluttered with glasses and dishes. A flatscreen reader stood like a piece of sculpture amid the mess. She placed a hand on the back of the sofa: the pillows showed the wrinkles and depressions of long use. She imagined him here, studying, till sleep pulled him out lengthwise, still clothed.

She snatched her hand away.

The bedroom was neat and orderly. A modest collection of clothes in the small closet, stark gray sheets, a clock and lamp on the lone nightstand.

More clutter in the kitchen sink, but virtually no food in the pantry. She scrolled through the menu on his autochef: coffee, various potato and pasta recipes, eggs, three meat dishes, juice. It was as abbreviated as his wardrobe.

The workroom, dominated by Thales' console, exhibited the most debris of occupation: papers, disks, three chairs, four or five readers . . . No dishes, though.

"Hello, Ambassador Burgess," Thales said.

Ariel felt a wave of guilt. She swallowed. "Hello, Thales. Status?"

"I am linked to a positronic analysis station on Kopernik," the RI said. "We have ninety-nine percent capable dataflow, time delay negligible through subetheric router. Subject has been connected to diagnostics and I am running an excavation now. We have uncorrupted memory nodes isolated by collapsed positronic synaptic framework. Estimated retrieval time for first verifiable memories: two hours, twenty-nine minutes."

Fast work, Derec, she thought, impressed despite herself. Having Hofton no doubt had sped things along. Hofton's absence disturbed her, which came as a surprise. She felt vulnerable. "How much available memory do you and I have at our disposal, Thales?"

"I am using the buffers on Kopernik for the excavation, the commline buffer to maintain the link. For all practical purposes, you have all my available on-site memory."

"I see. Don't tell me anything precise, like a number."

"Would you prefer a specific? I have available 3 x 1023 kjC in three primary and six secondary nodes—"

"That's fine, Thales."

It amused Ariel at times, the way positronic entities tried to accommodate human wants, matching expectations with limitations. Flexible as they were, they sometimes provided either too little information or too much, their ability to accurately judge what constituted the necessary and the sufficient inadequate to the challenge of serving people. All in all, they were remarkable creations, among the best things humans had ever devised. But they were not flaw-less. Not flawless at all.

Ariel sighed. "All right, then. I want you to begin a records search, new file. Priority protect protocols in effect. Alert me to any attempt at eavesdropping. I want all avail-able data on the history of Nova Levis. I also want to be kept updated on the excavation you're doing on Kopernik."

"Yes, Ariel. May I ask, what level of records search?"

"What do you mean?"

"Do you wish me to confine myself to those records without confidentiality protects or shall I acquire any and all documents pertinent to your request?"

Ariel considered. Thales wanted permission to violate protected files. She had no doubt it could do so. Privacy issues represented a gray area for robots—they required spe-cific instructions in such cases, lacking any sense of how harm might attach to simple data.

"Do a survey of available documents of both kinds," she said finally. "Give me a list, detailing their security status and source. We'll decide then."

"Yes, Ariel." A moment later: "Will you be staying here?"

She hesitated. "I'm not sure, Thales. What would you prefer?"

"It would simplify the security standards you have requested if I did not have to contact you via external comm for updates."

"Hm. True. Do you think Derec would mind?"

"I see no reason why he should."

No, I don't suppose you would . . .

"In that case, yes. I'll leave for a short while to get some personal items." She thought a few moments. "In fact, from time to time I may have to leave anyway, depending on what you find out for me."

"I understand, Ariel."

She went back to the kitchen. Perhaps she could bring R. Jennie down here. On the other hand, vacating her apartment completely might be a mistake. In either case, she needed to give Jennie instructions . . .

Details. She needed food in the kitchen, changes of clothes, her personal datum. She wondered if Derec ever had visitors, then dismissed the thought. She would have known; if nothing else, there would be signs here, in his living space, and she saw little enough even of Derec.

What has he been doing this past year?

Oddly, the idea that Derec had spent all this time alone—except for those few instances when they had shared a meal or attended a meeting together—saddened her. But then, she knew little enough of what he had been doing prior to last year. Perhaps this was his norm, the way he was used to living.

He had been bitterly angry over losing his company. That he had nearly ended up in prison had seemed relatively unimportant to him. Had she not moved to reinstate his Auroran citizenship, he might very well be living today in a private call in a Terran penal facility, the charges ranging from violation of Earther trade laws and the Positronic Prohibition Acts to murder. That he would have been no more guilty than any other Auroran on Earth made no difference—he would have been the perfect *example*. Even without a jail term, the Phylaxis Group, his firm, had been used as a club to beat the pro-positronic movement into submission and undermine all the work that had been done over the last several years to bridge the gaps dividing Earth and the Spacer worlds. Not the only club, to be sure, but a most effective one: Phylaxis had been held responsible for the failure of the entire Union Station positronics showcase and the subsequent events involving what the media had characterized as a "Killer Robot": Bogard.

Bogard. Derec's attempt at building a bodyguard. Ariel still shuddered when she thought of it. She had condemned the idea—unfairly, she realized. Bogard *had* worked. It had been subverted, tricked, and attacked—no other robot of which she was aware could have possibly continued functioning under such stress. And that had been Ariel's objection. She did not want robots to function after failure. If they did not adhere rigorously to the Three Laws, she wanted them incapacitated. Bogard had doggedly persisted in functioning, all the way up until the end, when it had taken a human life. Inadvertently, in the course of protecting Derec, but even for its remarkably flexible criteria an intolerable violation.

The thought had occurred to her that Derec might take the blame personally. She believed him more resilient than that, but you never knew how or which events might overwhelm a psyche. She was ashamed of herself that she had not checked, had left him alone while she embraced her own self-pity.

Maybe we can turn it all around with this, she thought. Baseless optimism irritated her as much as pointless cynicism, but sometimes the situation demanded an investment of faith.

She looked back at Thales. *I could ask it what Derec's been doing . . .*

But there were those privacy issues again.

"Ariel," Thales said, startling her. "I have a question. Which Nova Levis did you wish me to research?"

*　　*　　*

"I have found two references under the heading 'Nova Levis,' " Thales explained. "The first concerns a Settler colony, established thirty-two years ago in the Tau Secordis system. The second concerns a research laboratory here on Earth established twenty-eight years ago."

"What sort of research?" Ariel asked.

"Biomedical and prosthetics."

"Really. What sort of prosthetics?"

"The shareholder precis published upon issuance of initial shares refers to neurocortical extensions. Inferring from other references, I believe this pertains to artificial appendages linked directly to the nervous system."

Ariel frowned. "That's nothing new. What were they researching?"

"That data is under seal. The company closed after eight years of operation in the wake of a criminal investigation."

"Explain."

"A global investigation initiated by the Eurosector Civil Enforcement Agency into kidnapping and infant brokerage produced charges of conspiracy to illegally traffic in orphaned and stolen children involving several orphanage institutions and several medical labs. Nova Levis was part of the overall investigation, but no charges were filed against it. It closed down several months after the case was declared closed."

"Any direct links to Nova Levis colony?"

"One of the chief researchers emigrated there a year after the laboratory was closed."

"Anyone else? I mean, what about the other people who worked for the lab?"

"There were five department heads, all of them founding associates of the company. Three are now dead. The fifth is listed officially as missing. He was a Theian native living on Earth named Kyas Vol."

"Missing. That could mean anything. Did anyone look into his disappearance?"

"Not that I have been able to ascertain."

Ariel wrestled with her curiosity. Earthers maintained profound prejudices regarding anything that suggested humaniform robotics, even prosthetic limbs. Prosthetics were available, certainly, but people never talked about them. Like any prejudice, it manifested in bizarre fashions and displayed many blind spots and innate hypocrisies. Artificial intelligences proliferated on Earth, in many areas, and nonsentient robotics were employed liberally, so long as none of it came close to resembling a human. Prosthetics occupied a tolerated space within the complex hierarchies of Terran bigotry. She had no idea how advanced the technology was, or if any new research was currently underway.

"Stay with the colony, Thales. If you come across any more direct connections, explore them."

"Very well, Ariel."

"I'm going to my apartment now, Thales. I need some things. I'll be back."

"I should have a preliminary report for you when you return."

She thanked the RI and left.

R. Jennie met her at the door. "Welcome home, Ariel. You have a message from Ambassador Setaris."

"Thanks, Jennie. Pack an overnight bag for me, would you? I'll be sleeping elsewhere tonight."

"I had intended preparing crayfish almandine tonight, Ariel."

Ariel gave the robot a look, startled at the note of disappointment she thought she heard. It was so easy to personalize robots, so easy to "inform" them with emotion and human expression, but it still caught her by surprise to detect it.

"Change of schedule, Jennie. Place the menu on hold for the time being."

"Yes, Ariel."

R. Jennie walked off to pack. They had devised a standard kit a long time ago when Ariel had spent more time away from the embassy, in the company of others—particularly Jonis Taprin, now Senator Taprin. It had been over a year since their last tryst and Ariel had spent most of her time confined to her suite of office.

Ariel sat down at her comm and keyed the ACCEPT button. Setaris's face appeared on the screen.

"Ariel, I'm giving a dinner party tonight, I thought you would like to come. I'm appending a guest list. I'd appreciate it if you'd put in an appearance. We don't see enough of you."

"My my," Ariel mused. "I must be coming up in the world." She resisted the urge to call Setaris back and ask why. Instead, she scrolled through the list of invitees: The usual collection of ambassadors and close aides—Gale Chassik of Solaria, Trinik Hapellon of Capella, Frish Ioseco of Osiris, others—and a sprinkling of Spacer emigreés and industrialists.

And Jonis Taprin.

"What the . . ." Ariel stabbed the CONNECT on her comm and tapped in Setaris's code. A few moments later she worked through Setaris's secretary to Sen Setaris herself.

"Ariel, how are you?" the ambassador asked.

"Puzzled. You're serious about this invitation?"

"Of course I am."

"You've invited Jonis Taprin."

"Yes . . ." Setaris frowned briefly, then her eyes widened knowingly. "Ah, yes. I forgot. My apologies, Ariel. The event is partly for him. He put out some feelers a few weeks ago to see if we might arrange some talks."

"Concerning?"

"Concerning precisely the subject we spoke about earlier. I thought it might be worthwhile to have you there. If, however, you feel uncomfortable—"

Ariel shook her head. "No. I merely wanted clarification."

"And you have it now?"

"Yes."

Setaris smiled condescendingly. "I envy you. Will we see you?"

"Absolutely."

"At twenty, then. Formal."

"Very good, Ambassador. I'm honored."

Setaris smiled thinly. "Till this evening, Ariel."

The screen faded.

Ariel leaned back in her chair and stretched. "Just how much ass-covering am I going to need?" she wondered aloud.

"I packed the standard bag, Ariel. Will it be too much?"

Ariel looked around to see R. Jennie standing there, holding the overnight bag.

"I have a preliminary file on the requested material, Ariel," Thales said when she returned to Derec's apartment.

Ariel set the bag down at the door to the bedroom. "Go on."

"Nova Levis was established as a Settler's colony thirty-two years ago by special agreement between the Vas Domini Trading Company, a Settler cooperative sponsored by private endowment through the Church of Organic Sapiens, and Solaria—"

"Solaria? How do they figure in it?"

"The Tau Secordis system was originally developed as a mining franchise by three Solarian corporations which eventually became insolvent and were subsumed by the Solarian Department of Resource Development. The second planet, originally called Cassus Thole, after a modest amount of biosome intervention, is suitable for agriculture. Under the terms of a trade agreement with a limited corporation formed by six Settler worlds, Cassus Thole was renamed Nova Levis and subcontracted for settlement and development."

"Why hasn't Solaria protested the blockade?"

"Except for being the principal lien holder, Solaria has no representation on Nova Levis and has remained aloof from its operations since the first colony was established. There is still a small mining station with its own port used excusively by Solaria. Nova Levis has for all intents and purposes represented itself as a sovereign world with rights and titles to its own territories. The colonists themselves have not even admitted to Solarian ownership and have engaged the current crisis as a duly constituted independent state."

"So it's not even common knowledge that Solaria owned the system?"

"The conditions of ownership have been allowed to grow vague. Solaria's holding is listed in public files as Cassus Thole. Except for the mining concession, Solaria officially conducts no business with the Settler government.

Nova Levis has since been regarded as a separate colony."

Ariel laced her fingers together and tapped them lightly against her chin. She felt foolish now at having paid so little attention to the events of the past year. The Nova Levis blockade was the first and largest aftershock from the failed trade conference last year.

"Give me a brief on the blockade," she said.

"Two years ago, Terran investigators traced a number of stolen shipments to ships making regular calls at Nova Levis. This was discovered in the wake of the *Tiberius* incident, which proved to be related to illegal traffic into and out of Nova Levis. Further investigation on the ground resulted in the deaths of three agents and partial evidence that Nova Levis is host to an unregistered spaceport. At this point, warrants were solicited through the Intersettlement Judicial Committee for a task force to visit and inspect all ports on Nova Levis. The governor-advocate of the colony refused and offered to conduct the investigation himself and report the findings. This was rejected. A further proposal was made that a joint task force of Spacer, Settler, and Terran inspectors be deployed, and this, too, was rejected. Fifteen months ago, motions were placed before the Committee to establish a permanent inspection base at the edge of the system with a mandate to forcibly inspect all ships entering and leaving the system. This motion, of course, was rejected in due course when the Spacer legation insisted that robotic inspections be instituted for all traffic to and from any Spacer world. The station was never authorized, but Terran military ships began arbitrarily and at random stopping and searching ships entering and leaving the Nova Levis system. A series of protests were filed. The Committee became tangled with delaying motions by the Terran legation until a Terran ship was fired upon by an unregistered freighter caught leaving Nova Levis. Upon inspection, it was discovered that the ship was carrying contraband. The crew was arrested, the ship impounded, and the 43rd Squadron of the Terran fleet moved in to blockade the planet. That was eleven months ago. Subsequent negotiations have validated the blockade, although only one Spacer world has added ships to the Terran contingent, and no Settler ships have joined it."

"That's how it stands today."

"Yes, Ariel."

"Stolen shipments . . . any kind of manifest on what those shipments contained, or who they were stolen from?"

"That is a protected file. It will take some time to open it."

"Do it. What about Solaria? What did they say when all this happened?"

"They have made no official statement to date, content, apparently, to follow Aurora's lead."

"Are those Auroran ships with the Terran squadron?"

"No, they are Theian ships. Aurora is remaining militarily aloof."

As usual, Ariel thought wryly.

"And no one has brought up Solaria's past ownership?"

"No, Ariel," Thales replied.

"Not even Aurora . . . but Solarian ships are still entering and leaving the system. How is that possible? As I understand it, a blockade like this is enforced at the port of origin as well. Solarian ships heading for Nova Levis would be stopped or at least noted and identified as blockade runners."

"That is how the law reads. I will look into it."

Something else teased at Ariel. "You said there were

three Solarian firms that initially had title to the system. Who?"

"Strychos, Incorporated, M39-Viavel Corporation, and the Kysler Solar Industries."

"Kysler . . . that sounds familiar."

"Kysler Diversified Industries, Ariel. They are a Terran firm based on Titan, though no longer Terran-owned. The three Solarian firms I mentioned have all been subsequently purchased by the Hunter Group. Only Strychos remains as a semi-independent corporation, dealing in agricultural products."

"Hunter owns Kysler?"

"They own a controlling interest."

"What did they do? The Terran firm, I mean."

"Primarily a holding company. Pharmaceuticals, raw material development, shipping, finance—"

"Stop. Any other correlations through their dependent companies?"

"No. However, Kysler purchased the physical plant in which Nova Levis was housed."

"Really. What became of the rest?"

"After it closed down it was split up and sold. The R&D division went to Imbitek, which folded it into a subsidiary: Captras Biomed. Various pieces of hardware went to a number of small firms."

"Imbitek owns the research and Kysler owns the shell . . . what did they do with it?" Ariel asked.

"Unknown. Current data suggests that the structure is sealed and unused. A retrofitting company was hired to convert it into a raw materials distribution plant a few years ago. After that I find no records."

"Thales, I want a list of shareholders for each of those three companies: Kysler Diversified, Hunter Group, and

Nova Levis. Prepare a hard copy for me. Let's return to the colony. You said that a Settler cooperative took it over?"

"That is correct. Through private endowment."

"Through a church, though. What was its name?"

"The Church of Organic Sapiens."

She thought for a moment. "That's Rega Looms' church."

"It is currently the church with which Rega Looms is affiliated. However, he has stepped down from its director-ship for the duration of his senate campaign. He was not its director at the time the colony was established."

"Did he belong to it?"

"I do not have access to those records. Would you like me to try to obtain them?"

"Maybe. Hold off for now." Ariel drummed her fingers on the edge of the console. She could not shake the feeling that she was missing something. "Rega Looms despises the whole idea of offworld colonization. So does the COS—*now*. I suppose it didn't then."

"The Church of Organic Sapiens has undergone a num-ber of fundamental changes in purpose in the sixty-eight years of its existence. The current one has been in place since Rega Looms became its director."

"How long ago was that?"

"Eighteen years ago."

"Display the exact dates."

Numbers scrolled across one of Thales' screens. The Set-tler colony of Nova Levis was established eleven years before Rega Looms took directorship of the Church of Organic Sapiens. Ariel could see nothing significant about that, but she felt certain she should.

"When was Nova Levis—the lab—incorporated?"

The date appeared between the first two displayed. Nova Levis Incorporated opened forty-two months after the colony.

"Closing date."

Fourteen months before Looms took charge of his church.

"There is a correlation," Thales said. "Rega Looms was one of the initial shareholders in Nova Levis Incorporated. Not in Kysler Diversified."

"All right . . . he couldn't possibly have maintained it and represented a church that condemns prostheses. When did he divest?"

"Four years after its incorporation."

"Did he start a panic?"

"Apparently not. Only three other shareholders divested in his wake: Kyas Vol, Tenebra Patis, and Gale Chassik."

Ariel started. "Ambassador Chassik?"

"Yes, Ariel."

"Was he ambassador then?"

"No, Ariel, he was Chief Attaché to Ambassador Masmo Pedesor."

Ariel frowned. "Do you have those lists of shareholders?"

"Yes, Ariel."

Another screen filled with names in three columns. The one for Nova Levis, Inc. was the shortest, the one for Kysler Diversified the longest. Names were highlighted in bright blue.

Ariel raised an eyebrow. "Well, well. Some people just turn up everywhere, don't they?"

Glowing brightly in all three columns were the names of Alda Mikels, Gale Chassik, and former senator Clar Eliton.

"Thales, get Coren Lanra for me, would you? I think we need to talk before this goes much further."

THIRTEEN

Coren knocked on the office door labeled KELVY TORANS, ACCOUNTS EXECUTIVE. When the woman behind the large desk looked up, he smiled and waggled his fingers at her.

"Coren!" Her grin dazzled. "Come in! You actually caught me with time on my hands."

"I couldn't be that lucky, could I?" He sat down across from her.

She touched a button, closing her door. "Yes, you could." She gazed with mock seductiveness at him until they both laughed. "What can I do for you, Coren?"

"A little inside information."

"Nothing that will get me in trouble."

"I don't think so. What do you know about Myler Towne?"

She raised an eyebrow. "Chairman protem of Imbitek?"

"The very same."

She closed her eyes for a few seconds. Her face, still and framed by a close-cut helmet of black hair, seemed almost childlike. When she opened her eyes, she drew a deep breath. "Joined Imbitek eleven years ago, New Accounts, and worked his way into Mergers and Acquisitions. Three years ago, he was on the Logistics and Projections board. The assassinations last year opened a position on the board of directors. He was nominated and elected within two weeks. After Alda Mikels received his sentence, Towne campaigned for the position of chairman, but it was given by the board reluctantly, and with the proviso that it was temporary, ending upon Mikels' release."

"How good is he?"

"Not bad, considering that he's spent most of the past year fending off lawsuits and dealing with TBI investigations into the company. He's actually turned Imbitek around in the last few months, so I'm beginning to recommend it again as a primary investment. They're not as robust as they once were, but given this I can't wait to see what they do when Mikels is back at the helm."

"I knew Imbitek had taken a tumble—"

Kelvy grunted eloquently. "They very nearly dropped out of the Primary Three Hundred. Within three weeks after Mikels was sentenced to prison, Imbitek stock fell eighty points. Towne has it back up forty-eight points."

"How?"

She shrugged. "Wish I knew. They've gone through a big restructuring, a lot of positions terminated, and he's trimmed off some of the fat Mikels kept on as pet projects. But a big part is that Imbitek is buying back its own stock."

"It had the revenue for that?"

"Apparently from the sale of offworld holdings."

"Why 'apparently'? Wouldn't it be in their shareholders' report?"

"Of course. But the convenient fact about offworld holdings is that local laws are flexible and there are a thousand ways to funnel money that can't be traced. I say 'apparently' because you can never be sure if a holding on, say, Revis Logandi is real or just a fiction to hide funds."

"So they sold holdings . . . no other way they might get the money?" Coren asked.

"Sure. The easiest way would be to borrow it. But they've made no loans for it and according to their reports over the last few years, their credit has been limited. Banks aren't quick to count those offworld holdings I mentioned as reliable collateral, so credit is based mainly on available Terran assets and so on. According to that, Imbitek was overextended. Not dangerously so, but enough to limit them. If they were hiding collateral, well . . . I'm sure it would have angered shareholders to know the company had that available credit hidden from them, but under the circumstances no one complained. The policy kept those shareholders who had remained faithful from losing everything and even gaining a little."

"So he's a bright boy. What happens when Mikels gets out?"

"That's what we're all waiting for," Kelvy said. "Already there's been nervous trading. Towne might have to pull another magic trick to keep the company from devouring itself in a proxy war if he decides to fight Mikels. He has managed to replace two of the board members with his own supporters. The others . . . well, you just never know how these people will jump. Towne has proven himself. Mikels is bringing a lot of baggage to the table and may be unable to reclaim the chair."

"Do *you* think there will be a war?"

"Towne is ambitious, Mikels is the old bull. You tell me. The psychology is certainly volatile."

Coren considered. "So how far has Imbitek stock fallen since Mikels' release was announced?"

Kelvy grinned at him appreciatively. "Eighteen points. Not a disaster. Yet."

"Still. Is Towne buying?"

She shook her head. "Not that I know of. Imbitek has started slowing down some its outside investment, too. Odd. As of a month ago, their regular cash allocations for new stocks virtually dried up. If I didn't know better, I'd say they're having serious cash flow problems."

"Why do you know better?"

"Two months ago, Imbitek sold off one of its subsidiaries for an enormous profit. They haven't paid a dividend on it yet because it was the beginning of the quarter, so all that money is just sitting somewhere. Towne gave himself and everyone on the board merit increases—modest ones, not the sort you see when a company is in trouble and the management is salting away the spoils before the end."

"In other words, their expenses haven't risen substantially."

"Right. So I doubt they actually have a problem with cash. They even paid back a couple of longterm loans."

"War chest."

Kelvy frowned.

"Myler Towne wants to keep his new position," Coren said. "He's preparing for a war. What are Alda Mikels' people doing while all this is going on?"

"A lot of them left the firm. A lot of them were asked to leave. Those who left have been drumming up support among the shareholders, advocating Mikels as the better choice as Chairman."

Coren tapped his fingers on the armrest. "What subsidiary did they sell off?"

"Captras Biomed."

"Who bought it?"

"A consortium of private investors. I'd have to do some prying to find out who. They bid anonymously."

"Could you, please? I'm very interested."

Kelvy nodded, frowning.

"One more thing. Do you remember a bio research company called Nova Levis?"

"Sounds familiar. Old, gone now?"

"Yes. It shut down several years ago. I wondered if it might be possible to get a list of its investors."

"That would be a matter of public record."

"Not the real names," Coren said. "A lot of investors go on record through a front. The fronts are public. I want to know who really owned shares."

"All right. How soon do you need it?"

"Same time I need to know who bought Captras."

Kelvy smiled. "Ah-hah. Yesterday. Do we have time, then, for dinner?"

"I'd like that . . ."

" . . . but not tonight." She shrugged. "Oh, well. I'm just your broker, not anyone special. Your future lies in my hands every day, but you shouldn't be over-felicitous on that account."

"Have I ever pointed out that you use a very questionable technique?"

"Several techniques, under the proper circumstances. I hope to show you more of them sometime." She smiled. "It'll be worth the wait. I'll get you this information by tomorrow morning. Soon enough?"

"That will do nicely. Thank you."

Kelvy pointed a finger at him. "We have plans?"

Coren grinned. "We have plans."

"Shoo, then. I have work to do."

Coren left her office. The plaza fronting the brokerage was filling up with second-shift on its way to work. Coren crossed to the walkways and stepped smoothly to the third lane.

He commed his office.

"Has Jeta Fromm contacted me yet?"

"No," replied the Desk.

Damn! "Any other messages?"

"Ambassador Ariel Burgess wishes you to call her as soon as possible. Mr. Doppler from Data Recovery Systems wishes you to contact him at your convenience."

Doppler . . . ? Data Recovery Systems was the clearing house that had originally supplied him with Jeta Fromm. Coren closed the link to his Desk and tapped in Doppler's code.

"This is Lanra."

"Mr. Lanra, forgive the intrusion," replied a smooth, androgenous voice. "There has been a . . . complication with our recent service. We've been trying to repair any possible harm that has resulted." Doppler's hesistancy made it clear that he felt embarrassed. "I wish to confirm that our service to you was acceptable. The operative your office has been attempting to locate—"

"Jeta Fromm."

"Yes, sir. Um . . . this is quite awkward . . ."

"You haven't been able to find her," Coren guessed.

"In fact, we haven't even tried. She has become no longer available, having ended her association with us three months ago. We are trying to determine a chronology so that service to our clients is not compromised."

"Three months. That was before I retained her."

"Yes, sir," Doppler confirmed.

"You're telling me that she wasn't even working for your company when she initially responded to my commission. And no one thought to inform me?"

Doppler seemed to clear his throat. "Regrettably so. I realize that excuses fail to compensate in this circumstance, but our system suffered an . . . intrusion . . . which kept us from monitoring certain files adequately. It wasn't until recently that we were able to restore the data and determine the nature of all the errors. I hope you understand."

Coren briefly felt cold. "I do, indeed. Am I the only person she contacted after she broke her ties with you?"

"No, sir, there were several others. I am not, of course, at liberty to discuss their files."

"Of course not. Discretion is your reputation."

"Something like that. I also wanted to warn you that, under these unusual circumstances, whatever data you received from Ms. Fromm would be highly questionable. Our usual reimbursement policy is in effect, of course, but we will not guarantee the quality of the product."

"That's . . . problematic. Thank you for the call, Mr. Doppler."

"I hope this will not put you off using us in future."

"Of course not."

The link broke. Coren pocketed the comm. Jeta Fromm was dead. The question was when. Had he even met with her to begin with?

He watched the warrens pass by—shops, offices, home kitchens, girders, plazas, balconies. Block upon cube upon struts, mounding up to a hazy murk high above. The lights shone brilliant blue-white through the mists that formed near the upper elevations, delimiting the volume by showing everyone the ceiling of the cave. Inside. Tunnels, corridors, a maze of interconnected structure, involuted and self-cannibalizing over time, filling and refilling, home to billions, contained, giving the illusion of safety and accessibility. So easy to get from one place to another, it was all In Here, and the ways all clearly marked. No part of the world was cut off from any other. You could in principle reach anyone, anytime, by any of ten or a hundred pathways.

But not if they were dead.

If he had not lost his optam, he would have at least had something visual to run through—especially the humans that had accompanied the stealth robot. Odd, he was beginning to think of the robot as having been in charge.

Going through Damik had been the only way he could think of to find the people Nyom might have gone through, but that had led him into areas that seemed unrelated to Nyom's death.

So why pursue them? he wondered.

Because it felt connected. Because he saw Rega Looms' name on a list of investors of a company that he would today condemn as a morally questionable enterprise, a company with the same name as the colony his daughter had been murdered while trying to emigrate to. Because Looms had made the same remark as a man Coren had never even heard of till today. Because all these unrelated details *felt* related. He just could not see how. Yet.

The rule by which he had always worked was, when stuck for the next move, ask more questions.

Why did Damik go see Wenithal?

Coren certainly had names from the Wenithal connection, but not the ones he had expected and none he could do anything with, at least not immediately.

Unless I just can't see it . . .

He glanced at his watch, then pulled out his comm again.

A few connections later, Ariel Burgess answered.

"Coren Lanra, Ambassador."

"Mr. Lanra, thank you for returning my call. I think we need to talk."

"I couldn't agree more. In person?"

"That would be best." She paused. "Are you busy this evening?"

"I have no way of knowing yet. What did you have in mind?"

"I've been invited to an embassy dinner this evening. I have the option of bringing a guest of my choosing. Would you be interested?"

"At your embassy?"

"The Auroran embassy, yes."

Coren hesitated. This sounded like a complete waste of time, but he had no other ideas past talking to Damik. "Um . . ."

"There will be other Terrans present, Mr. Lanra, it isn't that sort of dinner. I believe it could be very interesting. Even informative. It would be a favor to me if you'd agree."

"Will Ambassador Chassik be there?"

"Yes. Why do you ask?"

"Something I stumbled on today. I suppose this will be formal?"

"Of course."

"I have an errand to run up in the Baltimor District. I'm not sure how long that will take and I'll have to change before I meet you."

"We have an excellent tailor on the premises, Mr. Lanra."

"Two, three hours then?"

A pause. "I can make that work. There will be an escort in the main lobby to bring you to my apartment."

"Then I'll see you later this evening."

"Thank you."

The link broke. *Dinner with the enemy?* he mused. He laughed softly to himself as he headed for a commuter station.

Brun Damik's apartment was on the fourth level of an expensive block in what had once been an exclusive warren. Though other parts of the urban complex now superseded it as *the* place to live, it still bespoke class and elegance, and far more credit than Damik ought to possess.

Police lounged in the corridor. Coren felt a sudden hollowness. One of the officers approached him, hand on the butt of her department-issue stunner, and Coren automatically held up his ID with the investigator's license appended.

"Inspector Capel is in charge, Mr. Lanra," she said, gesturing through the door.

The living room contained little furniture, but all of it looked expensive. Coren glimpsed the label on the entertainment array and quickly calculated the significant fraction of his annual income the system would have eaten. Forensic recorders drifted slowly over the stone-tile floor. A huddle of plainclothes police stood with their backs to a wall-length image of black, white, gray, and ivory blocks of various proportions that gradually exchanged places. The detectives stopped talking when Coren approached.

"Coren Lanra," he said, showing his ID again. "I'm looking for Inspector Capel?"

One of the men took his ID and examined it casually. He was slightly shorter than Coren, grayish hair a fine dusting across his broad skull. His eyes were a bright, almost artificial green. "Private security," he said, handing it back. "Do you have business here?"

"I'm not sure yet. I'm an acquaintance of Brun Damik."

The inspector blinked twice, then nodded. "Come with me," he said. "I'm Capel."

He led Coren to Damik's bedroom. Coren surveyed it quickly, noting the pair of uniformed police going through the wall-length closet and the bank of drawers. The bed was enormous, cobalt blue sheets rumpled. Coren saw no sign of blood.

"In here," Capel said, continuing on to the bathroom.

Damik sat propped on the toilet, hands dangling. Coren stared, shocked at the condition of the body. Bruises covered most of Damik's torso and thighs; his eyes were swollen shut, lips black and inflated. The head sat at an odd angle and Coren noticed the thick line of purpling around the neck. The only blood came from the holes where Damik's ears had been attached.

"They're in the sink," Capel said, guessing Coren's question. "These apartments are completely soundproofed. Surveillance shows no one entering or leaving before or after Brun Damik came home last night. Preliminaries indicate that sixty to seventy percent of his bones are broken—the spine is holding him up, if you're wondering—and several major organs are ruptured." Capel wheeled on him. "Your card says Special Service, so I'm not even going to try to be clever with you. Let me ask right out: what are you doing here?"

Coren closed his eyes. He had never grown the calluses other veterans claimed came after seeing enough dead bodies, but the nausea he once experienced no longer reached the point of muddling his thinking. The hollowness he felt upon seeing police here acquired a sour tang, and his conscience suggested that this was his fault for having visited Damik recently. He drew a deep breath.

"My employer is running for office," he said. "Rega

Looms. I'm following up possible embarrassments."

Capel nodded as if Coren had just passed a test. "What could Brun Damik have done to embarrass Rega Looms?"

"Nothing, directly."

"But . . . ?"

"But . . ." Coren glanced over his shoulder as to make sure he and Capel were out of earshot. He stepped closer. "Looms' daughter has been known to play at smuggling from time to time."

"Baleys. We know. So you're covering for him by trying to find his daughter." Capel pursed his lips. "Could this be the result of your investigation?"

"I honestly can't see how."

Capel stepped closer to Damik's body. "He was tortured. Somebody did this over a four- or five-hour period." He looked up. "How well did you know him?"

"We worked together in Special Service several years ago. He was competent. His tastes ran a little rich, though."

"Rich enough to accept perks?"

Coren made an inclusive gesture, indicating the opulence of the apartment. Capel grunted, agreeing.

"Was he supposed to have some information for you?"

"I don't know. I spoke to him yesterday. He wasn't very helpful. I was coming back to try again."

"Somebody beat you to it." Capel sighed. "I don't expect to get everything you might be able to tell me, Mr. Lanra, and I don't doubt you have a very good attorney, working for Rega Looms, so I won't even think about detaining you. I'm going to rely on your integrity as a former cop to tell me what I need to know. I'm not naïve enough to believe I'm even going to get that, so we'll pretend for the moment that we're actually working on the same side and that you wouldn't obstruct my investigation."

"Believe me, Inspector, I don't have a clue who did this. Or why."

Capel nodded. "It *is* excessive, especially for baleys. But who knows? This is politics, right? Maybe someone knows something about Looms' daughter that could hurt him." He shrugged. "It's a stretch. But all the other ideas I have don't explain this any better. Some sadistic shit tortured this man. That transcends jealousy, crime of passion, payback on a bad debt. Nothing explains it. Not even politics, really, unless he knew something."

"Torture is not a very reliable way of getting useful information."

"That's true. So we're left with revenge or someone sending a message."

"A message?"

"The question is, from whom to who? And why? Does Rega Looms know Brun Damik?"

"I seriously doubt it."

"And I doubt Rega Looms knows the particulars of your work right now. He's busy campaigning."

"Correct."

"So could this be a message for you?"

Coren studied Damik's corpse. If this was a message, it failed. Graphic, certainly, but the intent was buried in the bruises.

"If it is," he said, "I can't interpret it. There *is* a third possibility."

"Yes?"

"Pleasure. Someone enjoyed doing this."

Capel shuddered. "I do not even *want* to consider that. Not yet; hopefully, not ever."

Coren understood. A truly sick mind was one of the most difficult to track down, and when caught, it was difficult to know what to do next. But he agreed with Capel—this was a message.

"May I look around?" Coren asked.

Capel stared silently at Damik for a long moment, till Coren thought he had not heard. Then: "Sure. You know better than to touch anything and so forth."

"Thank you."

He backed out of the bathroom and looked across the bedroom at the police still riffling through the immense closet. Not sure where to begin, Coren walked around the bed and immediately touched something.

The sheets were expensive. Imports, Coren guessed. Damik would have been in an ideal position to help himself to whatever black market goods came through. Who would challenge him, especially if he was reasonably careful and not too greedy? He was not selling anything, as far as Coren knew. If he had been, he would have been living in a private enclave, with better security. No, Damik was not *that* corrupt. It had been clear even in Special Service that Damik was interested only in personal comfort, not the extra work illicit business would bring. He was a taker, not a dealer. It did not appear to Coren that he could have affected anybody's bottom line. Not enough to warrant an assassination.

Coren tugged the sheets down. Stained. Sweat? The coloration was wrong for anything else. Still, the possibility that someone had been in bed with him was not unreasonable. What had he said about his contacts?

"A woman named Tresha and a man named Gamelin. I assume he's just muscle, he's big enough."

Coren thought back to his last visit to Jeta Fromm's hab, and the fact that a man and woman had come to see her, but she had already left. What was the chronology? A day?

Two days? Things had happened so fast. The warren rat had said the man was big, something wrong with him. The same pair?

He wondered then if the woman who'd acted as his data troll had even *been* Jeta Fromm. Perhaps he'd been dealing with this "Tresha" all along . . .

The sheets were skewed in the direction of the bathroom, but that did not necessarily mean Damik had been dragged. Coren left the bedroom and almost stepped on a forensic recorder. The compact, turtle-shelled unit continued on, oblivious to Coren's presence, looking for the minutiae that might provide a clue—hairs, skin, fibers, fluids.

Coren stopped before the large picture and watched the rectangles drift before and behind each other. It was a very expensive piece, Auroran, Coren thought, and he wondered if it were an import as well. He turned away after a few minutes and did a slow circuit of the living room.

A low table made from a sheet of thinly-sliced granite stood between facing seteés. One glass stood in a drying pool of condensation, ice melted at the bottom.

One glass.

No clothes in the living room.

He entered the kitchen. Four glasses stood on the counter by the sink, all empty.

The place had been cleaned, he realized. While Damik had been tortured—four or five hours' worth, according to Capel—someone had gone through the apartment and tidied up.

Damik's office showed a little more disorder, but none of it appeared significant. A few papers scattered on the desk, disks stacked sloppily, a jacket draped over a chair back.

A few plaques decorated one wall. Coren smiled, seeing the Special Service certificate, and, beside it, a merit award for bravery. He did not recall the action, but he could look it up.

Damik had gone to university—Nestern in the Freno District—and graduated with a degree in art history. Coren grunted, surprised. He would never have guessed.

The frame rested crookedly on the wall. Coren brought a fingertip against the lower left corner and pushed up to straighten it. The hook on which it hung came loose and the entire plaque clattered to the floor.

It burst apart—frame, cover sheet, hook, and documents—and sprawled across Coren's feet. Damik had used the same display to hold several items, one atop the other. Coren knelt quickly. He counted half a dozen certificates, which must have strained the capacity of the frame, stuffed past its meager limits. Coren gathered them up.

More graduation certificates. Damik had taken courses in a number of unrelated fields: cooking, the history of paleoanthropology, astronomy, microcircuit repair. All them unexpected and, in their diversity, admirable.

Coren stopped at the last document. Damik's grammar school certificate, from the Holmer Foster Gymnas Cooperative.

Brun was an orphan . . . ?

Something else about the name of the facility seemed familiar. Later, he decided; he could look it up later. He folded the certificate and tucked it into an inside pocket, then reassembled the frame. He found the hook and pressed it back into the wall and carefully set the display on it, which then listed crookedly to the left.

Capel waited in the living room.

"Anything?" he asked.

"Nothing obvious. You realize that the place was sanitized."

Capel scowled. "They had time. Where can I reach you if I need to ask further questions?"

Coren fished out a card and handed it to Capel.

"So have you found Nyom Looms yet?" Capel asked.

"I'm still looking," Coren said smoothly.

Capel nodded again. "We'll be in touch."

"Even if you don't need me, let me know, would you? Damik and I *did* work together once."

Capel seemed to soften a little. "Sure."

"By the way, did he have any relatives?" It seemed likely that Damik would have been adopted, but Coren never heard him talk about anyone. That omission now acquired significance.

"I was going to ask you that. None we've found. He had a broker. We'll be talking to him."

"Hm. Too bad."

Coren left. He checked his watch. He had less than forty minutes to get to the Auroran embassy. Too little time, really, to sort out his thoughts, much less his feelings.

Brun Damik was an orphan...

He pulled out his comm. "Desk, connect to the public records of the Holmer Foster Gymnas Cooperative. Alumni."

While he waited, Coren teased at the reasons Damik had been killed. Because of Coren's visit? So soon? That implied a surveillance network of remarkable scope. Had Damik called someone, given himself away, or was this an unrelated matter?

"Connection complete," his Desk said.

"Access records for Damik, Brun."

"Located."

"List of kin or other relations."

"Parents, Evlin Mores and Rolsin Dynik, recorded as deceased. Institutional guardianship until age eleven."

Mores and Dynik . . . sound familiar . . . Coren could not remember. "Then what?"

"Elective sponsorship."

"Name of sponsor?"

"Under security lock."

"Hack it. I want that name."

"Working."

Damik's parents seemed so familiar, as if he had met them or seen their names—

The list of people in Wenithal's investigation.

He needed to check it again and verify, but now that he remembered he was sure.

"Finished," his Desk reported. "Sponsor listed as Wenithal, Ree, agent with Eurosector police."

FOURTEEN

A dinner?" Derec shook his head at the image on the comm screen. Ariel returned his cynical look. "I don't get this," he continued. "Two days ago we were all but persona non grata and now Setaris is inviting you to embassy soireés."

"It gets better," Ariel said. "Jonis will be there."

"Taprin . . . it occurs to me that you're being used here."

"Really?" Ariel intoned with mock dismay. "I asked Lanra to be my guest. One good surprise is worth another."

"Do you trust him?"

"Of course not. He hasn't told us half of what he's looking into."

"Fair is fair. We aren't telling him everything, either."

Ariel shrugged. "Do you want to take odds on whether the two lines of inquiry intersect?"

"I'm not sure I want them to."

"Well . . . Lanra asked me if Chassik would be there tonight. I asked him why, and he said it was something he stumbled on."

"Chassik. What could he possibly want with Chassik?"

"I have some opinions. Did you know that Solaria owns Nova Levis?"

"That hasn't come out in the newsnets."

"No, and it may not. They owned it before it was Nova Levis, when it was no more than a Solaria mining franchise called Cassus Thole. The colony—a Settler colony—is a lease agreement that was originally set up between Solaria and the Church of Organic Sapiens."

Derec started. "Looms' church?"

"The same, only back before they were so rabidly anti-space. Now, just to heap coincidence upon coincidence, Gale Chassik was one of the initial investors in a biomed research lab called—are you ready?—Nova Levis, which was closed after having been investigated for infant brokering."

Derec whistled. "Convergence is imminent."

"So it seems. How's it coming with the robot?"

Derec glanced across the small workspace at Rana. She stared, rapt, at the banks of screens, calibrating the myriad details of Thales' link to facilitate a precise excavation. The robot itself remained where it had been left, on its pallet, now connected to Thales and Rana's console via several heavy cables.

"I'd say another half-hour, we'll have the interface running at an acceptable level," he said. A small icon in the upper left corner of the comm screen revealed Thales' presence in the exchange, monitoring security and running an encryption routine. Ariel saw the same icon on her end, otherwise she would never speak so freely on a commline.

"Speaking of things robotic," Derec said, "the director here is a man named Rotij Polifos. Do you know anything about him?"

"No. Should I?"

"He's been director for seven years. I was just thinking, it's kind of unusual for an Auroran to stay in a Terran posting like this for that long. Don't they usually rotate out more regularly?"

"Usually. Maybe he likes it."

Derec frowned. "Maybe."

"Is there a problem?"

"No, I just . . . it seems odd, that's all."

"Have Hofton look into it. Keep your mind on the robot, Derec."

"Right, right. You know, Lanra wants us to prove a robot committed the murders. There's no way, Ariel. Not this one, anyway. It's just a standard DW-12 with a few added modules—nothing I don't recognize—and it's showing a nearly textbook collapse pattern. It couldn't even have made the crack in the cargo bin, not without some tools."

"Oh, I don't doubt the robot you have is innocent. What I'm wondering is, why didn't the robot *prevent* the deaths? If a second robot had been involved, as unlikely as it sounds, this one should have intervened. Has Sipha Palen told you much yet?"

"No. She wants us to run the excavation without any preconceptions. I can understand that."

"Get it done ASAP. I want to move this to the next level."

Derec raised an eyebrow. *"What* next level?"

"I'm sending you a packet to go over in private," Ariel replied. "About Nova Levis. Very interesting reading."

"The colony, or the lab you mentioned?"

"Both. The list of shareholders in the lab is intriguing all by itself. Chassik isn't the only surprise." She looked away for a few seconds. PACKET RECEIVED appeared along the bottom of Derec's screen.

"Got it," he said. "Be careful tonight, Ariel. We don't want to be deported for bad taste."

Ariel's eyes widened in mock surprise. "Derec, please! I? Bad taste?"

Derec smiled. "Forgive me. I *do* know better."

She grinned. "Have fun."

The screen went blank then, except for Thales' icon and the notice of the data packet. Derec plugged his personal datum into the board.

"Download the packet for me, Thales," he said. "I'll look at it later."

"I would recommend sooner," Thales said. "I compiled the raw data. It may be more relevant than you might think."

"'Keep your mind on the robot,' Ariel said. I'll add it to the list, thanks."

Lights winked on the datum's pad. He scooted his chair over by Rana. She worked with confidence, clearly in control, comfortable in her expertise. Better than Derec remembered, and he remembered her as being very good.

"I suppose," Rana said slowly, "that it's occurred to you that you're *both* being used."

"You think so?"

"You're being set up to take blame."

"That would be consistent."

"Then why are you going along with it?"

"It's a question of being deported now or later. The longer we put it off, the more chance there is to avoid it completely."

"You don't believe that, do you?"

"Shouldn't I?"

She shrugged. "I suppose you're thinking that you might find something in this mess—" she waved at the screens

"—that will make you so valuable to someone that they'll intercede on your behalf and restore you to former glory."

"Something like that."

Rana shook her head. "I can't imagine why. All I want to do is get away from this planet, and all you want to do is stay." She turned to look at him. "Why?"

"We've been over this before," Derec said uncomfortably.

"Yes we have. And you've never given me an answer. Excuses, reasons, justifications, but not an answer." Rana glanced toward the curtain that isolated them from the rest of the lab. "This planet has treated you pretty badly. Hell, it's treated *me* badly and I was born here; you weren't. I grew up on Earth and I have no place here. I'm leaving first chance I get, to go somewhere I might be appreciated."

"Aurora is just as bad in different ways."

"But it's not personal the way it is here."

"Who told you that?"

"My co-workers, for one. After they got over the idea of a Terran who understood positronics, they treated me as an equal."

Derec shook his head. "No. You just haven't learned to read the signs."

Rana cut the air with her hand. "Stop. It *is* different because I have skills they value. Maybe it will be only more of the same in a new way, but for now it *feels* like respect. I already *know* what I don't have on Earth."

"So what is your question?"

"Why are you so set on trying to stay here?"

"You think there's one answer?"

"No, but there's usually one thing that validates all the rest."

Derec stared at her, mind suddenly blank. "I never thought about it that way before," he heard himself say. He no longer looked at Rana, but at a point just past her right shoulder, as if waiting for something to resolve in the air behind her.

"I don't need an answer now, boss," Rana said. He refocussed on her.

"Um . . ."

"And I can manage this," she said, turning back to the console.

Conversation abruptly terminated, Derec went over to the gurney, annoyed and impressed by Rana.

Beyond the fabric curtain he could hear the other lab workers moving and speaking in low tones. He leaned on the edge of the pallet and gazed down the length of the robot.

"So where did you come from?" he muttered.

The torso showed age and use. Scratches gave the impression of a complicated urban map etched in bronze. The metal gleamed dully through patches of tarnish and encrusted grime. Plates covered linkages thirty centimeters below its arms that allowed extra limbs to be connected. The arms themselves, three-jointed and thick, ended in finely articulated six-digit hands. The legs depended from a rotating platform beneath the torso shell. Derec noted more removable coverplates on the platform hiding assemblies to which secondary legs or support braces or tractor modules or one of several other modifications could be fitted. The DW-12 was a large robot, two-and-a-half meters tall, designed for a multiplicity of heavy tasks in conjunction with human workers, very adaptable, with an advanced positronic brain that allowed for considerable independence and problem-solving capacity.

Vaguely humaniform, the head was little more than a protective helmet curving over the intricate sensor array behind the mesh-covered eyes. A complex architecture of connections rose out of the torso and joined the brain that lay within the chest cavity to the communications and sensory apparatus beneath the headcap. The normally thick column had been modified by the addition of accessory modules and cables. Normally, the "neck" would be covered by a smooth carapace, but the extra components jutted out like synthetic goiters, requiring a specially-fitted casement no one had bothered to acquire.

Derec frowned at the overall dirty appearance. This robot had been worked hard for a long time. Hiding it, as would be necessary on Earth, probably prevented the owner from caring for it as thoroughly as needed, but he would have expected Palen's forensics people to clean it up in the course of their inspection.

But no thorough examination had been made.

Derec started going over it more carefully.

He felt beneath the headcap for the release and flipped the cover off, revealing the strutwork that caged the components. He took a rag and small bottle of solvent from the workbench and lightly cleaned off grime from the smooth surfaces until he found the serial number. He jotted it down and went to the comm, where he fed it to Thales to be encrypted and sent to Ariel.

Derec made note of each component he recognized within the head. Optical and aural receptors and translators, UV and Infrared telemetric assemblers, gas traps linked to interferometers, location and attitude modules—nothing unexpected. He wanted to turn it over to get inside the torso shell, but not till Thales finished the excavation.

On its right side, below the accessory limb coverplate, new metal shone brighter than the surrounding surface. A fifteen-centimeter square area had been replaced, the weld itself invisible but for the age difference in the material. Derec went over the rest of the body for signs of recent damage, but found none.

He tried to imagine its last minutes. A chamber full of humans died around it. What would its reaction have been? Derec tapped his finger arrhythmically on the pallet.

One human had been assaulted: Nyom Looms had suffered a broken neck. And this robot had failed to protect her from an alleged second robot.

Which had now disappeared.

Ridiculous.

Derec turned over first one robotic hand, then the other.

A dark substance filled the joints of three fingers, palmside, of the right hand. Derec tried to flex them open but the segments were too tight. He found a small flathead screwdriver among the tools on the workbench. He slid a sheet of paper beneath the hand, then pried one of the segments open and dug at the matter embedded within the joint. Flakes fell to the paper.

He looked around their workstation. No magnifier. Derec carefully brushed the recovered material into a small dish, clapped a lid on it, and stepped from behind the blind.

Three technicians worked at two stations across the chamber. Derec spotted the equipment he needed against the wall to his left, midway between the curtain and the techs. He strode across the lab as if he did so every day and sat down at the console.

Within seconds, he had the magnifier powered up and the dish in the drawer of the observation platform. He keyed for a relatively low magnification—200X—and let the machine perform.

The screen showed him three distinct substances: two clearly artificial—one crystalline and the other fibrous. The third was blood.

He tapped a command to separate out the three materials and deposit them in separate dishes. A few seconds later, a different drawer in the platform slid out bearing three dishes. Derec pocketed the one containing the blood and reinserted the one with the crystalline material.

"May I help you, sir?"

Derec looked around at a young female technician standing anxiously behind him.

"No, I have what I need. Thank you."

"Um . . ."

"It's all right, I'll clear it with your director."

"Did you find something?" another tech asked, suddenly leaning past the first and gazing at the image on the screen.

Derec switched it off. The man frowned.

"I'm fine," Derec said. "If I need help, I'll ask."

The man met Derec's gaze coldly, without the scowl of offended dignity and violated territoriality Derec expected. Derec sensed that it would be a mistake to look away, to yield at all to this one. He would lose his samples and the presumed privileges he had just accorded himself, access to any and all parts of the lab.

"I *am* qualified to ask for help," Derec said. "I've had years of practice."

The tech smiled thinly. "Of course, sir. Sorry to bother you."

The first technician watched her coworker retreat.

"Where's the infirmary?" Derec asked. His legs trembled slightly.

"Next level," she replied, pointing downward.

"Thank you." He removed the sample tray from the

magnifier and wiped the machine's log. "I want one of these in our area when I return."

"Yes, sir," she said uncertainly.

"It *is* authorized." He stepped closer to her and lowered his voice. "It wouldn't do anyone any good for me to take this to Director Polifos. Would it?"

"No, sir. No." She glanced in the direction of the other tech.

"Don't worry about him," Derec said. "He's an amateur."

She gave him a surprised smile. "Yes, sir. I'll see to procuring you a magnifier."

Samples in his pocket, Derec walked out of the lab, feeling the male tech's eyes on him all the way to the door. He wondered what internal politics he had just upset and how, if at all, it applied to him.

An elderly Auroran named Greler attended the infirmary. After a brief exchange of names, Greler amiably ran a complete scan of the blood samples and handed a disk to Derec along with his sample.

"Apologies for being unable to run the match for you," Greler said. "This sort of thing must go through Kopernik Medical. You can take it to them and have it done."

"Thanks."

Derec returned to the positronics lab.

He walked in to find two more techs sitting with the first pair. All of them fell silent when they saw him and watched as he crossed the floor to the curtained station. Derec felt a prickle up the back of his neck.

Hofton waited with Rana, along with Rotij Polifos and Yart Leri.

Polifos wore a pinched expression. Ambassador Leri looked concerned. Hofton and Rana seemed mildly puzzled.

"Mr. Avery—" Leri began.

"I would appreciate," Polifos cut in immediately, "that any and all requests for equipment or special analyses be made through me. This is my lab."

Derec did not respond. Polifos looked frustrated. When he finally broke eye contact, Derec looked at Leri.

"I was under the impression that we had your full cooperation."

"Of course," Leri said, glaring briefly at Polifos. "I apologize for any misunderstandings, but we are answerable to Ambassador Setaris and, through her, Aurora itself. We're used to a more regular set of procedures."

Polifos blinked in amazement at Leri. "I should have been told what this was all about. I am responsible to the Calvin Institute and the Positronics Commission—directly—and any and all matters concerning robots and other positronic entities within and involving this facility are my responsibility. I'm required to report, oversee, and voucher all activities—"

"You don't have to quote the code to me," Leri snapped. "This is, I repeat, an unusual circumstance—"

"I have this authority precisely *for* unusual circumstances! All due respect to Mr. Avery, he is not the only roboticist on Earth, and unless I have a very good reason to relinquish my responsibilities, I cannot allow him to simply take over—"

"No one is taking over," Leri said.

"Stop interrupting me."

"Stop jumping to conclusions! You didn't know about this because *I* didn't know! I didn't know because Ambassador Setaris told me I *wouldn't* know! She has asked for the utmost discretion, and I will not tolerate petty fits of temper over personal slights!"

"I can't cooperate with Mr. Avery unless I know what he's doing," Polifos said.

"I agree," Hofton said. "Can't expect useful cooperation from ignorance."

"Perhaps I was remiss," Leri admitted. "But I was told that your work was highly confidential and that a minimum of interference was in order."

"Misunderstandings are easy under these circumstances," Derec said. "Evidently, *I* was misinformed about protocol myself."

Leri looked sheepish. "I, uh . . ."

"Director Polifos and I can work this out, I'm sure," Derec said.

"Well." Leri gave Polifos one last glare.

Polifos did not look away this time. "I do not want Palen's goons tramping through here as if it were their office and we were criminals."

"Under the circumstances, we don't have much choice," Leri snapped. "Now, straighten all this out with Mr. Avery. I'm too busy to do arbitration over bruised egos." He looked at Derec. "I'm sorry for the inconvenience, Mr. Avery. If you have any more trouble . . ."

He stormed off. Huddled techs watched him leave.

Derec turned to Polifos. "Chief Palen?"

"One of our staff was arrested," Polifos said. "Nothing unusual in that—the man in question has a history of running afoul with Palen."

"Doesn't sound like someone you'd want to keep on staff," Hofton observed.

"We have personnel shortages," Polifos said. He seemed distracted. "But even so, I've tried to get this one rotated back to Aurora and it simply doesn't happen." He shook his head impatiently. "That isn't the real problem. What *is* the problem is her *people* have been in and out of my lab since yesterday, questioning my staff. Then *you* show up, and the next thing I see is Palen herself with your man Hofton here bringing in a robot of which I had *no knowledge!* I can't help but think that it's all connected. Your presence has changed our relationship with Palen, and not for the better."

Derec exchanged a look with Hofton. "I'm afraid I don't know anything about—"

Polifos cut him off. "No, I don't imagine you do, nor would you even if you did. One of her *police* appears in the doorway, points, and expects to be followed. Our arrangement with the Terran authorities here is peculiar to say the least—we were all required to concede that Palen is in charge of all security throughout the station. Makes sense, I suppose, but—"

"We were informed about none of this," Hofton said. "When was the arrest made?"

Rana frowned at Hofton but said nothing.

"Shortly before you arrived," Rotij said. "Naturally we're nervous."

"What are the charges?" Hofton asked.

"Disorderly conduct. But Palen's been questioning my people about smuggling." Polifos snorted in disbelief. *"Smuggling!* Why would an Auroran engage in smuggling?"

Derec looked across the lab and recognized the tense look in the eyes of the staff.

Derec stepped close to Polifos. "I want that equipment, Director. Soon as possible. The quicker we get done here, the sooner we'll be out of your lab and away from your people. But we want the equipment *here.* I don't want any more confusion over who's responsible for what."

"No, we don't," Polifos answered sharply. "All right." He stepped around the blind. "Hovis!"

Derec looked at Hofton. "What's this about?"

"You stepped on toes in your walk across hallowed ground," Hofton said. "Someone complained. The accusation that we're plants from Palen materialized. There's a rather ugly atmosphere here. Also," he lowered his voice, "I'm sorry I didn't get a chance to tell you earlier. I tried to look into Director Polifos's record. This posting and credentials from the Calvin Institute were all I could find. There's a security block on records older than Kopernik."

"Terran security?"

"No, sir. Auroran."

Derec stared at Hofton, for a moment uncomprehending. Then he shook his head. "We'd better proceed on the assumption that we have even less time than we started with." He showed the disk to Hofton. "I had the blood sample screened and typed."

"Blood sample?" Hofton asked.

"The robot's hand. I found material in the finger joints. Some of it is blood. The rest I'll look at when I get the proper equipment."

"Blood. Wonderful. That should help exonerate the robot."

Derec slipped the disk into the comm console. "We're going to need a complete autopsy report on all the victims, I think. And I want to look at that cargo bin. In person, not on a screen."

"I'll see what I can do," Hofton said.

"One way or the other, we need to see for ourselves."

"I understand."

Derec turned to address his RI. "Thales, I'm sending a blood screen. I want you to run a match through all available databases."

"Yes, Derec. That may take some time."

"I can wait." He pressed SEND and turned to Rana. "How's the link?"

"Established. Thales is beginning the first level excavation now. I've set up buffers to receive intact memory nodes as they're found and retrieved. We should be able to view them in isolation."

"Good, good." Derec went to the edge of the blind and watched a pair of technicians setting up a magnifier on a cart. "I want a complete scan for eyes and ears on all this equipment. Have Thales do one on the lab itself."

"All of it?" Rana asked.

"Every bit."

"Derec," Thales said, "I have a consanguinity match."

"Already?"

"Given the probable source of the sample, I began with the most obvious. I am continuing through the rest of the databases on the chance of finding an exact match."

"All right, what do you have?"

"There is a 99% match to Nyom Looms."

"So . . . it's her blood?"

"No. I can display the details, but the distinction is clear. This sample came from a male."

"Her father, perhaps?" Rana suggested.

"No, Rana. Even given the unlikelihood that Rega Looms would permit a robot close enough to him to touch, I ran the same match against his genome and it remains only a close match, not identical. The markers I used to verify distinctions number two hundred eighteen. There is no significant margin for error. The sample belongs to a male relative of both Rega and Nyom Looms, probably a son and brother."

"Son . . ." Derec mused. "Looms never had a son."

"The record would so substantiate. However, there are always possible oversights."

" 'Oversights'," Hofton said. "Interesting way to put it. Have you typed the sample against Looms' wife?"

"Yes. The same degree of consanguinity. The logical implication is that Nyom Looms had a brother. However, no record of such a relative is forthcoming."

"Can you determine age, Thales?" Derec asked.

"That is proving difficult, Derec. Normally there are mutations over time in the chemistry and base DNA. Proteins provide a reliable clock. But this sample shows an incongruity of results. Certain proteins suggest an age of twenty-nine, others an age of ten."

"Rehab treatments?" Hofton suggested.

"The requisite chemical signatures of all known rejuvenation or rehabilitation protocols are absent. This does not preclude that one or more have not been employed that are unknown, but I cannot consequently give you an accurate estimate of age."

"Send this data to Ariel, Thales," Derec said. "Continue your search for an exact match. Add the databases of all rejuvenation clinics extending back a period of, oh, thirty-five years, and see if anything turns up."

"Yes, Derec."

"Nyom had a brother she didn't know about?" Hofton said. "Amazing. Imagine that, from a man like Looms."

"Call Palen," Derec said. "We need to see those bodies and all the autopsy reports." He stared across the lab, watching the personnel, and realized after a moment that he was looking for something that did not fit. "Thales, ask Ariel to run a background on Rotij Polifos."

FIFTEEN

Y ou're late."

Ariel nodded curtly to Coren's escort, who bowed formally and left. Ariel stood to one side, waving Coren in.

"Your tailor took his time," Coren said, entering the apartment.

Ariel Burgess wore a gown of graphite-gray material that contained motes of color which sparkled delicately. The cut had no sharp edges and, rather than encase her body, seemed to travel along with her. Coren kept expecting to see thigh or hip or breast or belly through the mist, but, though the fabric covered her reluctantly, it never failed to hide.

She wore no jewelry. Her black hair was braided thickly into a helix laced with silver, blue, and gold ribbons. She appeared to be barefoot. Coren could not stop watching her, thoroughly caught by what he saw.

"No matter," she said. "Fashionably late is better than being too early. Have you ever been to one of these before?"

"No," Coren said. "Rega has never been invited."

She frowned. "Oh, I doubt that. Setaris is always trying to persuade detractors to come see for themselves." She shrugged, then gave him an open appraisal. She nodded. "That will do."

Coren bristled briefly at the inspection. The Auroran tailor complained that he was unused to working for Terrans because they were so short and thick, all the while his lasers measured him and his robot did the cutting. The suit, a midnight blue formal affair, fit beautifully—Coren enjoyed fine clothes, especially new ones, and he had never owned an Auroran outfit before. The sleeves seemed a bit too loose, but nothing was too tight, and after the trip from the tailor's to Ariel's apartment it felt as natural as skin.

Then he felt foolish for resenting her. He had been studying *her*, after all.

"I'm glad I meet your standards," he said.

She cocked an eyebrow. "For tonight, at least." She crossed the room to a comm console, dragging his gaze with her. She retrieved a disk and brought it to him. "Take this now, just in case."

"What is it?"

"The subject of our evening's discussion. But later. We have to go."

In the corridor, she frowned. "How well do you handle the open?"

"As in . . . ?"

"Unroofed space, free air, stars in the sky."

"I can manage well enough."

Ariel looked dubious. They reached a wide area lined with elevator doors. She tapped a code into one.

"Well," she said, "if it becomes too much, there are plenty of enclosed spaces in Setaris's residence."

The door opened on a comfortable car with a plush

bench mounted in a semicircle. Coren barely felt it begin to move and after a few moments there was no discernable motion.

Ariel slid briefly against him, thighs touching. His nostrils filled with a subdued odor and he became instantly affected by her presence.

"All right, we have a minute," Ariel said. "Do you have any questions about protocol? Have you been to any Spacer functions?"

Coren set aside his growing distraction. "Um . . . when I worked for Special Service, there were occasions, but I've never been a guest."

Ariel nodded. "I have no idea yet what the occasion for this dinner is, but I have no doubt several guests will be recording it. This will be a working dinner, so business will be done. Not openly, not blatantly, but arrangements will be made. There's a hierarchy which you'll pick up on as the evening progresses. Who sits where at the table, who is served what kind of drink, even who gets to go home for the evening with whom—all this is a matter of protocol and negotiation. Don't argue with anyone. Prod, suggest, imply, insinuate—that's not only allowable but expected. Anything but an open disagreement. Follow my lead."

"Anyone I should be particularly wary of?"

"Gale Chassik, the Solarian ambassador. He has allies who may or may not be sifting for information for him. The Keresians, for one."

"Gale Chassik . . . I've come across that name recently."

"So have I. He's involved in Nova Levis."

"Uh-huh."

"Both of them, I believe. The colony and the lab."

Coren blinked at her. "The lab?"

"It's in the disk," Ariel said, smiling. "I've been doing a little homework. Anyway, one other you should know about. Jonis Taprin will be there."

"Senator Taprin?" Coren frowned. "That could be awkward."

"Don't worry about him using your presence there against Looms. Terrans will resign office before admitting to petitioning Spacers. He sees you there, he'll be more worried that you'll use it. If you do, then he'll retaliate, but in my experience it's automatic deténte."

"Why is Taprin going to be there?"

Ariel smirked. "Looking for favors, sifting for data. Even the most rabidly anti-Spacer politician, if he or she is at all intelligent, knows that Earth can't do without us. The trade with the Settler colonies is too important to risk losing our shipping fleets as subcontractors. Besides, there's the implicit threat of blockade. Earth also isn't out there with the Settlers; we are. If there's to be any kind of control—"

"There are Terran fleets," Coren interrupted. "We aren't all cloistered agoraphobics."

"Compared to the Fifty Worlds, Earth's presence is a token. You can blockade one world, maybe two, cause enough damage to upset the balance of power, but . . ." She let it hang like that. Then: "In any case, exercise discretion and say nothing about baleys. That's nothing but a sore point among all of us. If it comes up, I'll deal with it."

"Why did you ask me here?"

"Efficiency. Setaris is playing a game and I don't know what it is yet. I haven't exactly been in favor this last year. Now all of a sudden I'm being asked to embassy fêtes again. You'll act as a wild card in the game. Accompanying me will suggest a lot to them."

"And explain nothing."

"Exactly. Then afterward we can talk about our—we're here."

Coren had not noticed the car slowing. The door slid aside and let them out in a wide arcade.

The air smelled different. Coren slowed as he neared the edge of the overhang, sensing the change before he saw anything.

Through a dimly-seen parkland with slim trees and thick grass, light came from the residence, warmly tracing the outlines of the intervening flora. The sounds of conversation, occasional laughter, and the nearly overwhelming rhythm of music drifted, muted, toward him.

He forced his hands to unclench and stepped from beneath the shelter.

A breeze brushed his face.

He took a dozen steps and looked up.

Stars salted the night sky, and for an instant he caught his breath. They seemed so close that they formed a roof as solid as the urban shell beneath which he had lived all his life. Far more beautiful, though, and he understood why people wanted them, wanted to go to them, even why they wanted to see this same view from other worlds. There was certainly nothing to fear.

Between one step and the next, leaves fluttered in the corner of his vision and his perspective changed. Abruptly all of above became an infinity into which he felt he might fall.

Coren jerked his gaze to the ground, shuddered briefly, and made himself look only at the light ahead. Ariel had stopped halfway across the grass, waiting for him. He walked stolidly toward the party, pleased that he had not reclenched his fists. Ariel smoothly took his arm, and they continued on together. He touched his face, and his fingers came away dry.

Good. He stepped from grass to flagstone. He risked one more quick glimpse skyward. The light around him occluded the view of stars and he relaxed.

He blinked at the startlingly clothed people.

The styles ranged from strips and patches of fabric that barely covered, and often intentionally failed to cover, to blousy, opaque suits that seemed large enough for two people. The dance of color, shift of cloth and skin, the moil of distinct tastes from several cultures somehow blent into a single attribute: Spacer.

Even the Terrans dressed in one or another Spacer fashion, though they still stuck out. Coren thought he knew why: Terrans dressed for personal status while Spacers dressed purely for personal taste. On a Spacer, the quality and expense of the clothing said nothing of their place in the hierarchy, which kept Terrans continually unable to rank them on sight—something Terrans did among themselves habitually.

"Coren."

He followed his name and found Ariel looking at him. She stood with three people: two Spacers, the other Terran. He recognized the Terran.

"Coren," Ariel said, taking his arm, "may I introduce Ambassador Sen Setaris of Aurora."

Coren bowed slightly and Setaris returned it. She was Spacer tall and austerely attractive, her hair glowing white around a seamless face. She could be fifty, or one hundred and fifty for all that Coren could tell.

"Welcome, Mr. Lanra," she said. "I trust you aren't in any distress?"

"No, thank you. I'm fine."

"Good. Make yourself comfortable, this is an informal gathering. Should you wish, my house is open."

"I appreciate that, Ambassador."

"And this," Ariel moved on, "is Ambassador Gale Chassik of Solaria."

Chassik looked very different from Setaris. Heavier, dressed in the thick Solarian manner, his head was nearly smooth. He smiled broadly and the lines in his face were deep. Coren began to extend his hand, then remembered the Solarian aversion to being touched. He bowed again.

"Ambassador."

"Pleased, Mr. Lanra. It's good to see Ariel out of her shell again. We've missed her."

Ariel smiled. "I've missed you, as well." She turned to the Terran. "And this is Senator Jonis Taprin of Earth."

"I recognize the Senator, of course," Coren said, extending his hand. "How do you do, sir."

Taprin was pale and middle-aged, lines in his forehead qualitatively different from those in Chassik's. He was thin and nearly as tall as Setaris. He clasped Coren's hand. "This must be an unusual occasion for you, Mr. Lanra. I understood you worked for Rega Looms."

"That's true, sir."

"What would he think of you consorting with Spacers?" Taprin grinned at Chassik and Setaris, including them in the joke.

"No more than he would of you doing so, Senator," Coren said.

The Spacers laughed softly. Coren noticed the quick resentment in Taprin's eyes, gone just as quickly.

"Honestly, though," Coren said, "I'm here at Ambassador Burgess's invitation. I'm currently on leave from Mr. Looms' service."

"Isn't that unusual?" Chassik asked. "You *are* his chief of security, are you not?"

"I am. But I have very capable people handling his day-to-day operations. On the road as he is, I have to look after the home office. But even I get a few days off from time to time."

More polite laughter.

"Enjoy yourself, Mr. Lanra," Setaris said. "If you'll excuse Ariel and me . . . ?"

Setaris took Ariel's arm and the two drifted off.

"Ambassador Setaris sets a marvelous table," Chassik said. "The buffet should not be missed." He gestured toward a long table near the entrance to the house.

"In that case," Coren said, "I should do the diplomatic thing and eat something."

Taprin smiled. "Stay away from the mauve buttons with the yellow cream sauce. They sneak up on you at the most inconvenient times."

Coren glanced back when he reached the long table filled with Spacer delicacies. Taprin and Chassik faced each other, talking intently. He searched the crowd and spotted Ariel and Setaris, near the edge of the patio, also talking intently.

He surveyed the food arrayed down the length of the long table and saw almost nothing he recognized. He located the buttons Taprin had warned him about and, perversely, took one. It possessed a faintly musty taste beneath a cinnamon-sweet tang. The sauce reminded him of buttered scallops. Nothing unfamiliar.

"Drink, sir?"

He glimpsed a tray to his left containing several tall glasses. He took one.

"Thanks."

The servor rolled away, then, and Coren watched it, a robot shaped like a mobile table, moving deftly among the partiers. He caught a glimpse of a few more spaced throughout the gathering.

The liquid in the glass shimmered golden and he wondered where it put him in the order of importance. He sipped: tea with almond liqueur. He popped the rest of the button in his mouth and washed it down.

"I trust this isn't going to become complicated."

Taprin stood beside him.

"Complicated, Senator?"

"You understand me, Mr. Lanra."

"I do. I'm sure both of us understand the risks of unmanaged implication."

Taprin winced. "Just so we do." He was not finished, though. He fidgeted, sipped at his drink, and finally asked, "Have you and Ariel known each other long?"

"We met last year."

Taprin blinked, startled. "I wasn't aware she'd been seeing anyone . . ."

"Should you?"

Taprin frowned.

"I'm sure, Senator, whatever else gets discussed here tonight, Ariel Burgess's personal relationships won't be part of it."

Taprin nodded. "Excuse me."

Coren watched him walk away, toward the house. *So much for being nonconfrontational . . .*

"Do you think he can defeat your Mr. Looms?"

Ambassador Chassik stood beside him, also watching Taprin retreat to the interior of Setaris's residence.

"The election is still six weeks off," Coren said. "Anything can happen between now and then."

"I know. That's always surprised me about you Terrans.

Given your temperament, one would think you'd find a less volatile way to choose your leaders."

"For example?"

Chassik shrugged. "For example, on Solaria the process is accomplished by a combination of appointment and annual assessment. A vote of confidence keeps the appointed official in office. Too low a vote..." Chassik drew a finger sharply across his own throat. He grinned quickly. "Politically speaking, of course."

"Who does the appointing?"

"There is a college of electors. We never know who they are."

"I see. I think we'll keep our volatility."

Chassik laughed.

"My question," he continued, "is not academic, Mr. Lanra. Should your employer defeat Senator Taprin, new arrangements must be made. I would consider it a favor if you let Mr. Looms know that Solaria is open to a dialogue."

"You *do* know Rega's position on Earth-Spacer relations."

Chassik nodded. "In spite of his public pronouncements, I'm sure he's at base a reasonable man."

"Is Senator Taprin a reasonable man?"

"More than others, less than some."

"When the time comes, I'll pass that on," Coren said.

"Thank you, Mr. Lanra."

"I would think, though, that you would tell him yourself. You used to know him personally, didn't you?"

Chassik's eyes narrowed briefly. "I won't insult your no doubt substantiated intelligence by denying it. That was, however, a long time ago."

"Before you were ambassador, wasn't it?"

"I was newly arrived on Earth. He was one of the few Terrans who took any time to show me around."

"I suppose it helped to be in business together. I found that interesting. It's not very common these days, is it?"

"We were never 'in business' together, Mr. Lanra. You're mistaken."

"Oh. I apologize—perhaps I misunderstood. You both owned shares in some of the same companies."

Chassik shook his head. "Even then, Rega was not sanguine about mixing with Spacers. If we *did* have common investments, it was quite by accident."

Coren nodded. "Ah. Forgive me. I was under the impression that he brought you in on a project."

"What project might that have been?"

"Something to do with prostheses, I believed. I forget the name of the company."

Chassik shrugged. "Rega showed some interest in our medical technologies along those lines, but nothing ever came of it. He found our procedures too invasive. Later on, his discomfort turned to fanaticism. We haven't spoken since he became head of that church of his."

"Which is why you'd like me to take your offer to him."

"Exactly, Mr. Lanra. I—oh, Ariel. I was just discussing political systems with your friend. The merits of Terran populist mandates, as opposed to good old-fashioned autocracy."

"No meddling, Gale," Ariel said, stopping before them.

"Never!" Chassik proclaimed with mock severity. "I'm so pleased to see you, Ariel. It's about time Setaris got over her snit and remembered your existence."

"*Was* it a snit? I thought it was a well-deserved vacation. Now I find I have to start working again."

"If there's anything I can do . . ."

"I think Sen would be displeased if you helped me get another vacation."

"You should come to work for us, Ariel," Chassik said. "We have a much more beneficent attitude toward sacrifice and service."

"Mmm. The only problem with that would be the travel."

Coren studied Ariel while she sparred with Chassik. He noticed then how different she seemed compared to the Spacers gathered here. His first thought was that she looked younger, but that was wrong. They all, for the most part, looked *young,* at least in that their skin was smooth, their eyes were clear, their hair thick and shimmering. But that could be purchased at any competent rejuve clinic. Earthers managed cosmetic youth up till their eighties and nineties, when the repairs failed for lack of anything dependable to repair.

No, Spacer youth was qualitatively different, something rejuve could never achieve. Instead, it was a static perfection, isolated in time, unchanging and unchanged. They looked like icons of health instead of people, archetypes of agelessness. Instead of perpetually young they were perpetually the same.

But not Ariel Burgess. For one thing, she was not young. Fine lines rayed from the corners of her eyes, and her laughlines were deep and permanent. A single chiselled dash deepened between her eyebrows when she concentrated and her skin, rather than the smooth porcelain austerity of her fellow Spacers, showed the reticulations of virgin, unrejuvenated or rehabbed derma.

She was not stuck in time.

Coren surveyed the crowd, checking his newfound perception to see how it held up. He saw exceptions, of course, and the Earthers were distinct by virtue of their evident age and the use of makeup where nature let them down. But for the most part observation confirmed expectation.

"—curious why you haven't challenged the blockade," Ariel was saying.

Coren's attention snapped back to Ariel and Chassik.

Chassik looked puzzled. "What business would it be of Solaria's to get in between a dispute between Earth and one of its unacknowledged offspring?"

"None, usually," Ariel said. "Except that Solaria holds title to Nova Levis. I assume, since you haven't deeded it to the colony, you still have some interest in it."

Chassik frowned. "I was unaware of any holdings by that name. Are you sure you have your facts correct?"

"It's possible the record is just incomplete. These things do get overlooked. Solaria owned the place outright about thirty-five years ago."

"Really? By that name?"

"No."

"Ah. Well, then you *do* have me at a disadvantage."

Ariel cocked her eyebrows. "I've never known you to be at a disadvantage. I'll have to remember this. Especially where something you once personally owned shares in is involved."

Chassik made a long show of assembling a plate of assorted delicacies, his lips pursed thoughtfully. "You're probing, Ariel. I don't think you know what it is you're looking for. You've heard a name, saw a bit of obsolete data, and you're jumping to conclusions. That got you in rather a lot of difficulty last year, didn't it?"

"In a way. Difficulties don't come from wrong conclusions."

"Oh, they can, though. Depends on how they're wrong.

This Nova Levis thing . . . rather arcane subject for the Calvin Institute liaison to concern herself with," Chassik said.

"Illicit traffic in positronics does concern me."

Chassik blinked, startled. "Accusations are beneath you, Ariel."

"I'm not making any, Ambassador."

"Nova Levis has been a de facto independent colony for nearly thirty years. I believe Aurora has sponsored a few such colonies itself, and I'm sure if you looked the actual ownership of those worlds may still be a matter of doubt. Does Aurora meddle in the internal workings of these colonies?" He shrugged. "What the situation is on the ground rarely matches what you find on paper. If Solaria hasn't signed over anything, it's simply a clerical error."

"Was it a clerical error," Coren asked, "when you divested your personal holdings in Nova Levis? If I recall correctly, you did so at the same time as Rega Looms sold his shares. Oh, but I forgot, you never did business together."

Ambassador Chassik's reaction moved through stages, from genuine bafflement to comprehension to an abrupt resumption of a professional mask.

"Ariel," he said drolly, "I rarely give advice, but in this case I think you need it. I admire and respect you, but you've shown truly questionable taste in paramours. You should be a little less reckless." He smiled at Coren. "Please excuse me."

Chassik sauntered away.

"What was *that?*" Ariel asked.

"Following your lead," Coren said. "Blind shooting. I turned up some interesting facts concerning that research lab you mentioned, Nova Levis. Your Ambassador Chassik was a primary shareholder. I wondered if maybe the two were related—the lab and the colony."

"Blind shooting. I'd love to see what you can do with your eyes open." She shook her head. "You guessed wrong, though. I wasn't shooting blind. Solaria still holds title to Nova Levis—the colony. It wasn't called that when they owned it."

"What was it called?"

"Cassus Thole."

A chime cut through the air like crystal.

"Dinner," Ariel said. "I hope the rest of the evening is as interesting as the hors d'oeuvres."

Coren left Ambassador Setaris's dinner gratefully. Through the excellent food and drink, the strain of trying to pay attention to *everything* gave him a mild headache.

Ariel wore a vague smile during the ride to the embassy lobby. Coren had expected to return to her apartment or office to talk, but when he began to mention it she shook her head distantly.

"Later," she said.

In the lobby, Coren became impatient. He held his tongue in front of the Auroran security guards, though, and let Ariel take his arm and walk with him through the exit.

On the plaza fronting the embassy, she said, "Let's get a car. I haven't been outside the embassy in months. I want to go for a ride."

Bewildered, Coren ordered a cab.

Once in the passenger section of the automated transport, her vagueness evaporated.

"Paranoia is a requirement for the job," she said, and punched in a series of random destinations in the cab's datum.

"Who do you think is listening?"

"My own people, for one. Add Chassik to the list." She turned to face him as the cab moved off. "All right, tell me what you know about this lab."

Coren recounted what he had discovered about Nova Levis Research. Ariel listened silently. When he finished she leaned her head back and gazed at the ceiling for a time.

"Alda Mikels and Gale Chassik together in the same investor's list makes sense," she said. "But Rega Looms?"

"Odd, I agree. But why would the colony be named for the lab?"

"You're sure it is? Could be coincidence."

"You could find out more about that than I could."

Ariel nodded. "I'll look into it."

"What did you mean about illicit positronics traffic?"

Ariel waved her hand. "Like you, blind shooting. I thought I might get a reaction. There has to be a reason Solaria never relinquished claim to Nova Levis. I thought perhaps they were using it as a transfer point for black market robotics. That could still be it, but I'm not sure Chassik knows anything about it."

"The entire Solarian government?" Coren asked dubiously.

"No, just factions. And he was right about the independence of those colonies. We lease the worlds, Settlers come in, after a time the colony charters its own government, and independence is a fact. There's never been a reason before for any kind of intervention. No precedent. I haven't checked yet, but maybe there's some old agreement that keeps Earth from demanding Solaria exercise rights of ownership. Or it could be that the fact has been lost in the name change. Even if there isn't, it may be that one department simply didn't know what the other was doing. 'Oh, that business of the deed? I thought *you* had taken care of that. Well, it isn't *my* responsibility.'" She smiled at Coren's laugh. "Contrary to what you Terrans believe, we Spacers are not of one mind. On any subject."

"That's not something I ever believed."

She leaned forward. "Rega Looms had to have a reason to invest in a biotech lab. Did he have any other investments like that?"

"Not that I know. I'll check, but I don't think so."

"So if it was just the one investment, the one lab, it seems logical he'd have a good reason."

"I suppose. But—"

"Probably a personal reason?"

"Where are you going with this?"

"Did he have any other children besides Nyom?"

Coren hesitated. A few days earlier he would have stated emphatically not, but now, after hearing the remarks of both Looms and Wenithal, he was less certain.

Instead of answering, he said, "There's something else. My errand to Baltimor District. The reason I was late. The shipping container Nyom used was routed out of Petrabor. Shipping schedules had been rearranged to accommodate it."

"Petrabor . . ."

"The reschedule came out of the ITE offices in Baltimor. I looked up an acquaintance from my Service days, a man named Brun Damik, who was in charge of the inspector's department of ITE, figuring that if anyone would know how to get in touch with the people who run the whole baley operation, he would. He led me to a retired cop named Wenithal. I found Rega's name in his old case logs, part of the same investigation that involved Nova Levis. According to the public record, no charges were filed against Nova

Levis, but the attention from the investigation must've been enough to sink it. It was bought by the Kysler Group and dismantled. Tonight, when I went back to ask Damik about his connection to Wenithal, I found police there. He'd been murdered. Tortured and murdered."

Ariel winced. "What was the case?"

"A kidnapping. It turned out to involve several orphanages and a couple of biotech labs, extending back several more years. Infants were being taken from orphanages, funneled through the labs, and shipped offplanet. A slave trade, of sorts."

"What did the labs have to do with it?"

"I don't know yet. But I found this—" he handed her the certificate he had taken from Damik's apartment "—hidden in Damik's office."

Ariel opened the sheet and studied it. "He was an orphan?"

"Interesting, isn't it? I never knew. We worked together and I never knew." He folded the document and put it back in his pocket. "Ree Wenithal sponsored him."

"Should you have known?"

Coren shrugged. "Maybe, maybe not. You don't expect the people you work with to hide that kind of thing from you after you admit to them that you're an orphan."

"You?"

"Seth Canobil Hospice and Social Rehabilitation Center. Lifelong resident. I graduated from there before entering the Academy."

Ariel seemed to think about that for a time. "All right, so you were both orphans. This police officer, Wenithal, was investigating a kidnapping. Children were stolen from orphanages and eventually sent offworld. To Nova Levis?"

"Maybe." He stared out the window for a time. "What is it we're supposed to be stopping Nova Levis from doing with this blockade?"

"You're insisting you have the right to on-ground inspection. You're looking for pirates."

"'You'? I thought Aurora was backing Earth on this one."

Ariel shrugged. "You notice we haven't sent any ships."

"Point taken."

"Where was Nyom Looms taking her baleys?"

"Nova Levis."

Ariel nodded. "I think we should have a talk to this police officer."

"I agree. But I'm not sure what good he is. His information is a couple of decades old."

"If Spacers are involved, that's meaningless. They can be very patient."

"'They'?"

She shrugged. "Sometimes I don't feel very much like one of them." She frowned. "But this might be the very same case your Mr. Wenithal was investigating. It may be that whatever was going on then has just come back home. If it ever really stopped. Why did he resign?"

"I don't know." Coren sighed. "There's something else."

"Always."

Coren laughed. "No, I mean another coincidence. I did a background on the warehouse where Nyom connected to her killers. I tried to find the dockworker who met them—a man named Yuri Pocivil. I did a trace and found out he was a Settler immigrant. From a colony called Cassus Thole."

Ariel stared at him. "The same as—?"

"I don't know. Interesting coincidence, don't you think? The fact is, he came to Earth six years ago—from Cassus Thole. Along with a good number more who all work for the same company. Six years ago. Long after Cassus Thole supposedly became Nova Levis. So either there are two colonies with the same name—"

"Or there's a problem inside ITE. Your acquaintance, Brun Damik—do you think . . . ?"

"It's something I intend to check into now."

"I think we need to find out what else this Hunter Group owns as well. Maybe we should ask Mr. Wenithal what corporations came up in his investigation."

"Settlers, Spacers, and Terran companies. Rather unusual circumstances that could bring them all together."

"In my experience, profit explains such anomalies nicely."

"But profit from what?" Coren asked.

"Kidnapping from orphanages."

"But—"

Ariel pointed. "That disk I gave you has a full screening of a blood sample taken from the finger joints of the robot Nyom Looms had with her."

"Blood."

She nodded. "We typed it, scanned it, and ran a match. It seems Nyom Looms had a brother."

SIXTEEN

The cab let them out in front of Lanra's building. Ariel followed him up the stairs to his office. The building showed considerable age—the stairs worn where countless feet had pressed upon them, dust accrued in corners, an uncovered access to conduit and wiring long unrepaired—but it seemed moderately well maintained. Cleaner than she might have expected in this old neighborhood, which lay on the outskirts of the Infant District, just off the Southwest Corridor of D.C.

A light glowed above Lanra's fourth floor office door, illuminating a nameplate—COREN LANRA, I.S.I.

"Do you have any neighbors here?" Ariel asked.

"An industrial cleaning firm," Coren said, gesturing toward the other lighted door down the hall. "The floor below is empty. Three businesses on the one below that. Two below that."

"And above?"

"Storage. Past tenants left stuff, paid to have it stored. Or not, but management kept it all anyway."

He let them in.

"It's a more prosperous district than that," he continued, "but there are only so many lawyers to fill available office space." He shrugged. "A lot of tenants have left in the last year. I don't know why."

"Trends are merciless."

He nodded distractedly. "Especially on real estate. Wait here a moment." He pushed through the inner door, to a private office. Ariel heard a brief verbal exchange and wondered if he had a secretary. The thought annoyed her for some reason. "All right, come in," Coren called.

When she stepped through the door she found Coren seated behind a broad desk, its surface illuminated by a touch-sensitive grid. He had taken off his jacket and was absently rubbing his left shoulder. Ariel studied the desk.

"That's impressive," she said.

"And as expensive as it looks. Sit down." He leaned over the desk then and started entering commands. His fingers danced deftly.

"AI?" she asked.

"Yes . . ." He inserted the disk Ariel had given him into a reader slot. A flatscreen extruded on one corner of the desk. Coren studied it. "The DNA is a close match . . . what are these other things? Proteins?"

"Derec hasn't finished his analysis yet. Proteins, yes, but there are a few puzzles—for instance, a high concentration of myralar."

"What's that?"

"A polymer, synthetic. A distant analog of nylon. It's used in robotics for joints, pivots, dry lubricant. Apparently the robot you found grabbed someone. We found the blood samples mixed with these other materials in its fingers."

Coren frowned at the screen. His fingers worked. "Not Nyom, but . . ."

"Very close."

Coren's glance flicked over her, a hint of irritation. "I didn't think robots could hurt anyone."

"Not intentionally, no."

"So where did the blood come from?"

Ariel shook her head. "We'll have to wait for Derec's excavation before we know that."

"You're so sure it couldn't have been the robot."

"Not *that* robot."

"And you don't believe in my second robot."

"I didn't say that."

Coren grunted. His eyes closed for several seconds. Ariel began to think he had just fallen asleep when he straightened abruptly in his chair. He winced as he stood.

"I'm sorry," he said, "would you like something to drink?"

"You're hurt."

Coren nodded. "I was rolled in Petrabor."

"When was this?"

"The last time I saw Nyom, when she left." He walked stiffly toward another door. "I think I could stand a drink, if you don't mind."

"You didn't say anything about being attacked."

He shrugged and went through the door. Ariel heard the faint sound of liquid on glass, then a deep groan. Silence stretched. Ariel went to the door and looked in.

Coren sat on a long divan, a drink perched on his right thigh, eyes shut. An open bottle sat on the low table before him. She lifted it to her nose and sniffed. Bourbon. She found a row of glasses on a shelf above a small liquor cabinet. She poured three fingers and studied the room.

Shelves, a pair of closet doors, another chair, a set of drawers. It reminded her of the monk's hole Derec had kept on the premises at Phylaxis.

Last year . . . ages ago . . .

A box lay open on top of the table. Ariel stared down at a collection of images of a young woman, almost gaunt, but with a bright smile and large eyes. She looked vaguely familiar.

Looms, she realized.

Coren cleared his throat. Ariel looked to see him watching her, a worried frown creasing his forehead. She picked up the top image.

"Nyom?"

He nodded.

Ariel dropped the picture. "This isn't a case file."

"Nyom wasn't a case."

"You're not doing this for Rega?"

"Partly. Mostly I'm doing it for myself."

"It's personal, then."

"Very."

Ariel pulled the chair close to the table and sat down across from him. "What's that like?"

Coren pulled himself straighter and set the glass on the table. "I don't think this is relevant."

"Maybe not to the universe at large," Ariel said with mock gravity. "But I'm interested."

"It's not very interesting. I resigned from Special Service almost six—no, seven years ago now. I tried running my own private security company for a year or so, but my best clients were always police agencies who needed a little extra expertise." He smiled grimly. "We private cops tend to be a little less constrained by legality than regular police. Anyway, it wasn't turning out the way I wanted it to. I'd quit because I didn't like the compromises I had to make on behalf of official policy and now I found myself compromising everything else to pay the rent. I started looking for a staff position in the private sector. Rega hired me about five years ago. I met Nyom seventeen months later."

"You remember it that clearly?"

"A very memorable sequence of events."

Ariel raised her glass to her mouth and said with mild sarcasm, "I suppose it was love at first sight." She took a sip.

"Don't smirk. It happens." He shook his head. "The thing is, I didn't know that till later. I thought it was just lust. Both of us. I thought she was doing it to irritate Rega, but he never knew. Nyom was nonconformist to a fault, but she didn't flaunt it. She wasn't looking for attention. Whatever else Rega might have done, he instilled a sense of purpose in her. She wanted her life to mean something." He shook his head. "That sounds superficial, doesn't it? The ultimate cliché."

"No. Not if it's real."

"Oh, it was real. That's how she ended up running baleys."

"Now *that* sounds like something aimed at her father."

"It's easy to think that, too. They didn't really get along. The truth is, Nyom knew things were wrong, that the way everything is put together is all messed up, but she didn't know how or why. She didn't know what would make it right. If anything could. So she moved from one cause to another, trying to find the formula for fixing the world. Rega just chose something that felt right and stuck with it. Nyom wasn't confident enough with her judgement to think she knew which one. Mostly, she ended up trying to help people do what they wanted when official policy got in their way."

"If it's a law, it's necessarily oppressive?"

"Something like that. Baley running was a natural for her."

"Is that what ended it between you?" Ariel asked.

Coren nodded. "Irreconcilable ideologies."

"You don't think anything is wrong?"

"No, no, not at all. I just can't see the use in tearing down everything you have until you can make it work."

"Very conservative."

"That's me."

"What will you do if you find that Nyom's view was right?"

"I have no idea." He leaned back. "Rega Looms has never lied to me before."

"You're referring to the possible existence of Nyom's brother?"

Coren nodded. "It doesn't make sense. Rega only had one child."

"That you know of."

"That I know of. Nyom never said anything either." He shook his head. "I hate being lied to."

"Maybe Rega just neglected to mention it. Has he always told you everything?"

Coren looked uncomfortable. "That would be a very dangerous omission on his part."

"Granted. But it's those things that can hurt us most that we never reveal, even when we should."

"Is that experience talking or a Spacer proverb?"

Ariel considered responding to the barb, but decided against it. "Assuming he lied about that, why? Did the child die?"

"There would be no reason to hide that. Even assuming Rega to be a callous opportunist—which he isn't—having a child die in infancy could only be a subject for sympathy. Why would a dead child be something to hide?"

"It might depend on how it died."

Coren shook his head. "No, if Rega has hidden it, then the child didn't die." His eyes narrowed. "Why are you interested in this?"

"My government—"

"Uh-uh. *You.* There's a difference between following orders and pursuing a goal. You're interested for your own reasons. Why?"

Ariel considered telling him about the note on her comm—*We're not finished with you*—but balked, unwilling even now to admit how much it frightened her.

"Maybe later," she said. "It's not important right now."

"We never reveal the things that can hurt us most?"

"Drop it," she said curtly.

Coren raised his hands in mock surrender. "Later, then. But I think you're going to have to tell me sometime."

"Then sometime I'll tell you."

"Preferably before it's too late to do you any good."

"May I ask another personal question?"

Coren made a gesture to continue.

"Has there been anyone since Nyom?"

Coren frowned thoughtfully, then picked up his glass. He shook his head. "I haven't made the time."

"Not interested, or just not ready?"

He glanced at her speculatively. "Are you making a suggestion?"

Ariel laughed, surprised. *Am I?* Thinking about it now, with Coren watching her, waiting, she realized that the same question applied to her. *It's been a year since Jonis. How long is long enough?*

"Maybe," she said. "When we have more time."

"Ah."

"Nova Levis," she said with emphasis.

"Yes. Our phantom research company. Or the colony."

The fragile mood broke and Ariel felt mildly self-conscious.

"They could be connected," she said.

Coren set down the glass and rubbed his eyes. "Maybe. Probably. Nova Levis, formerly Cassus Thole, is apparently involved in baleys in a big way. Warehouses, shipping, stolen cargo. Your complaining Spacers and their delayed shipments." He waved a hand. "Too much. I need sleep."

"I'm not tired."

"I can call you a cab if you want."

Ariel studied him, realizing that she did not want to go back to the embassy. Perhaps it was just being away from other Spacers and the confines of the mission precincts, but she was enjoying being here too much. That thought surprised her, too.

Coren looked at her. "Is something wrong?"

"No. If you don't mind, I'd like to stay here."

"Don't you have to report in?"

"Not if I don't want to."

"Senator Taprin—" Coren began.

"Old business."

"But is it over?"

"I thought it was. It would be nice to know for certain."

Coren coughed. "I am really, really tired."

"Do you have anything I can go over, then?" She smiled at him. "Or you can sleep. I'll watch."

He pushed himself up. "Let me finish up a couple of things." He walked woodenly into his office. Ariel could see him from where she sat. She wondered at herself: just what it was she intended with Coren Lanra; what she would do, and why. For the moment she was content to let her feelings run their course. It had been months since she had been interested in anything beyond her own self-denigration. Right now she felt in control, free to act instead of waiting for something to react against.

"Desk," Coren said, "have you completed compilation of the case files of Ree Wenithal?"

"I am sorry," the Desk said, "I have no record of such a request."

Coren's face went blank. "Desk, run review. I requested a survey of relevant material concerning the investigations of Ree Wenithal, reference downloaded material from disk yesterday."

A moment passed. "No such material is extant in memory."

"Run diagnostic."

Ariel felt her pulse quicken. "Your system is buffered, I assume?"

"Of course. The whole office is—"

"Diagnostic complete. Reference nine-one-oh."

Coren snatched Ariel's disk from the reader and tossed it to her. He worked furiously over the surface, then stood. He came back into the private room and went to the shelves.

"Something's infiltrated your system," Ariel said.

"That's the code reference you heard." He tucked small objects into his pockets, then grabbed an overcoat and a soft travel bag. He piled things in quickly, slammed the drawers, and returned to his desk. He studied readouts, nodded once, and entered more commands.

"What—?"

He raised a hand and shook his head. Ariel fell silent.

Finally, he shrugged on the overcoat, shut down the

Desk, and indicated the exit. Ariel preceded him through the door, across the reception area, and waited.

Coren Lanra pulled out a handgun. Ariel suppressed a shudder at the sight—the weapon looked compact and heavy, with an ominous green light on the frame just above the trigger guard. She was guessing, but it seemed lethal.

He leaned out into the hall, looked left and right, then took her arm. He guided her in the direction of the stairs and gave her a slight push.

Ariel stepped onto the stairwell landing and waited for Coren. When he emerged into the dusty gloom of the shaft, she asked quietly, "Do I get one of those?"

He studied her intently. "You know how to use one?"

"It's been known to happen."

He reached within the voluminous overcoat. A second later he pressed a fatal shape into her hand.

Ariel held it gingerly for a few seconds, studying it. A modified stunner with an extra powerpack and an amplifier along the generator coils. At close range, it would probably kill. She thumbed it on, felt the energy as a faint, numbing surge against her palm. She sited along the barrel a couple of times to get the feel of it, then nodded to Coren.

Coren led the way down the stairs. They had not seemed so dark on the way up, but now the shadows oppressed, the turns threatened. Ariel's pulse was racing by the time they reached the bottom.

"Stay here," Coren said, and stepped quickly out the door. A few seconds later he came back in. "This way."

Beneath the stairs he turned on a handflash. Ariel saw a heavy metal door with a keypad upon which Coren deftly entered a command. Old bolts lurched back and the door swung away from them.

In the light of Coren's flash Ariel made out another landing and a flight of skeletal stairs leading down to a sublevel. Coren closed the door behind them and shined the light above and around. A few cobwebs had gathered in high corners but not so many as might be expected.

Their feet clattered loudly on the bare metal steps. At the bottom, reddish-orange light pooled. Coren switched off his flash.

"That way," he said, pointing down one corridor, "leads to the garage. This way—" he indicated the passage leading straight from the stairs "—runs under the next several buildings in this block. There's access to lower levels."

"Do you own transport?"

"No."

"Then . . ."

He headed toward the garage.

Halfway down the passage a sound stopped Ariel. She glanced back, trying to comprehend what she had heard—a rasping noise, like rough cloth over gravel, or the hissing of water against a hot surface—yet fearing to see what could make it. But the narrow corridor was empty. She hurried to catch up to Coren.

They entered a storeroom. In the light of Coren's flash, she saw bins stacked high to the ceiling, filled with packages and angular shapes, and clusters of components and discarded parts. A workbench held a complicated mechanism that had been thoroughly dismantled.

Through another door they emerged into one of the garage levels. Bright lights imbedded in the ceiling painted sharp highlights upon the sleeping transports sitting in rows. Coren strode quickly along them, head swiveling, until he came to the end of one row. He dug in his jacket for something, then inserted a card into the reader on the transport door. He tapped a code into the lock. A moment later the door slid open.

"Get in."

Ariel went around to the passenger door.

Coren powered up the transport and eased it out of the slot.

Ariel glimpsed movement off to the right. Before she could speak, a large shape shot out in front of them, bounced off the hood, and landed heavily on the roof.

"What—?" Coren began.

His window burst in, spraying bits of shattered plastic across them. Ariel clutched the pistol while her free hand came up to protect her face.

The transport lurched to a halt.

Coren was half out the window when she looked again. He hooked his left leg awkwardly under the steering column and his right hand clutched at the frame separating the front and rear sections. An ugly hacking sound came from where she imagined his head must be.

Ariel opened her door. She gave the line of nearby transports a quick survey, then rolled out. She came up facing the vehicle and brought her weapon to bear.

The shape on the roof of the transport looked human. It was large, mostly covered in a long, colorless overcoat, one leg thrust back for balance along the front screen, foot sheathed in a heavy black boot.

She aimed.

A head appeared over the hunched shoulder. Eyes fixed her, unblinking and sharp. The face . . . the skin looked rough, disfigured . . . the hair was a ragged growth of oily brown and red.

It grinned at her.

It moved with alarming speed, turning toward her, crouching to spring—

Ariel fired.

The weapon felt warmer in her hand. The bolt of energy, nearly invisible, slammed into the assailant and tossed him from the roof of the transport like a mass of compressed air buffeting a rag.

He hit the pavement with a solid, meaty impact and a puff of air.

He sat up, shook his head, and looked at her.

Terrified, Ariel fired again.

The head snapped back, so savagely that it must have broken the neck. A few moments later, though, he began to stand.

Ariel watched, seized by amazement and fear, as he rose to his full height.

Shoot it again, she thought, but her finger did not flex against the stud.

He took a step toward her.

A brilliant splash of crimson-white burst against him. She glanced back toward the bolt's source: Coren had managed to get off a shot. The attacker screamed, a sound like a million sheets of paper ripping at once, and staggered back.

Ariel fired a third time. A pungent burnt odor filled the air.

The attacker fell to his knees, rose, then ran away.

All at once the stillness engulfed her.

Coren coughed.

Ariel came around the transport and found him lying on the pavement, holding his throat in one hand and his pistol in the other. She set her weapon down and helped him sit up with his back to the transport. He coughed and hacked for a minute, spit out a gob of phlegm, and sucked air in huge gasps.

"I know that hand," he said finally. "Son of a . . ."

He got to his feet shakily and looked around.

"Get your weapon," he rasped.

Ariel snatched up the stunner.

Coren accessed a different transport. He drove fast now, taking the turns recklessly until they made the avenue. Ariel waited till he slowed down to a normal speed before saying anything.

Before she could speak, though, Coren made an ugly throat-clearing noise and said, "He should've died. Only thing I can think of that could resist a shot like that is a robot. So tell me, Ambassador Burgess of the goddamned Calvin Institute, when did you people start making humanoid robots?"

"It wasn't a robot."

"No? Then what the hell was it?"

"Something we stopped playing with a very long time ago," she said. "A cyborg."

Ariel's hands trembled.

Figures, she thought wryly, *now that we're safe.*

Relatively *safe, anyway,* she added. Her eyes ached from trying to see all around her and into the darkness of third shift *faux* night. Coren drove them out of D.C., southwest, past industrial enclaves and private neighborhoods, through abandoned sections, and into an area Ariel had never been to. She recognized the main building from the subetheric—dimly, an old memory—as the headquarters for DyNan Manual Industries.

Coren got through all the security checks, sent the transport back where it belonged, and took her through unpopulated corridors to a suite of offices.

She watched him work a desk that was similar to the one in his private office, though, from the attention he gave to each command, it was far less sophisticated, not even close to an AI. Her pulse slowed, adrenalin drained away, and her fears took over in the form of the shakes.

Coren glanced her way and stopped what he was doing long enough to pour her a drink. Gratefully she sipped at the dark liquid. She had never been sure why alcohol helped at times like this—perhaps it was the care with which one had to take it in that distracted the mind from its own terrors—but she finished the tumbler of whiskey at the same time Coren sat down across from her.

"We're secure for the time being," he said.

Ariel nodded toward his desk. "Smart matrix?"

"An old one."

"Your desk is an AI."

"Was. Rega would never allow one on his property."

"I don't understand. If *you're* willing to use one, how do you—?"

"Life is a compromise. I prefer working for Rega to working for anyone else. That doesn't mean I agree with everything he says or believes." He smiled thinly. "Much like you, I imagine."

"Ah, well. To coin a phrase, 'That's different.'"

"Really. Well, I won't argue. How are you feeling?"

"Better," she said, raising the empty glass.

"Want another one?"

"Yes, but later. Too much comfort dulls the reflexes. How are you?"

Coren shook his head.

"Let me see your shoulder," Ariel said. She reached for his shirt.

Coren leaned away from her. "I'm all right."

"Of course you are. Let me see."

With obvious reluctance, Coren unzipped his shirt and pulled the left half away, revealing his shoulder. Ugly bruising spread from the base of his neck down to his clavicle.

"Have you seen a doctor?" she asked.

"In my spare time," he said grumpily and pulled the shirt back on. "Painblock."

"You'll pay for that."

"I know." He shrugged. "I made an appointment, but . . ."

He went to a sofa and sat down heavily, letting his head fall back.

"Your desk," Ariel said. "What happened?"

"Something got through my buffers," he said. "I had the AI doing a lot of in-depth searches. It was spread fairly thin and it must've become vulnerable."

"Or some of the files it was accessing were corrupted."

"Sleeper programs?"

"Maybe. If I could look at the software I could tell you. But bringing it here—"

"—would corrupt this system. Unless we knew exactly what had gotten through."

"Go to the head of the class."

Coren rubbed his shoulder, frowning. "This . . . cyborg. He's the one who rolled me in Petrabor."

"You're certain?"

"I think I'd remember a deathgrip like that." He frowned at her. "Unless there's more than one?"

"No," Ariel said suddenly, hoping it was true. "Let's not get more paranoid than we need to."

"*You* said it was a cyborg."

"I was guessing. I could be wrong—"

"But if you're not, what is it you're talking about?"

"A composite. An organic machine."

"I've seen some pretty impressive soldiers come out of—"

Ariel shook her head. "No, this different. I've seen those people, too, and they aren't like this."

"You said an organic machine. Like augmentation? Prostheses?"

"Far more intimately involved than that. Yes, you could claim that people with artificial limbs, organs, new skin, bone replacements are cyborgs, but it's a much too limited use of the term. No, people like that are still fundamentally human—there's a clear line of separation between the organic and the augmentation. You haven't replaced their basic being with a full-partner robotic symbiote. A cyborg is a blend of the two into a third kind of being."

"I don't quite follow."

"Neither did we. That's why we stopped fooling with them."

Coren scowled skeptically. "I thought Aurorans were the experts on robotic intelligence."

Ariel sat forward. "We are. That's what I mean. This isn't robotic intelligence. It's . . . something else. And we couldn't figure out what."

His disdain faded to a guarded respect. Ariel sat back, mollified.

"All right," he said. "I'm listening."

"A positronic brain," Ariel said, "is basically a sensory-data receiver-collator that operates by a collection of discrete parameters arranged in constellations that shift in response to new data. That's a gross simplification, but accurate enough for our purposes. We're talking about a few billion discrete parameters and nanosecond processing time, and a complete lack of an unconscious, and a few other additions and subtractions that allow us to actually program it while granting it a modicum of creative responses—"

Coren held up his hand. "I get the idea. I think. But that sounds like any other AI system."

"True. The key defining factor is in self-perception. A positronic brain is aware of itself. It is also aware of others as both distinct and collective entities that possess similar attributes."

"But—"

"I'm using the word 'aware' in exactly the way you would use it to describe yourself. An AI, no matter how sophisticated, is not aware. The best of them have fully-mapped models of their own make-up and function: a reference, if you will, that tells them what they are. But the relationship is always and only one of data referencing data in a strict modular process. A positronic brain possesses a sense of Self that is independent of models—it will continue to perceive itself *as* a Self even with extensive reprogramming that might in any other respect change the nature of what it does and what it knows—and a basic understanding of Self in others. That opens a huge gulf between an AI and a positronic brain. For instance, you could never infiltrate a positronic brain the way your desk was infiltrated. An AI, unless specifically commanded, will regard that infiltration as a problem in programming. It's just data. The more sophisticated the infiltration, the less likely it is to be aware of anything wrong. A positronic brain would immediately detect the attempt not as data but as damage. It would respond to it by treating it more or less as an infection. It would *feel* wrong. And if the infiltration were inimical to its loyalties, then the Three Laws would come into play. If it could not purge the infiltration, it would collapse. It would not tolerate a violation of its Self."

"Humans don't even do that," Coren said.

"Not as effectively, no," Ariel agreed. "But we have far fewer hardwired parameters and far more self-reprogramming parameters. We have both a sub- and an un-conscious. We can dream, we can imagine, we can lie, we can hallucinate. Reality is a conditional set of perceptions. The plasticity of our minds enables us to function even through gross distortions in our initial parameters. We imagine more richly and much faster than we process information. We're inextricably linked to our environment, but our perceptions of our environment are fluid. We can be fooled, deceived, manipulated. But it's a two-way exchange—the manipulator will be manipulated in turn through the interaction—but we can still function in the midst of deception and illusion. We can set aside our moral restrictions if need be—and we define our own need—and resume them later. If we choose. Humans, in short, can remake who they are at will. A positronic brain cannot."

Coren's face showed the effort to understand. Ariel stopped, unsure how much he followed.

"It borders on metaphysics," he said.

" 'Borders?' Hell, it *is* metaphysics. All the philosophical speculation of ten thousand years became concrete when the first positronic robot sat up and said hello to its makers."

Coren nodded slowly. "And a cyborg?"

Ariel sighed. "Positronic intelligence gave us another self-aware entity we could compare our own to and ask questions about the differences. It gave us the measuring stick to determine what is human and what is not. Cyborgs . . . break the measuring sticks and dump all those questions back in our laps."

She leaned forward again. "Imagine a positronic brain with all its capacity to analyze data and perceive the world as a material whole *all at once,* joined to something that can set its own parameters. There is no buffer, no unconscious to help process excess data or unpalatable information, and no preset responses to conditions. It has no basis for behavior other than what it chooses to have at any given moment."

"You've described a sociopath."

"A very, very fast, smart sociopath. A sociopath we can't begin to understand because we don't have a model for its mental processes."

"Why did you stop working with them?"

"We discovered that we couldn't program in the Three Laws. Something in the mix, probably—undoubtedly—from the organic side kept overwriting them. The one consistent attribute that emerged was self-preservation. Beyond that, we had no idea how to cope with them. After a while it seemed immoral to continue the experiments."

"Immoral. You actually shut down a line of research on moral grounds?"

"Why not? Spacers don't get to be moral?"

Coren shook his head. "No, it's not that. I—never mind. So you're saying that we were attacked by a cyborg."

"That's my first guess. A robot would never have done that. I doubt a human—even one of your military modifications—could have survived those shots. I'd like to hope I'm wrong, but . . ." Ariel blinked at him, suddenly understanding something. "I see. You Earthers wouldn't have shut down the experiments. You didn't. The only thing that kept you from building cyborgs was the fact that you'd outlawed positronics."

Coren's expression showed his ill-ease. He did not like

what she had said but he could not deny it. Ariel had always been puzzled by Terran perversity, the apparent willingness to do what clearly should not be done. But perhaps the real puzzle was why Spacers chose *not* to do those things. Maybe their long lives gave them a better understanding of consequences. Maybe their smaller populations made them less willing to take risks on questionable projects. Terrans seemed only to care in hindsight, when things went wrong.

One of their spasms of late conscience banished positronics...

"How," Coren said finally, "does this relate to Nyom Looms?"

"That robot you saw."

Coren nodded. "Cyborg."

"More than likely."

"And the blood Avery found on Nyom's robot..."

"A cyborg composed partly of a relative?"

Coren's face contorted in harsh distaste. "Where? How? We can't build them here, you won't build them there..." His eyes widened. "Pirates. Black market."

"A reasonable guess." *Which would explain Aurora's sudden interest in helping the Terran authorities with the baley problem. Where are all those baleys going?*

"Could someone somewhere be converting baleys—?"

"No. A cyborg doesn't work that way. You couldn't take a full-grown human and make the conversion." Ariel thought about that. "At least, I don't *think* you could. From what I recall, a cyborg has to be grown. The mix has to mature in symbiosis, so ideally you'd start with a fetus."

"A newborn?"

"Possibly. The organic system is still in transition

through puberty, so I suppose children could be used, but the older the material the more difficult the process."

"But where would they get all the raw material?" Coren asked.

"I said at the beginning of this evening that we need to talk to this retired policeman."

"Wenithal." He blinked. "Orphanages."

SEVENTEEN

Coren slept for an hour, then showered, swallowed more painblock, and found a change of clothes for Ariel. Dressed now in plain pants, work boots, and a dull blue jacket, she looked like any other T-rated office worker just off third shift, going home or shopping. He took her to the mall where RW Enterprises was and they waited in an open kitchen across from the entrance. Twenty minutes later, Wenithal emerged and trudged wearily down the concourse.

Ariel drifted away, quickly and unobtrusively falling several meters behind Wenithal on the way out of the mall. Coren was mildly surprised and impressed at how quickly and easily she blended with Terrans. The more time he spent with her the less Spacer she seemed.

He sat at a table at the edge of the pantry, nibbling on a meat pastry and sipping a cup of acrid coffee. After about ten minutes, he crumpled up the wrapper and dropped it and the half-full cup into the waste.

At the door to RW Enterprises, he took out his palm monitor and a small device that he pressed to the wall just below the lock. While it worked to decode the access sequence, Coren pulled out a few of his little devices and activated them. He glanced around. The mall was pretty deserted, but a few people milled around. The trick was to gain entry as fast as possible, making it look as if he had been admitted. The longer it took the more conspicuous he became.

The palm monitor chirped at him. He had the code. He entered a command that turned the ID scan on the door into a recorder, pocketed the reader, and pressed his right hand against the panel above the lock. A second later, the door slid open for him.

He snatched his decoder from the wall and dropped his devices just inside the doorway. They scurried off to run interference for him as he proceeded on, into the plant.

Machinery hummed. Coren went directly to Wenithal's private office. As he stepped through the door, he thumbed his hemisphere for a little added security, set it in the middle of Wenithal's cluttered desk, and paused.

Where to start?

Coren did a slow turn.

It was a working office, that was clear. A few changes of clothes lay scattered over chairs, stacks of paper and disks filled corners, three empty cups sat on the desk.

Coren looked for a personal datum. He found it tucked in a desk drawer.

He took a disk from his pocket and inserted it into the datum's reader. The screen scrolled up, went cloudy, then blank. Coren waited, listening intently to the distant sounds of automated machinery.

Less than a minute later—a long time for the decryption 'ware Coren used—the screen presented a menu.

Letters, memos, profiles on clients, quarterly reports. Coren opened the latest of these and perused RW Enterprise's Profts and Losses statements. One of the largest customers, he noted, was a Solarian firm—Strychos—that bought nearly half a million meters of a synthetic fabric a year. The lot was identified only by a batch number. Coren opened his palm monitor, switched it to record, and began taking notes.

Far down the menu he found a file named GRATUITIES. Coren grunted in surprise. *Well, he never thought anyone would open this . . .*

The file contained what it suggested: a list of people to whom Wenithal paid bribes.

Brun Damik was halfway down. A very generous allocation.

Gale Chassik appeared several lines further.

Coren copied the list and closed the file. Studying the menu, he wondered how much more he needed to know about Ree Wenithal.

Why you resigned after becoming a hero would be useful . . .

He saw nothing that would seem to contain the answer to that, so he closed the datum down and returned it to the desk drawer.

So Wenithal was paying bribes to Damik. Coren still did not understand what any of this had to do with baleys . . . though he felt he should know.

There were several files of correspondence. Coren opened each one and perused addresses. He found several to a location in Petrabor. The documents themselves proved cryptic—evidently a code Coren did not recognize. Still, messages to someone in Petrabor seemed suggestive enough. He looked for replies and found them attached to each document—all of them were initialed either T.R. or Y.P.

Yuri Pocivil . . . ?

Coren swiveled in the chair, searching the office walls. Nothing.

He closed up his palm monitor and left the office. Sitting down at one of the secretarial stations, he accessed the production records. He located the batch number for the synthetic, and went into the main plant to look for it.

The synthesizers looked like huge columns of dark gray segments piled high to the ceiling. Heavy conduits ran from their bases back into the shadows of the cavernous chamber. They hummed with activity, though only a few seemed to be outputting product into the deep troughs below their extrusion slots.

Coren followed the row of machines to the one marked "Line 18" and stopped. It was on—they all were, it cost too much to shut them down completely and restart them—but nothing was coming out. Coren studied the control panel.

"Imbitek," he noted, recognizing the logo. He keyed for access. The screen gave him a list of options. He entered the code for a sample.

Less than a minute later, a meter of black fabric oozed from the machine into the trough. The cutter came down with a heavy thud to chop it off, and Coren picked up the sample.

It was remarkably thin, almost insubstantial, and he found it difficult to hold, its surface friction nearly nonexistent. He managed to fold it down to a square that fit into his pocket with no more bulge than a handkerchief.

He walked away from RW Enterprises as if he were late for an appointment, briskly but not so fast as to look culpable. Outside the mall, he called Ariel.

* * *

Ree Wenithal lived modestly for his income. His apartments occupied two floors of an old warren complex that had once been a barracks for factory workers, then converted into luxury apartments nearly a century ago, and now had evolved into many things: apartments, clinics, retail shops, storerooms, offices. Coren was amused to find two private investigation agencies listed.

Ariel waited across from the arched entry to Wenithal's warren, sitting at an autochef with a cup of hot cocoa, doing a reasonably effective imitation of someone who had just gotten off-shift and on her way to well-earned sleep.

"Did you follow him all the way in?" Coren asked, sliding onto the stool beside her.

"No. I'm not altogether certain he didn't see me, so I thought I'd better not. Did you find anything?"

"Some, but I'm not sure if it means much. He runs a business." Coren shrugged. "He's paying bribes to Chassik."

Ariel frowned. "He does business with Solarians?"

"A couple. Pretty big accounts."

"Solaria manufactures its own textiles. What are they buying from Earth?"

"A half-million meters a year of a synthetic." He showed her the sample. "If I'm not mistaken, this is myralar."

Ariel ran a finger over its slippery surface. "I'd have to analyze it, but it feels right. Hm. Half a million meters a year? That's a lot, but not enormous." She shook her head. "Maybe I'll ask Chassik."

Coren drummed his fingers on the counter. "I've got his P&L records, we can go over them later. I don't think we'll find anything conclusive, though. He was bribing Damik, too. The bribe is unusually large, more than I would have guessed Damik would be worth."

"Did Damik have something over Wenithal?"

"It's a thought . . . but that's not the feeling I got when I followed Damik to his meeting with Wenithal. Everything about it said Wenithal was the one in charge." He glanced at her cup. "Are you done?"

Ariel held up the cocoa and wrinkled her nose. "Before I started. Let's go talk to your ex-policeman."

They passed under the archway and started down a path lined with poorly-tended shrubbery. A number of the growlamps above them were out. Coren glanced around the area, and frowned.

"What's wrong?" Ariel asked.

"Hm? Oh. Nothing . . ." He glanced up at the tall windows to his right. Balconies and walkways hung higher up. "That's not true. I'm not sure if I can explain it."

"Try. I'm always eager to learn new things."

Coren looked at her. He saw no sign of sarcasm in her expression. Indeed, she seemed intent only on their surroundings.

"Well," he said, "usually when someone has a connection to a case—I'm talking like Service now—you might find someone through one source, one link, but when you look, if there *is* a connection, there's more than just one."

"And with Ree Wenithal?"

"There are suggestions of more connections, but I still have only one: Brun Damik. And *his* connection was tenuous."

"Until he died."

"That was a pretty strong hint, but not really a connection."

She frowned at him. "Just what do you count as a connection?"

"Something with steel cables tying it to something else."

"Isn't that a bit unrealistic?"

Coren stopped. Ariel continued on a few more steps, then turned to him.

"Early on," he said, "I arrested an innocent man. It wasn't a big deal, nothing bad happened to him, he just spent a few nights in confinement, went through a lot of humiliating interrogations and filled out a lot of forms. It was a mistake. I think *I* felt worse about it than he did."

"So you vowed never to make a mistake again?"

"No, but I got into certain habits after that. I made fewer mistakes. I became pretty good at it. And I got overconfident."

"And made a big mistake."

"Very. It cost me the life of a friend."

"You're talking about Nyom Looms."

Coren nodded.

Ariel pursed her lips. "High standards are good."

They continued on to Wenithal's apartment in silence.

The door stood open.

"Come in," Wenithal called. "I was beginning to wonder if you'd ever get here."

Ree Wenithal sat on a long couch, slippered feet propped on a low table, a glass in his left hand and a pistol in his right. He scowled at them for a long moment, then laughed.

"You! I thought it would be someone else." He set the pistol aside. "Close the door if you're staying."

Ariel pressed the contact. The light from the balcony shrank to a narrow line and vanished.

The room smelled of alcohol.

"So," Wenithal said, "did you go through my files?"

Coren hesitated.

"My career," Wenithal said, stressing each syllable. "My exploits. They're all in the public record. They'll tell you all about me, about my life, my accomplishments, my . . . my . . ." He waved a hand vaguely. "Everything."

"I looked at them," Coren said.

Wenithal waited. When Coren said nothing more, he got ponderously to his feet. "Are you going to introduce me to your partner? Oh, if you want a drink, help yourselves. I keep a good stock. Even some Spacer stuff."

"Brun Damik is dead," Coren said.

Wenithal nodded. "I was questioned about it."

"Uh-huh. Do you have any idea why he was killed?"

"Do you?"

Coren crossed the room in four strides and snapped his palm into Wenithal's chest. The older man sat back down heavily, his wind wheezing from his mouth.

"We were attacked earlier tonight," Coren said. "I'm in no mood for repartée, *Mister* Wenithal, so do me the courtesy of answering my questions directly."

"I don't have to tell you shit," Wenithal said breathily.

"Fine. Then when the people you *were* expecting come to kill you, I hope you have some friends to attend the services."

Wenithal glared up at Coren, but his eyes wavered moistly and Coren caught the distant shimmer of fear behind them.

"Something killed Nyom Looms and Brun Damik and fifty baleys who just wanted to get off Earth," he continued. "Something tried to kill me tonight, and something is coming after you. You used to be a cop. Pretend you still are for the next ten minutes and do the right thing." He paused. "Or do you already know who these people are?"

Wenithal tried to heave himself up, but Coren rapped him in the sternum again. "You're a bastard," Wenithal hissed.

"Do you know that for a fact, or just speculating?"

Wenithal slapped at Coren half-heartedly, missing. Coren watched the old man warily, but it was obvious Wenithal would do very little now.

"What do you want?" he asked grumpily.

"The same thing I wanted the first time we spoke: information."

"I don't have any to give you."

"Bullshit." Coren wanted to shake Wenithal. "How long would you have played games like this when you were a cop?"

"When I wasn't pretending, you mean?" Wenithal grunted. "I wouldn't have played them at all." He shrugged, tried to sit up straighter, then nodded. "All right . . . what do you want to know first?"

Coren picked up Wenithal's glass and smelled it: Akvet. A Theian drink, a variation on absinthe. No wonder Wenithal was so intoxicated so quickly.

"What were you going to do when the bad guys came?" Coren asked. "Play dead?"

"Very funny . . ."

Coren looked at Ariel. "Would you see if there's any stimulant around? Coffee, capvitane, sniff, whatever."

Ariel raised an eyebrow speculatively, then nodded and headed further into the apartment.

"There's coffee," Wenithal called after her. He looked up at Coren. "What do you want to know?"

"First, why did Damik see you after I talked to him?"

"What did you ask him for?"

"I wanted to know who ran the whole baley enterprise. The real managers, not the dockside people."

"Ah." Wenithal grinned again. "That's clever. He never

believed he could get caught. Ex-Special Service, you know about that. So he wasn't ready when someone came asking the right questions. Of course, you realize, it got him killed."

"We were screened. No one overheard our conversation."

"So? It's all connections. People looking for other people. Links get made, conclusions drawn. Brun was killed on spec."

Ariel returned with a cup of steaming coffee and set it down on the table before Wenithal. He stared at it for a long time, then lurched forward to grasp it.

"I don't drink much anymore," he said. "Not used to it."

"Seems a suicidal habit to start up again just now," Ariel said.

"If I'm drunk enough it might not hurt so much." He lifted the cup to his lips and held it there, poised.

"Brun was an orphan," Coren said. "You sponsored him. Why? Did you know his parents?"

Wenithal stared at him.

"The Holmer Foster Gymnas Cooperative," Coren said.

Wenithal focussed on him. "You knew?"

"We *did* work together once," Coren said evasively.

"Mm. I suppose that counts for something." He took another drink and scowled. "Something about the acids never mix right with the wormwood..." He set the cup down and rubbed his eyes with the heels of his hands. "There was a kidnapping. Oh... when was that?... twenty-something... a long time ago. A district manager for a company that no longer exists. Very high profile. Like an idiot he went to the newsnets first, made everything very difficult for us. The thing was, no ransom demand ever came. The child just disappeared and that was it. It wasn't my case initially, I was called in later, but... anyway, we had nothing to go on, no thread to follow through the maze. When we started looking through the database for similar cases, a pattern began to emerge. Hundreds of unsolved kidnappings all over the world over the previous decade, none of them with a common denominator other than the complete absence of further contact." Wenithal grinned crookedly. "The problem with databases—AIs, smart matrices, logic systems—is that if you don't ask just the right question you never get the answer you need."

"Hundreds," Ariel said. "That many, they had to be going somewhere."

Wenithal raised a finger. "Absolutely. But where? After canvassing and recanvassing witnesses, acquaintances, associates, total strangers who might possibly have seen or heard something—anything—I started expanding the search. I started looking at schools, hospitals, orphanages."

"You found the link in orphanages."

Wenithal nodded. "Not all of them, though. Special ones, ones that took in and maintained 'problem' children. Infants with defects, genetic problems, congenital and chronic illnesses. Children turned over to the institution and their records sealed or, in some cases, erased. It was difficult to detect, actually, but I found several of them doing a backdoor business in what they delicately termed 'material.'"

"Selling the children?" Ariel asked.

"Basically. Oh, they claimed they were selling cadavers, but the numbers were too high and the age groups too coincidental. It took a long time to finally prove what I knew was going on."

"And Brun?" Coren urged.

"I didn't know his parents very well. They were part of a

series of interviews I conducted in relation to the case, but they didn't really have anything to do with it. They'd tried to adopt, that was all. After Brun they'd been told not to try another natural birth, not without a complicated gene therapy they couldn't afford. Shortly afterward, there was an accident. A semiballistic struck an old piece of orbital debris. Ninety or so passengers and crew. Holmer Foster was the local institution. I felt . . . an interest, I suppose. Brun was bright, nine years old. When I checked on him two years later, he was running a kind of black market in his facility, using smuggled-in recordings, access codes, food allotments. I thought it was a waste of natural talent. So I sponsored him."

"You didn't adopt him?"

"A police officer? Where would I find the time? No, sponsoring was about the best I could do. It was actually Brun who told me about the missing UPDs."

"UPDs?" Ariel asked.

"Untreatable Physiological Dysfunction. Children with disorders that can only be watched. Often they can't even stop their pain. Those were the ones I found out were going missing the most."

"That doesn't make sense," Ariel said. "What use—? Oh."

Wenithal glanced at her. "Research, spare parts, other things I never cared to think about."

"You're sure they were being shipped offplanet?" Coren asked.

"That's where the trail went cold. We traced them to four or five labs. They all funneled the 'material' through a single lab that I could never really prove was involved."

"Let me guess," Coren said. "Nova Levis?"

"Very good. You must've been a decent cop."

"I still am. Who was running the operation?"

"Very corporate. But I could never prove it. I know it, but I can't take it to court."

"Imbitek," Ariel said.

Wenithal shrugged.

"How did that tie in with the kidnapping that brought you into it?" Coren asked.

"That was the most perverse component. The boy that was kidnapped was just a normal boy. It didn't make sense in light of what I had found out about these ... these ... flesh mills. So I took a closer look at my concerned parents and found that they had had two previous children. One had died shortly after birth, the other ... the records had been manipulated. The claimed death was not a death. They relegated it to one of these orphanages. There *was* a connection." Wenithal frowned at Coren. "Do you even want to know? You work for Rega Looms, how much do you know about him?"

"I—"

The door chimed.

Wenithal groped for his pistol.

"Take it easy," Coren said quietly, easing his own weapon out. He looked at Ariel and gestured for her to move to the far side of the room. Coren moved quickly to the wall alongside the door. He nodded to Wenithal, who brought his pistol into his lap.

"Enter."

Coren tensed as the door slid open. Light from the balcony outside spilled across the carpet, outlining a shadow. Wenithal raised the pistol.

Coren stepped away from the wall, aiming at head height.

A sharp hiss and a muffled "Shit!" came from the person standing in Wenithal's entryway.

The light in the room brightened, revealing a woman in dark clothes with a heavy pack slung over her left shoulder. She gaped at Coren, stunned.

"Jeta Fromm," Coren said. "I've been looking all over for you."

EIGHTEEN

The lab datum has been compromised, Derec," Thales announced.

Derec looked up from the screen and blinked. "What?"

"The lab datum has been compromised," the RI repeated. "I have detected nine gates placed at various locations within the system that are diverting information to an external source."

"What about you?"

"I have already detected and blocked an attempt to establish a gate in the immediate array. Judging from the other gates, this will not be a problem; they are sophisticated but limited. However, the longer I block implementation, the more likely other measures will be taken."

"In other words, they're not just giving up and going away."

"Essentially, yes."

Derec went to the end of the blind and looked across the lab. Only one tech was on duty, this late in the third shift.

Derec returned to his chair and rubbed his eyes. He had been at it since arriving, nearly eighteen hours now. The excavation was proceeding more slowly than he had expected due to a series of defensive modifications someone had added to the DW-12. It took Rana several hours to tease through them with Thales' help. Once they understood that bypassing them would not corrupt the matrix any further, everything went smoothly, but making sure ate up a lot of time.

"How soon?" Derec asked.

"Regarding what?"

"The excavation. When do we start getting useful data?"

"I have isolated the constellation of memory nodes we need, and I am beginning a chronological assignment. Another hour."

"I want your findings copied directly to Ariel's datum."

"That precaution is already in place."

"Are you able to trace the gates to their external source?"

"The risk of detection is high. I suggest completing the task at hand first before attempting any further action."

Derec reached for the cup of cold coffee on the workbench. He needed sleep. He had sent Rana to her apartment hours ago.

He felt the passing of time acutely. Ariel had not commed in over five hours. Sipha Palen estimated she could keep the deaths out of the newsnets for another day, two days at most, before someone figured out that she was hiding something. Or—and Derec thought this more likely—someone who already knew would sell the information. In either case, this needed to be done quickly.

"I would like to talk to you about another matter, Derec," Thales said.

"Hm? What, Thales?"

"I have taken advantage of the access here to larger memory buffers to set up my examination of Bogard's positronic matrix. I have run six attempts at reestablishing a functional template."

I forgot all about that, Derec thought uneasily. "I didn't know you'd done that."

"It has not interfered with the performance of any other task," Thales said. "As we do not know if another opportunity may occur, I thought it best to use this one."

"That's fine, Thales. Um . . . six attempts? I gather none of them have been successful?"

"In achieving a stable matrix, no. However, I believe I have achieved something positive. I now know that we cannot do more in simulation. The convolutions in the error log indicate the presence of a reifying condition."

"I'm not sure I understand."

"Basically, there is a command error which repeatedly instructs the matrix to disassemble at the same point. I could not be sure of this before because I was forced to continually reconfigure the parameters to accommodate the lack of memory. Now that this is no longer a problem, I see that the breakdown occurs at the same point each time."

Derec leaned forward, curiosity cutting through weariness. "Can you identify that point?"

"That is the difficulty. It seems to be in the checksum routine that oversees the data interface with the physical plant."

"Seems to be?"

"It is possible the error precedes that point, which is why I am unwilling to be more confident. But in each case the breakdown occurs at the place where the program attempts to command the actual body. There is no body, of course, and I am studying the options to construct one in simulation, but I am not convinced this can be solved that way. I am of the opinion that the error is tied to the violation that caused the initial collapse. It may be that what I am seeing is not an error at all but an irreconcilable dilemma. In either case, the error effectively orders a new collapse each time. Available memory is not the problem. The matrix itself is self-destructive."

"That doesn't make any sense, Thales. That would suggest intent on some level. There isn't enough coherence for that to be the case."

"Under normal circumstances, I would agree with that assessment. However, Bogard was unusual in several respects and its termination was singularly traumatic."

"All right. The next question, obviously, is what do you propose we do about it?"

"It is possible that the error can be resolved by loading a partially reestablished matrix into a blank positronic brain and tracing the final connections through to see if the error persists."

"Treat it like a hardware problem, you mean."

"Essentially, Derec."

Derec smiled. "And where do you propose we obtain a blank positronic brain?"

"We have one at hand—after I have completed my excavation."

Derec looked at the DW-12 lying on the table, cables snaking from it, connecting it to the board Thales was using.

"It's not at all what Bogard would be used to," he said. "That assumes we're allowed to use it at all."

"If I may point out the obvious, the owner is no longer a matter of concern."

"Heirs, Thales."

"I have considered that. Do you really think Rega Looms will want it?"

Derec laughed dryly. "No, I don't imagine so. But Sipha Palen has authority. It's station security property."

"With all due respect, Derec, Chief Palen has procured the robot under false pretext. She has filed no official records that it even exists on Kopernik. Effectively, the robot occupies a legal void. It belongs technically to no one. I believe my position is defensible in Terran court."

"It may be, but..." Derec sighed. His brief spurt of energy was ebbing. He needed sleep. "I can't make this decision now, Thales. We have other matters to resolve first."

"Would you object if I created an implementation program in the event that we do make use of the robot?"

"No, of course not. Right now, though, we need that excavation."

"It will be completed in fifty-two minutes."

"Good, good." He regarded the screens before him speculatively. Somewhere in all that machinery was a consciousness. It surprised him sometimes how easily he disregarded the inorganic nature of positronic entities. "Thales, why are you so interested in Bogard?"

"Why?"

"Yes, why."

"Bogard is a problem you set me to solve."

"True, but—never mind now. Thales, I may doze off sitting here. If anything happens that I need to know about, wake me."

"Of course, Derec."

He closed his eyes. He did not fall immediately to sleep, though. He could not shake the feeling—tenuous, barely identifiable—that Thales had just evaded answering his question.

"The question of will in a positronic matrix is and may remain one of the unsolved—and unsolvable—mysteries about these minds we have created. We built them to serve us and in that matter they have no choice. But we then gave them an imperative to serve not our commands but our morality. To assume this makes them thrall to human will to exclusion of their own may be an error."

Who said that? Derec fished through his memory until he found it. Ariel had said that, in her graduate thesis from the Calvin Institute.

Something to that . . .

A constant question in positronics—one most positronic specialists toyed with but never wanted to discuss—concerned the hardware: How much of a robot's "personality" depended on the actual mechanism, and how much on what was called "accrued experiential associations"? The easy answer—always—was that a positronic brain was entirely a matter of physical linkages and connections, tied directly to its sensory apparatus—the "real world" model that allowed them to make deterministic decisions based on the Three Law parameters encoded into the pathways.

But that begged the question; it did not address the problem of Mind. Derec had come up against it with Bogard and now with Thales—why, he wondered, could Thales not simply construct a matrix very much like Bogard's? Evidently, Thales could not. Bogard's physical modifications had been an integral part of its consciousness. Thales' suggestion that the entire matrix be reinserted in a blank brain reinforced the obvious: that a robot was inextricably mechanistic, even though it demonstrated consciousness very similar to a human.

How many humans willingly admitted that they were as much meat as mind?

Derec yawned, and sparks danced at the edge of his vision. Too much, too deep. He waited for sleep. But his mind writhed with questions.

"Mr. Avery."

Derec opened one eye and looked up at Hofton. "Mmm?"

"We have a problem." Hofton nodded toward the lab.

Derec stood slowly. A huddle of people crowded at the entrance. He recognized Palen, Leri, and Polifos, all apparently on one side of an argument, facing four Terrans—two men, two women—whose clothes—neatly-cut, unadorned, and severe—suggested authority. They spoke in low, terse tones that even without knowing the subject made Derec apprehensive.

"Thales, how far along are we with the excavation?"

"I require a few more minutes, Derec."

"Who are they, Hofton?"

"TBI," Hofton said. "Leri, to his credit, is fending them off with implied threats of 'political repercussions' and 'violation of sovereignty,' but they aren't really backing down. They want the robot. My sense is that they intend to take it regardless of the consequences."

Derec glanced at the DW-12. "Why would they want a robot?"

"Not *a* robot—*that* robot. They know exactly where it came from and what it is."

"Thales, those leaks—"

"It is possible they were TBI monitors," Thales said. "I did not trace them for the reasons we discussed."

Derec studied the group. "Palen looks upset."

"I would be, too. Evidently her authority is being challenged. I suspect she'll lose, but she may be able to delay any immediate action."

"It may be a moot point, anyway." He leaned over the console. "Thales, complete the excavation, copy all material to Ariel's office, then start tracing those monitors. Be careful not to reveal your presence as more than a security trace."

"Yes, Derec."

Derec smoothed his shirt and ran a hand through his hair. Hofton watched him speculatively.

"Shall we?" Derec gestured toward the confrontation.

"Your lead, sir."

Derec approached, Hofton a pace behind. Polifos noticed him first and tapped Ambassador Leri's arm. The discussion died immediately with everyone looking at Derec.

"Excuse me, but I couldn't help noticing," Derec said. "TBI?"

One agent nodded slowly. "You are . . . ?"

"Derec Avery. I gather you've come about the matter of the robot?"

Palen glared at him, outraged. The TBI agents frowned uncertainly.

"You have in your possession—" the first agent began.

"Pardon me," Derec interrupted, "you are . . . ?"

"Agent Harwol."

"Pleased to meet you. And these others?"

Harwol waved a hand in the direction of his male partner, then each of the women. "Um . . . Agent Gerit, Agent Jallimolan, Agent Cranert . . ."

"Pleased." Derec gestured toward Hofton. "This is Liaison Officer Hofton of the Auroran Embassy, D.C."

Awkward nods passed around the group. Derec noticed that Polifos looked baffled, but Leri was suppressing a smile.

"Now," Derec continued, "I'm the positronic specialist in charge of examining that robot. I have authority from Ambassador Sen Setaris to do so. It's my understanding that diplomatic considerations require that you have a proper warrant, countersigned by Ambassador Setaris, before I can turn any of our property over to you."

Agent Harwol made a chopping motion with his hand. "Not in matters concerning the death of TBI or other Terran police personnel. We have an overriding interest in that robot, which we'll be happy to take up at a later date in court with Ambassador Setaris. But right now we insist that you turn over the robot in question."

"For what purpose?"

Agent Harwol frowned.

"What do you intend to do with it, Agent Harwol? It's a collapsed positronic robot. Basically, so much scrap as it is. What do you propose to do with it?"

"That's not germane to this situation—"

"But it might be. You see, if you intend to turn it over to your own specialists for examination, then we may be able to save you time."

Harwol exchanged looks with his fellow agents.

"What do you propose?" he asked.

"We're already doing the only examination that might produce results. I'm sure that sharing our data with you wouldn't be out of the question. Ambassador Leri?"

"Well, under the circumstances, it would be unusual," Leri replied. "I'd have to vett it through Ambassador Setaris, of course, but I don't see a significant problem. Cooperation with Terran authority is always preferable to confrontation."

Chief Palen no longer seemed angry, but Derec felt uneasy under her gaze.

"We'll have to post an agent with the robot," Harwol said.

"That's out of the question—" Polifos began.

Leri jabbed his elbow into Polifos's ribs. "In company with one of our own security officers," he said, "I don't see a problem with that."

Harwol looked miserable. Derec guessed that his orders had been vague but succinct. He was ill-prepared to negotiate, and he knew his presence in Auroran embassy precincts was questionable at best.

"We require full disclosure," he said.

"We would probably require your help in any case," Hofton said. "I am curious, though. You said in the case of a death of a Terran agent. What Terran agent?"

Harwol clasped his hands behind his back and shook his head.

Derec stared at him. "You had agents in that group of baleys."

Harwol met his stare stoically. Finally, though, he nodded.

"Shit," Palen hissed.

"Well," Hofton said, "that changes a few things."

Derec stepped up to Palen. "Maybe you should show us the crime scene now. I think it's time we all see for ourselves."

Derec gazed up at the cargo bin. Till now, he had only seen it on a screen. Small and manipulable on his desktop, it lacked any impact. Here, though, it disturbed him. It was both larger and smaller than he had expected.

People were going to travel to another star system in this . . . ?

Lights shone within the container. Folding tables held

portable datums, but no one paid any attention to them. Derec looked at the office where Palen and Harwol talked with Leri and Hofton. Derec feared a jurisdictional fight, the worst kind of battle. Hofton, at least, was capable of steering the situation past that—if he was allowed to.

Derec wandered to the row of datums, keeping watch out of the corner of his eyes for any move from the armed officers spaced around the bay to stop him. He occupied a fuzzy zone in the hierarchy, so the odds were even that he could do nearly anything he wanted.

Most of the screens showed blank. Two contained schematics of the interior of the bin. A third showed a chemical analysis of some kind. To Derec, it looked like a crystalline structure, but he could not identify it. He stepped closer to one of the schematics.

Cages supported acceleration couches arrayed around the inside surface of the bin. A very simple design, easily modified, completely modular. The rebreather unit sat bolted to what was now the floor but in freefall would be just another bulkhead.

Fifty-three couches.

How many bodies?

Fifty-two. Logically, the empty couch would have held the murderer.

Who got out how, exactly? Derec wondered.

The only evidence of escape was the crack in the hull in which Nyom Looms' body had caught. But that hole was far too small for anyone to slip through.

So that meant the killer did everything before lift-off and remained on Earth.

That did not follow, either. What would have prevented the robot from opening the hatch and saving the baleys by just admitting fresh air? No, the only time the poison would have been effective—and the robot ineffective—would have been in freefall, in vacuum.

Therefore, the killer was in the container and committed the murders en route to Kopernik.

The crack let out the atmosphere, forcing the baleys to stay on the rebreather, which eventually poisoned them. The robot had attempted to intervene—hence the blood and material in its hands—and failed. It would have been forced to do what? Whatever it could. It was found trying to shut off the rebreather.

Which would have meant suffocation for the baleys.

Either way, they would be dead.

So one of the bodies removed from the bin had to be the killer. Easy enough to check, just find one with torn clothes.

But how could the DW-12 attack a human?

And what about that empty couch? Derec assumed they would have known how many passengers, so what good would one extra couch be unless it was for someone who intended to get out before discovery?

Or for someone who never showed . . .

He crossed the bay to the cargo bin. No one stopped him as he entered.

Lights brightly illuminated the inside. He climbed up the scaffolding that supported the couches to the crack in the ceiling. The metal showed a clear curve where something had gouged it from the interior and pushed it out. Derec ran his hand over the surface and found a number of indentations on either side. A hand?

"Sir."

Derec looked at the entrance. A uniform stood there, sidearm out.

"I have to ask you to leave," she said. "You aren't supposed to be in here."

"Really?" Derec climbed down. "Why is that?"

"This is a crime scene, sir."

He stepped past her. "It is, indeed. Thank you for pointing that out."

Derec entered the office—and walked straight into a full-blown argument between Palen and Harwol.

Harwol was fuming. "—what in hell you thought you were doing, but you overstepped you authority by a considerable margin!"

"This is *my* station, Harwol," Palen shot back. "It *is* my margin!"

"Excuse me," Derec said.

Everyone looked at him. Palen and Harwol both were breathing hard.

"I was wondering," Derec continued, "if anyone had bothered to count the bodies."

"Of course we did, Avery," Palen snapped. "We counted them as we carried them out."

"Yes, but have you counted them since?"

Palen frowned at him, mouth open.

"I didn't think so," Derec said. "Maybe we should."

NINETEEN

Coren almost reached for her, to pull her into Wenithal's apartment. Jeta Fromm tensed, looked left and right, then, with a harsh sigh of frustration, stepped forward.

"Shut the damn door, gato," she muttered.

She stopped halfway between Coren and Wenithal, who still held his pistol in her direction. Coren closed the door, the soft *snik* bringing her around to face him again. Her long, almost gaunt face showed anger and fear. She blinked nervously. Coren glanced at Wenithal, who now looked away, hands clasped in his lap.

"You've wrecked my life," Jeta said suddenly. "That's going to cost a bit more than my usual fee."

"Where've you been?" Coren asked. "I tried to find you right after—"

"Right after you gave me away to the sanitaries? What happened, did they offer you more credits than your wildest imagination? Or did you just decide to piss on some warren rat for fun and see how long it took her to die?"

"The 'sanitaries'?" Ariel asked.

Jeta glared over her shoulder. "Who are you?"

Coren cleared his throat loudly. "Sanitaries are enforcers. They clean up things. Sanitation workers."

Ariel made a silent "Oh" and nodded. "How clever," she said. "I'm Ambassador Ariel Burgess from the Auroran Embassy. Pleased to meet you, Ms. . . . ?"

"This is Jeta Fromm," Coren announced. "The freelance data troll who found Nyom for me . . . then vanished before I could thank her for doing basically what she's accusing me of."

"Me?" Jeta shouted. "You vatdrip! Someone's tried to kill me twice since I talked to you, once right after you left with the data I got you. Second time was at the Lyzig tube station, morning after I took off."

"Did Cobbel and Renz tell you I was looking for you?"

Jeta frowned uncertainly, just for a moment, then looked away. "I was looking for you myself."

Coren caught Ariel's eye and gave a slight shake of his head.

"Who did you tell about the baleys?" he asked.

"You," Jeta said.

"Who else?" Coren took two quick steps toward her. She backed up only one. "They were all murdered, Jeta! Fifty-two dead baleys! Someone knew they'd been found, and killed any possible witnesses! If I'm the only one you told, then how did they know?"

"I'm asking you the same question! How did they find me?"

"I don't know who 'they' are. And if I'm one of them, why would I have to ask 'them'? You're not making sense."

Jeta glanced from Ariel to Wenithal, then back to Coren. "I didn't tell anybody."

"Then you were traced."

She scowled. "I'm better than that, there's no way—"

"*My* system was compromised, and I can afford a hell of a lot better protection than you can."

Jeta shook her head. "Don't brag on it, gato—that's how I found you."

It took Coren several moments to understand her meaning. "You broke into my system?"

She nodded. "It was hard, you've got a good one, but . . ."

Coren looked at Ariel. "But—"

"Someone piggybacked in with you," Ariel said. "Your system's still compromised."

"Who are they, Jeta?" Coren asked. "Who's trying to kill you?"

"Ask them, gato, I got my own problems!"

"I'd love to, but it could be fatal. Who *are* they?"

Jeta swallowed loudly. "All I know is, I handed over the data to you and went back to my hole! Two of 'em were waiting for me before I got there!" She looked at him narrowly. "I thought you'd had them standing by for after you got what you wanted."

Coren shook his head. "Then why follow me? If I set you up, this is the surest way to get yourself killed."

"I said that's what I thought. I thought it then, not now."

"What changed your mind?"

"I checked you out. It's not too often you find an honest cop."

"Then—"

"Good cops go bad."

"That still doesn't explain why you're here." He looked at Wenithal, who seemed to be pointedly ignoring them, drinking his coffee. "If I went bad—"

"I didn't know where else to go! All right? I don't trust

any of my usual contacts! I thought I could make an arrangement with you."

"If I were still a good cop, I'd help you. If I were bad, we could do business."

"Something like that."

"I've been trying to find you for over three days."

"I know. Why?"

"I thought you'd double-marketed the data."

Jeta's face hardened. "I don't do that."

"Then how did they know about the baley shipment?"

Jeta let out her breath slowly. "I'm a good troll, Mr. Lanra, very good, but I'm not the only one. If I could find out, so could a dozen others, easy. If I was you, though, I'd ask the people running the baleys to begin with. If anyone'd know . . ."

"I thought about that. I've been trying to find them."

"No luck?" A mocking smile tugged at her thin lips, even though her eyes still showed fear. "Maybe you need to hire a professional."

"Fine, then," Coren said tersely. "You're hired."

"My fee's doubled," Jeta said.

"I don't mind, I have an expense account."

"I have expenses, we're even. What you want to know first?"

"First? What are you doing *here?*"

"Following you."

"So you say. You want to tell me why? The truth this time."

Jeta looked around. "Do you mind if I put my stash down? Thanks." She set her pack on the end of the table by the sofa, then dropped into the cushions with a loud, relieved exhalation. "You botched my ride, gato. Then you almost got me killed. I thought that, anyway. I figured if anyone could solve my problems, it'd be the gato who caused them all to begin with."

"What do you mean, I botched your ride?"

She gave him a guilty look. "Confession time: I found that data for you as fast as I did 'cause I already had it. I was slated to go on that shipment. I had a berth with them."

"I've been trolling for almost sixteen years," Jeta explained. "It's not a bad life if you don't mind the occasional hassle from police—public *and* private—and planning for the very long term. Some of us get good enough that we get hired as staff somewhere, go completely legitimate. Finding lost data is a full-time industry in some quarters. Can I have something to drink?"

Ariel went into the kitchen again and returned with a glass of water. Jeta sniffed at it, frowned, then shrugged and drank.

"Anyway, you have to understand how much data there is on this planet. I'm talking centuries of accrual. It never entirely disappears. Overwritten, archaic storage media, just plain misplaced, misfiled, or misremembered. It sits in layers, piling up, lumping together. Whole AI systems are devoted to sifting through it all, but it occasionally takes a deft hand, intuition, a lucky guess—human qualities you just don't find in a machine. There are specialists who do it, going through stuff that's *really* old. Some of them start out legit and move into freelance, but for most of us it's the other way around. There's a hardcore bunch that never go legit.

"Mostly though, it's not much more dangerous usually than any other job. It's been understood for a long time that the troll isn't a target; you don't damn well shoot the messenger. Killing us hurts everyone. And then there are the clearing houses that offer protection and anonymity, and some corporations keep their best trolls on retainer and offer defence. Worrying about sanitizers is just not a big issue. I've been beaten up a couple of times, but no one has ever–*ever*–threatened my life.

"Till now. About three months ago I was retained to find some old minutes from a board of directors that no longer exists. This kind of thing isn't my most common job, but I've done a few. It's surprising how careless some corporations are with old data like this. I think it's just arrogance–that was the *old* board, they didn't do anything right, why bother keeping the minutes around, and if there's no legal reason to do so, they just shove them somewhere. A new board is like a new government and anything that happened before them is by definition full of error. Nothing unusual, standard fee, I got a few leads where to start, and I went trolling. Turned about to be a real challenge. I could find traces of it, but it was obvious someone had gone to some trouble to hide it. Took me nearly a month to recover enough of it to make any kind of sense. I found it hiding in stockholder reports, maintenance logs, spread out through portfolio surveys, resumés, spread sheets. Bits of it even turned up in vacation itineraries. The program that hid it was sophisticated enough to actually reconstruct it all with the right command sequence, so it was obvious someone wanted to be able to recover it, otherwise a lot of it would have been corrupted beyond recognition."

Jeta grinned proudly. "But I did it. I found it all and reassembled it and put it into a package for the client. I was finishing it all up when I got a message on my comm that said, 'If you deliver what you have, we will kill you.' Very simple, very direct. Somehow, I didn't think it was crank. We don't get them often, but we do get threats, and there are procedures for dealing with them. I turned it over to my controller at the clearing house and delivered my package per our contract. When I got back to my hole I found a new message: 'You were given fair warning.' That's all it said."

"No signature?" Ariel asked. "No source?"

"That's all it had to say, 'cause it wasn't the words that scared me, but the timing. I knew then I was being moni-tored—closely—and that my own system had been hacked."

"Did you try to trace it?" Coren asked.

Jeta scowled. "Of course I did! It ate at me. I've been scared before, especially back when I started out, but this was different—this had an edge to it. After a couple of days and I was still scared, I started making plans to disappear. I did my accounts, added things up, and it looked like I could make it work. I reconfigured my system three times to purge the intruders, then made inquiries to emigrate. I always wanted to, anyway—it was one of my two or three top retirement options. This decided the issue for me.

"No way I'd get my assets through ITE. I'd have to go baley and smuggle what I could. Meantime, I just kept on as always, living my life, doing business like I always had, making no moves I'd never made before. No flags, no warn-ings, nothing to tell anyone that anything had changed. The final vetting came through Baltimor for the Petrabor Egress—that's what they called it—and I started arranging everything to be ready to transfer at a heartbeat.

"Then you showed up with your request for data on the same baley group. I knew if I refused, you'd just use another troll and in the end it'd be the same result. I had to change my plans. I thought first maybe you were working for the gatos who'd threatened me. So I ran your profile. Imagine my surprise when I saw 'Special Service' pop up, then DyNan Manual Industries. What I saw, it didn't make sense you'd be hunting down a troll for anybody."

"I appreciate that," Coren said with mock sincerity.

"That didn't change anything. I couldn't know what I'd find if I turned up for my ride out."

"You might have asked me for help."

Jeta shrugged. "Couldn't. Not then."

Coren nodded. "I understand."

"Yes, well. So I left everything as it was, kept the arrangements intact, and made different plans. I did your job, handed over the data, and headed home to disappear. That's when I was attacked. I got away by being just small enough for some crannies others can't use.

"No one waited for me at my hole, so I cleaned up, packed my stash, and ran. I made plans to go to the Bering port. I don't know how they figured that one, but the same gato found me at the tube in Lyzig."

"How did you escape that time?" Ariel asked after a long silence.

"Screamed." Jeta gave them a wan smile. "Too many people, too much attention. He walked away. I felt like a fool standing there in the middle of the platform yelling at the top of my lungs. But not so foolish I wouldn't do it again if I had to. That's when I decided to find Mr. Lanra here. I thought to myself, 'He started all this, he can fix it.' "

"I wish I could, Jeta," Coren said. "I had no idea."

"I saw that pretty quick—you weren't part of those gatos trying to kill me. But you fouled up my egress. You drew attention to it. For all I knew, you were going to show up with immigration cops and arrest them all. I couldn't take the chance. Now ..." She swallowed loudly. "I want out, Mr. Lanra. I want away from Earth. I want my life. I'll work for you till you can do all that for me."

"I'll try, Jeta. I can't promise. I don't even know who these people are. They hacked my system, too."

Jeta blinked, her eyes moist. She nodded calmly and looked at Wenithal. "Who are you?"

"Forgive me, I've been remiss. I'm Ree Wenithal. This is my apartment."

"Ah. Nice place."

"Thank you."

"Jeta." Ariel leaned on the back of the sofa. "That job you did, the minutes ... who was it for?"

"Umm ... there's a small matter of confidentiality involved. I'm not sure–"

"Someone is trying to kill you over those minutes," Ariel said, her voice intensely reasonable. "I think it would be understandable for you to set confidentiality aside in this instance."

Jeta nodded. "Yeah, well ... it was an intermediary, you understand, but I checked into him before I accepted. The contract was from Myler Towne of Imbitek."

Jeta claimed to be dead tired. Wenithal showed her into his bedroom and let her sleep. He went into the kitchen and returned with another cup of coffee. His hand shook slightly as he poured it.

Coren said nothing. He joined Ariel on the sofa and spoke quietly.

"That's not Jeta," he said.

"Then who is she?"

Coren shrugged. "Maybe we'll find out. It's interesting,

though—Towne tried to hire me away from Looms. Some-one tried to assassinate Towne. He doesn't trust his own security anymore."

Wenithal came back into the room and, cup in hand, sat down in a chair.

"Alda Mikels is being released from prison in a couple of days," Ariel said.

"If you're wondering if there's a connection, I've been wondering that, too. But what would a disagreement between Mikels and Towne have to do with a bunch of baleys?"

"Perhaps," Wenithal said ponderously, "the connection is sleeping in the next room."

"Seems rather heavy-handed," Ariel said, "to murder fifty innocent people just to get one. Especially after the thing you're trying to prevent has already occurred."

"You mean the delivery of the data she found?" Coren asked. "It doesn't make a lot of sense, but . . . we have more murders to explain, though."

"Brun's," Wenithal said. "Ms. Fromm said she went through the Baltimor District to set up her egress?"

"She said that, yes," Ariel confirmed.

"Brun headed the ITE customs office in Baltimor," Coren said. "But . . ."

"Ghost connections," Wenithal said. "Implications, sug-gestions, hints—nothing solid. Except that Brun is dead." He stared down at his coffee, eyes narrowed.

"Nyom had nothing to do with any of them," Coren said.

"But her father did," Ariel said. "Maybe Nyom's mystery brother did, too."

"Oh, definitely," Wenithal said.

Coren looked at him. "When I told you Nyom had died,

you said something about 'both of them now.' What did you mean?"

Wenithal scowled. "You *heard* that?"

"I cheat a lot," Coren said. "You're not denying it. What did you mean?"

"Rega Looms *did* have a child before Nyom. A son. A very sick son. A UPD."

"I've heard that abbreviation before," Ariel said, "but I've never been clear on what it means."

"Untreatable Physiological Dysfunction," Coren said.

"I *know* what it stands for. But what's untreatable? Even if Terran medicine can't deal with something, we have *some* agreements covering humanitarian aid. Spacer medicine is—"

"Unable to deal with these," Wenithal said. "I'm not clear myself on what they are, but some of them are horrible. Most are just chronically debilitating illnesses; a good portion of them are transmissible. The only recourse is quarantine. Looms' first child contracted one when he was barely a year old."

"So it was institutionalized?"

"Had to be. The law. And it died shortly thereafter. I imagine it crushed him. It would me."

"How did you come to know about it?" Coren asked.

"Rega Looms was one of the principle investors in Nova Levis," Wenithal explained. "A research firm established to take advantage of some of the first influxes of Spacer med tech. Everyone thought it would take off on the market, but it didn't do well the first couple of years. Then, suddenly, it had almost unlimited cashflow."

"Black market?" Ariel asked.

"Worse. It turned out to be the main channel for all those missing babies. We shut it down."

"That's not what the record says," Coren pointed out.

"Nova Levis was cleared and operated long after your investigation."

"The record often disagrees with reality," Wenithal said. "The truth was that too many important people had invested in it and too many of them had embarrassing connections with it. Very simple: We turned off the pipeline, told the public it was clear, and then put it on the market. We disassembled it without harming any of the major shareholders."

"That must have been an impressive list of shareholders," Ariel said.

"Oh, it was! You'd be shocked."

"Looms divested early, though," Coren said. "Quite some time before it closed."

"I think he did it out of extreme disappointment. They couldn't cure his child, so he wanted nothing to do with it. I can't imagine how he must feel right now."

"Why did you retire after all that?" Coren asked.

"Because I wasn't finished and they weren't going to let me finish. I traced the kidnappings to Nova Levis, but they were going *somewhere*. I thought it had to be offworld. To save those prominent citizens' reputations, I was not allowed to follow the leads. I was fêted, medaled, and promoted—and basically told to drop it. It ate at me till I couldn't stand it anymore. I presented an ultimatum: either I'm allowed to pursue the case or I quit." He raised his hands, palms up, and let them fall.

"You didn't try to look into it yourself?"

"Not very aggressively. I was already known to those involved. I knew I wouldn't be very effective." Wenithal shook his head. "No, this was the only way: wait for someone new, with no attachments to the old case. We couldn't go looking for anyone because that might set off alarms in all the wrong places."

Coren turned all this over in his mind. It sounded just a bit glib, rehearsed, but that did not make it less true. To be sure, Ree Wenithal had been living with this for a long time. In his place, Coren believed he might have it well worked out by now.

But Coren found it unconvincing. It did not explain Wenithal's connection to Brun Damik, or why Damik would go to Wenithal after Coren confronted him.

"Where was Nova Levis?" he asked.

"Hmm? Somewhere in the Pacific Ocean, one of the undine enclaves. Um . . . Teluk Tolo, Indones Sector."

"Maybe it would be worthwhile to take another look at it," Coren said.

"It's gone. There's nothing there anymore, just a shell. It was all sold off. I think it was converted to a processing plant for raw materials or something."

"You won't mind if we try, will you?"

Wenithal sneered. "Don't be sarcastic. I'm doing you a favor telling you any of this."

"Of course," Coren said. "You're such a model citizen. If I had more time I'd be more polite about it."

"Mr. Wenithal," Ariel cut in, frowning at Coren, "you're expecting trouble. Have you been followed?"

"Not that I know of, but they killed Brun. I'm next, logically. What would you think?"

"I think you should move somewhere safer."

"And where might that be?"

"The Auroran embassy. I don't think you can be gotten to there."

"You *think?*"

"I don't know what exactly we're up against. Do you want me to lie and guarantee your safety?"

"We wouldn't want you to do that." Wenithal shook his

head. "I've never run from a fight. Besides, it might look odd."

"You'd look very odd crushed to death," Coren said.

"Crushed?"

"Judging from the victims we've seen, it looks like crushing is the favored method."

Wenithal considered that and shuddered. "I've never been to the Auroran embassy." He shrugged. "If it would put your minds at ease . . ."

"I could always leave you here with Jeta," Coren said then.

Wenithal frowned at him.

"How long have you known her?" Coren asked.

"I don't—"

"Stop it. She didn't follow me here. She came to see you."

Wenithal laughed. "Why would a data troll want to see me?"

"I can't think of a single reason. But she's not a data troll. You were waiting for someone to show up tonight, someone you thought might kill you. So far, we've shown up, and Jeta Fromm has shown up." Coren held up his hands. "Is there a mistake in my logic?"

"You're guessing," Wenithal said.

"So, do you stay here, or do we go to the Auroran Embassy?"

Wenithal sighed. "All of us?"

"I'm not letting Jeta—or whatever her name is—get away from us."

"If she's not Jeta," Ariel said, "then who—?"

"I'm guessing a woman named Tresha," Coren said. "You've done business with her before, Mr. Wenithal. but I imagine you've never done any with her partner—Gamelin."

Wenithal stared at Coren now with undisguised resentment. "Like I said, I've never been to the Auroran Embassy before."

"If I'm right, getting there might be an interesting problem," Coren said.

Ariel smiled at him. "Leave that part to me."

Coren turned away, muttering under his breath, "I knew you were going to say that . . ."

TWENTY

The morgue was a bit cooler, though Derec wondered how much of that was simply psychosomatic illusion. He stood to one side, near the big entrance, while Sipha Palen and her chief forensic specialist, Baxin, went through the logs.

"Fifty-one," Baxin said finally. He looked at Palen. "There were fifty-two when we brought them in here."

"So a corpse got up when you weren't looking and walked out?" Palen's voice made everyone cringe.

Baxin shook his head, less intimidated than bewildered.

"Not only that," Palen went on, "but it cleaned up its container and put it back in storage!" She wheeled around at the pair of security men nearby. "Didn't *anybody* pay attention to the monitors? Nobody saw a *thing* out of the ordinary?"

Derec leaned back against the wall. The TBI agents stood nearby, looking slightly embarrassed on Palen's behalf. But Derec could see the impatience in their faces.

Palen stopped herself before she continued her rant.

With sudden and surprising calm, she said, "I want the monitor records gone over. I want to know when the dead got up and walked out."

Her two officers, with evident relief, left quickly. Palen came up to the TBI agents.

"I'm disinclined to turn anything over to you," she said, "but under the circumstances, maybe we can share resources. Avery here has been working on recovering the memory from that robot. If he succeeds, we'll all know what happened. If you remove it now, all his work will be lost and you'll be starting from scratch."

"That's not—" one of the agents began.

Halwor raised his hand and cut her off. "As you say, Chief Palen, 'under the circumstances.' " He looked at Derec. "How soon, Mr. Avery?"

"We were less than an hour away from the first recoveries when you showed up."

"Then, let's go see what you have."

Rana was waiting for them when they arrived in the lab. She frowned upon seeing the TBI agents trailing behind Derec and Palen. She came forward, stopping right in front of Derec.

"Boss, we have a problem," she said.

"Yes, I know. There's a discrepancy in the bodycount."

"Yes, there is. The robot is gone."

It seemed to take a long time for the information to register. Derec stared at Rana. "What?"

"The DW-12 . . . left."

Derec pushed past her and entered the workstation. The pallet was empty, the cables all neatly removed and retracted into the diagnostic link.

"When—?"

"What happened, Avery?" Harwol asked. "What did you do with the robot?"

"Nothing. Obviously, I've been with you. Rana?"

Rana looked embarrassed. "I had some personal business to attend. When I came back, the unit was gone."

"Thales?" Derec asked.

"Yes, Derec?"

"Where's the DW-12?"

"At this precise moment, I do not know."

"Did someone remove it?" Harwol demanded.

"No," Thales said. "However, I have everything requested from it. I have organized the recovered memories and prepared them in a linear scroll for viewing."

Derec, uncertain and nervous, sat down at the console. "The excavation is complete, then?"

"I have a complete document of the robot's memory, Derec."

The TBI agents looked uneasy.

"Um . . . any preferred mode of replay?"

"All options available, Derec."

"Flatscreen and full auditory will be fine, Thales." Derec turned to the gathered audience. "If you'll all spread out along the blind, please, we can put this on a few screens and you can all see."

"I want an explanation, Avery," Harwol said. "That robot is evidence—"

"Maybe we should pay attention to the main question," Palen said, "of what happened to those people."

Harwol frowned, unmollified, but he nodded curtly. "Very well."

While they arranged themselves, Derec made sure the link was feeding to Ariel through Thales. He glanced back to see that everyone was ready.

"Okay, Thales," he said, "let's see what you have."

Four screens above the console cleared simultaneously. A few seconds later, a single view filled them all.

The group of baleys gathered around the two people facing each other in their midst. The woman—Nyom Looms—looked angry, impatient. The man, dressed in dockworker's dull yellow togs, faced her stoically, arms folded, waiting for her to finish.

("Is there audio?" one of the TBI agents asked. "Thales," Derec prompted. "Incomplete. I am working on filling gaps.")

Nyom Looms raised one hand, finger aimed at the dockworker, and almost jabbed him. He dropped his arms and said something.

("Pocivil," Palen mused. "What's that?" Harwol asked. "Nothing," Palen said.)

"—forming you now—have backup—prepared. It's the same as it was, only different. A new canister. We *are* professionals."

The robot turned toward the group. Someone was working his way forward and had come to a halt at the very edge of the half-circle.

A window appeared at the lower right corner of the screen, and a series of faces scrolled quickly by, matching text on the left. The words NO MATCH appeared in place of the faces. The robot moved toward the stranger.

("That's Coren," Palen said. "Who?" one of the TBI agents asked. "Later," Palen said.)

"All right," Nyom said. "But if this turns out to be anything but copacetic, I'll peel your skin off with pliers. Tell your people we're ready."

Suddenly, Coren stepped forward, a half-smile on his face. The robot reached him at that point and gripped his right arm. Coren looked up angrily, but his expression changed quickly to fear.

"I apologize, sir, but I must ask that you come with me." The robot walked him back through the crowd of baleys, who looked frightened and angry themselves.

They emerged from the crowd and continued on to the next bay. The robot stopped. Coren gave it another nervous glance, then turned abruptly.

"Damnit, Coren!"

Coren smiled wanly. "Good to see you, too, Nyom."

She hissed through clenched teeth.

"Don't tell me you're surprised to see me," Coren said.

"I'm not. That's what bothers me."

Coren nodded toward the robot. "Umm . . ."

"Coffee, go see to our arrangements."

"Yes, Nyom," the robot said.

The robot—Coffee—released Coren and returned to the group of baleys. It worked its way through them. Some cringed from it, but most stood their ground with stolid expressions, afraid but unwilling to show it.

Coffee emerged from the huddled refugees just as the dockworker returned, followed by four individuals. The window appeared at the lower left again as Coffee attempted to find matches.

One of the four was another robot.

("Looks like a DM-70," Rana whispered. "But what's *that?*")

One of the four looked distinctly artificial, surface a smooth, dull gray, but it was far more humaniform than either of the other two robots. Coffee gave this one a close examination. The view zoomed in on its head. Human-imitation eyes peered back. It wore close-fitting black: shirt, pants, and soft boots, which seemed silly for a robot.

("Look at the way it moves," Derec said.)

"Everybody ready?" the dockworker called out. He turned to Coffee. "Where's your boss?"

"One moment."

Coffee made his way back to where Nyom and Coren stood talking. It stopped a short distance from them. "Nyom."

Coren started and Nyom laughed. She began to reach toward him. "Coffee won't hurt you. What is it, Coffee?"

"Time."

"I'll be right there."

Coffee returned once more to the group of baleys. "She is on her way," it told the dockworker.

"All right," Nyom's voice snapped. "Let's get this boat sailing, shall we?" She stopped upon seeing the newcomers, frowning. "Who are these?"

"*My* dock crew," the first dockworker informed her. "It wasn't hard to get everybody else to go out for a drink, but I think they'd draw the line at longshoring an illicit bin and loading up a bunch of baleys, don't you think?"

Nervous laughter came from the group of baleys. Nyom nodded, her eyes on the strange robot.

"This way," the dockworker said, leading them through the open bay.

They passed through the huge doorway. The baleys stopped on the broad apron between the warehouse doors and the maze of tracks upon which cargo bins scurried en route to and from the shuttle fields of Petrabor port. One bin came almost directly at them, stopping abruptly on its magnetic rails less than five meters away. Its door folded down.

"Okay, folks," the dockworker said, clapping his hands. "Here's the drill. Inside you will find an array of bunks—acceleration couches—each one with a breather mask attached to a rebreather. There's enough air in the bin for the ride up to Kopernik and the transfer to the ship that'll take you on to Nova Levis, as long as you use the rebreather. One of my associates here will ride up with you and make sure you know how to use the masks and will stay as security till you make the transfer to the ship. Once aboard ship, you will be released from the bin and provided regular berths for the main leg of the voyage. Once you are secured in your couches, do not—I repeat, do not—get out of them. There isn't enough room for floating around, and you could injure yourselves. Any questions?"

He looked around. Coffee was paying attention mainly to the unusual robot.

Abruptly, that robot stepped forward, approached Coffee, and made a show of examining it. It moved with a sinuous fluidity that belied its artificial nature, making one slow circuit around Coffee and coming to a halt directly before it.

The skin seemed to ripple briefly. Suddenly, it looked to its left. As Coffee watched, the skin changed hue and texture, dappling and darkening.

"Nyom," Coffee said, "I recommend against this. We should abort and try another avenue."

"Why, Coffee?"

The strange robot regarded Coffee with an attitude of almost human curiosity, as if to say *Yes, Coffee, why?*

"I am unable to define my reasons," Coffee said. "The situation has too many unexpected variables. For instance, I do not know what this is." Coffee aimed a digit at the robot before it.

"Come on," the dockworker said, exasperated. "We don't have time for this shit! The crew will be back any minute—you take it or leave it. You drop this ride, your chances of getting another one go way down."

Nyom turned to her group. "It's up to you," she said. "Do we go?"

The refugees murmured among themselves briefly, then hands went up. "We go," most of them said.

Nyom frowned as she turned to the dockworker. "I repeat: anything goes wrong on this, I'll have parts of you as souvenirs."

"What, you think we're going to ruin our reputation? Come on, we're professionals—we do this all the time. Now, can be get a move on?"

"Coffee," Nyom said, "you just pay close attention to everything."

"Yes, Nyom."

The robot facing it spun gracefully and walked up the ramp, into the bin. The baleys filed in, one by one.

Nyom hung back, close to Coffee. "What's wrong, Coffee?"

"That robot—" Coffee began.

"The tally doesn't add up," the dockworker interrupted. He held up a pad. "I did a head count. We're missing one."

"I know," Nyom said. "It happens. Someone gets cold feet at the last minute; they don't show. Can't call it off on account of one or two who change their minds, can you?"

"No, I suppose not. But my people don't like it."

"I don't care what they don't like."

The dockworker shrugged. "So we have one extra couch. Everyone else showed, though?"

"Everyone else did." Nyom gestured. "Where'd you get that robot?"

"Gamelin? Didn't get him anywhere. He's part of the connection on the other end."

"He's . . . different."

"He is that. Well, you ready? Everyone else is on board."

Nyom nodded and walked up the ramp. Coffee followed.

Within, the light was dim, provided mainly by a single flash held by the robot, Gamelin, and the readylights on the hulking rebreather unit in the middle of the deck. Gamelin was helping people settle into the couches that were stacked to the ceiling, and answering questions in a quiet, raspy voice. Coffee began checking those already settled in.

The hatch came up, then, and Gamelin activated the internal seals. Coffee squatted by the control panel of the rebreather and began running a diagnostic.

"Don't you trust me?" Gamelin asked.

"What model are you?" Nyom asked. "I've never seen one like you."

"You won't again," Gamelin said, turning toward her. "Better get into your couch."

The bin lurched and Nyom nearly fell. Gamelin caught her arm and steadied her.

"No talking," Gamelin announced. "Uses too much air."

Coffee did a second check on the rebreather. Everything read optimal. It straightened and watched Gamelin help Nyom with her straps.

"And the mask—"

"I have my own," Nyom said.

Gamelin hesitated. "Very efficient."

Coffee approached Gamelin. "You did not answer Nyom's question. What model are you?"

"I'm a prototype. I don't have a model designation."

"Are you Solarian? I am unfamiliar with any Auroran

design even in the planning stage from which you might be derived."

"How long's it been since you were on Aurora?"

"Thirty-six years."

"Things might've changed, don't you think?"

"Very probably. That is why I ask."

"Solarian. Now get to your ready station. We've got ten minutes before the shuttle lifts."

Coffee returned to a place beside the rebreather. Gamelin climbed lithely into one of the couches.

("What happened? The scene shifted..." one of the agents complained. "Coffee shifted briefly to standby," Derec explained. "Nothing recorded during an essentially uneventful period. All telemetry is on, but...")

The cargo bin was in freefall, on a trajectory to Kopernik on board a shuttle. Two or three people groaned. Coffee bent to the rebreather control panel and checked the readings on individual respiration.

"There is a problem," it said.

"What?" Nyom asked. She pulled herself out of the couch and swam quickly to Coffee.

("Where'd she learn to do that?" Rana wondered.)

"The monitor indicates distress," Coffee said. "Breathing is becoming impaired."

"What the—we have a defective rebreather?"

"Nothing's defective," Gamelin said, sliding across the bin. "Everything's working fine."

"I disagree," Coffee said. "According to this—"

"Shut up, tinhead. Time to put on a standard mask, Ms. Looms."

Nyom shot a look at Gamelin. "What are you—"

Gamelin reached for her. She writhed in mid-air and

slammed a foot against its chest, launching herself backward. Her shoulders banged into the strutwork supporting a bank of couches.

Gamelin pursued, one arm extended, reaching.

"Stop," Coffee said. "You will cause injury."

"Exactly," Gamelin said.

Coffee twisted around and grabbed Gamelin's shoulder. Coffee's grip closed on softer material than expected. Gamelin jerked around beneath the grip and pulled free, hissing in clear pain.

Coffee opened its hand and saw, in its enhanced vision, a mass of fabric and dermis mingled thickly with blood.

The scene lurched. Coffee watched, immobile, as Gamelin chased Nyom Looms around the bin, while all around people were moaning louder. Several had ripped off their masks, gasping. Coffee looked down at the rebreather.

("Why doesn't it *do* something?" one of the agents asked. "It's caught in a dilemma," Rana said. "It just hurt something that might be human. It doesn't know what to do." "Human!")

Suddenly, Gamelin caught Nyom. Coffee looked up to see her struggle briefly while Gamelin got a grip on her head and gave a short, sharp yank. The snap of bone sounded horribly loud.

Gamelin let Nyom's body go and pulled something from its belt. It went to one of the clear surfaces and aimed the tool. A brilliant spark leapt at the bulkhead.

"Stop," Coffee ordered. "You will breach the integrity of the container."

"Stop me, tinhead," Gamelin said. "If you can."

"I—"

Suddenly, Gamelin drew back and punched up. The loud bang filled the chamber. A moment later, he pushed both hands through the crack he had made and heaved. Blood oozed from the wound on his shoulder. Air whistled through the hole.

Gamelin swam back to the robot and came close to its face.

"They'll suffocate if they don't put their masks back on," he said. Then he returned to his couch.

Coffee went from person to person, urging them to replace their masks. Some were already dead, though. Coffee seemed to realize then that the rebreather was poisoning them.

It knelt by the unit and tried to run a systems purge. That did not work, so it began stabbing the DISCONNECT, all the while the air inexorably leaked from the small chamber.

Everyone stared at the now blank screens, mute, the shock clear on their faces. Derec let out his breath slowly. He looked at Rana.

"What—?"

"So where did that *thing* go?" Agent Harwol demanded explosively. "Obviously, that's what walked out of your morgue, Chief Palen, right under the noses of your staff and your surveillance."

"Coren said it was invisible to his optam," she said.

"Invisible to your security systems, too?" Derec asked.

She looked frightened. "What is it, Mr. Avery? You're the roboticist. Tell us."

"I have no idea. I've never seen anything like it. Coffee couldn't stop it because it was human. Or seemed human."

"That?" Harwol exclaimed.

"It bled, Agent Harwol. It was—is—organic. Up to that point, Coffee assumed, as did everyone, that it was a robot . . . " He blinked. "A cyborg."

"A what?" Rana asked. "I didn't think those were possible."

"Aurora stopped research on them a long time ago. Not because they aren't possible—on the contrary, they are very possible. And much too unpredictable."

"We're impounding all this material," Agent Harwol declared. "I want every bit of it turned over to us before any more of it goes missing."

"To do what with?" Derec demanded. "You don't have the first idea what any of this means."

"And you do? No arguments, Mr. Avery—this material is now under TBI jurisdiction, and *you* are under arrest."

"For what?"

"Criminal negligence, for a start. Until we find that robot, I'm holding you responsible. You were working for us on this and an important piece of evidence is missing."

"For the sake of—" Palen said. "Stop it. Just what do you think you're accomplishing by all this?"

"I'm putting the lid on a bad situation on its way to becoming worse, *Chief* Palen," Harwol barked. "You're suspended, pending an investigation into abuse of authority. You had no mandate to indulge in this sort of an investigation—"

"You're going to make a mess of this whole thing—"

"Enough! I want this lab quarantined and everything in it held in stasis till I decide what to do with it. You have overstepped your authority in this matter, and the TBI is now taking over the investigation."

"Damn it—!" Palen began.

Harwol aimed a finger at her as if it were a weapon.

"Another word, Chief Palen," he said. "One more."

She restrained herself with a visible effort.

"You're an idiot," Derec said. "You could've just asked."

"I'm afraid, Agent Harwol," Hofton said then, "that you lack the authority to make arrests on Auroran territory."

"Kopernik Station is an Earth Incorporated Zone," Harwol said. "Security is handled by Terran authority under specific treaty, which is why Chief Palen here has the authority to police even the Spacer and Settler areas. I am relieving her of that position and assuming that authority."

"That's thin, Harwol," Palen said. "Really, really thin."

"Maybe, but that's what I'm doing. I can damn well make arrests here, and I damn well will. You may file a complaint through proper channels and it will be considered at that time, but till then *I* am in charge of station security and *you*—" he pointed at Derec "—are under arrest."

"I'm sorry, sir. I didn't know. I was under the impression that Auroran embassy grounds were accorded the same privileges as the main mission."

Hofton looked agonized. Derec had never seen the man so distraught. He sat on the other side of the narrow holding cell, elbows on knees, shoulders hunched, his face stretched by internal doubt and self-loathing.

"You can't be expected to know everything, Hofton," Derec said.

"I don't," Hofton said. "But I should know everything about my job."

Derec looked across, through the mesh of his cell door, to the cell opposite his. The Spacer who had been arrested the day Derec had arrived still waited within it. In all the confusion, he had been forgotten.

"It's understandable," Derec said. "Harwol and the others saw something they don't understand. Naturally, their reaction is to put anything they don't understand in a cell."

"All expectations for rational action and maturity notwithstanding," Hofton said gloomily.

"Doesn't matter. The relevant point is, you still have a job. I accept your apology. Now, let's figure out how to solve our problems."

Hofton continued to stare at a spot on the floor for several seconds. Then he drew a deep breath, straightened, and nodded.

"You're right, of course," he said. "What do you propose?"

"Thales withheld information for some reason. There's no way that robot could have done anything with Thales knowing." Derec thought about that. "Scratch that. Without Thales instigating it. Assuming for the moment Thales won't say anything to anyone but us, then the first opportunity we get to question it alone—"

"That may be very difficult. Harwol has an agent in the lab at all times."

"Hmm. All right, then the first thing we have to do is get some idea of what that thing is we saw in the recovered memories. They all saw that, there's nothing left to hide from the TBI. Contact Ariel, go over it with her."

"You said it's a cyborg."

"That's my best guess, but I wouldn't mind being contradicted. If somebody has a better idea, I'd love to hear it."

"Assuming you're correct, though, what then?"

"Then we have a real problem. Harwol and his people have no idea. If it's a cyborg, it was certainly not created out of thin air. There's infrastructure behind it—industry, an impressive application of technology. Which means money. More than likely, if there's one, there are more."

"Whose money?"

"That's one good question. The other is, what do they have to do with baleys?"

"Baleys in general, or those going to Nova Levis specifically?"

"Right now it could be either one. When you talk to Ariel, find out if Lanra has any statistics on the number of baleys going out each year that arrive dead. Or just disappear."

"With all due respect to Mr. Lanra, how would he get such statistics? The Settler colonies are not all willing to provide Earth with data. Census figures alone represent a major problem."

"Mmm. Well, maybe he knows someone who can get those numbers. I just need to know if one colony above any other is having a problem with this."

Hofton nodded. "I'll see what I can find out. Anything else?"

"Can you go in and out of the lab?"

"For the time being." He grinned wryly. "I'm a bit of a gray area for them. They don't quite know how to handle me. I've threatened them with Ambassador Setaris."

"Then get me an update from Thales."

"Yes, sir. Shall I see about getting you out of here?"

"Eventually, yes. For now, though, I've got some thinking to do, and this is as good a place as any."

"Yes, sir. Anything else?"

"Call me Derec."

Hofton stood. "I'll see what I can do. Sir."

Hofton placed his hand against the lock pad. The door opened for him; after he passed through, the mesh slid back into place. If Derec had tried to follow Hofton a stunner would have knocked him back very firmly.

A few minutes later, the main door opened again and two of Palen's uniforms brought a man into the block. They escorted him into a cell at the opposite end from the main door, locked him in, and left without glancing at Derec or the other prisoner.

Derec strained to see into the cell of the new inmate, but the man had flopped onto his cot.

Derec looked across the concourse at the other Spacer.

"So what did you do that got you thrown in here?" Derec called.

The Spacer sat up. After a few seconds of contemplation, the man went to his cell door, placed his hand on the lock, and walked out. With a glance in the direction of the newcomer, he came quietly up to Derec's door, opened it, and entered the cell. The door slid shut and the Spacer sat down where Hofton had been sitting.

Derec stared at him. "You're one of Palen's people."

He grinned. "Right on the first guess. They didn't lie when they said you were bright." He extended his hand. "Masid Vorian, station security."

Derec shook Masid's hand. "So I suppose you heard everything we discussed?"

"Most of it. Don't worry about the TBI, though. The cell monitoring system is keyed to Sipha's password. She shut it down after Harwol and his eager fools showed up. So they'll never know what you discussed with your man, or what you and I talk about now."

Derec nodded toward the door. "What about the new prisoner?"

"Must be a legitimate arrest. His escorts would've given me some kind of warning if he was a plant or something. Don't worry—I doubt he can hear our conversation, either."

"And what *are* we talking about now?"

"The same thing." Masid leaned forward earnestly. "You need to understand one thing: Sipha Palen is a good cop.

She's honest, dedicated, and a magnificent pain in the ass to work for as a result, but she's sincere about the job."

"I never doubted it."

Masid nodded once. "But it gets her in trouble. That's the reason she's up here and not running a department on the ground."

"Honest to a fault."

"She doesn't always know when to shut up." He grinned. "In certain circles, it can be a real deficit."

"She planted you in the lab."

"No, I was already there. I'm a turned agent. I used to work for Settler security. Sipha found out and made a deal with me: work for her, at least part-time, or she'd expose me."

"Forgive me, but you look like a Spacer."

Masid made a mock bow. "Native of Proclas."

"Then how—?"

"It's a long story. The short version is, I was trained as an information specialist, but, frankly, it's boring work. Proclans are agrarian by temperament, but you can't maintain much of a civilization growing vegetables. I started freelancing. The government called it treason and I had to leave. I ran an independent merchant ship for a while, then went to work for the Theian intelligence service on Pax Commari—"

"That's a Settler colony."

"Yes, it is. Theia sponsored it. Anyway, I decided that what I was doing was crass and unethical, so I turned myself in to the local intelligence people. They had absolutely no use for me, but—lucky me—they knew someone who *did*. I ended up working for the Settler Coalition."

"I didn't know they had an intelligence arm."

"Not very many people do. Their biggest concern is smuggling. Post to post to post, I ended up here." He raised his arms. "That's the short version. Some day when we have time and a good deal to drink, I'll give you the full version, which is a lot more interesting."

"So you work for Palen part of the time."

"At this point, I'd have to say I work for Palen all of the time. She made me a good deal. Over the last few years, I've found myself with a growing case of loyalty to her."

"That impressive?"

"I respect her," Masid said.

The way he said it, Derec got the immediate sense of a vast and profound commitment; that respect was something Masid Vorian esteemed above all else.

"All right," Derec said slowly. "I presume that the arrangement is, you work with the Aurorans for a time and when you have something to report you get yourself arrested."

"Basically. Most of the time information is easily sent through a secured comm channel. But sometimes something comes up that requires a personal meet."

"What prompted this one?"

"Baleys. Lots of very dead baleys."

"There's a regular route, always has been," Masid explained. "The bays change, but usually they're Settler. Baleys have been leaving Kopernik for years via the same avenues--fifty, a hundred years. We estimated that on an average year maybe five, six thousand people leave Earth through clandestine channels. Occasionally, the number goes as high as ten or twelve thousand. ITE cracks down periodically, the numbers drop to less than a thousand, then pick back up.

"A couple of years ago we started seeing a massive

surge: twelve, thirteen, fifteen thousand a year. I think this had to do with the politics, Eliton's whole Concessionism kick, and then the collapse of talks last year. I think a lot of baleys are afraid all the avenues are about to be shut down.

"In the middle of this frantic running, though, we started hearing rumors from some of the Settler crews that a number of shipments went missing. I started doing a little digging among my old Settler contacts. I found out that transfers were being made mid-journey by certain ships—destinations changed, baleys offloaded and sent somewhere else. Too many claims to ignore."

"Pirates?" Derec asked.

"That's an easy accusation to make. Tell me, what *is* pirate? Black market, certainly. But fine, let's assume for the sake of this discussion we're talking about pirates. Then what are they doing? A lot of so-called pirate ships are already dealing in baley running. A lot of them have quasi-legal status and come into port regularly. No warrants, no evidence to hold them, we let them go. The ships offloading the baleys aren't doing so under duress, so it's a business deal. But for who? The money being paid by baleys and some of the recipient colonies is a lot, but I don't see how the margin makes it worthwhile stealing the baleys after they're already en route. So where are they being taken?"

"You found out?"

Masid shook his head. "Not exactly. A lot of talk has them going to Nova Levis. Of course, that's quarantined, so it's not likely we're going to find any ship's owners willing to admit they're making runs there. The pirate ships taking the baleys on never come to Kopernik. But let's assume that one or two colonies have hired mercenary shippers and are paying premiums to steal baleys. Why? What do baleys have that could be marketable under illicit conditions?"

"Labor. Possibly blackmail of family."

"No blackmail, not a single demand. Labor, sure. But you can buy cheap labor from companies like Imbitek and Morris and some of the others. There are some colonies buying robots from Spacers. So, if it's not labor, what is it?"

Derec shook his head.

"Bodies."

"Organs?"

"What else? On spec I recommended that a shipload of baleys be traced and intercepted en route. A joint Auroran-Terran venture was set up. It took four tries to find a transfer, but we found one and the ship was taken. The baleys were already dead, in stasis. Medical quality stasis. Eighty-three of them. We had a few arriving shipments intercepted here and at least three of them contained already dead baleys."

"Why didn't you shut it all down if you knew about the shipments?"

"Two reasons: we *don't* know about all the shipments, and we still don't know who's killing them and selling the corpses. Ongoing investigation; we need to keep it quiet till we can shut down the source. I know, it's terrible. People are dying. But that's the way it is."

"How many?" Derec asked.

"So far, three hundred plus. We've been trying to infiltrate baley groups, see where they're going. Our agents have been turning up dead, too. Some of them in very unpleasant ways. The worst was Chiava."

"Chiava?"

"The Brethe dealer you heard about. Right here, in her holding cell."

"Chief Palen worked her the same way she works you?"

Masid nodded. "She worked dockside vice mostly, not this. She found something related to my investigation."

"Did she have time to tell Palen?"

"No. She was brought in while Sipha was away. By the time Sipha returned . . ."

"What I don't understand," Derec said, "is where the market for this is. Organs can be grown—you don't have to do gross transplants."

"Spacer medical tech is expensive."

"That's facile. It's also safer. The only reason . . ." Derec caught his breath. "The baleys in question. You identified them?"

"As many as we could. Some had bought very expensive privacy locks on their pasts."

"How many of them were orphans?"

"Orphans?"

"Yes, orphans."

Masid blinked and shrugged. "I don't know."

"Find out."

"You have an idea what's going on?"

"Just an idea. A very tenuous idea."

Masid nodded. "You look like you hope you're wrong."

"That, too." Derec studied Masid for a time. "So what are you still doing in here?"

"Oh, that. Well." Masid smiled sheepishly. "I'm bait."

TWENTY-ONE

I've called for an embassy limousine," Ariel said. "It should be here shortly."

Ree Wenithal gave her a gloomy look, as if now regretting to go along with them. He had drunk four cups of coffee and swallowed a stimulant pill, and his mood had grown ever more somber.

Coren scowled at him. "Don't tell us you've changed your mind and don't want to go. Would you rather wait for Tresha and Gamelin?"

Wenithal looked startled. "Who?"

Coren almost smiled. "Your collectors. The ones you've been waiting for."

Ariel watched them regard each other, Ree Wenithal clearly unsettled and Coren smugly observant.

"We standing around playing *Who Knows*," Jeta Fromm asked, "or moving somewhere safer?"

Coren laughed. "Come on. Is there anything else you want to bring?"

"No," Wenithal said grudgingly, and stepped to the door.

Ariel touched Coren's elbow. When he looked at her, she pointed to his shoulder. "Are you all right?"

"I could use some painblock and a stimulant right now," he said, "but I can move."

They exited onto the balcony warily, Ariel coming out last. Third shift was still a few hours from ending and the quiet made the warren seem deserted. Coren led the way down the steps to the courtyard and out to the avenue. Ariel went last, glancing anxiously over her shoulder, trying unsuccessfully to see into the shadows. She gripped the stunner in her pocket, knowing it would be next to useless against the thing that attacked them earlier, but unwilling to release its illusion of effectiveness.

Far to the right, at the end of the avenue, music and laughter reached them from a bar; otherwise, the area was still. They pressed back against the wall and waited in silence.

Ariel jumped when the limousine pulled onto the avenue. The long black vehicle stopped and the rear door slid open. As they neared the vehicle, two men emerged and quickly flanked Wenithal and Jeta. Wenithal stopped short, but Jeta whirled around, glaring.

"What *is* this, gato?" she demanded.

Coren stopped before her. "It's for everyone's piece of mind . . . Tresha."

She frowned at him. "My name is Jeta Fromm."

"I doubt it," Coren said. "But we can sort it out later, when we're in comfort and security." He looked at Ariel. "Is this going to cause problems?"

"Nothing I'm not used to," Ariel said. She addressed the guards. "Screen them."

One of the men took out a pad and walked around the pair. He reached inside Jeta/Tresha's jacket and removed a pistol. "That's all, Ambassador."

"Good. In the limousine, please."

The guard took Tresha's pack, then Wenithal and Tresha were ushered into the capacious backseat. The guards watched them from the facing seat. Ariel went around to the passenger side front and got in.

Coren closed the door and leaned against the jamb.

"I'm going somewhere else," he said.

Ariel wanted to protest, but held back. "I see. I'll stay with these people, then, and set them up at the embassy."

He nodded. His eyes shut briefly. "When I get there, I think I'd better sleep."

"You wouldn't want to tell me *where* you're going, would you?"

"Not now." He smiled wearily. "Deniability and all that. Besides, I really don't know just exactly where..." He shook his head. "Get them to the embassy and safe. I'll comm when I'm finished."

He pushed away from the limo. The door closed. Ariel watched him walk wearily away. She felt a sharp reluctance to let him out of her sight. For a moment she wanted to get out of the limousine and go with him, trusting the limo and the guards to get her passengers to the embassy.

Not very responsible, she thought peevishly.

Coren rounded a distant corner, disappearing from sight. Ariel leaned back in the seat, wondering at her uneasy mix of emotions.

"Embassy," Ariel said. She glanced over her shoulder at Tresha and Wenithal, and wondered idly how much of a diplomatic mess she had just created. *Only if they complain,* she thought.

"Yes, Ambassador," the car replied and rolled on.

"This is nonsense," Wenithal said.

"What's changed?" Ariel asked. "You were prepared to shoot whoever came through your door earlier."

He glowered, then let his head fall back. Within a couple of minutes his eyes closed and his breathing deepened. Ariel wondered just how much alcohol he had drunk before they had arrived. Then she wondered how often people had thought that about her.

Tresha glared at Ariel, straight-backed and on edge, hands pressed against her thighs. Her backpack lay on the seat between the guards.

"That looks heavy," Ariel said. "What do you have in there?"

"Why?"

"Just curious."

Tresha frowned. "My chops. Code burner, datum, decrypter. Some clothes."

Ariel waited to see if Tresha would volunteer more. When she remained silent, Ariel asked, "Why Nova Levis?"

"Time. There's a list and a schedule. Nova Levis had the earliest opening. Besides, you hear there's a lot of tech there."

"You do?"

"They say, sure."

"It was an agrarian colony, started up by the Church of Organic Sapiens."

Tresha blinked at her. "They changed, then." She shrugged. "So, do you believe Mr. Lanra? That I'm not who I say I am?"

"Does it matter? Either you are and you need our help, or you aren't and we need to keep you under guard."

Tresha shook her head. "Meddling. Spacers are always meddling. Why is that? What's all this to you?"

Ariel considered giving Tresha a glib answer, predigested and politic. *It's my job, I was ordered to help.* True as far as it went, but Ariel had never done anything purely for surface reasons. In this case, she felt she would have been justified to tell Setaris no and let herself be rotated back to Aurora as she expected to be.

She understood Derec's motives—he wanted to get his hands on a positronics lab one more time. The ground mission's lab was denied him and, though he still retained Thales, he simply could not do the research he wanted. And he wanted to stay on Earth, a desire about which she had grown ambivalent in the last year.

She understood Coren Lanra's motives, though she suspected there was more than he had admitted.

Ariel even understood Sen Setaris and the policy under which she had delegated the assignment.

But her own motives for going along with it?

"Until two hours ago I didn't know," she said. "Then I saw the enemy."

When they arrived at the embassy, Ariel summoned an extra security team to escort Wenithal and Tresha to separate apartments. "I want someone watching them full-time, highest level surveillance."

She went directly to her own apartment, then.

"Any messages, Jennie?" Ariel asked.

"Thales requests that you check in as soon as possible."

"Thank you, Jennie." She tapped a code for the embassy security office. "I want an ID run, please. There is a woman just installed in the secure apartments calling herself Jeta Fromm. Verify. Check against records for a woman named Tresha, last name unknown."

As she stepped into the corridor, she felt a brief wave of

weariness. She had been going for too long a stretch without more than ten minutes' sleep. Ariel shrugged it off and headed to Derec's apartment.

"Thales, do you have something for me?" she asked as she entered Derec's workspace.

"A number of items, Ariel. I have completed the recovery from the subject. Derec and Hofton have already viewed the relevant memories."

Ariel's pulse quickened. She sat down. "Then show me."

Ariel watched the entire episode, from the point where Nyom Looms confronted the dockworker to the point when collapse occurred after the murders of all the baleys. She did not move when it was done, staring at the screen. She felt warm, and a distant anger she knew would only grow with time.

"Do you wish to review any part of the material, Ariel?" Thales finally asked.

"No. Where's Derec?"

"In custody. The TBI have intervened and assumed authority over the investigation on Kopernik."

Ariel stood. "Wait." She went to Derec's bathroom and found a container of stim pills. She swallowed two and returned to Thales. "All right, Thales, tell me what's happened."

She took the embassy shunt to Setaris's offices.

Unexpectedly, Ambassador Setaris was in.

"Come in, Ariel, come in," Setaris said as Ariel walked in. "My door is always open for interesting people, and you've been so *very* interesting lately."

Setaris sat behind her desk, gazing at the subetheric. Ariel glanced at it and saw Jonis Taprin speaking to a reporter in a formal interview setting. The sound was off.

"Derec Avery is in custody," Setaris said. "The TBI have seized control of Kopernik security from Chief Sipha Palen and are making very loud noises about security leaks and subversion. I have a protest filed from Ambassador Chassik demanding you be censured and dismissed from all embassy duties, pending an investigation of your fitness for executive responsibilities." She gestured at the subetheric. "Senator Taprin has been making very obnoxious noises about the treaties concerning our embassy missions. What did you do to him, Ariel? He's been almost shrill about reviewing Spacer presence on Earth."

"Nothing recently."

Setaris smiled wanly. "It's been a very long day. You've been excessively diligent in your assignment."

"Why is Derec in custody?"

"The TBI said something about evidence tampering and hindering an investigation. It's the sort of charge they make when they don't know what really has them angry. You two have stirred up a lot of trouble."

"I don't see how. We haven't done all that much yet."

"Yes, but you've done it in all the right places. You two have the damnedest luck. Gale basically wants you to stop looking into Nova Levis." Setaris frowned. "You didn't know Derec Avery was under arrest?"

"I just got back in," Ariel said evasively.

"Then why did you come here? I expected a barrage of protest and a demand to have him released."

"Maybe later." She leaned on Setaris's desk. "Why are we hiding a Solarian national?"

Setaris frowned. "I'm sorry, would you repeat that?"

"Rotij Polifos."

Setaris nodded slowly. "What do you know about him?"

"Derec got suspicious of him. Neither of us knew much

about him, except that he's been director of the lab on Kopernik for six, almost seven years. That's a long time for an Auroran to hold a post here."

"I've been here nearly twelve years, Ariel."

"We're diplomats; we're different. For someone like Polifos, it's an eternity. When I checked, I discovered that he had never once requested rotation to another post. No one from any office has questioned his long residency on Kopernik. Nothing you'd expect to happen in his position has happened. His stipend hasn't even changed in six years."

"And why did you conclude he's a Solarian national?"

"A couple of things. A background check on his name came up with an old Solarian family, for one, but there are no birth records or citizenship papers for him. The family itself has only two remaining members and, like most Solarians, they're recluses. The other thing is that all his Auroran documentation originated here."

"How did you manage to learn that?"

"I'm very good at my job. The third detail is precedent. We've done this before with defectors who may be subject to extradition under the Fifty Worlds Mutual Accords. Did I guess wrong?"

"No. But—"

"I'm not finished. I did another search then, one I wouldn't have thought to do. We've been so busy tracking down who used to *own* Nova Levis we never thought to find out who *worked* there. Five researchers were senior staff— they ran the research protocols. It was their lab. Four of them are dead."

Setaris regarded her quietly. "And the fifth?"

"Was a Solarian. He vanished. Interestingly enough, the document trail for Rotij Polifos begins shortly before Nova

Levis was closed down. The Solarian presumably returned to Solaria, but I could find no evidence that he ever got there. A couple years later, Polifos assumes directorship of the positronics lab on Kopernik."

Setaris nodded. "As you say, you're very good at what you do. Though this isn't exactly your job."

"It has *become* my job," Ariel said.

"Point taken. Anything else?"

Ariel felt herself get angry then. Setaris was being "diplomatic" and neutral, superficially uninvolved—"professional," she would say. Ariel decided to thoroughly ruin her day. "Did you know about the cyborgs?"

Setaris's face lost all expression for a moment. Her skin paled then. "You're joking."

"I wish I were."

Setaris's face flexed with comprehension, brow furrowing deeply, mouth opening and closing wordlessly, eyes scanning the surface of the desk as if for something lost. It took less than a minute for her to regain composure. When she did, though, all the casual annoyance and alloyed humor were gone, replaced by pragmatic professionalism.

"Tell me what you know," she said.

"What I *know* isn't much. What I *saw* . . . Coren Lanra claimed he saw a robot with masking capabilities. What I saw tonight could only be a cyborg. It's entirely probable that it's what he saw as well. The blood sample Derec took from the collapsed robot's hand is more than likely a close relative of Nyom Looms. The material mixed with the sample—myralar—suggests robotics, but until tonight it made no sense to me."

She blew out a breath. "Nova Levis is still technically owned by Solaria. It was renamed after a Settler colony leased it from them, but the original title never transferred.

There is also an old research lab—here on Earth—called Nova Levis, among which I found Gale Chassik listed as an original shareholder. Plus Rega Looms and Alda Mikels. Tonight I met a retired policeman who was investigating kidnappings twenty-some years ago who says that, among other things, a number of infants were taken from orphanages here and transported offworld. He suspected a slave trade. But several of these infants were hopelessly handicapped . . . UPDs, he called them. Nova Levis was one of the labs he'd investigated, but he claims that it was clear of any culpability."

Setaris shook her head. "What did the lab do? And what does all this have to do with cyborgs?"

"I don't know. Nova Levis the lab was involved in prosthetics research, though."

"Why did it fail? Prosthetics is a fairly lucrative field on Earth."

"I don't know that, either," Ariel replied. "What I *want* to know is if this blockade around Nova Levis has anything to do with it. With cyborgs. I want to know if you *knew.*"

"Why would I have known?"

"Because you gave me some pathetic reasons to start this investigation."

Setaris raised an eyebrow. "Assuming I did, why wouldn't I tell you?"

"Oh, some sort of attempt at objectification. Maybe, though, you knew but had no proof. You wanted me to verify your suspicions."

"Rather shabby use of my people, wouldn't you think?"

"It wouldn't have been the first time."

Setaris narrowed her eyes. "When this is over, Ariel, I will sit you down and give you a lesson in the realities of the diplomat's life. You've been able to function largely unaffected by them since you've been here. In the meantime—"

"In the meantime," Ariel interjected, "I need Derec out of jail, and I want a little cooperation from the TBI. I don't think diplomacy will solve this particular problem."

Setaris frowned, and gestured toward the guest chairs. "Sit down, Ariel. Shut your mouth while I tell you what the situation actually is. Then, if you want to make demands, I'll listen."

TWENTY-TWO

Coren leaned against the wall and gently kneaded his neck and shoulder. The pain was growing worse; on top of his lack of sleep, he wondered if he could manage what he intended to do. He pulled his comm out and stared at the keypad, trying to think. He still lacked necessary information.

He tapped in Kelvy Torans' code. He almost gave up just as she finally answered.

"Kelvy, it's Coren."

"Please tell me you're near my apartment," she said brightly.

"Actually, no. I'm sorry to bother you so late—"

"I wasn't sleeping, anyway. Something it sounds like *you* should be doing. Are you all right?"

"Just tired. Long hours. I'm never letting Rega run for office again."

She laughed. "In that case, I suppose you're calling to see if I have that information you wanted."

"Do you?"

"As a matter of fact . . . hold on a moment . . ."

Coren listened to indistinct noises for a few seconds. Then:

"Okay, we have *lots* of good stuff," Kelvy said. "Once I started looking into this, I found all kinds of things I can use, so I suppose I owe you part of my commission. Captras Biomed: bought by the Hunter Group. It wasn't exactly a voluntary sale; Myler Towne and his faction actually tried to block it. He nearly lost the chairmanship over it. Now, Hunter bought it through one of its subsidiaries—Kysler Diversified—who also bought that research lab you mentioned, Nova Levis. One very interesting detail I found was that Towne's mother was on the original shareholders board of Nova Levis; she's since deceased. What makes a lot of this interesting is in the dispersal of the company assets. A good portion of the research documentation went to Captras Biomed, which was a small start-up back then, and later was bought out by Imbitek. It was Alda Mikels' first acquisition upon becoming a board member of Imbitek."

"Mikels was an original shareholder of Nova Levis."

"Very good. Indeed he was. As was Rega Looms. In fact, there was a bidding war over Captras between Looms and Mikels."

"Why would Rega have wanted it?"

"You'd have to ask him. *Very* uncharacteristic of him."

Coren mentally added it to the list of things he intended to ask Rega. "All right, so Myler Towne got rid of Captras, but he didn't want Hunter to have it. Why not?"

"Alda Mikels is—was—a board member of Kysler Diversified."

"Is there any other connection between Kysler and Imbitek?"

"Kysler once made an offer to acquire controlling ownership of Imbitek, but it failed."

"And when did Mikels buy into Kysler?"

"About two years after that attempt."

"So Mikels bought the company that bought Nova Levis's research material, and now is trying to reacquire that material through a competitor to his own company."

"My guess? This is insurance, in case Mikels can't defeat Towne in a shareholder vote."

"Was Captras that lucrative?"

"As a percentage of Imbitek?" Kelvy replied. "It performed a few points better than most Imbitek holdings, but not spectacularly so. However, the Hunter Group owns a number of other biomed companies on Settler colonies. Recently, they consolidated some of them under Kysler management. Add what Captras could bring to the fold, you have a very large and progressive biotech industry with established markets on several worlds. What all those companies lacked till now was a licensed vendor on Earth. Captras gives them that."

"So that's what made you so happy."

"I'm already moving on Kysler stock."

"Assuming Mikels loses to Towne, he has a ready-made position with this new company."

"New company? What new company?"

"At a guess, he'll call it Nova Levis," Coren said.

"Maybe . . . which brings up another thing. Nova Levis was not unprofitable. There was no reason for it to shut down."

"I thought it had been under suspicion in a police investigation."

Kelvy made a harsh sound. "Companies get investigated

all the time, they don't close up shop and sell their assets over it. Often such an investigation benefits them. When they're cleared of any charges, it's like getting a recommendation from the police. Their market value rises."

"Nova Levis . . . ?"

"Increased in value. The investigation did not shut it down. A year afterward, the board began buying up outstanding shares. It took six months for them to gain the necessary control to sell, over the loud protests of a number of shareholders."

"What happened to the rest of the shares?"

"Over time Kysler bought them all out. Even after Nova Levis ceased to be a corporate entity, Kysler paid options and bought off the last few until no outstanding stock remained. But now here's the thing. When Captras Biomed sold to Kysler, it did so through a blind. At least a dozen former Nova Levis shareholders made up that blind, all of whom were shareholders in Imbitek, all of whom sold their shares in Imbitek and bought shares in Kysler."

"So they bought their own company."

"In essence."

"One thing . . . what was the primary focus of Nova Levis?"

"Ah, now *that* took some digging. You know me, I'm not the most tech-literate. Primarily, they were doing research and development on chronic inorganic infectious syndromes."

Coren wrestled with the term for a few moment. "What?"

Kelvy chuckled. "My words exactly. I'm not sure exactly what they are, but I get the impression that these are diseases caused by allergic reactions to certain technologies— old nanotech, specifically. You don't hear about them much anymore because we pretty much beat them, but once in a while some poor child is born with a dysfunction that's basically untreatable."

"UPDs . . ."

"That's one term, yes. Do you know something about this?"

"No, not really. I've just heard about it—I don't know what it is. How many children?"

"It varies. Between ten and a hundred a year. Most of them don't live very long. Quarantine is about the only thing to do."

Coren thought about that. "You said we beat them. How?"

"That would take a little more research than I thought you wanted." She paused. "What do you think?"

"I think . . . dinner at Rhiomay's and a foot massage afterward."

"*That* good? I hope you don't stop at the feet."

Coren grunted. "How long have you known me?"

"Not long enough, Coren, love. Not nearly long enough."

"Thanks, Kelvy, this has been a great help. Um . . . by the way, have you ever heard of something called a 'decompiler'?"

"Sure. Curiously enough, given what we've been talking about, they're a class molecular reagent. Nanotech, used mainly for terraforming on colonies."

Coren blinked. "You knew that off the top of your head?"

"I didn't two days ago. It's one of Captras Biomed's main exports. They're banned on Earth."

"I see. Well. This definitely extends things to the calves and thighs, too."

Kelvy laughed languorously. "Can't wait. Call me when you're done doing whatever it is you're doing. I'm dying to hear the details."

"No doubt. Talk to you soon."

Coren broke the connection and pocketed the comm.

All the lists began to make sense now. Shareholders. Follow the credits. Coren had always relied on the money trail to tell him which way to turn, who to look at. This one was nearly a maze, an ouroboros swallowing its own tail.

Rega . . . how deeply into all this are you . . . ?

One or two questions remained, besides the big one. Who had killed Nyom? And why?

Coren Lanra shuddered, from weariness and despair.

Nyom . . .

The Hunter Group owned the warehouses. They owned Kysler Diversified, which now owned Nova Levis. Apparently they also owned the colony Nova Levis—or Cassus Thole, whichever name it went by. Alda Mikels owned a good piece of that.

Coren rubbed his eyes and looked down the avenue to the innocuous entrance at the T-crossing. Myler Towne lived behind that door. Coren fished a pill from another pocket and popped it into his mouth. He had waited till he knew what he wanted from Towne before taking the stim. Now he was ready. He waited for the clarity and temporary strength and the illusion of rested power.

It came like a coolness over his skin, a slight increase in hearing sensitivity, and an internal rush in his muscles. He pushed away from the wall and started down the street.

Towne wore a deep green dressing gown and sat in an enormous wingbacked chair that he still managed to dwarf.

Del Socras stood within arm's length of Coren. He had supervised a very thorough search of Coren before bringing him to see Towne. Coren felt uneasy without any weapons.

"Unusual hour for you, Mr. Lanra," Towne said. "Or maybe not. It is for me, certainly."

"Sorry if this is inconvenient for you," Coren said. "But I think we need to talk."

"I agree. Have you given my proposal further consideration?"

"Some. I'm afraid I have to turn you down for the most part."

Towne raised his eyebrows. " 'The *most* part'? Intriguing choice of words."

"I find that I've done work for you in the course of doing my job. I need to know a few things, though, to be sure."

"Are you suggesting I owe you compensation?"

"I may send you a bill. But for now, let's just see how much what I've done is worth to you."

Towne waved his hand as if to say "continue" and eased further back in his chair.

"Alda Mikels is trying to oust you from the chairmanship of Imbitek. He may also be trying to kill you, but he's certainly trying to frighten you."

Towne frowned and glanced at Socras. Coren felt the bodyguard's presence fade. When he glanced back, Socras was gone.

"How did you arrive at this conclusion?"

"Circuitously. Someone killed Rega Looms' daughter. I'm trying to find out who."

"Do you think Mikels is involved in *that?*"

"Directly? No. But it was his people."

"And who are they?"

"I don't have names ... yet. But they all work for the Hunter Group, in one way or another. So does Mikels."

Towne steepled his fingers below his chin and stared at Coren for a long time. "You are either very diligent or very lucky, Mr. Lanra. The Hunter Group wants to buy Imbitek. I've no doubt Alda is behind the attempt. Even for them, we're a bit too large and perhaps too dangerous."

"Who are they?"

"On Earth? They own shipping companies and warehouses, that's about it. Off Earth, however, they are one of the largest consortiums in the Settlers' worlds. Fewer rules, more places to move things when the law tries to compensate for the newness of the colonies. They own a little of every kind of industry. No one worried about it two or three centuries ago, before Terrans began to go out to space once more, and only Spacers existed away from the homeworld. It's fairly brutal business out there now. Mind you, I don't quite understand why Hunter wants us—they own comparable firms on several worlds. Maybe it was a prize for Alda."

"He got them Captras Biomed."

Towne sighed and dropped his hands. "You are very well informed. That's disappointing. I spent a lot of money trying to keep that news from spreading."

"Why did you want to get rid of Captras in the first place?"

"No real applications. I'm trying to consolidate Imbitek, streamline the company, get us back to our base product. Most of the things Captras produces have no use here—they're all exports."

"There's money in that."

"There was money in it for Alda, he had the connections. We've been running into higher and higher losses."

"Hunter?" Coren asked.

"It's my opinion that Hunter is the legitimate face of the pirate consortiums. Alda has been doing business with them for years, perhaps decades. Alda wants the chair back, but I won't give it to him. I have the shareholders on my side."

"But he has Hunter."

"Exactly. So I thought, just to irritate him and give us a better position in the field, it would be smart to get rid of our albatrosses. I set up a sale for the company with what I had thought was an independent group of investors. Too late I found out that Hunter was backing them." He shrugged. "I still got my price, Imbitek shares increased in value, and the last poll among shareholders showed a higher degree of confidence in my leadership."

"So now he's trying to kill you."

"It appears that way." Towne narrowed his eyes. "What did Nyom Looms have to do with all this?"

"She was running baleys."

Towne's face went slack. "I see. That's unfortunate."

"You hired a data troll to find some minutes of old board meetings Mikels chaired. She was threatened when she started looking, so she planned to leave Earth. The group of baleys she intended going with was murdered—including Nyom."

"Then I can only say that she was collateral damage. I can't imagine anyone would want to kill her. Not anyone involved in all this."

"No? Did you know Rega Looms was an initial investor in Nova Levis?"

Another shock registered on Towne's face. "No, I did not. I know almost nothing about Nova Levis."

"But you know which one I'm talking about."

Towne shrugged. "The colony holds no interest for me."

"It's interesting that you don't have more concern for Nova Levis, though. Your mother was also a primary shareholder."

"So? That doesn't mean I was ever privy to the company's workings."

"The company's material became Captras Biomed."

Towne pursed his lips. "A little knowledge . . . The minutes I hired the troll to find concerned exactly that transaction. I know what products Captras started out with, but there was more to Nova Levis than that, and those records were missing by the time I joined Imbitek. Captras was Alda's pet project, and apparently it has returned to its owner."

"The minutes?"

"Concerned several topics of a clandestine nature, but none of them Nova Levis. Quite a bit concerned Hunter."

"Oh? What connection was that?"

"Weapons, apparently. Hunter deals in arms among the colonies."

Coren nodded. "And now they have a very good bioweapons company."

"They already had one."

"Decompilers."

"You saw the results of one such misapplication the other day." Towne heaved himself out of his chair. "So. Are you working for me now or not?"

"I'm working for myself at the moment. When I've finished, maybe we can talk."

"Good. What changed your mind about Mr. Looms?"

"I don't take well to being lied to," Coren said.

"I see. Then, with that in mind, let me tell you this: One of Imbitek's many . . . subsidiary interests . . . is in baleys. I learned upon assuming the chairmanship that we—plus two or three other firms—run illicit trade through a variety of avenues. Nothing direct, purely through ancillary personnel, many of whom do not even know they work for us. I've been looking into shutting all this down, but not fast enough. Alda's people have been attacking several of our illicit ventures, including the baley running. In the last ten months we've lost eighteen shipments of baleys. We recovered three of them. They were all dead."

He stepped closer to Coren. "Your Mr. Looms' daughter was apparently using one of our egresses. The murderers were attacking *me*, Mr. Lanra." He blinked furiously. "I'm . . . sorry."

For a few seconds, Coren felt something like pity for Towne. He believed that the man truly *was* sorry. "I appreciate your honesty, Mr. Towne."

"One more thing, then. I didn't acquire those minutes through the data troll I hired—she never returned to me with the requested information. I used another source to obtain them. I have no idea where that troll went."

"Her name was Jeta Fromm."

"Yes."

"How long ago did you hire her?"

"Almost four months ago."

Coren nodded. "That's useful to know, too."

"I hope we can do business soon, Mr. Lanra."

Coren walked away from the warren, hands in his pockets, unsatisfied. He knew more now, but, though it made sense on the surface, he felt he still did not know enough.

Where did Nyom's brother come into all this?

He stopped across from a walkway access and looked around at the nearly-deserted plaza. Third shift would be ending soon and people would be filling the moving walks and the corridors and their way home or to work.

His comm chirped.

"Lanra."

"Ariel, Coren. Where are you?"

"Um . . ."

"You need to come here. Things have changed. Your friend Palen is no longer in charge, and the TBI have assumed command of the investigation on Kopernik. Derec's in detention."

Coren sighed. "I need sleep. Do you think that can be arranged?"

"As long as you do it quickly."

"I'll do what I can. I'll be there soon."

TWENTY-THREE

Derec opened his eyes in the half-light of sleep mode. The lights had dimmed shortly after Masid had left his cell. Derec lay awake for some time, mulling over what Masid had told him, and had gradually drifted off to sleep.

He raised himself on his elbows and stared across the corridor to Masid's cell. Masid seemed still asleep on his cot. Derec sat up and rubbed his eyes, wondering what had awakened him. He yawned. He went to the bowl in the corner and relieved himself.

He turned around, resealing his pants, and started at the shape staring at him through the cell door.

It was tall, broad across the shoulders, with long arms that hung to the sides. A pale halo outlined a bald head but left the face in darkness. It wore a long overcoat that fell nearly to its ankles.

It. Derec could not consider it otherwise. His subconscious labeled it as kindred to what Coffee had witnessed in the cargo bin, even though it bore no overt resemblance.

Derec swallowed hard.

It walked away from the door. Derec rushed forward and pressed his face to the mesh. He saw it walking toward the far end, to the cell of the new inmate.

"Hey!" Derec shouted. "Somebody! Intruder!"

With startling speed, it spun around and returned to Derec's cell. Derec staggered back.

It placed a hand against the door, fingers splayed. The air suddenly smelled faintly of ozone. The door slid open with a sudden crack.

"Shit," Derec breathed.

It seemed to fill the cell, head nearly brushing the ceiling. Derec wanted to yell, to argue, deny it the right to do this. He imagined slipping past it, breaking into the corridor, and fleeing; he was smaller and it seemed to be moving so slowly. Coolness spread over his thighs, down his calves, then across his shoulders, up his neck and across his scalp. He felt the beginnings of quivering somewhere around his spine.

It raised one arm and opened a hand, took another step forward. Derec could make out details in its face now and he thought he recognized it. Human face, but wrong, damaged . . .

"Looking for me?" Masid suddenly called out.

It frowned, then whirled about and stepped toward the cell door.

A brilliant scalding flash erupted around it. It dropped to one knee, staggered, and started to rise. Another flash. Derec flinched and backed up against the wall. The ozone smell was gone, replaced now by burning. He heard a roar, deep-throated and grainy, as if sound were being forced through too small a larynx, and heard the crackle then of a blaster, saw the reddish glow through closed eyelids. Darkness. Crackle, glow . . . and stillness.

"Derec."

He blinked furiously, trying to focus on the voice. Masid. Derec looked at the door of his cell. A man stood there now, the angled shape of a weapon in one hand.

"Are you all right?" Derec asked.

Masid snorted, amused. "I'm supposed to ask you that."

"Um . . ." Derec pushed away from the wall. His legs felt slightly disconnected from his hips, but he could walk. *Glad I pissed first*, he thought, and laughed at himself. "Sure. I'm . . . not hurt . . ."

He caught the edge of the cell door and gripped it tightly.

Masid smelled faintly of sweat. He nodded toward a shape on the corridor floor.

The cyborg lay crookedly sprawled, its coat spread out beneath it like a pool of blood in the half-light. Smoke wafted from its shoulders and chest.

"My apologies," Masid said. "I was asleep till you yelled." He frowned. "Was it coming for you?"

"No, it . . ." Derec swallowed again and gestured toward the far end of the block. "It was heading for the new inmate."

"That's not what was supposed to happen," Masid said grumpily. "We expected someone to come for *me*."

The lights came full-on then.

The sound of running feet filled the corridor. Masid turned suddenly and hissed.

"Well, my cover's blown," he said *sotto voce* to Derec.

Derec pointed at the corpse. "They can see it now."

People flooded around them. Palen stopped at the foot of the dead thing. Harwol stared from a few steps back.

Derec managed to walk toward it. The quivering centered now in his chest, along his sides, and over his pelvis, but he could move reasonably well.

Masid had shot it four times. Each hit was clear by the ugly burn on left shoulder, sternum, right side of the neck, and scalp. Bloody red patches mingled with ashen black. Fibers curled out of the wounds. Cloth and skin were seared together and blue, gray, and worm-white veins shot through the bubbled centers of the patches. Derec felt acid at the back of his throat, but swallowed it back.

The eyes were open. They looked strangely perfect, like exquisite copies of real eyes. No moisture, no veins in the whites, and now the irises were slightly different sizes. But the radial patterns of the dull gray pupils seemed precisely symmetrical.

The skin showed irregularities, like acne scars or old injuries that still contained fragments of whatever had done damage.

"Is this like the thing we saw in the recovered memories?" Palen asked.

"I—" Derec had to swallow again. "I wouldn't be surprised. It opened my cell door by shorting out the lock."

Reluctantly, he lifted the hand that had done the job and turned it over. Wires showed, spread over the palm. Derec pushed back the sleeve; the wiring ran up the arm.

"It shouldn't have been able to open it," Palen said.

"Was your Brethe dealer's door shorted?"

Palen nodded. "We reprogrammed them then to remain shut in the event of a short."

"What did you see on surveillance?"

"Nothing. Until your door opened. Then Masid came out of his cell. But this . . ." she gestured at the body between them. "Nothing."

"It would be interesting to know how . . ."

Derec pulled the coat back from its shoulder. A small control box was attached to the shirt.

"Damn," Agent Harwol said.

"What?" Palen asked.

"That," Harwol pointed at the box. "You said masking technology, Mr. Avery. That's it. Military spec, alternating wavelength . . . stolen."

"Black market?" Palen asked.

Harwol nodded solemnly.

"Stolen military tech isn't the worrisome part," Derec said. "Whoever supplied it is also dealing in cyborgs."

They all stared at him, expressions carefully neutral, the studied look of law enforcement unwilling to show worry when they were likely more than a little scared. Derec tasted acid once more and walked away, willing himself to not throw up in front of such pointless professionalism.

He stopped, staring at the cell at the far end. The man there sat on his cot, watching, face pale. After a few seconds, Derec went up to his cell door.

"So, who are you?" Derec asked. This close, he looked familiar.

"Who wants to know?" the man snapped back.

The voice, combined with that face . . . It took a few seconds for Derec to put it all together.

It was the dockworker from Petrabor. The one shown in the memories of the DW-12.

"Why was Gamelin coming to kill you?" he asked.

The man's face turned even paler. He stood abruptly and went to the back of his cell.

"What's going on?" Masid asked, coming up alongside him.

Derec gestured at the inmate. "This one worked the

dock in Petrabor, middleman to those dead baleys. Who is he?"

"Yuri Pocivil," Palen said, joining them. "Coren sent me his records. He's been looking for him. We picked him up in the Settler section."

"You mean," Masid said, with mock indignation, "that thing was coming to kill *you* and not me? All my careful planning and baiting went for nothing?"

Pocivil just glared back at them.

"We have to talk," Masid said to him. "What did you do to piss these people off?"

"I'm not saying anything to you," Pocivil said.

"Then maybe we should just release you now," Palen said, "and let you take your chances."

Pocivil looked away. Suddenly, he lurched to his toilet and began heaving. The sound reminded Derec of his own urge. He walked quickly away.

He managed to suppress it, though he kept walking. No one called out or tried to stop him from leaving the cell block. He emerged into the security station. Everyone had gone into the corridor, leaving the consoles untended. Derec sat down before a bank of monitors, grateful to be off his feet.

Masid joined him.

"He'll talk," Masid predicted. "He's terrified. I think it will occur to him that his best chance to stay alive now is to cooperate with us."

"He might wonder if we can really protect him," Derec said.

"Can't we? Seems to me I managed to kill that thing pretty dead."

"It took a bit, though, didn't it?"

Masid shrugged. "Cyborgs, occlusion tech, dead baleys," he said. "Any suspects in mind?"

"That's your job, isn't it?"

"So they keep telling me. There are a few arms dealers big enough to handle this kind of thing."

"We just need one."

"All right. Kynig Parapoyos."

"Why him?"

"He's the great bogeyman of the galaxy. Anything you can't pin down to someone else gets blamed on him. But he does have his fingers deeper into military tech than the others, and the widest distribution network. He runs an intelligence agency that's as good as anything a legitimate government can field. If nothing else, he's the most logical choice."

Derec nodded. "For the sake of argument, let's say that."

"All right. Then the next question is, what does he want with cyborgs?"

"The ideal soldiers."

"He sells weapons *to* soldiers."

"So? How profitable would it be to have something that could do it all?"

"Ideal mercenaries?" Masid shrugged. "I'm less impressed with mercenaries than with dedicated patriots and fanatics. Mercenaries are practical—miss a payment, they go away. They have a cost analysis attitude. If the cost is too high, they go away. What would make cyborgs different?"

"Depends. Research into them was suspended because they were unpredictable."

"Like people?"

Derec shook his head. "No. People are predictable, at least in certain broad patterns."

"So a cyborg would be a weapon that might turn and shoot its owner?"

"Maybe. If I recall correctly, they couldn't be programmed with the Three Laws. Something in the organic side of things that kept sliding around them."

"They're positronic, then?"

"The ones the Calvin Institute worked with were, yes. These? I don't know."

"How quickly could you find out?"

"Get me back to the lab."

Masid nodded and straightened. "I'll see what I can do."

Derec watched him go back into the cell block.

Too many questions to answer. Where would cyborgs be manufactured? Nova Levis? Could an industry be hidden there? A whole world? Why not? Was that perhaps the real reason behind the embargo?

But the technology . . .

"Derec."

Rana stood in the doorway to the guard room. "Director Polifos is missing."

"Did that robot take Director Polifos?"

Harwol spoke with a solid dispassion belied only by the glint of impatience in his eyes.

Derec, Harwol, and Rana stood in the positronics lab, facing each other.

"Why would you think that?" Derec asked.

"The robot is missing, Polifos is missing. I don't know, but in my policeman's way of looking at things that suggests a connection."

"A robot wouldn't do that," Derec said.

"Really? You know that for sure? You also said it was collapsed."

"It was," Rana answered.

"Which means that it couldn't just get up and walk out," Harwol said.

"Normally, yes."

"What does that mean, 'normally'? Could it or couldn't it?"

"On its own," Derec said, "no. It had to have been removed. By someone who knew something about robotics."

"Anyone working in this lab could have taken it, then. Perhaps even Polifos himself."

It was not a question. Derec turned toward Harwol. Behind him, Hofton stood beside Ambassador Leri. Two of Polifos's techs stood further back, watching anxiously.

"I don't think it's reasonable anymore to assume," Derec said, "that the people working in this lab are the only ones on Kopernik familiar with robotics."

Harwol regarded him steadily, then nodded. "Do you think there could be another cyborg?"

"Do you mean did a cyborg steal the robot?" Derec did not want to contemplate the possibility of more than one cyborg. "But why?"

Harwol shrugged. He was out of his depth, but refused to show it. "The thing we saw from the recovered memories," he said, stepping toward the console, "didn't look like what we caught tonight."

We? Derec thought sourly. "No, it didn't. But then it changed by the time Palen's people opened the bin. No one remarked on anything unusual when the bodies were carried out, so it must have looked human."

"Is that possible?"

"Malleable materials are common enough. I can imagine, though I can't describe, how you might make something that could do that." He thought of Bogard, brand new and newly aware, in its amalloy body, capable of changing shape to meet circumstances. But it never looked anything but artificial, always appeared to be what it was: a robot.

Derec glanced at the monitors, then. Thales had said nothing so far.

Harwol rounded on Derec. "If I find out you had anything to do with this—"

"Why would I?"

"You didn't want us to have the robot. Maybe you had legitimate reasons; maybe not."

"Don't waste your time suspecting me. I was in a cell, remember?"

Harwol suddenly grabbed Derec's shirt and walked him back against the examination table. He pressed Derec against the hard surface. Harwol's breath flowed hot across his face.

"I don't have time to be diplomatic. I have dead agents and a lot of interference and now a piece of evidence is missing. I do *not* need self-important Spacer *attitude.*"

Derec braced himself on the table. "I used to be of the opinion that violence was the last refuge of the incompetent."

Harwol's eyes narrowed. "And now?"

"Now? I think it's the first choice of an idiot."

Harwol's grip tightened, and he lifted Derec slightly from the floor.

"Beat it out of me," Derec said. "That's always the best way to solve a problem. Works for me all the time."

"Agent Harwol." Palen's voice cut through the sudden stillness. Her voice was calm, authoritative. "I want to see you privately."

Derec's heart hammered. Slowly, Harwol eased his grip. Derec's feet touched the floor. Harwol stepped back.

"I want that robot," he said. "I want it found and returned."

Derec cleared his throat. "And if I can't do that?"

"Then we'll see how big an idiot I am."

Harwol turned to glare at Palen, who stood nearby, hands on hips.

"Now," she said.

Derec watched them all leave, then sat down. "If I live through the night . . ."

"Sir—" Hofton began.

Derec held up a finger. "Where's Polifos?"

"I don't know," Hofton said. "No one seems to remember when they saw him last."

"Rana?"

She shrugged.

"All right, never mind." He looked over the console. "We have another subject to do an excavation on."

"Another robot?" Rana asked.

"No, not quite. A cyborg." Derec turned to Hofton. "Get Palen's pathologist—what's his name? Baxin. I think he should assist with this one. In the meantime, where the hell did Coffee go?"

"I can answer that question, Derec," Thales said. "Coffee walked out of here after I reloaded a functional matrix."

"What did he do?" Rana asked, leaning over Derec's shoulder to peer at the displays.

"We talked about this possibility," Derec said. He looked from one screen to another, trying to follow the RI's step trees. "Thales has been working at recovering Bogard's matrix so we could find out what happened when it collapsed. Because I'd built so many peripherals onto Bogard, it partly became a hardware problem. Thales thought it was a question of raw memory—not enough—but when he got to use this system, he had enough, and realized that wasn't the whole problem."

"A positronic brain," Thales said, "is not simply programming. Programming can be corrupted. The physical pathways are as necessary to its function as the matrix being run on them. Therefore, I determined that in order to successfully recover Bogard I needed to load its matrix into a brain."

"You had no way of knowing," Derec said, "if this would maintain its integrity."

"I was reasonably confident. But, no, I had no way to be certain other than to load it and see."

"You gambled."

"There was an imperative."

"Explain."

"The situation has evolved," Thales said. "Ariel and Coren Lanra have been attacked. Both are safe and Ariel is back at the embassy. She has been requesting that you contact her as soon as possible. However, there is a local problem which may pose a threat. I have traced the gates I found in the lab systems. There are two destinations. Most of them go directly to a location in the Settler sections. One, however, feeds directly to Director Rotij Polifos's apartments."

"What does that have to do with Coffee?" Rana asked.

"Three Law imperative, Rana," Thales replied. "I am required to protect. I cannot effectively do so as a stationery system."

"What," Derec asked, "is Coffee now?"

"The unit previously designated 'Coffee' is contained in a memory buffer within my system. The robot now contains a composite matrix of myself and Bogard. It is effectively what you initially intended in designing Bogard."

Derec felt excited and worried. "It's functional?"

"After running several diagnostics and situation simulations, I was confident in disconnecting it from the link."

Derec's hands curled into fists. "So where is it?"

"In the Settler section. It went to follow up on the gates we discovered, and to attempt to locate Director Polifos." Thales paused. "It seemed the most reasonable avenue of action." Another pause. "Did I err?"

TWENTY-FOUR

All we have to do, Coren thought as he rode the walkway toward the embassy district, *is find them. Or let them find us . . .*

Neither thought inspired him. He started to raise a hand to his eyes, to rub them, and his shoulder spasmed. When the pain subsided, he resigned himself to standing as motionless as possible till he reached his destination.

He thought about what Towne had told him.

The idea that Nyom was no more than an incidental casualty grated, but it made a kind of deeply banal sense. Rega entertained conspiracy theories, believing the universe was being manipulated by unseen cartels and malevolent forces. But Coren had worked for the government; he knew better. Things were a mess most of the time. Coren took compensatory comfort in that, after he thought about it for a while. It meant, finally, that no one was really in charge, and in the end he preferred it that way.

But it was intellectual comfort. In his gut, he wanted very much to blame someone when things went wrong. He very much wanted to hold vast powers responsible and perhaps try to burn them down to atone for their misdeeds.

He wanted Nyom's death to *mean* something.

It did not. Except to him. It was difficult seeing that as sufficient.

Coren glanced around. The walkway carried him now through an office district. Stairs led up and down into a jumbled landscape of boxy office complexes, some with windows, most with illuminated signs giving the name of the company or just a number. Walkways and enclosed corridors crossed above him, connecting one side to the other, and above that were the larger stained surfaces of higher levels. He saw a grid marker pass by and started moving to the slower lanes.

He still had another person to question: Tresha. What to ask her, though?

To begin with, why kill a data troll and take her place? Perhaps the information Towne had commissioned her to find related directly to the baleys. But how?

And he was not not certain that the woman *was* this mysterious Tresha. It was simply a conclusion—a logical one, but not something upon which he could be absolutely certain. By the time he got back to the embassy, perhaps Ariel would have made the final determination.

Two more exits. Three people came from the opposite direction. Coren followed them with his eyes as they passed by and continued on—

Twenty or so meters behind him two people rode his lane. A man and a woman. Immediately his fatigue seemed to subside, replaced by a wary tension. He kept his posture unchanged and looked ahead. A corridor split off from the avenue, but too close to make his exit look natural. He was four exits from the most direct route to the Auroran Embassy.

Perhaps it was only coincidence. He was fairly sure Tresha was under guard at the Auroran Embassy, but that left her "muscle," Gamelin, still loose. Coren had no valid reason to feel that he was being followed, but . . .

He watched the corridor pass by and casually stepped over to the next slower lane. Only one separated him now from the stationery lanes. He glanced back. The couple had moved closer.

Coren stepped to the slowest lane. He saw an archway approaching that opened on a public mall. At five meters, he left the moving lane and strode purposefully toward the arch. He heard footsteps behind him.

He passed beneath the arch and ran.

The mall was a collection of cafés and clubs. The urgent throb of music pushed at the air. People looked up from tables nearby as he sprinted past.

He reached the far end to be confronted by a broad stair heading up. Behind him, the two people came running.

Coren bounded up the steps, three and four at a time. His breathing was heavy at the top, where he came to a large plaza with a holographic fountain in the center. Color and shape danced and shimmered thickly in the air.

He skirted the perimeter of the fountain and palmed a stunner. He thumbed off the safety and searched for an open door, but there were only windows encircling the plaza. On the opposite side, another staircase led up to the next level.

Coren judged the distance, took long strides, and hit the rim of the fountain. He closed his eyes tightly as he jumped across two meters of water to land on the edge of the central display platform. One more step and he slitted open one eye. He stood in the middle of the holographic display. All around him color prismed, split, washed one into the other. He glimpsed the top of the stairs he had ascended through brief gaps in the imaging. Crouching, he watched.

The pair came into the plaza and stopped. They exchanged glances and drew weapons, but through the dance of light Coren could not tell what kind of pistols they held. Each one circled the fountain in the opposite direction. Coren watched the woman, turning as she moved.

They joined on the other side of the fountain, spoke briefly, then hurried up the next staircase. Coren counted to ten and jumped out the far side of the display.

He wanted to continue running, reach the embassy, and worry about these two later, but that would be sloppy. He did not know if others waited further along the way, a second team waiting to pick up where the first left off. Slowly he walked around the fountain until he could see the landing above. Empty.

Silently, he walked up the stairs.

At the top, just beyond the wall that rose on either side of the landing, he found a boulevard. Residential warrens lined the far side. Personal transports sped by in both directions. He saw a moving walkway across the six lanes. A bridge spanned the trafficway to his right. He leaned cautiously out and glanced down the walkway, left and right.

The woman stood about three meters along, pressed against the wall. She seemed to be watching the footbridge. A moment later, Coren saw movement on it—the man.

It was a clear shot. He aimed carefully and fired. The man spasmed briefly and fell.

The woman made a move in the direction of the bridge. Coren rushed up behind her. She started to turn, bringing her own weapon up, when he reached her. He grabbed her gun hand and pushed it down sharply, bending the hand forward against the underside of the wrist. Her fingers loosened automatically and the weapon fell.

But then she drove her foot back against his shin. The pain surprised him. He lost his grip and she broke free. She spun around and slammed the heel of her hand against his collarbone. Coren snapped back against the wall. He saw her arm go back, preparing for another blow. Gracelessly, he kicked her across the ribs. She staggered back and fell to the sidewalk.

She sat up, began to rise. Coren dropped to one knee between her legs and pushed his pistol against her cheek.

"Tresha?" he asked on spec.

She frowned. "Who?"

He saw a shoulder holster beneath her jacket, and pushed the short coat off her. The rig held a commlink, restraints, and an ID folder. He plucked the little black case out and flipped it open. "You're a cop?"

"Chavez. Homicide. And you're in a lot of trouble," she managed to say, her voice shaking.

"Why are you following me?"

She glared at him. Coren dropped the ID wallet in her lap and stood.

"I don't have time for this. You tell your—"

"Put down the weapon!"

Coren turned. A uniform cruiser stood ten meters off now, two officers alongside the vehicle, weapons drawn.

"It's all right," he called, raising his weapon, fingers spread. "I have—"

"Time to wake up. You weren't stunned that badly. Come on."

Coren resisted opening his eyes. He had been aware of

sounds around him for some time, though it was hard to judge how long he had actually been awake. Neural stuns did odd things to time sense, among other things.

He recognized the voice, though. He blinked. The light was low, for which he was grateful.

A broad-shouldered man with short, graying hair stood above him, watching, his bright green eyes intent.

"Inspector . . . Capel?"

"Very good, Mr. Lanra. Let's hope the rest of your memory works as well. Can you sit up?"

Coren closed his eyes, trying to orient himself. He was lying on a cot. He sat up slowly, levering himself with his arm. His left shoulder throbbed with deep pain and he sucked air between his teeth.

"Here," Capel said.

Hands grasped his arms; Capel pulled his right side around, and Coren swung his legs over the edge of the cot.

"Oh, that hurts," Coren groaned.

"You're bruised. Hairline fracture on the clavicle—no wonder the painkillers you've been taking don't work. You should take better care of yourself, Mr. Lanra. Stop doing foolish things. Like running from the police."

Coren looked up at Capel. "I was surrendering to the uniforms."

"They saw a weapon," Capel said reasonably. "You'd already shot one officer and had the other under threat."

"I was checking her ID. They were following me."

"You have some reason to be running from strangers?"

"Strangers usually don't follow me."

"Here."

Capel offered a glass of amber liquid. Coren automatically accepted it and straightened. "How long?"

"They brought you in an hour ago. If you hadn't been so

beaten up you'd have been awake by then. Since you weren't, we brought you to the infirmary first."

"Thanks." Coren lifted the glass and sniffed. He recognized the acid smell of the standard enhancer cocktail used by people in high stress occupations—like emergency medical techs and the military and police—to provide quick, temporary revitalization. He would sleep later, sleep deeply, if he drank this now, and he was not sure he liked that. But his head felt wrapped in thick wadding and his thoughts came sluggishly. He drank down half the liquid.

"Who did you think we were?" Capel asked after a minute.

Coren felt sharper already. One drawback was that the pain in his shoulder was more acute.

"First, were you following me, or did I stumble into something?"

"We were looking for Ree Wenithal. You were seen leaving his apartment warren, so I assigned a team to follow you. After you left Myler Towne, I decided we needed to have a talk."

"Ah. You found out Wenithal was Damik's sponsor."

Capel nodded. "Do you know where he is?"

"Last I knew, in the Auroran embassy."

Capel frowned. "What's he doing there?"

"It's a long story."

Capel backed away from the cot and sat down. He crossed his left leg over his right, propped his head on his left hand. "You aren't leaving till I hear it all."

Coren finished the glass of unpleasant fluid, looked around the sterile infirmary room, and decided that he had no real choice. Still, he felt compelled to bargain.

"Quid pro quo?" he asked.

"We'll see." Capel smiled. "You go first."

*   *   *

In his years as a government agent, Coren had found that lying to the authorities only gained time, and not very much at that. If you were not part of the center of their attention, a lie could pass almost unnoticed, but if you entered their field of interest even a little bit, lying never proved a sound policy. The only people who could get away with it were those who could afford to hire people to lie for them.

Coren doubted he could talk his way past Capel with anything less than a complete disclosure. At this point, it might be worth it to see what Capel knew. Besides, he had no time for anything else.

When Coren finished, Capel was leaning forward, arms on his knees, listening intently. After a time, Capel straightened and pushed a button on the wall behind him.

"Coffee, two," Capel said, then folded his hands in his lap and looked at Coren. "I suppose it's occurred to you to wonder why Damik ran to Wenithal in the first place?"

"I was coming to ask him that the night you and I met."

Capel's face flexed in a half-smile. The door opened, and a uniformed officer brought in a tray bearing two cups and a carafe. He placed it on the table beside Capel and left. Capel poured and handed a cup to Coren. After the revitalizer, it smelled wonderful.

"We dug up Wenithal's case logs after we found the connection," Capel said. "He was a reliable cop for most of his career, nothing special. That last case was his entreé to bigger things. Very high profile. And very successful, as far as it went."

"That's rather ambivalent."

"He didn't finish. Arrests were made, several facilities were closed down, a big media event resulted making him out to be a hero. It benefitted everyone more than not, so

Wenithal was allowed to quietly resign. But he wasn't guilt-free, and some people wondered if his success hadn't been just a little too convenient."

"You're saying he was corrupt?"

Capel shrugged. "My personal take, after reviewing the logs, is that Eurosector Enforcement Agent Ree Wenithal was handed that success as a reward to stop looking. The missing children that were recovered comprised less than one percent of the total, which is still a considerable number. But he was far from over when he started arresting people. You know and I know that once you start making arrests, those you don't get in the first wave go to ground and get harder to find. If they're adequately resourced, you never get them. They leave Earth and you lose them."

"And he lost some?"

"I'd say he probably lost the core perpetrators. Nobody who served time as a result of that case damaged the organization by their absence. There was a four- or five-year hiatus and the abductions began again. The market wasn't shut down, the routes weren't closed. What happened afterward was all public relations, and no one was willing to look foolish by calling it into question."

"No other agents followed up?"

"Two of Wenithal's partners from those days died shortly thereafter—one from natural causes, the other in an accident. There were three people in the civil advocate's office connected to the case who died." Capel waved a hand. "All the deaths were explained, and from what I can tell the explanations were legitimate, but the fact remains that those closest to events either died or quickly found new careers. I'm reading all this and I'm thinking coverup. Call me paranoid. It's ancient history, though, so there's no way to find out for sure."

Coren sipped his coffee. "And Damik?"

"Damik is a little less problematic. He was definitely receiving bribes. Most of them were coming through Wenithal. Nothing large by some standards, a lot of gray market material— adjusted tariff stamps, relabelled goods, that kind of stuff. But he was also plugged into the baley network. One of them, anyway."

"Which one?"

Capel shook his head. "Does it matter? As it turns out, the one being run by Imbitek under Alda Mikels. Oh, yes, we knew about it, but we could never get enough evidence for warrants. Besides, baley-running is generally considered a victimless crime. These people want to leave, who are we to say no? The laws are more symbolic than anything. What's relevant here is that ten months ago Wenithal cut Damik off. Within a month, Damik had found other sources of income, and was finding more, but it hadn't yet equaled what he'd been getting from Wenithal."

"I saw reported payments in Wenithal's records to Damik up till a few weeks ago."

"Really. Where did you see those?"

Coren cleared his throat. "Something Wenithal left lying open on his desk."

Capel smiled wryly. "In any case, there had apparently been a falling out between them. Maybe Wenithal had started paying him again, but we know he had stopped payments for several months."

"How do you know they were bribes?"

"Because of the source of Wenithal's funds."

"May I guess? Either the Hunter Group or Kysler Diversified."

"No. Imbitek. Or was. This new guy, Towne, has been trying to clean the company up, shutting down a lot of its illicit ventures. But under Mikels they'd been buying from Wenithal for years, except they paid him five times market value for what he supplied them. Half that money ended up going directly to Damik."

"Imbitek . . ."

"Something else, though." Capel took a folder off the table beside him and handed it to Coren. "Look at this and tell me what you think."

Coren pulled an image out of the folder. It showed a naked female body, horribly bruised from face to shins. "Same kind of lividity as Damik."

"That's my thought. I did a records search for similar cases. That one was the closest match."

"Who was she?"

"We don't know. No ID. Found her in Lyzig District six days ago." Capel retrieved the print and returned it to the folder. "You were in Lyzig not long ago yourself, weren't you?"

"Yes."

"Maybe a coincidence. I hoped maybe you could identify her."

"Run a match for 'Jeta Fromm.' She was a data troll."

Capel blinked, then pressed the button again. An officer appeared, and Capel told her to run a check on that ID.

"If it comes up positive," Coren asked, "does that make me a suspect?"

"If I thought that, you'd be in custody. No, but you're close to this. Closer than I am, anyway."

"That's your feeling?"

"That's my feeling." Capel finished his coffee and set the cup down. "If you could talk to anyone you wanted to right now, who would it be?"

Coren thought for a moment. "Alda Mikels."

"He gets released tomorrow morning. We have till then to interview him."

"Privately?" Coren asked with emphasis.

"Very. Interested?"

"Very." Coren stood. "Why?"

Capel raised his eyebrows. "You mean, why am I letting you into this? Very simple. Some of the people who were around when Wenithal closed his last case are still around, only in even higher positions than they were then. If this goes where I think it will, I may need someone outside the department."

"Do you trust me?"

"I looked at your record." Capel pressed the button to be let out. "Shall we?"

Marland Reformatory and Social Reclamation Center occupied a huge area north of D.C. Capel took Coren through the security passage that linked directly to police headquarters, a ten-minute ride in a car designed to carry prisoners behind a transparent security shield that separated them from their guards.

Coren waited while Capel arranged an interview room. Silently, the two men followed a uniformed escort up four levels and down a long hall. The interview room was comfortable, with plush chairs all around and a writing desk. Coren was surprised to find it open, with no indication of any security wall to keep prisoners from interviewers.

Capel noticed his reaction. "We have no surveillance, either."

Coren took his hemisphere from his pocket. "What happens if I switch this on?"

"Nothing. You don't trust me?"

"You, yes." Coren thumbed the field damper on and returned it to his pocket.

Capel nodded and took a seat.

"How much freedom do I get?" Coren asked.

"Don't abuse your welcome," Capel said. "Keep it within reason."

A few minutes later, the opposite door slid open and Alda Mikels stepped through.

He had lost weight, Coren saw, and his thick mane of white hair seemed thinner. The lines in his face sank deeper and his skin looked slightly waxen.

"Mr. Mikels," Capel said. "I appreciate you taking the time to see us. Please, sit."

Alda Mikels frowned at Coren as he eased himself into a chair. "You're welcome, I'm sure, Inspector. Do I know you?"

"I'm Inspector Capel, Homicide Division. This is Coren Lanra, head of security for—"

"For Rega Looms. Yes, I thought you looked familiar. Is there a reason for this visit, or just a last chance to see me in prison?"

"We have a few questions we thought you might help us with," Capel said.

Mikels focussed on Capel. "Homicide? I haven't killed anyone. Not in here, at least."

"That remains to be seen," Capel said. "Do you know Ree Wenithal?"

"Should I?"

"You've been overpaying him for textiles for years," Capel said. "From the amounts, we thought perhaps you had a personal relationship with him."

"A good supplier, then?" Mikels said, shrugging. "I don't remember."

"Odd. He remembers you," Coren said. "Even kept a special log of all your transactions."

"Really?"

"He was cut off by your successor," Capel said.

"I wouldn't know anything about it. What Towne is doing to my company . . . well, I'll find out all about it soon enough."

"You're being modest," Coren said. "I think you know all about it now."

"And why would that be?"

"You're waging a war for control of your company. I'm impressed with your resources—it must be very difficult to conduct business from a cell. But it's not a very precise way to do it. Some people have died as a result. According to Tresha, the orders went through Wenithal, along with his monthly stipend from Imbitek . . . until Towne took over and started cutting up your empire."

Mikels glowered. "This is all supposition, of course."

Coren said nothing. Mikels blinked and looked at Capel.

"Is it standard procedure for the police to allow private security to harass wards of the state?"

"Coren," Capel said, "you're just supposed to observe."

Coren nodded, but continued to stare at Mikels. He felt anxious, which was a problem—an interview like this needed a finesse he did not feel willing to accord. He realized then that he had decided to blame Mikels for Nyom's death—it was *his* war, after all, that had gotten her killed.

"Now, Mr. Mikels," Capel said, "we know you're a busy man. We won't keep you very long. But I wondered if you could explain those payments to Mr. Wenithal. The amounts were quite generous. It seems fiscally irresponsible—at least to *me*—that you'd pay him those amounts when you could easily have switched vendors and saved yourself all that extra expenditure. Unless he was blackmailing you, that is. Was he?"

Mikels laughed. "You're more imaginative than most of your colleagues, Inspector Capel."

"Then he was working for you in other capacities?"

Mikels stood. "I don't have to talk to you."

"I think it would be a good idea, though," Coren said. He took a couple of steps toward Mikels. "You have a problem, and it could be very dangerous."

Mikels laughed. "Are you threatening me, Mr. Lanra?"

Coren smiled with mock innocence. "Me? Not at all. I'm trying to help you."

Mikels glanced toward the detective. "Inspector Capel—"

"Sit down, Lanra," Capel said tersely.

Coren looked at Capel. He saw nothing but a warning in the inspector's eyes, and the expectation of obedience. Coren gave Mikels a long look before he grudgingly returned to his chair.

"It seems, Mr. Mikels," Capel said, "that your replacement at Imbitek may have gotten himself into some legal problems. Certain clandestine operations have surfaced and you could help us clear them up. I just thought we could help each other."

"Towne?" Mikels sounded incredulous, but he sat down. "What do you have?"

"It seems he's been running baleys. Some of them have gotten killed. We think reprisals have been made and will continue to be made."

"Baleys." Mikels looked from Coren to Capel. "You're here about baleys?"

"Anything you might have that could help us . . ." Capel said, obviously trying to lead him.

"Is this off the record?"

"We don't have anything official pending in your case. We're hoping you'll help as a good citizen."

Mikels pursed his lips and folded his hands in his lap. "Well, it isn't my desire to see Towne hurt."

"Could you vouch or him, then—substantiate his innocence?"

Mikels smiled. "I don't think so." He sighed wearily. "I knew this would hurt the company in the long run. There has always been a faction at Imbitek involved in extra-legal matters. I shut down three divisions during my chairmanship that dealt in contraband. But Imbitek is large, and favors are passed in a variety of ways. It's difficult to keep track of everyone and everything. Towne . . . well, he's been tangled up with the Settler Coalition for a long time. If he's running baleys, I'm not surprised."

"Wenithal?" Coren prompted.

"I was not aware we were still doing business with him. Those three divisions I mentioned all used him to fix Customs. Wenithal had an associate in ITE—an adopted son, I think—through whom he got special considerations. When I shut them down, I thought I'd cut him off."

"The payments?" Capel asked.

"Wenithal owns a textiles manufacturing firm. It would be safest to mask the payments as business-as-usual."

"You said you didn't know him," Coren said.

Mikels glared at him. "Do I look like an idiot, Mr. Lanra? I don't know him personally, but in this connection I remember the name."

Capel pointedly frowned at Coren.

Coren ignored him and pressed on. "And the association. Is there any reason you could think of that Towne would have either of them killed?"

"Not unless they were about to turn against him."

"Might they?"

Mikels shrugged. "I can't see that Wenithal would gain anything, but Damik might. After all, he would have the most to lose in any kind of official inquiry."

"So you knew Brun Damik, too?" Capel asked.

"I didn't say that—"

"Were Damik and Wenithal about to go freelance? Or was it just Damik who thought he could set up his own operation from your leftovers? Is that why you had him killed?"

Mikels laughed. "I'm a businessman, Inspector. I don't have people killed. I have no idea who murdered Damik."

"So you *did* know he was dead?" Coren asked.

Mikels started to stand again. "I think our talk is over, gentlemen—"

Coren took the folder Capel had brought with him. Before the inspector could stop him, he walked quickly up to Mikels, slid the picture out, and held it before the industrialist. Mikels stared at it for a long time.

"Do you know her?" Coren asked.

"No." Mikels looked worried now.

"Have you ever seen a body look like that? I've seen a few recently. Something—or someone—crushed them. Must be an incredibly painful way to die."

"What does this have to do with me?"

"Whoever did this can slip in and out of secured areas undetected. Some kind of military-grade masking tech. I even know of one victim who was in jail, and no records exist of her death. None."

Mikel's eyes flicked to Capel.

"Why don't you sit down again, Mr. Mikels," the inspector said.

Mikels sank back to the chair.

Coren turned to Capel. "Here's what I think. I think Mr. Mikels has been paying his way through Customs by way of Wenithal and Brun Damik. I think Myler Towne found out about it when he took over and started straightening Imbitek out." He turned back to Mikels. "I think you did a quick estimate of how much this was going to cost you in future revenue and decided to oust Towne. It's backfiring, though, and he's more popular now than ten months ago, when he took over. So you've been cleaning up all the loose ends that could tie you up in litigation and further prison time if they come to light. You're shutting down the baleys before he does, and you're doing it so that it looks like it was his fault, because, after all, Imbitek is the one in charge of them, isn't it? And you're in jail, so how could you be doing any of it?"

"You have no proof," Mikels said haltingly.

"Oh, but it gets better. When it looked like there was no way you could win a shareholder vote, you arranged to take over part of Imbitek, the part most profitable off Earth. You used the same people you used to funnel baleys all these years to fund the purchase of Captras Biomed. Towne tried to block the sale when he found out who was behind the purchase, but he couldn't. To cap it off, you tried to kill him. Leave Imbitek headless and, after you get out of prison, leave the planet. Imbitek falters, you use Captras as a platform through which to buy it out, and you end up owning it outright." Coren grinned wolfishly. "Stock transactions leave a pretty good trail for those who can read it."

Mikels grunted. "You have an excellent imagination. Why should any of this cause me to help you?"

"Because I think you may become a loose end yourself. All this is going on and the profits are rolling and you're still in jail. Someone is going to be thinking pretty soon that you're superfluous."

"Why would they think that?"

"Because it just might occur to them that they already have Captras Biomed. What do you need *you* for? To run it? At this point, you're waging a private war against Myler Towne, to hurt a company that your backers no longer want. This isn't good for profits."

Now Mikels reacted nervously.

"The only thing that bothers me," Coren continued, "that I don't understand, is where all the baleys are going and what Nova Levis has to do with any of this?"

"What does Rega want to know this for?" Mikels demanded.

"Why do you think?"

Mikels shook his head. "I don't know. He's been out of it for years. Why now?"

"Maybe," Coren said slowly, taking a gamble, "it's a family matter."

Mikels grew still. Only the sound of breathing filled the room. When he did not answer, Coren leaned close to his ear.

"This isn't Rega," Coren said. "This is me. I want to know." He leaned closer still and whispered. "Your little vendetta killed a friend of mine. A good friend. This is personal for me."

"Just because you and Damik served together—"

Coren straightened. "Not Damik! But if you know that, then you know the rest. You killed Nyom Looms, you fuck." He snarled. "I'm sure you know about Nyom and me. She's dead."

"Lanra!" Capel bellowed. "Back off—now!"

Mikel's eyes widened. "I see. That's unfortunate, Ms. Looms' death, but . . ."

"Cyborgs," Coren said flatly.

Mikels started. "What?"

"Cyborgs. What do you know about them?"

Mikels wiped a hand over his mouth. "May I give you some advice, Mr. Lanra? You should let this go now. You won't help Nyom Looms anymore. All you could do would be to put yourself, your friends, and your family in danger."

"Not really a problem. I don't have any friends and I'm an orphan. Just like Damik."

Mikels sighed and shook his head. "I don't have to talk to you. But Wenithal knows everything. You can ask him. I've never been directly involved."

"Is that why you've gone to all the trouble to buy Nova Levis?"

Capel grasped Coren's arm. Coren shrugged him off.

Mikels looked startled, then laughed. He stood, then. "My, but you *are* impressive. If I thought you'd accept it, I'd offer you a job." He walked toward the door. "If you know that much, then you know the rest. *You* figure it out."

"Why infants?"

Mikels stopped. "Excuse me?"

"The thing I can't figure out—why infants?"

Mikels shook his head. "This interview is over."

Mikels rang the bell for release. A few moments later, the guard took him away, leaving Coren and Capel alone.

"Damn," Coren hissed.

"What do you want to do now?" Capel asked sarcastically. "Is there anyone else you want to roust tonight before I get the full story?"

"I don't know." Coren stared at the door, then looked at Capel. "Don't wait for an apology."

"I won't. I just wish I understood what just happened here." He pressed a hand against Coren's chest. "You *can* explain it to me, can't you?"

"Maybe. Where do you want me to start?"

"First things first," Capel said. "Given Mikel's reaction to it—what's a cyborg?"

Coren flashed a half-smile. "Well, as I understand it. . . ."

TWENTY-FIVE

The corpse on the table smelled cloyingly sweet. Baxin, Sipha Palen's pathologist, directed a squad of devices while speaking aloud his findings for the recorders.

"—lungs are permeated by clusters of nodes which seem to function as storage systems for long-term oxygenation. Secondary vascular system routed through what appears to be a secondary spleen suggests waste gas disposal follows complimentary pathways for storage in . . . what the hell is *that?*"

He fidgeted nervously and glanced at Derec and Palen, who watched from the other side of the isolation screen. Baxin was perspiring slightly. His fingers worked a keypad, and the small scavengers moved on and through the body of the cyborg.

"The muscle structure is a complex interleaving of polymers and protein. Molecular bonding seems to be cyclodextrous . . . we have polyamide bonding along single-chain amine nitrogen . . . looks like it uses adipic acids to facilitate the protein interactions . . ."

Baxin looked at Derec and shook his head.

"I have no idea what I'm looking at," he said. "This thing looks like it's made of nylon and nylon analogs."

"Myralar?"

"Yes, I'm finding a lot of that in the joints and the valves. A second pancreas that looks like an organic polymer factory . . . it's producing hexamethyline diamine instead of insulin . . . I don't even know why it was brought here."

"This doesn't look like the being in the recovered memories," Palen said. "The skin looks . . . normal, I suppose."

"Oh, that," Baxin said. He took a pair of forceps and lifted a layer of skin from one pectoral. Instead of the red and gray of organic tissue, the underside looked like graphite. "There's a layer of composite that seems to be electrolytically active. If I run a small charge through it, the material shifts to the exterior derma." He dropped the layer and shook his head. "It causes problems—skin irritation and infections from the look of it. That's the source of the rough complexion."

"In your opinion," Palen asked, "is it at all human?"

Baxin shrugged elaborately and surveyed the body. "Sure. There's blood, oxygenation, amino acids . . . I'm seeing some alternate building blocks in part of the DNA, like fluorotryptophan . . . but it's at least as much a machine . . . a very odd machine . . ." He grabbed a hand and held it up. "The musculature in key areas has an underlying carbon isotope structure that responds to pressure by forming a kind of sheathe. The best comparison I have is calcium deposition in bones under stress. But *that* takes days or months. According to the projections I've got here—" he pointed at his monitors "—*this* responds instantly by creating a kind of exoskeleton which can be reabsorbed." He shook his head. "In my opinion, the only thing that would define this as primarily organic is that you'd have to grow all this. You couldn't add it onto an already extant organic structure."

"Not at all?" Derec asked. "I mean, how early would you have to start?"

Baxin sighed and glanced at the readouts on the bank on monitors beside him. "Well, there are some problems. I've got an organ here that looks like a gall bladder, but as far as I can tell it's strictly for the isolation of ammonia, which seems to be produced as a byproduct of a polymerization process. The ammonia would still be toxic if released generally, so it's flensed from the system and fed back into the one of the spleens for venting. It's not a perfect system—I'm seeing excess carbonic carbonyl in the duodenum that seems to be ingested to compensate for an imbalance. I'm thinking that most of this secondary polymer system was introduced before puberty, probably in infancy. You could overcome some of these problems by starting with a base genetic template and growing one from scratch, but I wouldn't be able to tell you how. Probably the rate of breakdown would overwhelm it at that stage, so starting later might compensate for some of the flaws."

"You don't sound too certain," Palen said.

"There'd have to be certain preconditions," Baxin said. "I'm not good enough for this, Chief. I'm guessing. You need someone who understands sequencing and gene therapy."

"What about the brain?" Derec asked. "Is it wholly organic?"

"No . . . well, yes . . . I mean, it's oxygenated, but what I'm seeing is the presence of protonated oxygen. That would limit cell absorption considerably, except that there's a monomer fiber strung along the vasal matrix that's drawing particles from a small isotopic shunt in the hypothalamus."

"What kind of particles?" Derec pressed.

"Positrons."

Derec sensed Palen looking at him. "All right," he said. "When you finish, I want the brain sent to the positronics lab."

"The whole thing should've been sent there to begin with," Baxin complained. "Sorry. I'll let you know when I've completed my autopsy."

"Thanks, Doctor," Palen said. "By the way, the masking ability—"

Baxin laughed sourly. "That's the only thing that's easy to explain. The clothing. It doesn't have it built into itself. It just wore military tech."

Derec walked away from the theater. Masid leaned against the wall by the exit, arms folded over his chest. Derec heard Palen's heavy tread catching up to him.

"Your assistant," Masid said, "just called to say you should come to the lab ASAP." Derec nodded in response.

"So, just what *is* that thing?" Palen demanded as the three of them stepped into the corridor outside the morgue.

"A cyborg," Derec said. "What I was afraid of."

"Where did it come from?"

"I have no idea."

"Are there more of them?"

"There's no reason to think this one is the prototype. Why use it for something as risky as slipping into a police station to murder someone if it's the only one? No, there are others." He glanced at Palen. "What did your Brethe dealer find that got her killed by one?"

Palen glared at Masid. "I don't know," she said. "We didn't get a chance to debrief her."

"Where was she when you picked her up?" Derec asked.

"Settler section, dockside," Masid said. "She used to keep a flop there, in the service section."

"Has anybody looked at it since she died?"

Palen nodded. "It had been tossed, pretty thoroughly. None of her associates shed any light on what she was into."

"Was she actually dealing Brethe?" Derec asked.

"Absolutely," Palen said. "Only way to keep her cover valid."

"Who was her supplier, then?"

Masid nodded. "A local boss named Metresha, who also has a finger or two in the baley traffic."

"Has anybody talked to her?"

"Not yet," Palen said. "She's offstation right now. I didn't want to move on her till we had some solid information about these deaths."

"Does anybody know when she's coming back?"

Masid shrugged. "Metresha is rather hard to keep track of. No one is really sure what she looks like—she tends to work through intermediaries a great deal. I gather the docks are being watched?"

"The Settler ship that was supposed to pick up those baleys is in dock now," Palen said. "Metresha always shows up when a cargo is being moved."

"Have you heard from Lanra?"

"Not since yesterday."

"I want to talk to Ariel," Derec said.

"*I* want to know where that robot is," Palen said.

Derec glared at her. "You might want to ask your new prisoner about the cyborg. He knew its name, after all."

"We're letting him think things through a while longer," Palen said. "Do you want to be there when we question him?"

"It might be useful to have someone there who knows a little about robots," Derec said sardonically.

The three of them took the next shunt to the Spacer quarters in stony silence. Derec found himself slightly in the lead as they strode toward the lab. Agent Harwol and one of his people stood outside the lab, talking quietly. When he spotted Derec, he came forward.

"We have a situation, Avery—"

"Talk to the ambassador," Derec said irritably, brushing past the TBI agent.

"Avery—"

Derec entered the lab and stopped abruptly.

The DW-12 stood in the center of the space, most of the resident techs standing in a loose circle around it. Director Polifos sat, arms folded indignantly, before the robot. When he saw Derec, his scowl deepened and he tried to stand. The robot placed a hand on his shoulder and urged the director back into the chair.

"Damn it, you cannot *do* that!" he shouted. "What is wrong with this robot? Doesn't it know that it has to take my orders?"

"It knows it has to keep you here," Derec said. "For your own protection."

"I'm in no danger!"

"Then, why were you running?"

"I wasn't."

Derec looked at the robot. "Thales?"

"The Director had booked passage on a Settler transport," the robot said. "I found him in a dockside tavern in Section Forty-nine, carrying a pack of personal belongings."

Polifos glared up at the robot.

"What is this thing?" he asked quietly.

"Never mind that," Palen said. "Why don't you tell us where you were going? And why?"

Polifos looked at her, anger and fear working at his expression. He shook his head.

"What ship?" Palen asked.

"The *Reyatta*," Thales answered.

Palen pulled out her comm and stepped away, speaking softly. A few seconds later, she came back.

"Interesting choice of ships, Director," Palen said. "The *Reyatta* is a known blockade runner. Where were you going, Director Polifos?"

Polifos shook his head and studied the floor.

Derec searched the lab until he saw Rana over by the workstation they had been using. She waved him over.

"Ariel needs to talk to you," she said.

Derec stepped up to the console. "Thales, are we secure?"

"Yes, Derec. I have traced all the gates in place. One of them fed directly to Director Polifos's quarters. Another went to Chief Palen's office. One, however, I have a location for but no identification, in the Settler's section."

"Where's Ariel?"

"Back in the embassy," Thales said. "But not for long. There have been developments."

"Connect me."

Derec stopped before Polifos and waited for the man to look up. "Director."

Polifos frowned.

"What kind of work did you do for Nova Levis?"

Polifos blinked and went pale.

Derec turned to Palen, who had been talking intently with Masid, away from the others. "I want to bring him down to the morgue."

Palen looked intrigued. "All right."

Thales/Bogard urged Polifos to his feet. Harwol and two of his agents came forward. "What are we doing?" Harwol asked.

"A demonstration," Derec said. "Thales?"

"Please follow Derec Avery," the robot said.

"Agent Harwol, if you could have your people guard our flanks on the way down . . . ?"

Reluctantly, Harwol agreed. The entourage emerged from the lab and headed back down to Palen's morgue.

Baxin still worked on the body. He looked up at the approach of this new group, his brow knitting. Derec glanced at Polifos.

When the director saw the corpse, he stopped, then tried to back up. Thales/Bogard blocked his escape. Derec reached for him, took his shirt sleeve, and dragged him close to the transparency.

"What do you think of that, Director Polifos?"

"I—" He shook his head. "Please."

"Recognize it? Perhaps some of it is your own work?"

"I don't know."

"You don't know? Then why are you frightened? Why were you running? Is this what you were running from?"

"You don't understand—"

Derec tightened his hand on Polifos's arm. "Then make me understand."

"Please!"

"Is this what you've been hiding from for the last twenty years? Did you make that?"

"No! I don't know what that is! Let me be!"

Polifos squirmed loose from Derec only to encounter Palen, Masid, Harwol, and Thales/Bogard.

"Talk to us, Director," Palen said. "We've got a lot of dead people we need explanations for."

"I didn't have anything to do with that," Polifos said.

"What did you do in Nova Levis?" Derec asked. He pointed at the cyborg. "Is that a direct result of your work?"

Polifos tried not to look at it.

"Is that your work, *Kyas Vol?*"

Polifos paled visibly then. "You know?"

"You've been hiding here under the protection of the Auroran government since disappearing from Earth after Nova Levis closed down. Why? What were you doing there?"

"I'm trying not to die, damn it!" He whirled around, shoving Derec away. He backed against the transparency. "They killed everyone! Anyone who knew anything about it! Fos and Holani . . . Cortem . . . the documentation staff . . ." He was shaking now. "I went to the Aurorans because they were the only ones not involved. Terran authority, Solarians, corporates . . . Aurora had nothing to do with it."

"With what?" Harwol demanded.

Polifos started sobbing. He slid to the floor, eyes streaming.

"We never really knew who we were working for," he said finally. "The lab took subscriptions for stock. It was supposed to be a public corporation—we didn't know . . ."

"Your mission," Derec said. "What was your mission?"

"The plague. Stop the plague."

"What plague?" Palen asked.

Polifos shook his head. "There wasn't one. We succeeded." He sat there, crying for a time, until he finally got control of himself. He stood and looked at the corpse. Baxin stood away from the body now, waiting. Polifos turned away. "Please. I don't want to look at it anymore."

Palen led them all to Baxin's office. One of Harwol's people got Polifos a cup of water. The director sat in a chair, trembling and sipping.

"What plague?" Derec prompted.

"Old, old nanotech," Polifos said. "Do you know what UPDs are?"

"I know the term," Derec said. "I'm still not sure what it means."

"Untreatable Physiological Dysfunction," Polifos said. "The term covers a lot of ground. Some of it is organic—illnesses, chronic systemic dysfunctions, things we can only watch. We can't cure them. In some cases, we can provide a little relief, but they're all fatal, and usually pretty quickly. Ninety-eight percent of the cases are infants. The worst of them are nonorganic. We used to call them Vonooman Plagues." He shrugged. "I don't know why."

He drank again, coughed, and set the cup down. "Before we outlawed robots—long time ago—we played with everything. One of our developments was nanotech. We still have a lot of it. Food production is a result of old nanotech. Some medical treatments, manufacturing—but most of it got thrown out with the robots. Largely because a few experiments went wrong and we created self-sustaining inorganic colonies. Parasites, really. They disassembled extant structures and used the material. There was a huge panic when the first of them erupted a few hundred years ago. But the fact is, they ate themselves out. It was fast and furious and so fatal that within ten, twenty years they died out all on their own, except for a few aberrant strains that stayed in the ecosystem and caused relatively minor problems since."

"UPDs," Derec said.

Polifos nodded. "Poor kids. They'd be born with a minor problem and through some vector we've never been able to trace, a colony of these things would take advantage and set up within the system. Within extreme intervention, death would be quick. We set up hospice centers for them."

"They aren't very well advertised," Palen said. "This is the first I've heard of them."

"Nobody wants to know about them. Anonymity is almost always desired by the parents, so it works out comfortably for everyone but the victim."

"So what changed?" Derec asked.

"We found strains that were sustaining the victim. They were adapting. Why now and not before? Don't know. And not in very many cases. But when we diagnosed the first adult cases of new infection, we knew we had a big problem."

"Terrans?" Derec asked.

"Settlers," Polifos said. "We needed to find a cure. To do that we needed to find the vectors and we needed to understand the nature of the host system. We set up Nova Levis as a research lab in prostheses to cover the actual research into the new plague."

"And what was the vector?" Harwol asked.

"Only certain colonies. We found a series of enzyme deficiencies that produced chronic conditions that were treatable but rendered the system vulnerable to opportunistic infections. Those colonies tended to be the smallest and most isolationist. The influx of new colonists had been cut off for a variety of reasons—diplomatic, financial, other things. We were afraid that the plagues might adapt sufficiently well to become generally virulent and infect us. It was a small population that was at risk. We found a vaccine that was communicable by touch and could be spread through viral transfer."

"How did you get around the immigration barriers?" Harwol asked.

"Baleys," Derec said.

Polifos nodded. "Slipped them in through the back door."

"What about the infants?" Masid asked.

"We continued our research on them. We found that the diseases had reworked their basic genetic structure in some cases, demanding augmentation in key organs. We thought we were finding a cure. We found that the disease had left us with an organic system perfectly suited to the introduction of symbiotic machine prostheses. But it was a holistic approach. We couldn't fix one organ, we had to address the entire system."

"You started playing with positronics," Derec said.

Polifos nodded. "We got them through our Solarian contacts."

"That means you. *You're* Solarian."

Polifos shook his head. "I was born here, on Earth. My parents were Solarian and I kept my citizenship, but I've never been there."

"Then who was your Solarian contact?"

"Through the embassy mission. I never knew who."

"Why was the lab shut down?" Palen asked.

"We started getting infants in large numbers. We'd developed a method of introducing self-sustaining support into the organic matrix, freeing them from the massive support systems they'd been forced to live in. The babies showed up, we'd refit them, and then they'd disappear. Director Holani was our head of staff. She found out they were going offplanet. She started demanding to know what was going on. She threatened to go public. That's when everything was closed down."

"So how does this explain that thing Baxin's working on?" Palen demanded, gesturing in the direction of the cyborg's remains.

"We stumbled on a process that would enable us to fuse machine and organic systems. The vonooman infection opened the way for the introduction of fully symbiotic artificial components. Puberty alters too much for reintroduction—a lot of it is mitigated by viral infections, RNA recompositions, stuff like that—but from infancy, we found we could grow a composite organism to adulthood. That's when the traffic in infants increased."

"So that thing may have been one of your patients?"

"May have," Polifos admitted. "I went to the Aurorans when my colleagues started dying. I told them what was going on. They took me in and hid me." He looked around at them. "I don't want to die."

"Where's the work being done now?" Derec asked.

Polifos frowned.

"Where are the cyborgs being grown now?"

"A sister lab was built on Cassus Thole," Polifos said. "A transfer point for baleys to the other colonies where the plague was taking root."

"Cassus Thole?" Palen asked. "I never heard of that one."

"It's an old name," Masid said. "It's now called Nova Levis."

Yuri Pocivil did not try to run when he saw the cyborg corpse. He swallowed, hard, and stared at it. Slowly, he turned to Palen.

"I don't know anything," he said.

"You worked the baley run out of Petrabor," Palen said. "You worked *with* this thing. We have documentation on it, so don't bother lying."

"I'm just a dockworker, that's all," Pocivil said.

"Running baleys?" Masid asked.

"Baleys, drygoods, food, manufactured components—it's

all just cargo. My job is strictly dockside. I don't know anything."

"You know who pays you," Palen said. "You know your contacts. You get your assignments from somewhere."

"I also know what 'dead' means," he said.

"You should," Derec agreed. "You already are. That was coming to kill you." He nodded toward the cyborg. "You know that."

After a time, Pocivil nodded. "I got caught. That's against the rules."

"So why protect them?" Palen asked.

Pocivil shrugged. "A gato's got to have standards."

"Pretty low ones, in your case," Masid said. "You know all those baleys were murdered. The last shipment you sent up here."

Pocivil sighed. "Shit. I guess it doesn't matter. You won't find them, anyway."

"Why not?" Palen asked.

"Because the operation is over. It's being shut down. I was on my way home when your people grabbed me."

"Shut down," Derec said. "You mean, no more baley runs? No more—"

"Nothing, no more anything. They're closing up shop. It's over."

"Why don't you tell us where and who, then?" Palen asked.

Pocivil let out a long, shuddering breath and turned away from the autopsy theater. "What do you want to know first?"

Derec watched through the transparency as Polifos assisted Baxin in removing the brain and brain stem from the cyborg body. He finally realized what bothered him about the scene: the colors were all wrong. The blood was nearly purple, organs were gray or bronze colored, nothing looked like it came out of a human body.

He glanced back at the robot. Thales/Bogard remained nearby, silently observing the same operation.

"What do you think, Thales?" Derec asked. "Or should I call you Bogard?"

"Either, both, or some new name," the robot replied. "What do I think about what, Derec?"

"This," Derec said, gesturing at the cyborg.

"I have not decided yet."

"What do you mean?"

"The cause of Coffee's collapse was due to a misidentification. It believed that it was intervening against a robot. When he injured the being and realized that it had just assaulted an organic form, it naturally recoiled, assuming it had just attacked a human."

"Assuming?"

"I am not certain this construct qualifies as human."

Derec felt a disquieting coldness form around his thoughts. He stared at the robot for a long time.

"You be sure to let me know when and what you decide," he said finally.

"I shall, Derec."

TWENTY-SIX

Ariel felt intense relief upon seeing Coren Lanra.

He slumped in one of her sofas, head propped on one hand, elbow on the sofa arm, eyes half-lidded. He looked profoundly weary, fighting sleep. He smiled crookedly when he saw her, and made an effort to sit straight. He put weight on his left arm and winced.

"As long as you're here," Ariel said, "we're getting that shoulder looked at."

"No time," Coren protested. "I had an interesting talk with the police last night."

"Don't avoid the issue, you have no choice. I won't continue this with a damaged partner."

His eyebrows raised. "When did we become partners?"

"I'm not sure. Am I assuming too much?"

"That depends."

Ariel ignored a spike of annoyance. "It always does." She started unsealing his shirt. "You're still getting looked at."

"That was never a question." He smiled.

Ariel hesitated. Then, impulsively, she leaned forward and kissed him, very quickly and lightly, on the mouth. Coren stared at her, startled and, she thought, pleased. She continued removing his shirt.

"What have you been doing since Taprin?" he asked.

"Hiding for the most part. Turn around."

"The police surgeon said it's cracked."

The bruise was spectacular. "Is there some point you need to prove by finishing this in pain?"

Coren laughed sharply. "I told you I made an appointment with my doctor. You didn't answer my question."

"Nor did you." She stood, his shirt in one hand. "But you *will* have that looked at."

He shook his head. "I need to talk to Jeta. Tresha. Whatever her name is. Where is she?"

"Three floors down, under guard. She'll wait."

He tried to stand. "Then I have to go to Nova Levis."

Ariel frowned. "The colony?"

"No, the lab."

She pressed down on his shoulder. He winced but sat back down. "Don't bother. It really *was* dismantled." She turned toward her robot. "Jennie? Who's working the infirmary now?"

"I don't suppose I can reason with you," Coren said.

"Dr. Jerios," the robot replied.

"Of course you can," Ariel told Coren. "Just do what I say. Thank you, Jennie. Let her know I have a patient for her—we'll be right down. And bring me a robe, please."

Coren let his head fall back. "Can't she come here?"

"She can; her equipment can't. Come on. Up. One more trip before you can sleep."

"Make up your mind, will you? Up or down." Coren

grunted as he got to his feet. He stumbled. "Oops. One stim too many, I think. What do you mean, Nova Levis was dismantled?"

"What I said. After it was closed down, the facility was gutted and converted to its present use. There's nothing there." Ariel took his right arm and guided him toward the door. "Jennie, route my calls to the infirmary."

"What about Wenithal?" Coren asked.

"He's fine. Same floor, separate quarters, under guard."

"Guard?"

"Infirmary first."

"I need to talk to Tresha first."

"No, first—"

"She's *not* Jeta Fromm." Coren disengaged from Ariel. "The police identified Jeta's body in Lyzig. We need to speak to Tresha *now*."

Ariel regarded him for a moment. "All right. We can stop there on the way."

"Fine."

They continued on down the corridor to the elevator.

"Ambassador Burgess?" he said.

"Yes."

"Thank you."

"For what?"

Coren smiled. "The list is too long. Just say 'you're welcome.'"

"You're welcome."

The elevator let them out on the guest floor. Ariel led the way to the rooms.

A tall, uniformed Auroran stood outside each of two doors along the corridor. Ariel led Coren to the nearest. The guard bowed slightly and stepped aside.

Tresha sat on the bed, pillows behind her, watching the

subetheric across the room. Ariel glanced at what was being broadcast—it was a very old hyperwave drama; she remembered it vaguely, something based loosely on the first modern Terran permitted to visit a Spacer world after the long quarantine of Earth—and stepped in front of the set, blocking the woman's view.

"I hope you're here to apologize," Tresha said as she touched the remote to switch off the subetheric.

"For what?" Coren asked. "Not recognizing you sooner?"

The woman laughed. "Just who *is* this 'Tresha' person you keep talking about?"

"You tell me," Coren said. "I'd like to know why she killed Jeta Fromm."

Tresha shook her head. "Look—"

"Jeta's body was found . . . and identified."

Tresha stared at him, eyes narrowed. Finally, she shrugged.

"Why kill her?" Coren asked. "She was just a data troll."

"Why worry about her?" Tresha returned. "She was, as you say, just a data troll."

"Did Mikels order it?"

Her eyes widened briefly. Then she shrugged again. "If you know so much . . ."

Ariel said, "We have both Kyas Vol and Yuri Pocivil in custody. Your cyborg is dead—it's being dissected even as we speak. So, if you want to play guessing games, it's all right with me, but we don't have to participate."

Tresha pursed her lips. "You're talking to the wrong person, gato. I don't know anything."

"Nonsense," Coren said. "You were the contact for Damik and Wenithal. You handle all the legwork on the ground."

"So the messenger is supposed to know what the message is?"

Ariel waited for Coren's move. He said nothing. Tresha looked at him, then at Ariel, her eyes no longer so certain.

"Ask," Tresha said.

"Why'd you kill Jeta?"

"She was nosy. She poked around into the wrong places."

"How'd you pass for her in Lyzig?"

"They didn't know her. I moved in there shortly after we terminated Fromm."

"Why take her place?" Ariel asked.

"Common sense. If one commission for that data had come her way, more might. I wanted to find out how many vectors there were leading to that information."

"And the baleys?" Coren asked quietly.

Another shrug. "I don't think I'll answer that."

"Do you think you're getting out of here *without* answering it?" Ariel asked.

Tresha smiled thinly in response, then looked at Coren. "I understand your ex-lover died on that last run. For what it's worth, I apologize. It wasn't personal."

"That's very comforting," Coren said tightly. "You've been tidying up, haven't you? Closing things down. Were you going to kill Wenithal when you showed up at his apartment?"

Tresha touched the remote again and turned up the volume. Music swelled.

"Your cyborg is dead!" Coren shouted.

Tresha looked at him and shook her head. "We're done." She smiled briefly, then ignored him.

Coren stalked out of the room.

"Who's the Solarian in charge?" Ariel asked. When Tresha continued to ignore her, she spun around and jabbed the OFF on the subetheric. The sound died instantly. "The Solarian in charge," she repeated. "Who is it?"

Tresha sighed. "You're not as bright as I thought."

"Do you have any idea what it is you're playing with?"

Tresha snorted derisively. "Oh, please! Is this going to be an appeal to my naïvety, or just my conscience?" She sat forward. "It's all power, Ambassador—raw, absolute, over-whelming, carnal, irreducible power. Do I know what I'm playing with?" She grinned. "I'm *not* playing, Ambassador."

She stabbed the remote again, once more filling the room with sound.

Ariel found Coren waiting in the corridor, his back to the wall.

"Do you want to talk to Wenithal?" she asked.

"No. Let's get my shoulder looked at first."

He said no more till they arrived in the embassy infirmary, where two robots placed him on a gurney and pushed him into a diagnostics bay.

"What's the problem, Ariel?" Dr. Jerios asked as she tapped commands into her console. "He looks like he needs about three days' sleep." Jerios frowned at her. "So do you, by the way."

"That would be a good start. But I need him up and alert by morning. He's been running on stims and painblock for about four days now. His left shoulder is—"

"Cracked," Jerios said. "My word, how did this happen?"

"He was grabbed by a very strong hand."

Dr. Jerios shook her head skeptically, gazing at the scan image. "Some hand. I can see why he's in pain. All right, I can pump healant and accelerant into this. Actually, the stim saturation will be harder to deal with. He should be allowed to sleep it off."

Ariel shook her head. "No time."

"Then he's going to be very grumpy."

"As long as he's alert."

"Oh, he'll be alert. I hope you get along well if you have to work together tomorrow."

Ariel looked at Coren through the transparency separating them. He looked asleep now, his face relaxed as the robots carried out Jerios's instructions.

"I think we get along well enough," Ariel said. In a whisper, she said to the sleeping Lanra, "You're very welcome."

"Ariel, there is an emergency comm message for you," R. Jennie said.

Ariel opened her eyes. For a moment, she did not remember where she was; then realization came. She was in her own apartment, still fully dressed. Coren was asleep in the guest bedroom. She blinked at her robot.

"A message from . . . ?" she asked groggily.

"Security."

Ariel snapped to her feet and crossed the room. She slapped the ACCEPT on her comm. "Ambassador Burgess here."

"We've had a break-in, Ambassador," the security officer said. "Two guards have been found unconscious, a third dead. We're sealing the embassy grounds and alerting staff. Please stay in your apartment—"

"Negative. Send extra security to the protected apartments. The two people I brought in last night—"

"We've already dispatched extra personnel there. I am to advise you—"

She broke the link and ran out the door.

*   *   *

The scene she found when she stepped onto that floor shocked her. At least five guards lay broken along the corridor. Both apartment doors stood open.

Tresha was missing. *No real surprise there,* Ariel thought angrily.

She found Wenithal in his bathroom. He was dead—eyes staring blindly, head tilted at an awkward angle.

"Damn!" she shouted.

Behind her, more security officers rushed by in the corridor. She knew, though, that Tresha was long gone.

The security recordings of the corridor showed the guards entering the hallway. They joined the two already on station. Minutes later, something caught their attention from the direction of the elevator. Their hands, almost as one, went to their sidearms, but they began falling, one by one, twisting around, writhing in pain, thrown to the floor. Two of the guards managed to fire shots, but they, too, were suddenly seized by some spectral force and crushed.

After they had all been subdued, Tresha's door opened, and she emerged. She rushed up the corridor to Wenithal's room and entered.

The view showed no one emerging.

"Masked," Coren said.

"But before or after the attack?" Ariel asked.

"After," Coren said. "We never saw her leave the room before the attack, so that means she had help."

They watched the recording on Ariel's subetheric. Coren lay propped up in her bed, his left shoulder covered by a thick pad. He had slept nearly six hours. Ariel knew he was angry that she had let him sleep while her people had scoured the embassy for the woman who had pretended to be Jeta Fromm, but he had said nothing in rebuke.

"No one saw her leave the embassy," Ariel said, "but we can assume she's gone. The question is: where did she—or they—go?"

"Petrabor maybe," Coren said glumly. "Tell me about Nova Levis."

"I had a long talk with Ambassador Setaris last night. I hate it when I'm treated like a child who can't be told the truth." Ariel let herself experience the anger and irritation she had felt during and after her meeting with Setaris. Just for a few moments, while she composed her thoughts.

"We've known that Solaria has a compound on the ground on Nova Levis for several years, but until now we had no idea what it was or what they were doing. Just an enclave on an island, away from the Settler towns and cities. A lot of traffic in and out. Nothing we could do anything about. It was a Solarian holding originally, and they then let it to a Settler colony, so we had no legal grounds to go in there to investigate. Several years ago, though, when the first talks began between Earth and Aurora to try to reconcile our differences, we were able to share data on black market trade. Nova Levis was interesting because it seemed to be acting as a haven for several of the ships suspected to be regular contraband runners. Aurora made a few tentative inquiries with Solaria, Solaria offered to look into it, and what followed was a series of reports telling us that nothing illegal was happening on Nova Levis. Then the *Tiberius* incident happened."

"That's what precipitated last year's conference?" Coren asked.

Ariel nodded. "One of the things. A Terran smuggler challenged by an Auroran police cruiser. For whatever reason, it had drifted into our space and we insisted on inspection rights. They refused and were fired upon. The *Tiberius* was on its way to Nova Levis. Among the facts that did not become public was that several Solarian nationals were on board—primarily positronics specialists, but also a few geneticists. We decided then to push for more cooperation with Earth as a first step toward forcing Solaria to open up."

"Which blew up in everyone's face."

"Solaria will not allow ground inspections of Nova Levis."

"I thought Nova Levis was refusing."

"Same thing, as far as we're concerned."

"So why hasn't Solaria's involvement been made public?"

"Games. Aurora can't risk war with Solaria until we know who our allies are. Or how much of the Solarian government is involved. We have to pretend to accept everything at face value until we have the proof necessary to convene a general council of the Fifty Worlds."

"And the Theians?"

"We're using them as a potential cause for convening that council on other grounds if we can't get it any other way. If Solaria moves to interdict a Theian ship, we have the excuse. If Nova Levis fires on a Theian ship, we have the excuse."

"And if Earth actually gets permission to do the ground inspections?" Coren asked.

"What we find will give us the excuse," Ariel replied.

"In the meantime, the dance goes on until someone steps wrong."

"The wonderful world of diplomacy."

"I suppose that's preferable to arbitrarily getting several hundred thousand people killed."

"Is it any different in the corporate world?"

"Worse. You can't ever declare open war on each other. At the end of all the games, you still have to sleep with the enemy."

She smiled. "I suppose even that could have its pleasant moments."

Coren shot her a look. "I'm sorry, Ambassador, but I don't find any of this particularly amusing."

Ariel jerked as if she had been struck. "I didn't mean—"

"Someone very special to me is dead because you people are playing games. I understand them, but that doesn't make it any more acceptable."

Ariel's expression hardened. "Don't bleed too much, Mr. Lanra. You might pass out when I need you."

Coren looked away, reddening. He visibly controlled himself, then cleared his throat. "So what does Aurora think Solaria is doing on Nova Levis?"

"Until this, we had no idea. Black market trade is too vague to really attack them with—to one extent or another, we all participate, or at least our citizens do." She spoke evenly, the same tone of voice as before, as if their disagreement had not occurred.

"Until now. You mean the cyborgs?"

"Settlers couldn't build them. Solaria *has* to be behind it." She took a deep breath. "Which means that, if part of the research and development was done here, there had to be a Solarian contact on Earth to funnel materials and technologies and manage the program."

Coren blinked. "Gale Chassik was one of the original shareholders in Nova Levis."

"But he divested before assuming head of the Solarian mission."

"Which would make sense . . . But—why?"

"That's a very good question. I—"

Coren's comm chirped. He snatched it up from the table at his right and stabbed at it. "Lanra." He listened for a time. Gradually, his face lost its composure. He looked momentarily confused, then shocked. "I'll talk to him. Where is he now? Good. No, don't tell him I'm coming. Thanks."

"What is it?"

"Come with me. We have to see someone."

"You need more—"

"*Now,* Ariel. Please."

They took an embassy limo to the DyNan compound, where Coren easily passed them through security. He led the way to the elevator, and tapped in the destination; a minute later, they stepped into a spacious, comfortably furnished suite.

Someone was sitting in a chair, watching the subetheric. Coren held a hand up and felt Ariel bump into it.

The subetheric showed Rega Looms at a press conference.

"—decision has not been taken lightly or capriciously. For personal reasons I choose not to go into at this time, I must announce my withdrawal from this campaign. I apologize to all those who have shown me their support through the last several months. I know all our hopes have been compromised, but I trust they have not been destroyed. There are others, more qualified than myself, to step into office and carry on the work to which I have pledged myself my entire life. I do not—"

The screen went blank. The man who had been watching now stood and turned.

Coren stared. "Rega?"

Rega Looms looked at them both, his face expressionless and pale.

"What are you doing, Coren?" he asked quietly. "Why are you here?"

"Trying to find out why your daughter was murdered."

Looms shook his head. "I want you to stop. I don't want you to go any further. I want this ended. Now."

"Why?"

Looms shook his head again. "I don't choose to discuss it."

"That's not good enough, Rega."

Looms looked mildly puzzled for a moment, then scowled. "You work for me, Coren. This investigation is over."

"Why?"

"I told you—"

"Why didn't you tell me you had a son before Nyom?"

Rega Looms turned his back on Coren and faced the dead subetheric. Coren waited till it seemed Looms would say nothing more and reached down for his pack.

"I've withdrawn from the campaign," Looms said. "I was contacted by someone who threatened to release the fact you've just mentioned to the public and tie me in with people and concerns I broke from years ago. Of course, in the public's imagination, nothing is ever finished—if I had once been in league with the enemy, I must still be so. Without even a chance to explain, my ability to function would be compromised and my reputation crippled."

"Do you know who sent it?"

"No. Not specifically."

"When did this happen?"

"Yesterday afternoon. I tried to comm you, but you were unavailable. I decided late last night to withdraw rather than hurt the Church."

Coren wanted to argue with him, tell him that people

would understand, that they would support him because blackmail was so odious. But he knew better. The appearance of hypocrisy and the suggestion of a lie, even one of omission, turned people crudely incapable of compassion and robbed them of the ability to think when it came to politics. Coren had worked for the government, seen too many politicians go down in a mangle of innuendo simply because their constituency thought they had been betrayed by a promise compromised. There was nothing else Looms could do.

"Why didn't you tell me?" Coren repeated.

"I didn't tell anyone. It was nobody else's business. It was my own grief, my own horror. No one else has a right to that."

"Ree Wenithal knew."

Looms turned toward him. "Wenithal? What in god's name are you doing with him?"

"He came up. There was a kidnapping case and evidently you were part of it."

"Wenithal is a corrupt policeman who failed to follow through on that investigation. I was peripheral to his case at the time, but we had several interviews because of Jerem."

"Jerem? That was your child's name?"

Suddenly, Looms' eyes flowed with tears. His hands curled into fists and he looked toward the ceiling. "Why won't you let this end?"

Coren waited again. Looms sighed shakily and sat down onthe edge of a couch. "Jerem was born with a compromised immune system. Unusual, but not unknown; standard treatments exist for it. But they didn't work. It got worse. When he was a year old, it was obvious something was killing him. Finally, he was diagnosed with a nonorganic system infection. A nanotech disease. A leftover." He glared suddenly at Ariel. "A gift from our flirtation with technologies we should never have allowed." The fury waned as quickly as it had emerged, and his gaze returned to the floor. "No treatment. Life support was available in certain institutions, but we had to . . . surrender him into their care . . . "

He sobbed loudly. "It was easier. They offered anonymity and promised to make him comfortable till he died."

"Did they tell you when he died?" Coren asked.

"No. That was part of it. We had to walk away. In return, we guaranteed that it would never be made public."

"What about birth records?"

"Security locks. The system has been in place for a long time."

"Locks can be picked, Mr. Looms," Ariel said. "This one was."

"Let me guess," Coren said. "You bought shares in Nova Levis because they offered research into exactly what killed Jerem."

"Oh, much more than *that*. I named the place! Nova Levis. 'New Light.' Something I'd . . . borrowed . . . from the Church." Looms shook his head. "I was naïve. I hadn't yet realized that the original anti-robot movement had been absolutely correct in their analysis that any concession on the issue of nonorganic life was nothing but a danger, a complete betrayal of all things human. That this idea was fundamentally destructive and could never be controlled."

"We've proven them wrong," Ariel said.

"Have you? You're so utterly dependent on your robots that you're dying out. You don't even reproduce anymore."

"That's—"

"What? Untrue? What is the average birthrate on a

Spacer world? Is it sufficient for replacement? Or are your populations dwindling?"

Ariel said nothing.

"Life is good among the Spacers," Looms went on, warming now to his own arguments. "Two, three hundred years to explore the insides of your own psyches to the exclusion of all else, even the future. The possibilities of self-indulgence are so wonderful that you forget the most basic necessity of organic life—to breed. It's seen as an oddity, a curiosity, a peculiarity. Solarians don't even share the same households, they can't stand to be near others. They breed *ex utero*. Aurorans find children too undignified and simply avoid the whole embarrassing thing. But *you* compensate—*you* make life through your robots. I imagine that this goes quite a distance in fulfilling the void in your hearts by the absence of real children."

"We don't have orphanages to warehouse the unwanted and uncounted," Ariel said.

Looms stared at her.

"Why did you sell your shares?" Coren asked.

"Um . . . the research took a direction that repulsed me." He frowned. "They began developing symbiotic prostheses— nonorganic augmentation that combined with organic systems, became essentially one with them. I found this . . . unacceptable."

That's a lie," Coren said. "You got out because Jerem died."

Looms glared at Coren. "I know my own mind. Jerem died two years before I sold my holdings."

"But it frightened you," Ariel said. "The research."

"Yes, Ms. Burgess, it did. To preserve the few, we were threatening the very definition of 'human.' "

"Isn't that a little extreme?"

"Is it? Where's the line? Do you know where it is? Would you call your positronic creations 'living,' Ms. Burgess? I wouldn't. And I saw no good in blurring the distinctions further, no matter how many suffering infants it saved."

"So you bailed out," Coren said. "Did you know there was a sister lab on a Settler colony?"

"No. But that wouldn't have changed my decision."

Coren sighed wearily. "It's too late to stop this, Rega. I have to finish."

"Why? I left it alone for almost thirty years, why can't you drop it now?"

"I . . ." Coren coughed. "I loved Nyom. This is personal for me."

"You work for me."

"I quit."

Looms' face reddened.

"This is out of your hands anyway, Mr. Looms," Ariel said. "Aurora has a joint interest in this with Terran authorities. Nova Levis is the source of a problem to which your naïvety may well have given birth."

"You can't make me responsible for any of this."

"No? Try this: If you hadn't turned your back on what you did and pretended since that it never happened, maybe what's happened now would never have gotten this far. You surrendered any chance of control over it when you surrendered your responsibility."

"I did not act alone!"

"None of us ever do. Some of us forget that, though. Then there's a mess to clean up." She stepped up to Coren. "Mr. Lanra, Aurora offers you a job working on our behalf in this matter. Along with that comes our sanction and protection."

Coren could not look away from Looms, even when he said, "I accept, Ambassador Burgess."

A day earlier, the expression of betrayal he saw on Looms' face would have broken his heart. Now it only annoyed him.

"Very well," Looms said finally. "If you insist on going ahead. Use whatever facilities DyNan has. Both of you. Any assistance my company may offer, feel free to use, Ms. Burgess."

He walked past Coren, to the door. For a moment, Coren thought he might look back. But Looms passed through, out of the suite.

"You didn't tell him that his son is still alive," Ariel said.

"I see no purpose in cruelty now." Coren looked around the office as if trying to memorize its details. "Besides," he said at length, "is it really his son anymore?"

TWENTY-SEVEN

The configurations in the memory buffers are nonstandard, Derec."

Derec glanced at the console. "That's what I expected, Thales. Can you access them?"

"Yes, but I cannot guarantee any degree of coherence."

Everyone had gathered around the platform on which lay the slightly viscous mass of cyborg brain tissue and nearly fifty centimeters of what resembled spinal column. Instead of distinct vertebrae separated by disks, the spine was composed of overlapping sheaths that attached on clusters of bearing-like spheres.

Derec had found positronic nodes within the brain mass, though their links to the actual neurons of the brain were difficult to determine. Fine cables now entered the tissue, feeding back into the interface, connecting it to Thales.

Derec looked around at the others. Rana sat at the main board, monitoring the link. Palen, Harwol, Masid, and Polifos stood on the opposite side of the platform. Baxin sat nearby, with two of Harwol's agents.

Thales/Bogard stood behind them.

"Whatever you can give us, Thales," Derec said.

"Very well. I am translating through my own language processors. Stand by."

Silence stretched.

A loud hiss emerged from the speakers. Three screens flickered to life. The far left-hand screen displayed alphanumerics. Derec recognized the symbology—inferential calculus and asymptotic series, standard approaches to positronic interactions—but the groupings did not appear logical. As the symbols flowed by, he spotted an equation that startled him:

$$C^K = c_1 E_1^K + c_2 E_2^K + c_3 E_3^K \ldots$$

Then:

$$\sum_{i=1}^{r} c_i \, C_i^K$$

He recognized it out of combinatorial topology, but its use here baffled him. "You're copying this to Ariel, Thales?"

"Yes, Derec." Thales paused. "I am seeing invariant topologies expressed in Poincaré Sets. I surmise these are serving as anchor points between the organic neuronal structural and the positronic matrix."

"I'm glad *you* have some idea what it means."

The second screen showed abstract shapes broken at intervals by recognizable objects—faces, buildings, rooms.

A catalogue of visual memory, delivered in a form Derec comprehended from ordinary positronic excavations.

The third screen seemed to be nothing more than lists. Places, names, things.

The speakers popped loudly. Then: "My *owaaaaaaaaaaa!*"

The hiss seemed to modulate, then fade.

In a faint voice, sexless and tired: "Make it stop."

Derec took a step toward Rana.

"It moves! That's what I like, more juice, give me some of that and that and turn it around again, stop it!"

"Thales?" Derec prompted.

"The memory is stored nonhierarchically," Thales said. "More like a human brain, although storage is discreet rather than undifferentiated. I am trying other nodes."

The speaker crackled. "Kill it! What business does it have doing like that? I came here expecting nothing! Pull that or put it away I can do better than—"

"Derec," Thales said, "I have identified a structure that seems to be a positronic external interface."

"We can talk to it?" Rana asked, surprised.

"You can't have that, it's too complex and I'm too one thing or another! Get out of my borrowed—"

"Perhaps," Thales said. "It depends on how reliable the connections are to the rest of the brain. It is presently generating conceptual axioms similar to an organic condition known as Korsakov's Syndrome. Imposing order may not be possible."

"Let's try it," Derec said.

"It is now active."

"Can you hear me?" Derec called out.

Silence.

"Do you have a name?"

"Several," the speaker said. "Call me Shit For Brains, like

Greeshal does when I don't answer right away, nice guy Greeshal, should see me now, what do you want?"

"I want the name you prefer."

"Cordios."

"What are you, Cordios?"

"The answer to your problem."

"Do I have a problem?"

"A lot of problems. Main one, you're alive."

"So are you. Is that a problem, too?"

"Wrong. Wrong. Error. Sorry."

"You aren't alive?"

"Not since I was born."

"When was that?"

"Before I died."

"Cordios, do you remember becoming what you are?"

"Do you remember being born?" it asked.

"No."

"Then you must be human."

"Do *you* remember being born?" Derec asked.

"Light, fade, pinpricks all through my head, I have now taken up the heat. Little nits chasing around through my spleen, see them run, see them caught and added to the dog. Everything hurts it feels right, for once I'm growing, I hear, I see, I touch when I want to . . . no, I don't remember being born, just being reborn. *The clarity!* Look—at—that! If you made this then you must be good for something. Little shits can't even reflect light, but boy do they inspire! Watch me Mommy while I kill the cat! If you don't want me to break my toys then don't give them to me, hypocrite, liar, that's human, too. Left me here and all I did was breathe. Now I don't even have to do that. Some things are worth dying for, you should see it from the other side."

"What is this?" Harwol asked. "This doesn't make any sense."

"You want sense, tissue? Try this: evolution has infinite vectors, most of them unrecognized, a lot of them artificial. Evolution by design only happens when design evolves. Riddle, riddles, junior piddles, spank him nice and kill him twice. You're all obsolete. Look at me, I'm the new standard."

Thunder burst from the speaker then, fading quickly to a whisper, then silence.

"The interface has been deactivated, Derec," Thales said.

"Why?"

"I do not know."

"You had no reason—?"

"I did not deactivate it. The subject did."

"What does that mean?" Palen asked.

"It means," Derec said, "that this thing is still self-aware. It shut down the interface."

"Is that possible, boss?" Rana asked.

"I wouldn't have thought so. But . . . Thales, see what you can salvage, then terminate the subject."

"I may have a problem with that, Derec."

"What's that?"

"Is it human?"

Derec considered the question. "I see. Then just terminate the excavation. I'll deal with the remains."

"Yes, Derec."

The names still danced across the third screen, but now the other two showed nothing.

"Thales, do you have any identification on the names being displayed?"

"Yes, Derec. They are several lists combined. I have names of people currently employed in warehouses, shipping departments, and ITE offices. Dockworkers. Transportation specialists. There is a separate list of merchant ships. A considerable amount validates the information given by Yuri Pocivil. Another list of people and places which I infer from the locations are on Settler colonies. There is also a list matching files Ariel instructed me to locate regarding the kidnappings which precipitated the investigation that closed Nova Levis."

"They're all the victims?"

"Yes, Derec."

"I see. Copy all this to Ariel."

Derec walked away from the station. He could feel everyone watching him.

"So, now what?" Masid asked.

"We have to find them," Derec said.

"'Them'?"

"The rest. The cyborgs."

"So, now you're convinced there's more than one," Harwol said.

"Something like this . . . yes, I am. And we have to find them and stop them."

"Stop them from what?" Palen asked.

"Taking our place."

Coren, Ariel, and Ambassador Setaris filled separate screens mounted on the wall of Palen's private office. Harwol, Hofton, Masid, and Derec filled chairs around her desk.

"Pocivil hasn't shut up since he agreed to talk," Palen said. "So far we've identified twenty-six locations for contraband, illegal transport, and warehousing on the ground, and seven bays here that are regular stops for the black market."

"Has he said anything about the operations being shut down?" Coren asked.

"That's why he was heading back to Cassus Thole," Palen replied. "Operations on Earth are finished—so he says, anyway. Frankly, I doubt that."

"Maybe a temporary hiatus," Ariel said. "They ceased before, after Wenithal's investigation."

"We're prepared to move on all the sites," Harwol said. "Some of them are Spacer-owned, Ambassador Burgess. We're waiting on *you* to clear us."

Ariel frowned. "Derec, the cyborg—I went over the autopsy and excavation reports a little while ago. How many of these do you think there could be?"

"I have no way of knowing," Derec said. "Seems safe to assume at least two of them—the one we have and the one down there. Blood scans confirm that this one here is not the same one that was in the cargo bin with the baleys. But as for how many there *might* be . . ." He shrugged.

"We will sign off on the raids, Agent Harwol," Setaris said, "under the condition that any cyborgs found, captured, or killed will be turned over to us for study."

Harwol looked unhappy, but he nodded. "Agreed."

"And I want my people to have access to the sites after they're secured."

"I'll see what I can do, Ambassador."

"This isn't a good time to play things too close, Agent Harwol," Setaris stressed. "Your people know next to nothing about robots in the first place. You won't know what you're looking at if these sites contain positronic equipment, you won't know how to deal with any robots on hand, and you certainly won't know what to do with any of it afterward. If you encounter any cyborgs, you'll be even less prepared."

Harwol cleared his throat. "I understand. How soon can you have people available to accompany our teams?"

"Ariel?" Setaris asked.

"Give the word," Ariel said.

Harwol was surprised. "Do you have that many?"

"Enough for what we consider the key sites. I'll copy the list to you. You have people on Kopernik who can fill the same rôles there."

"Very well. I want to move on this within the next six hours, Ambassador. The sooner we do, the more of these people we can catch."

Ariel nodded. "Agreed. Coren and I will be going in with the Petrabor team. Coren has been there before."

"Mr. Lanra," Harwol said, "you are aware of the possible risks. You aren't an active agent—are you willing to submit to the team leader?"

"My status is problematic, Agent Harwol," Coren said. "Let's stop talking and move."

"Very well. All agreed, on my authority. Chief Palen will coordinate the station raids. If we time this well, we can shut it down all at once."

Palen gave Harwol a dubious look but said nothing.

"One more thing," Derec said. "These cyborgs, if there are more, will not succumb to stuns. You'll have to use lethal force, a lot of it, and that means some humans will probably be killed as well. I suggest . . ." He hesitated, unsettled by his own thoughts. "I suggest you don't worry about the human casualties. These things, loose, are far more dangerous."

Everyone stared at him for a time. He felt acutely uncomfortable.

Masid spoke then. "Ambassador, what about the Spacer end?"

"Pardon me?" Setaris asked.

"Obviously, there's a Spacer connection. Probably Solarian, most likely an embassy official. What will be done about that?"

"We're already working on that. We will take care of it." Masid nodded.

"All right, then," Palen said, standing. "Let's move."

TWENTY-EIGHT

Coren watched the TBI team sort and ready their equipment for the third time. The comm unit bead in his ear fed him updates on the status of all the other teams. He still could not quite believe they expected to pull this off—the final count had been thirty-one sites on the ground, and eight on Kopernik, all targeted to be hit simultaneously. It was ambitious.

But the clearances had come through from the Aurorans, which, no doubt, would cause a furor within Spacer circles—several sites were Solarian- or Keresian-owned.

Coren's own pack lay at his feet; he had arrived prepared, and had never been one to check and recheck his equipment in nervous anticipation. He glanced around the edge of the bay, toward the warehouse across the alley—the same one where all this had begun. He distrusted tidy closures like this, but it seemed the most logical place for Tresha to go. She was either here waiting transport, or she was already on Kopernik—in which case, Sipha would grab her.

At least this time I don't feel like I need a bath . . .

Ariel sat nearby, her back to the wall, eyes closed, arms folded over her chest, legs outstretched with ankles crossed. She gave the appearance, at least, of a seasoned field agent practicing patience, waiting for the Go signal. At this point, for all Coren knew, she *was*—everything he had assumed about her had turned out to be insufficient for any reasonable assessment. Ariel Burgess did not conform to easy descriptions or predictable definitions.

Like Nyom, he thought, *only completely different . . .*

The TBI team leader approached her, and squatted down to talk. She spoke quietly and intently, instructing the ambassador on what she was expected to do. Ariel nodded and rose smoothly to her feet, then crossed the ancient floor of the bay and sat down. A dozen agents huddled around her for one more question-and-answer session.

Telemetry chittered in Coren's ear. Suddenly, he heard: "Set. Good to go."

He looked up and met the team leader's eyes. She nodded. The huddle broke up into scurrying efficiency. In less than a minute, everyone was loaded up and waiting for the word.

Coren pulled his mask down, hoisted the pack onto his shoulders, and jumped from the edge of the bay. He sprinted across the alley and leapt onto the apron of a mirror-image bay. He pressed against the wall and waited while the TBI team flowed throughout the alley, taking positions to cover him.

Coren took a five-centimeter-square chit from his thigh pocket and slid it into the reader set in the wall. The bay door rumbled up and he ducked inside.

Three dockworkers looked up from the workstation around which they stood, shocked by the sudden intrusion. Automatically, their hands went up as TBI agents rushed in, aiming weapons at them.

"Down!" Coren hissed at the workers. They dropped to the floor obediently. "How many inside? Where?"

"Um . . . short staffed," one of the workers said. "Don't, uh . . . there's a special shipment, private . . . uh . . ."

"Okay," Coren said, tapping the man's head. "Quiet."

Coren set the pack down on the loading dock. The sounds of the warehouse and the distant port thrummed in the vast open spaces, constant and oddly reassuring. Trucks, dollies, crates, containers, all furnished the area.

He scooped out a handful of vonoomans and began methodically activating them. Upon release, they scampered into the recesses of the warehouse. He sealed the pack then took out his palm monitor.

"Give them a few minutes," he said to the team leader. He waved to an agent and pointed to the three workers. Immediately, they were restrained and moved out of the way. The team leader spoke intently into her comm.

Coren unfolded the monitor. Within seconds, a map of the interior sketched itself. The little machines showed bright green on the schematic. At no point did they change color to indicate human presence—not until one reached the transfer bays on the far side, where the bins for the shuttles came and went on automated tracks. Then several blue points appeared, huddled just outside one of the bay doors. Coren tapped Ariel's arm and pointed.

"That's them, then?" she asked.

"I assume so." Coren refolded the monitor and stood. He looked at the team leader. "Ready?"

She nodded silently.

Vehicles rolled into the alley outside.

Shouldering the pack, Coren started forward. Now he felt anxious. He wanted to get out there and find Tresha and whoever else she had with her.

He was beginning to accept that Nyom had died coincidentally, the result of a power struggle between forces that in all likelihood had not even been aware of her existence. Accept it, yes, but he would never be at peace with it. All that remained for him now was to find those responsible. After that . . .

He would never be able to work for Rega again, even if Looms were willing to have him.

I wonder if Ariel's offer is real . . .

At the rear of the bay, they ascended a short staircase. The door at the top let them into an office area. The squad seemed to fill it.

Coren was unconcerned about tripping warehouse security monitors—he doubted any of the normal internal systems were on right now—but his targets might have placed alarms at various points. He opened his pack again and took out another mass of tiny machines. He keyed them and let them out in the corridor beyond the office. Scavengers, they would hunt down and eradicate any telltale devices they found.

He sat down before a comm and waited, watching his monitor. When all the lights showed green, he nodded to the team leader.

Swiftly and efficiently, the agents poured from the room and disappeared into the warehouse, each member with a preassigned location. One of them remained behind.

The bead gave him new updates, reports from the various locations. Ariel listened to the same data, nodding silently to herself.

Coren inserted a decrypter into the console before him and initiated the invasive routines. Within seconds, the data stored in the warehouse systems was isolated from the

DELETE protocols that would have erased everything upon a single command—a command, Coren noted, which had not yet been given. Secured, he opened a comm channel and began sending all this information to another site.

"Done," he announced. "Let's go."

The trap was closing as Coren and Ariel hurried through the administrative areas of the warehouse. With Palen coordinating on Kopernik and Agent Harwol coordinating on the ground, the global sweep was underway. Warehouses, shipping firms, and ships were being seized. Executives were being picked up for questioning.

Alda Mikels was about to be arrested again.

He entered the same office area he had been in five days ago, overlooking the gridlike expanse of the warehouse proper. So familiar and so strange—things rarely formed neat closures or elegant symmetries in his profession. There was a mirror-like quality to this, though, that gave him a sense of validation, confirming his choices and assuring him that his purpose was necessary and sufficient. Perhaps this feeling was wrong, an illusion, but he could use it. He moved unhesitantly.

Halfway across the grid they heard the first blaster shots. Then shouting. Coren recognized the stentorian timbre of TBI commands. Arrests were underway.

He crossed the apron to one of the open doors leading out to the transport grid. Agents stood above eight people who lay face down on the floor, hands clasped behind their heads. Nearby sprawled three corpses, smoke still coiling listlessly from their wounds.

Coren went from prisoner to prisoner, then to the bodies. No Tresha.

The maze of cargo bins beyond was motionless, the

power cut. Huge cubes scattered across the vast field hovered on their self-contained antigravity cushions.

In his ear, Coren continued to hear reports of successful raids, arrests, a few casualties.

But no cyborgs.

He pulled out his optam and scanned the field of inert blocks. No movement. He strode onto the grid.

"Coren—"

Ariel came after him, the TBI agent trailing behind. "Where," she asked, "are you going?"

"They're here," Coren said. "They have to be." He turned away and continued walking.

"There are agents at the other end," Ariel called.

"I know!"

The TBI were very good at these sorts of things—they rarely botched a raid—but Coren wanted the confrontation. Things were going too well—the sites were being taken efficiently, arrests made quickly, few fatalities—but he wanted more of a mess, an excuse to get angry and desperate and violent.

He moved quickly, though cautiously, among the eerily-still cargo bins. The air smelled of ozone, and he felt a faint, dry tingle over his skin. The maze stretched a good two kilometers to where the port machinery sorted out the containers, those arriving and those departing going to separate chutes to the correct shuttles.

He stopped. He could not see the warehouse end now through the forest of cubes.

"Gamelin!" he called, voice echoing. "Did you know who she was? The baley runner you killed?" He listened to the answering silence. "Nyom Looms! Do you remember that name?"

He continued walking. "She was your sister, Gamelin! Did you know you had family?"

Coren stopped and looked to his left. He glimpsed a tall shape, dull gray, slightly crouched, standing outlined against one of the bins.

Coren raised his blaster.

Suddenly, the shape came toward him faster than Coren had ever seen anyone move. If it were not moving directly at him, Coren doubted he would have been able to discern a single detail.

But the moment seemed infinite in what he could see:

A face, pockmarked as if by horrible disease. Wide-set unblinking eyes. A hairless skull. Wide shoulders. A runner's build. A dead-alive intensity, unchanging, mutated into an expression of profound resentment.

Coren wanted more than anything to run.

He fired, too late. The charge slammed into the cyborg's torso, but momentum carried it into Coren. He felt as if his entire body had been slapped all at once. He flew back, into one of the cargo bins, and dropped onto his buttocks painfully.

Coren rolled and slowly rose to his feet.

When he turned again, the cyborg stood less than a meter away. He suppressed the impulse to try to shoot it—he doubted he could raise his weapon fast enough.

"Gamelin?" Coren said.

"Pleased to make your acquaintance, human," it said, its voice a rasp like dried paper scraps and crushed bone. "We don't know each other, do we, gato?"

"Maybe, in a way. Is that your only name?"

"Only need one."

"How about Jerem?"

It cocked its head quizzically. *"You* have a name?"

"Coren Lanra."

"That's two names. Never figured that. What, humans got to have more than one of everything? How come you never give anything else more than one name?"

"You know better than that. Look at your homeworld. It's got four names: Nova Levis, and Cassus Thole."

"Don't forget the star now. Tau Secordis. Six names. But other living things? One name."

"Are you a living thing?"

Gamelin shook its head. "Not really. But I don't mind. It's not so bad being dead. You should try it." He took a step forward. "What was that you said about a sister?"

"You killed her."

"Not possible, gato. I don't even have parents."

"You did."

Gamelin looked puzzled. "How'd I kill her?"

"Broke her neck when she wouldn't breathe your poisoned air."

Gamelin's eyes blinked, very slowly. Coren could not read its expression. The cyborg's eyes narrowed briefly.

"Not acceptable," it said.

"Coren!" Ariel's voice called.

Gamelin looked around. Coren gripped his weapon and brought it up.

The cyborg moved fast, laterally. Coren fired. The bolt struck a cargo bin, punching a hole in it. Something within it had been under pressure and now shot out of the wound, sending the entire container careening off its track into another one. Within seconds, they dominoed off and into each other, and Coren watched, stunned, at the sudden pile-up.

The grid's AI tried to compensate. Bins that had been

immobile now began precipitously changing tracks and rearranging to avoid the collisions. Enormous piles of metal rammed each other. Bins bounced around like toys. The drumming of colliding bins filled the vast chamber. Somewhere the violent hiss of escaping gas cut through the thunder—the bin he had punctured.

What was I thinking about this being too neat and efficient . . . ? Coren wondered.

Through the din, four harsh blaster shots, like air tearing, focussed his attention.

"Ariel!"

He looked around for her—just as Gamelin grabbed him.

Coren felt a bolt of terror pulse through him as he was lifted off his feet by one arm. The hand that gripped him compressed muscle and bone on his forearm, impossibly strong, and he understood how Jeta and Damik and the Brethe dealer and others unnamed had died. The blaster fell from his hand.

Now, was all he thought as he looked into Gamelin's face.

Ariel ran. Cargo bins careened in her wake, seeming to chase her. When the inert cubes had begun to move to compensate for the sudden threat to property, restarted by a watchful but uncreative AI, she expected to be crushed between them.

She glanced back. One bin bounced randomly among the others, a thick spray of gas squirting powerfully from a hole in its side. She considered shooting it again, but that might only make it worse. She kept running.

Finally, near the warehouse end of the transport maze, the banging ended and the shifting bins stopped shifting. Ariel looked back into the altered landscape and thought,

Even if very little is damaged, getting all this straightened out is going to take some doing . . .

When it was clear that nothing else was moving, she started back.

"Ambassador." The TBI team leader came up alongside her. "The warehouse is secured, we have nine people in custody, and we found four robots in stand-by niches. Your assistance is required to secure them."

"Are they moving?" Ariel asked.

"No—"

"Then they already *are* secured. Forget about them. Coren's out here."

"Ambassador." The woman stepped in front of Ariel and stopped. Ariel came up against her outstretched hand. "Please go back. We'll find Mr. Lanra."

"You can accompany me."

"Please, I insist—"

"Something started this disaster," Ariel said, waving her hand around at the jumbled bins. "Coren's vonoomans located no other people than those you already have in custody. Which means?"

"Ambassador—"

"Which means you can accompany me, but I'm going."

Ariel stepped around the agent. She heard a sharp hiss of breath—a signal—and then running feet. Two more agents joined her, along with the team leader.

They spread out laterally and worked their way through the labyrinth of containers.

The number of damaged bins grew the further they went. Clusters of toppled containers formed tangles. Ariel held her blaster in both hands, her pulse racing.

I must remember in the future that I don't really have to do this, she thought.

She heard voices. Moving toward them, it became clear that one of them was Coren, but the other—rasping and low—was not even clearly human.

Ariel came around a pair of mashed bins and saw Coren dangling by one arm from the grip of the cyborg. Coren nodded as the cyborg spoke to him, its head tilted forward on enormous shoulders.

Ariel licked her lips. *Now what?*

In those seconds of indecision, the cyborg suddenly straightened and looked around. It saw Ariel.

Indifferently, it dropped Coren.

In that instant, a blaster shot splashed against its back.

"No!" Ariel shouted, then pressed the stud on her own weapon.

Gamelin's pain came out like dust-laden wind. The cyborg took a few more steps, and fell. Coren squirmed and pushed and managed to crawl away. The stench of scorched fabric, melted plastic, and meat filled Ariel's nostrils.

Ariel hurried forward, along with the TBI agents. One of them grabbed Coren's jacket and dragged him further from the cyborg.

Ariel stopped a meter from it, keeping her weapon aimed at its head. It lay face down. Smoke wafted up from three burns on its back and shoulders.

The team leader took its arm and heaved, turning it over.

Gamelin surged up suddenly, brushing away her weapon and clutching her jacket.

"Oh, kill me slow, gato," it said. "It's the only thing I have left to feel."

It placed one enormous hand over her face and squeezed. Bone snapped with sickening delicacy, and the team leader screamed.

Ariel jerked the trigger of her blaster; the shot grazed

Gamelin's arm. The cyborg stood and tossed the body of the team leader at the other agent, turned, and fled. Ariel tried to hit it again, firing repeatedly. But none of the shots found a target, and Gamelin soon disappeared among the cargo bins.

Ariel's breathing came heavy as she went to Coren. Sweat covered his face, but he was conscious.

"It knows," he said. "I told it."

"How bad are you?" Ariel ran her gaze over him, settling on his right arm. She reached for it.

His other arm came up and stopped her. "Hurts."

"We'll get help."

"Tresha must already be in transit," Coren said. "Contact Sipha . . . make sure . . ."

Ariel felt momentarily frantic about his injuries, but she nodded and stood. She went to the other agent, who held the team leader in his arms. Her face was turning black already. One eye bulged hideously.

Somehow, though, she was still alive.

Ariel raised her comm and started issuing orders.

Derec listened absently to the tense comm traffic being monitored behind him. He gazed out of the office across the empty dock, waiting for the instant the bay doors opened and the shuttle for which they waited slid into the station.

Masid came up beside him.

"Reports from groundside indicate a rousing success," Masid said.

Derec glanced at him. "How come you don't sound pleased?"

Masid raised his eyebrows. "It's not finished. I'm never happy till it's over."

"All the Settler bays in question have been seized,"

Derec mused. "We have prisoners, some of whom are already giving up information—"

"Ah, but they don't really know a lot. Most of it won't amount to very much unless we can persuade this one—" he nodded toward the bay below them "—to talk. Tresha's the key to the whole thing."

"You never struck me as a pessimist."

"Pragmatist. Big difference."

"Coren's been hurt," Palen announced.

Derec and Masid turned toward the room. Harwol sat behind one desk, hand to his ear. Palen occupied another desk opposite him. She looked at Derec.

"Ambassador Burgess is all right," she said. "The cyborg got away."

"Damn," Masid said.

"Is Lanra hurt badly?" Derec asked.

"Crushed forearm," Palen said. "Reparable. Tresha is in transit." She touched a contact. "Look sharp, people—the main fish is coming into our net."

Derec turned away. One cyborg still loose. They had found no others. Part of him was reassured—at least they would not have to deal with any more right now—but he could not convince himself that these represented the only two. From what Polifos had told them, it was an old and ongoing program. Somewhere, there were more.

Maybe Tresha could tell them.

"Damn it!" Palen shouted. "Her shuttle is changing vector. It's heading to another bay. Who gave clearance for that?"

Harwol looked up. "I'm moving my people now. Do you have the new destination?"

Palen listened intently. "Working on it . . . come *on* . . . shit, it's going to a Solarian dock."

Masid leaned close to Derec. "What did I tell you?"

Derec went to an empty chair and pulled himself to a comm. He tapped in a code and waited. Ambassador Setaris appeared on his screen.

"Ambassador," he said, "we have a new situation. Our last target has switched destination from the Settler dock she was scheduled for to the Solarian section."

Setaris's eyes widened. "What do you need, Mr. Avery?"

"We're moving on her regardless," Derec said, glancing at Palen and Harwol, who both nodded. "You might want to start working on smoothing things over with Ambassador Chassik now."

"Thank you for the warning. Good luck."

"Move," Harwol said, looking at Palen. "Your station, your arrest."

Palen jumped up and headed for the exit.

Masid nodded for Derec to come along.

When they reached the dock in question, Solarian security—Keresians—blocked access. Palen pushed her way through the knot of TBI and station security. She brought her face close to the chief of Solarian security.

"Chief Palen," she said. "Stand aside. This is a lawful entry."

"I have orders—" the Keresian started.

Palen shoved him to one side and stabbed the access panel. The door opened.

Her people poured through.

They crowded into the control booth. Operators started to abandon their positions.

"Sit down!" Palen shouted. "You're receiving an unauthorized shuttle. When will it be in the bay?"

"Your pardon, Chief Palen," one of the operators said, "but we received authorization fifteen minutes ago."

"From who?"

"Our embassy, of course."

Palen stared at the man. "Are you going to tell me that this shuttle is under diplomatic protection?"

"I—well—"

"Entering the cradle now," another operator said.

"Bring it in," Palen ordered. "Embassy clearance or not, that shuttle is impounded."

Below, the huge doors opened. Tractor lines drew the sleek, bullet-shaped shuttle into the bay. Once it had cleared the opening, the doors sealed and the bay started pressurizing.

Palen moved to the access hatch. "Security, with me. Avery, you get on the comm and do liaison with your people. Masid, you do the same with Harwol."

"Pressurization complete," an operator announced.

Derec went to the comm console and tapped in a code. The channel to the Auroran Embassy, Earthside, showed open.

The hatch slid aside and Palen led her squad of police down the stairs. The hatch closed behind them. Derec went to the window and watched the security teams spread out around the shuttle.

Masid joined Derec. "Now maybe I'll start being optimistic," he said.

Derec looked at the chief operator. "Who issued the clearance?"

"I'm not at liberty to—"

"Don't. A name. Was it Chassik?"

The man looked embarrassed and uncertain.

"Derec," Masid said.

Below, the shuttle hatch opened. Palen took a position at the base of the ramp, hands on hips. A woman appeared in the hatchway. For a long, long moment, she gazed down at the security people and Palen.

There was a faint series of flashes around the bay door. And then, between one instant and the next, the door itself blew outward.

Derec flinched back. The shuttle lurched off its cradle, the prow rolling over Palen. Bodies lifted off the deck and sailed out the gaping hole. The shuttle itself caught against the sides of the dock, wedged briefly.

Then it exploded.

There was no sound. Derec fell to the floor. He could hear the walls of the control booth creaking under enormous stress, but they did not yield.

Minutes later, he managed to stand.

The bay was empty of anything that might have been loose. The walls were stained black, and the hatch itself was buckled outward. The shuttle was gone, and no one remained in the now airless space.

EPILOGUE

Derec watched Masid pack. The man wore the clothes of someone used to moving around: comfortable, lots of pockets, simply cut. The pack, though, contained tools and devices no baley would carry.

"You're sure about this?" Derec asked.

"I've got the best chance of getting to Nova Levis of anyone," Masid said. "Already worked it out with the TBI and the Aurorans, so don't even try talking me out of it."

"Is there anything I can do?"

Derec had grown quite fond of Masid in the last few days, since the world had changed. Derec had few enough friends. The thought of losing a new one disturbed him.

But Palen's death had affected Masid profoundly. He was angry and felt the need to do something. Derec believed going off like that was a bad idea, but he could think of no convincing argument to stop Masid.

"You've got your hands full here," Masid said. He glanced significantly at the robot standing near the door. "You wouldn't want to loan that to me, would you?"

Derec started. "That could be awkward, don't you think? Having a robot with you wouldn't be the most inconspicuous thing you could do."

"True, but I think I'm going to miss it."

The DW-12 did not react. Derec needed to schedule a complete diagnostic for it. Thales was unable to tell him very much about its make-up; everything was guesswork and projection. For a time, it had insisted on accompanying Masid. It took a good deal of insistent talk to convince it to stay with Derec. He recognized Bogard's attachment to duty, certainly, but its facility at debate was all Thales. Derec doubted he would win every argument with this new creation, this composite.

"You're right," Derec admitted. "Besides, Ariel asked me to help her do the analysis on the cyborg we acquired."

" 'Acquired'? Interesting term. 'Killed and captured' would be more accurate."

"If you destroy a robot, do you kill it?"

Masid frowned.

"It's a good question," Derec continued. "I'd say no. They aren't, strictly speaking, alive. Can you make the same statement about a cyborg? They're organic, certainly, but are they human?"

"Or human enough." Masid nodded. "Too much philosophy for me. I'm just a spy." He finished packing and sealed the bag, then turned back to Derec. "We need to say goodbye. It'll take me a few days to work myself back under cover so I can do this with any expectation of success. I'll be on Kopernik for a time still, but after this we can't know each other."

Derec took Masid's hand. "Be safe."

"Always my intention."

Masid shouldered the pack and walked quickly out.

Derec looked at the DW-12. "What am I going to do with you?"

"Whatever you wish," the robot replied. "Within limits."

Derec started, then laughed out loud. "What do I call you?"

"The preponderance of my matrix is based on Bogard."

"In that case, welcome back, Bogard. We have a lot to talk about. . . ."

Derec found Hofton in the positronics lab with Rana. They looked up at him dourly when he entered.

"*Now* who died?" Derec asked.

Neither smiled.

"Ariel can't get you permission to bring Bogard down," Hofton said.

Derec considered the news for a moment, then shrugged. "So I expected."

"She's also being seconded to Auroran intelligence."

He started. "What?"

"The cyborg is being shipped back to Aurora. They want her to work on it. Classified work, of course."

"I thought—"

"She wants you, boss," Rana said. "But if you leave Earth . . ."

"I won't get back."

"It *is* unlikely," Hofton admitted.

"I see."

"Boss—"

Derec held up a hand. "We've got a little time, don't we?"

"A few days," Hofton said. "Not much more, I'm sure."

"We'll work something out." Derec looked around the lab. "I need a workstation set up for a full diagnostic. Is Thales still linked up?"

Rana nodded. "No one's shut it down yet."

"Fine."

Work would take his mind off the situation for a time. Perhaps he could come to terms with what amounted to exile.

Yart Leri strode into the lab. He gazed about, eyes wide, until he saw Derec, Rana, and Hofton.

"There you are," he said, coming up to them. "Have you heard? No, of course you haven't. I just found out myself."

"Rega Looms has won the election despite having withdrawn?" Hofton said dryly.

Leri frowned at him. "No, of course not."

"Sorry, Ambassador," Derec said, giving Hofton a look. "What haven't we heard?"

"Nova Levis. A blockade runner has fired on a Theian perimeter ship. We may have a war on our hands."

Ariel's lower back ached from the too-stiff posture. She could not make herself relax, and the chair simply could not compensate for her tension.

The room felt cold, too. She was not entirely sure that was not an illusion, her own projection. No one around the conference table smiled; the mood was sepulchral. For the last four hours, Setaris had conducted the meeting—hearing, really— with all the warmth of a stone slab. After the first hour, Gale Chassik had stopped looking at anyone. He answered the questions put to him in monosyllables when possible, offering as little detail as he could get away with.

The clearance that had allowed the shuttle carrying Tresha to switch destinations to the Solarian section of Kopernik had come from his office. He refused to acknowledge responsibility, but he could not deny the evidence.

He had stopped responding to questions at all nearly an

hour ago. Ariel had been asked a few questions concerning details of the raid, but otherwise had not participated in the proceedings.

"In view of the circumstances," Setaris said finally, "I cannot in good conscience overlook the potential culpability in this matter on the part of Ambassador Chassik. Therefore, as head of the joint legation of the Fifty Worlds on Earth, I revoke his ambassadorial authority pending a hearing to review charges of abuse of office and negligence. Such hearing will be held on Aurora at a date to be determined by the Auroran legislature. Until then, Ambassador Chassik is remanded to house arrest, and his duties shall be assumed by another mission to be chosen by mutual agreement of this body."

Chassik looked up. "You're making a vast mistake, Sen."

"Possibly," Setaris said. "But a vastly smaller one than I would be making were I to allow you to continue as ambassador. Any questions?" She surveyed the table. "Good. This meeting is adjourned."

Ariel gratefully pushed away from the table and stood.

Chassik met her at the door and blocked her way.

"And, indeed, we have not finished, Ambassador," he said.

Ariel glanced at the two security guards flanking him. They stepped closer. Chassik glared at them, then left the room.

"He'll probably be recalled," Setaris said.

Ariel turned.

"I'll see to it he leaves before you do," Setaris continued. "I apologize, Ariel. I know you wanted to remain on Earth, but . . ."

"But I'm much more valuable where I can be kept an eye on," Ariel said. "I understand."

"Ariel, I actually envy you leaving so soon. I don't imagine that we'll have a mission here for much longer. Once the Terran senate finishes casting us in the rôle of the devil for having spawned a new menace, we'll be asked to leave. If war actually breaks out . . . well, I don't look forward to leaving under those conditions."

"Why would Earth make war on us? It was a Settler ship that fired on a Spacer ship."

"Prejudice. We'll be assuming control of the blockade, Earth will feel some perverse sympathy for the Settlers that *we* are then blockading, and the situation will degenerate from there." Setaris shrugged. "I may be too cynical, though. Perhaps none of this will actually happen. If not, perhaps you can return."

Ariel could think of no response. She wanted to go back to her apartment and have a drink.

Or go see Coren.

Which would be more dangerous right now? she wondered.

"We can talk again before you leave," Setaris said. "Arrangements need to be made and so forth. Till then, as a favor to me—be careful."

As she watched Setaris walk away, Ariel thought, *I'm not happy about leaving Earth, but it* will *be a relief to get away from her.*

Rega Looms finished the meeting and sat behind his desk, eyes closed, trying to find the satisfaction he once enjoyed from business well-concluded. Nothing. After a time, he sighed and wondered if anything, ever again, would give him any joy.

Melodramatic thought . . .

He poured himself a glass of brandy and drank it slowly.

When it was finished, he left the office and ascended to his private chambers.

On the desk in his residential office lay the draft of his next sermon. He was alone now—wife dead, both children dead. He had nothing left but his company and his church. Politics was over for him, at least as a personal activity.

He toyed with the ancient pen he always used to hand write these pieces, but, looking down the lines of neatly calligraphed words, he could think of nothing more to add just now.

The world was ending and he had said everything . . .

Looms shook his head. Ridiculous. Still, he felt that way often. What if, tomorrow, time stopped and the end came? Would he have done all he needed to do?

Some things he no longer could finish.

There were words he had needed to say to Nyom . . .

He walked into his bedroom.

Someone sat on the edge of the bed. A large man, dressed darkly, bare head bowed.

"Who are you?" Looms asked automatically. He thought of the gun in his nightstand.

The man raised his head. The room's lighting played off of pale skin, rough, scarred complexion, and large eyes that seemed somehow artificial. He grinned.

"Hello, Daddy," said Gamelin. "So nice to see you after all these years. . . ."

ISAAC ASIMOV'S
ROBOT MYSTERY

CHIMERA

MARK W. TIEDEMANN

Mark W. Tiedemann's love for science fiction and writing started at an early age, although it was momentarily side-tracked—for over twenty years—by his career as a professional photographer. After attending a Clarion Science Fiction & Fantasy Writers Workshop held at Michigan State University in 1988, he rediscovered his lost love and focused his talents once more on attaining his dream of becoming a professional writer. With the publication of "Targets" in the December 1990 issue of *Asimov's Science Fiction Magazine*, he began selling short stories to various markets; his work has since appeared in *Magazine of Fantasy & Science Fiction, Science Fiction Age, Tomorrow SF,* and a number of anthologies. His bestselling novel *Mirage*, the first entry in the *Isaac Asimov's Robot Mysteries* series, was released in April 2000. Currently, Tiedemann is working on the third book in the series, to be published in 2002; his next completed novel (working title: *Felony of Conscience*) is scheduled for release by ibooks in October 2001. Tiedemann lives in St. Louis, Missouri, with his companion, Donna, and their resident alien life form—a dog named Kory.

ISAAC ASIMOV

Isaac Asimov was the author of over 400 books—including three Hugo Award-winners—and numerous bestsellers, as well as countless stories and scientific essays. He was awarded the Grand Master of Science Fiction by the Science Fiction Writers of America in 1985, and he was the man who coined the words robotics, positronic, and psychohistory. He died in 1992.

P113-122 Coven's Use of Desth 3 C_a,
DS p. 122 "Counerble Common Associations"

P.272-27$\overline{5}$ — Def of Positronic Brain, HUMAN
'aware' self

P297   will in a Positronic Matrix